Alexander Besher was born in China to Russian parents and raised in Japan. Now based in San Francisco, he is the auther of the Rim trilogy – *Rim, Mir* and *Chi.* He is currently writing a new series of futuristic thrillers – The Hanging Butoh trilogy.

D0551883

ALEXANDER BESHER

•CHI•

ORBIT

An *Orbit* Book

First published in Great Britain by Orbit 1999
This edition published by Orbit 1999

Copyright © 1999 by Alexander Besher

The moral right of the author has been asserted.

A CIP catalogue record for this book
is available from the British Library

ISBN 1 85723 859 1

Typeset by Hewer Text Limited, Edinburgh
Printed and bound in Great Britain by
Mackays of Chatham plc, Chatham, Kent

Orbit
A Division of
Little, Brown and Company (UK)
Brettenham House
Lancaster Place
London WC2E 7EN

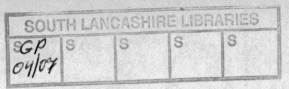

For Shurinka, my beautiful red butterfly

For Koize, the keeper of the bees

For Nicky, the Monkey-King

Bolshoya Spasiba to Fima and Ada

And For the Family Everywhere

Acknowledgments

I would like to thank the following for their assistance, inspiration and input: Joachim and Jenny Burger in Xiang Gang, always there for me; Nury Vittachi ('Lai See') of the *South China Morning Post* for his ever-trenchant insights into life in Xiang Gang; Christopher Moore in Bangkok, for his crystal-clear depictions of Thai 'heart-think' in his novels about Thailand; Peter Kaelli in Baan Taling Ngam for his gracious assistance and hospitality at Le Royal Meridien in Kho Samui; my son, Nicholas Besher, for assisting me with research; Greg and Geoff Leach, my Tokyo co-conspirators; Alexandra Moari, for helping make most of the writing as effortless as applying sunscreen at Ziggy Stardust in Bhoput; Serafina Clarke, my agent in London; Tim Holman, Lisa Rogers, and the terrific crew at Little, Brown/Orbit for all their wonderful support; and for all the 'children of *Chi*' whom we crossed paths with on the journey.

Contents

Frontmatter   **xi**

Phase 1: Larva   **1**

Phase 2: Pupa   **127**

Phase 3: Chrysalis   **189**

Phase 4: Butterfly   **263**

Epilogue   **285**

Chi (pronounced 'chee;' spelled 'qi' in Pinyin): *The Chinese name for the vital force or energy that is believed to enliven all matter; the pre-atomic constructs of energy. Also known as Ether (Aristotle), Prana (India), Ka (Egypt), Ki (Japan), Manu (Hawaii), Aché (Yoruba), Mumia (Paracelsus), Primary Energy, Space Energy, Zero Point Energy, Gravity Field Energy, G-Field Energy, Eloptic Energy (Dr Thomas Gale Hieronymous), Tachydon Field (Prof. G. Feinberg), Morphic Field (Dr Rupert Sheldrake), Higgs Field (Peter W. Higgs), X-Force (Dr Eerman), Neutrino Sea (Prof. P.A.M. Dirac), Radiant Energy (Dr T.H. Moray), Soft Electrostatics (Nikola Tesla), Orgone Energy (Wilhelm Reich), Bio-Cosmic Energy (Dr Brunler), Living Water (Viktor Schaunberger), Odic Force (Baron Von Reichenbach), Animal Magnetism (Franz Mesmer), Vril (the universal plastic medium of occultists), Anima Mundi (alchemy), Fermi Sea (Dr Enrico Fermi), The Force (Obi Wan Kanobi in George Lucas' film Star Wars), The Shit Hitting the Fan of Evolution (Anonymous)*

Source: The Aeonian Press

PHASE 1

· · · · · · · · · · · · · · · · · ·

Larva

The *Katoey* Butterfly

Kho Samui, The Gulf of Thailand
April 12, 2038, 10:30 p.m.

Butterfly, the transsexual *katoey*, knew the routine
and sniffed the air outside the door of her
bungalow. It was heavy with the smell of orchids and
jasmine and of sweaty *farangs*, those foreigners reeking
of coconut oil from their day at the beach.

Most of the *farangs* who lived in the row of cheap
bungalows (100 *baht* a night, $4) were still asleep since the
afternoon siesta, although the *katoey* couldn't imagine how
they coped with the heat and the mosquitoes in their airless
one-mat cells.

Zonked on Mekong whiskey probably, or on Sangthip,
the local Thai rum, or passed out from the *ganja* which
they smoked in prodigious amounts, and which Butterfly
sold them in little Thai medicine Zip-lok bags at an inflated
price.

Butterfly heard one of them moaning in the hut next to
hers, as if he were waking from a bad dream. Waking up,
now *that* was a bad dream— She frowned. She didn't want
any part of their bad dreams. Someone else's bad dream
could rub off on you if you weren't careful.

Butterfly shivered as the bad feeling came upon her. *Sang
hoon jai.* A sudden premonition that something terrible was
about to happen.

Bullshit, it would pass. She spat on the ground. She
couldn't afford to let a *farang*'s nightmare bring her down.

Not tonight when so much was at stake. Soon she'd be
out of here; maybe she'd open up her own bar in the
Patpong. She could lose herself easily in Bangkok. That was
a million miles away, up north.

Katoeys – 'she-boys' – had more respect there. Here, they
had to peddle their ass at the Coffee Boys' Club, or

someplace worse. She'd done that herself before she latched on to something better.

Like this job, for instance. It involved some risk, but the pay-off was ten times what you got for strutting your silicone tits on stage in drag or lip-synching your asshole to some ditzy Broadway show-tune.

Butterfly sniffed again. The revelers would soon be on their way. They would be coming along at any moment. *There*. They were coming now. She could see them heading across the bridge.

It was time for Butterfly to get to work. A *katoey*'s work was never done, especially when there was so much stuff to harvest. She had her quota to fill.

Kroon, her boss, who owned the Rasta Palace, was the local police chief, among other things. If she fucked up, worst case, he'd have her beaten up and deported to Laos.

Worse than the worst case, she didn't want to think about. Look what happened to Pung. What *had* happened to Pung? Another tragic *katoey* tale. Rumor was she wanted to sample the goods herself. She rigged up her own lab, dug up the buried treasure (knowing Pung, she probably stashed it behind her bungalow in the brush just off the path), and was either caught in the act by Kroon or by one of his goons, or short-circuited herself in the process. Fucking idiot.

Transferring *chi* from a *chi*-implant wasn't exactly like giving yourself a self-service brain-scan, which is what Pung allegedly did just to get up to snuff with the latest in medical technology.

She'd gone to see some quack medic in Chaweng, who specialized in treating *farangs* (concussions from traffic accidents, diving mishaps, sexual diseases, that sort of thing), and he'd given her a quick lesson in siphoning *chi*. They all did that to a certain extent.

It was a side-line of the local tourist industry, ripping off the bootleg *chi* that the *farangs* paid so dearly to have implanted in the fancy clinics on the mainland.

A *chi*-implant in Surathani, across the Gulf of Thailand, cost 125,000 *baht*! Five thousand U.S. dollars! You could live for a year on that – and support your family, too, in the provinces. Or go into business for yourself by opening up a *katoey* bar in the Patpong or in Soi Cowboy or at the Na Na Plaza . . .

Butterfly felt her pulse quicken. All that was so much closer now, within reach, actually attainable. *If* she played her cards right.

For the *farangs*, the *chi*-implant offered the promise of eternal youth, and all the delights that go with it. Sex, drugs, endless vitality, and no possibility of overdoing it. *A no burn-out guarantee*. They could afford short-time immortality at that price. So what did it matter if some poor Thai, nose pressed against the window of their exclusive club, took a little hit from them now and then?

If they borrowed some of that charmed life and recycled it back into the indigenous population? Just a little bit of it . . .

Of course, Kroon took it a step further. That's why Kroon was Kroon. *The Boss Bitch*. Nobody messed with him. Not the local authorities, not the generals, not the politicians (all of whom got their cut – Kroon saw to that) – and certainly not anyone who happened to work for Kroon at the Rasta Palace.

Like Pung, for instance. Pung who was gone for ever. Or like Butterfly. Butterfly, who was ready to spread her brightly colored Spandex wings and to fly away – far, far away – to some place where the jungle would leave her in peace.

Butterfly stepped into the shadows outside her bungalow wherein one open plastic suitcase, clothes strewn over the mat, a kerosene lamp, and a calendar were the total of her possessions.

She walked swiftly through the palm grove, past the heaps of decaying garbage, nauseatingly sweet in the humid night air, and put on a happy smiley face.

Another rasta temple had once been erected in this clearing, but it had burned down long ago leaving only the stumps of bar stools and the charred fresco of Bob Marley's face on the solitary wall left standing.

She paused for a moment to straighten the straps of her blue halter-top and to coax her breasts to form the right indentation in the Spandex bra to entice the *farangs* with her cleavage.

Then she moved briskly down the path to where the action was.

The *boom-boom-boom* of the Rasta Palace reverberated across the lagoon in the tropical night. The reeds rustled in the breeze and the army of croaking frogs grew silent, blinking away the night forces with horny skinned disdain.

A bit earlier that evening, before the reggae music began blaring from the mega-speakers built into the giant Polynesian *tiki* sculptures that stood guard outside the club, the frogs had been engaged in a chorus with the *kerbau*, the water-buffalo that was tethered to the banyan tree.

It had been a manic, frenzied foreplay of sound – the throaty razzing of the frogs and the ecstatic, receptive lowing of the *kerbau*. It would have turned anyone 'on.'

Now the real music of the night was beginning another round of orgasm in which they had no role. They could only absorb the vibrations through the swampy backwash of water.

The long rickety wooden bridge that led from the village to the disco-island swayed and creaked under the weight of the arriving mopeds. Those who traveled on foot paused in single file to let the *putt-putting* mopeds pass. Then they resumed their procession of bare feet, rubber flip-flops and four-step drive Teva sandals as they headed in the direction of the enormous palm-thatched Thai pavilion that was wreathed with fairy-tale strings of light.

The *farangs* were single men mostly: young, middle-aged and old, from Europe, America, Australia, New Zealand,

and from the richer regions of Asia, with enough *baht* in their pockets to promise them a good time on the other side of the bridge.

Some of them brought their girls with them, young Thai joy-girls hired for the short-time, whatever that short-time was, a night, a week, two weeks, as long as their lust and their *baht* held out.

Or they brought them with them from the 'other side' – from Surathani, Phuket, Krabi, the Phi Phi Islands, or even Bangkok.

The girls were pretty, winsome, and delicate, some as young as fourteen but most of them in their early twenties, with long black hair, sea-shell-shaped brown eyes, dressed in tank-tops, sarongs, and tight white shorts that revealed their chocolate-brown thighs.

Those that rode behind their *farang* lovers had their arms clasped around their waists, perched like birds on the back of a speeding cage.

They unselfconsciously lifted the plumage of their tails, displaying their coconut-shaped buttocks on the sweaty seats of the Hondas and Kawasaki motor bikes.

Butterfly was waiting for them at the end of the bridge, by the stalls that served up skewers of *satay* and barbecued shrimp, next to the outdoor VDO cinema playing the current garbled film which only the most dazed *farangs* and their girls would watch, just to catch a breather or to dry off their sweat from the action on the floor.

Butterfly was already on the job, mingling with the *farangs*, clocking their *chi*. She had her *chi*-meter hidden inside the macramé purse that she wore tied around her thin neck.

The scanned results were transmitted to Kroon's operatives in the back-room of the club where they were analyzed for fair black-market value and rated according to the daily print-out of high-priority items sought for export.

There were so many different kinds of *chi* life-force

energy for sale. Different qualities, different band widths, different hues and shades of human desire, human potential, brainpower, sex appeal, and sentient Web-sites tattooed on the body. Each one had its own special price, quality of work, and designated life-span.

Each type of *chi*, therefore, had its prospective buyer somewhere on the black market, be it in Singapore, or Kuala Lumpur, Beijing, or in Brussels, London, New York, or Moscow.

Kroon's network was vast. He was connected with every major syndicate and *chi*-broker around the world. It was a multi-trillion dollar industry.

Occasionally, a *farang* would walk into the Rasta Palace and the *chi* reading would go off the wall. There would be something special about the implant, perhaps something proprietary, something that could lead to something else that would provide the *real* pay-off.

Perhaps it might be the secret account number of an arms-dealer in an off-shore bank in the Grand Turks or the Caymans. Or the formula for some new biosoft pharmaceutical that could be sold to a rival company, or even part of an algorithm that when combined with some other little thing – an enzyme, a string of DNA – could fuel a massive new industry or send the price of shares skyrocketing.

That *farang* would never walk out again. Kroon's girls, or boys, would go to work on him. Eventually, he'd be lured upstairs to one of the short-time 'guest suites' that Kroon maintained for that purpose. D.O.O. – 'dead on orgasm' – is how Kroon put it. Kroon would allow them that much, before dispatching them.

He had designed the device himself, perversely calling it the 'death oyster.' The designated joy-girl or boy would insert the oval-shaped cylinder into their orifice. Sexual friction – and the lunging – would release the poison-needle into the head of the penis. It was the look of horror – more than pain, it was the look of *horror* on the *farang*'s face, of that final, fateful realization – that appealed so much to Kroon.

Kroon was an old *katoey* himself. Sixty years old, but with the body of a twenty-year-old, a platinum-blond Thai girl with a body to kill for, or which would kill for him.

Sometimes, just to stay in practice, he would entice the *farang* upstairs himself. Other times, he would watch the show through the two-way mirror, and video-tape the snuff-scene. That was another side-line of Kroon's. He had a list of wealthy private collectors all around the world, each of whom paid handsomely for such death-soaps.

The dead *farang*'s body would quickly be iced, the *chi*-implant removed and air-couriered that night to a trans-shipment point on the mainland for international delivery the next day.

Butterfly noticed the *farang* right away, even before Tan, Kroon's Number One *chi*-reader, was able to analyze the data and come up with the correct diagnostics. She just had that feeling about him the moment she set eyes on him.

Butterfly went by her sixth, or was it her seventh sense? That same sense which made her a hustler – not a very successful one, admittedly, but just enough to make her a survivor – had once run deep and proud in her family tree.

Generations ago, one of her ancestors was a village medicine-man, a *maw pii*, who did his work among the hill-tribes of the Lao. He was a bone-spirit specialist, who could set the dead free from their bones (or else they lingered on the earth-plane, making trouble for themselves and for their relations; hungry ghosts were angry ghosts).

Sometimes even, for a price, the *maw pii* would bring them back to life again through a mixture of herbs and some artful astral counseling.

Butterfly felt her great-great-grandfather awaken inside her, as he spread through her fibers, pausing to adjust to the *katoey* foliage of her skin.

No, Butterfly didn't need a hand-held *chi*-reader to know

that this man was somehow different. Somehow he was not even a *man*, on some level. He did not *belong* – not in the same way that a *katoey* does not belong to either sex – but on some more tangible, palpable level.

Beyond *katoey* – beyond this body, but still in the same form . . .

In any case, he was smiling at her as if he knew. He *knew*. He knew what she was doing! He was blond, this *farang*, and tanned and well built, and young. He looked as if he did not belong at the Rasta Palace. It was not his quest for pleasure that was stalking her or anyone else in this godforsaken hell-hole.

Not joy-boy, not joy-girl. Not any of that. Not for him. Butterfly restrained a shiver of belated recognition.

Not for it? The real it?

His eyes were green, somewhat incandescent, tinged with a cloud of luminosity almost like algae, with a glint to them of the forest and the sea. He was dressed in a simple white cotton Thai shirt and loose-fitting cotton pants. His feet were sunburnt and golden hair sparkled on his muscular forearms. His hands and fingers were well proportioned, square yet tapered.

He stood before her and spoke to her in Thai, which was unusual enough for *farangs*, who had not yet lost themselves enough to find roots in this land of smiles.

'Brother sister,' the man addressed her in a quiet voice that seemed louder to Butterfly's ears than the blaring of the reggae music from the speakers on the *tiki* totems.

'You were thinking that perhaps this was the night you would steal the *chi* you need to get away from here and to start a new life.'

Butterfly gasped. She had stolen one of Kroon's death-oysters and was wearing it now inside her. The lubrication trickled down her back-hole. *How could he possibly know that?*

Butterfly stared at him, the sorrow in her own eyes washed by the tide of some strange new feeling. A feeling that her life as she knew it was about to end, but that it would be just as easily replaced by something else, some new wonder that did not require her to ration her happiness or to dwell on the undwellable pain of living.

Was this what her earlier premonition of *sang hoon jai* had been about? Something terrible, something beautiful was about to impose itself on her life.

The blond *farang* sounded almost shy now, as if he were about to propose something that he could not find the words to express. 'I was passing through here, on the way to someplace else,' he explained. 'But I *felt* you. I felt you calling. That's why I *had* to come—' His chin jutted to a dimpled exclamation point. '*I had to come here*—'

He gave her another look, and it flooded her with courage, the often misleading courage to hope again. He spoke to her again softly, kindly. 'You wanted to steal, perhaps even to kill for it. I am here to *give* it to you. It is yours already. You possess it even now. It is in *your* eyes. Can't you see the difference? The rest – all this—' He opened his hands around him, 'is false. It is not *real*. Not the real *chi* . . .'

The *katoey* saw. More importantly, she *understood*. Then she said to the man quickly, bluntly, 'You must leave here right away. If I must, I will find you. If that is the way. But you must go. *Now*.'

She glanced behind her at the entrance to the Rasta Palace. The *farangs* and their Thai joy-toys were jostling up the stairs, drawn to the beat, drawn to the blazing torches that burned inside where the towering plaster-of-paris idol of Bob Marley stood with his hands raised up to the cavernous rafters of the dance club.

'*It's hot-hot-hot, feeling hot-hot-hot*—' The snake-dance was already jumping to the sounds of the band on stage. Kroon's men had not yet appeared, but Butterfly was sure that they would at any moment.

When she turned around, the stranger was gone. She thought she saw him crossing the long bridge across the lagoon. But in the mêlée of motor bikes and the rumbling of the *songthaews*, the canopied mini-truck taxis with their hard-seat benches which were unloading their drunken passengers at the entrance to the Rasta Palace, the moment's confusion drowned Butterfly's senses.

Then she saw Kroon, and his two side-kicks, Doom and Krik, with their writhing blue Chinese dragons tattooed down their arms, and they came for her, and Kroon slapped her hard in the face.

....

Bangkok Rain

Wing Fat raised an eyebrow, such as it was – a fine enameled line that etched the almond crescents of his black opiated eyes. He was on his fourth pipe of the evening, and that growing sense of detachment, which usually set in at this point, was confounded by the possible irony of it all.

Not a minnow, he told himself, *but a dragon . . . But weren't they all dragons in disguise? Those little revelations that amounted to some greater, bigger big truth along the way? Or was that just Madame O. tweaking his credulity with the promise of a big catch?*

Wing Fat lay stretched out on his rosewood opium couch in his vast air-conditioned living-room. T'ang dynasty figures stood illuminated under watchful spotlights in the four corners of the ante-chamber, a small terracotta army of soldiers wired with laser-spitting spears to protect him against intruders.

Priceless rugs from Samarkand lay strewn on the gleaming teakwood floor. A thin plume of rare sandalwood incense wafted from a bronze urn placed in front of the Kwan Yin figure in the alcove.

The Goddess of Mercy may as well have been just another employee in the House of Wing Fat. He had long since tired of mercy . . . He needed deliverance at this point in his life, and that was what the pipes were for . . .

What *was* he really? Wing Fat considered the options. He was a fat wealthy successful businessman dressed in a diaphanous black silk Chinese robe. *Be honest.* How fat? Six hundred-and-fifty pounds.

He had servants to cater to his every need. For his meals, for sex, and for chauffeuring him around in his specially constructed sedan-chair through the clogged streets of Bangkok.

His Nissan-built Water Buffalo had hydraulic horns for butting the three-wheeler *tuk-tuks* out of the way, with a mag-lev option for navigating the lattice-work of aerial freeways that criss-crossed the city.

Wing Fat had his own private elevator that led to the thirtieth floor of his luxury highrise apartment overlooking the bustling Chao Phraya river in the exclusive Chinese district of Balamphung.

The elevator was intelligent, and picked up all the gossip about his fellow tenants in the building. They were fellow Chinese millionaires, canny traders who had their fingers in a thousand different businesses, some of which impacted his own line of work.

Wing Fat paid his elevator a handsome salary, buying it stock options in Otis Asia. One day it would control the entire network of Otis elevators in the region. He considered it money well spent.

'Long Neck' was one of his best informants.

He also had servants like Little Min, who had been with him since childhood. Wing Fat was thirty-two years old. Little Min was his right hand, literally. He prepared his pipes for him. He knew Wing Fat's limits and facilitated his going beyond them. It was a daily exercise, to exceed the given boundaries.

Decadence *was* a martial art, no matter what anyone

said. Then Little Min would reel him back in again safely, back to *this* world.

Little Min was the only person whom Wing Fat trusted to operate the wired spirit-house for him, to bring him his dispatches, to arrange for the artful presentation of the *chi* specimens, then to effect their transmission to his roster of foreign clients around the world.

Little Min cheerfully absorbed the abuse that Wing Fat liberally bestowed on him without the slightest hint of complaint. He projected the perfect equanimity of the slave who accepted that his true position in life was to 'lie still beneath the mountain.'

That position offered Little Min the most panoramic view of the world. Besides, he could always move the mountain whenever he chose to. He knew all the acupressure points of Wing Fat's psyche.

Like now, when he brought him the latest samples from the spirit-house . . .

Little Min had just finished unscrambling the coded package, and brought it to his master on a black lacquer tray. He unwrapped the silk brocade that covered the holo-DNA sample in the petri dish and bowed.

See how the mountain was stirring, even after four pipes? It was amazing to witness all that bulk and girth transform itself into the agility and cunning of an acrobat on stage in a Shanghai cabaret . . . There was an entire city contained inside that man, with a population of thousands, just like Wing Fat's many moods . . .

That night, after Wing Fat had devoured his two-dozen courses of dinner, his chopsticks moving speedily over this dish and that – sparrow's tongue, the sautéed gall of tiger cub, the delicious serving of barbecued bear's claw, the spooning of live monkey's brain – he had drunk too much as usual.

Too much cognac, too many bottles of iced Singha beer, too many pots of Soochow tea, and he could not contain it any longer. His bladder demanded immediate relief. Little

Min barely managed to rush Wing Fat to the lavatory in time.

'Hurry up, hurry up,' Wing Fat ordered in a fit of pique. 'I can't wait, you idiot! Get it out quick, or I'm going to piss all over myself!'

Little Min fumbled with his master's silk robe, and even at top speed was unable to locate Wing Fat's equipment under his massive folds of flesh.

'*Min! Hurry!*'

The fat mountain sprang hot tears of frustration. He was such a child at times like this. He even required Little Min's neutral hand to effect congress with his stable of concubines, like a carpenter of lust who specialized in fitting joints of flesh together to make the 'spring rain' come . . .

'I'm sorry, master,' Little Min blustered (he knew when and how to exact these exquisitely delicate moments of revenge). 'But I can't seem to find your *pee-pee* . . .'

'A thousand curses on your ancestors, Min, *you* had it last!'

Without a word, Little Min delivered the goods, aimed the master's water-cannon at the bowl, and Wing Fat closed his eyes in ecstasy for three or four minutes until his bladder was completely empty.

'Don't do that to me again,' Wing Fat warned him, slapping the back of Little Min's head with gratitude born of customary disdain.

Now Wing Fat was lying on his couch, fishing among the dreams of his childhood. He was the scion of a scion of a scion. His ancestry traced itself back to the Qing Dynasty in the nineteenth century. His forefathers had been compradores to the *tai-pans*, the drug lords of the British Empire, who had been engaged in the opium trade on their island enclave of Shamian, upstream from the busy South Chinese port of Canton on the Pearl River.

Wing Fat's forebears retained their own share, of course – moving the product themselves wherever they saw fit, sometimes to the mainland, sometimes shipping it through their widespread network of clan members who were scattered all over Southeast Asia.

So what had changed since those days? Wing Fat accepted the fifth pipe from Little Min's hand and inhaled the sweet smoke. His own branch of the family had settled in Thailand, in Bangkok, where they milked the opium tit of the Golden Triangle.

But Wing Fat had diversified the family business. Educated at Stanford – a doctoral implant in the field of bio-energy pharmaceuticals – he was a *chi*-broker extraordinaire.

He was able to detect the finest quality *chi*, to appraise it with the palate of a connoisseur who knew his array of teas, each leaf of quivering consciousness brewed to its ultimate perfection.

'This just came in?' his voice, although husky with smoke, was rising to the occasion of deliberate thought.

One thought at a time, through each eye of each needle, until the embroidery of the full realization was complete. Such elaborate thought! It was wearying sometimes to layer each tiny abstraction into its delicately fritted *cloissoné* until it emerged as a complete work of art.

'Just now, from the spirit-house,' Little Min answered him. Each Thai house, each Thai business had a spirit-house on its premises, with offerings to the gods placed in front of the altar. Without that acknowledgment or obeisance to the gods, bad *joss*, misfortune, would result.

Wing Fat's spirit-house stood on its crimson pillar on the balcony outside his living room and office.

It contained a satellite-linked Toshiba Cray bio-supercomputer within its inner sanctum. You could practically transmit a human being through its DNA-fax board. At least, you could reconstitute one, but it was still cheaper to fly the Dragon Air Concorde, in Wing Fat's opinion.

Thirty stories below Wing Fat's apartment, the barges,

long boats, and ferries criss-crossed the sinuous arm of the
Chao Phraya River, with its splayed arteries of *klongs*, the
canals that fed into the abnormally bloated heart that was
the city of Bangkok.

'Source?' Wing Fat's eye told him this specimen was
something he had never encountered before. *Never
encountered before.* Which either meant it was something
entirely new, or it was so real and so new as to be bogus.
An ingenious deception, which was all too common in this
business.

Unfortunately, some things were *too good to be true.*
Wing Fat sighed.

'From Kho Samui. From Kroon,' Little Min replied
warily.

'Not another one of those miracle life-producing *chi*
spores from one of those fabled Isles of the Immortals, eh?
Fungus for fools, in other words.'

Little Min blinked impassively. He was as familiar with
those ancient legends as anyone who had grown up
listening to Chinese fairy-tales about the Taoist Immortals
from the mythic past of the Middle Kingdom.

'All right then, let's conduct the usual test. If we're to be
fools, let us be fools within the glorious idiocy of our
privacy. Get Xiaoling out here. She's been a little bitch
lately. She shit on the carpet this morning. Dropped her
precious pearls on a Ming dynasty treasure worth a billion
baht.' Wing Fat laughed darkly. 'And *that's* on the black
market, mind you. I bought that rug through the back-door
of the Palace Museum in Taipei just last year . . .'

Little Min bowed and left the room. He returned a
moment later with a squirrely tongued Pekingese dog that
was panting drops of saliva onto her silky grey sharkskin-
hued fur.

Xiaoling was another acquisition of Wing Fat's. She was
directly descended from one of the litters of Pekingese dogs
raised by the Dowager Empress Tzu-Hsi in the Forbidden
City. She had the face of a fluffy carp and the arrogance of

a eunuch who held the keys to the storehouse of imperial treasures.

'Set her down on the table,' Wing Fat ordered.

Little Min caressed the head of Xiaoling, but held her firmly under his arm. He looked at Wing Fat who nodded his assent. Little Min squeezed the tiny throat of the Pekingese. It shuddered briefly, but it was dead before the next strand of saliva reached its chest.

'Is it dead?' Wing Fat asked.

Little Min nodded. 'Its heart has stopped.'

'Now inject it.'

Little Min brought out the apparatus, loaded the sample into the applicator and squeezed the aerosol *chi* into the animal's nostrils. Both men waited. Wing Fat was too jaded to be curious. Little Min was too curious to show any obvious signs of interest.

'Nothing,' Wing Fat said after a moment as he surveyed the inert form of Xiaoling. 'Another fairy-tale. We've been hearing a lot of them lately. Tell Kroon he's been getting sloppy and dock his commission eight per cent from the next shipment. *That* will be a fairy-tale he will believe in—'

Before the words even left Wing Fat's lips, the *chi* infusion completed its spiral cycle through the vital center of the dog. The flow of its drool re-commenced. Xiaoling opened its watermelon-seed black eyes and stood a bit awkwardly on all fours. It whined as if it had been interrupted from swinging on the temporary perch of its life. Then it peed over Wing Fat's opium pipe, dousing the embers in the bowl.

Wing Fat smiled in disbelief. He could not readily accept what he had just witnessed. He turned to Little Min and said to him cooly, 'I know you like to play tricks on me sometimes. This is not one of them, is it? Because if it is, it will be more amusing for you to admit the joke now than it will be for me to kill you later.'

Little Min stared at his master and shook his head. That was enough for Wing Fat. He was familiar with the lies and the manipulation of his manservant, but that look on his face was all the assurance he needed. This was the real thing. Perhaps it *was* a fluke, but it was still the real thing.

'Get in touch with Kroon,' Wing Fat said. 'Tell him that we – that *I* – appreciate his gesture, and his sharing this gift with us. Tell him we need more. We need the actual source. He will be greatly compensated. He is an old friend. A valued and trusted friend—'

Wing Fat paused. 'Then when we have more to work with, we can get in touch with our *other* valued friend. In America.' Wing Fat's eyes narrowed to almost imperceptible slits, and the hulk of his face suddenly lost its effeminate contours. 'That D.D. woman will be pleased with this. She will be very, very pleased, I am certain of it.'

Little Min bowed and turned to leave the room with the panting Pekingese under his arm.

'One more thing—' Wing Fat's voice stopped him cold. It had that reedy quality to it now, a sing-song cadence that always implied threat.

'Before you leave, clean up this mess—' He nodded at the opium pipe, and at the puddle on the table inlaid with mother-of-pearl kingfisher feathers.

Little Min brought the rag out of his house-jacket pocket, the one he used for spills that his master made. But Wing Fat stopped him again. 'Before you wipe the table, wipe the dog—'

Little Min did not hesitate. 'Yes, master,' he replied. He walked over to the sliding glass-door to the balcony, opened it, and dropped Xiaoling thirty stories down below into the flowing darkness of the Chao Phraya River.

Little Min understood that the warning was meant for him. Xiaoling was a very, very precious dog. By comparison, Little Min's own life was a cheaply manufactured commodity like the bootleg *chi*-implants that were peddled by hawkers in the back-alleys of Silom Road.

He looked up as he felt sudden drops of rain hit his face. It was one of those instant tropical rainstorms that materialized out of nowhere, out of the fury of nothingness.

It was Bangkok rain.

'Is there anything else, master?' Little Min inquired as he stood motionless on the balcony that had turned into a raging waterfall. Wing Fat let him feel the full force of the deluge for a moment. Nature had spoken for him beautifully and eloquently.

Perhaps you could not control nature, *yet* – but you *could* play at being ventriloquist with storms and thunder and other natural forces. It was the illusion that counted anyway.

Just like this *chi* specimen which had confounded him. Whether it was real or not, it had *worked*. That was the important thing. Even better if it worked its magic on the *farangs* in the West. The Chinese would still control the pipeline. Wing Fat would be more than rich. He would own the intellectual property rights to immortality.

'No, that will be all.' Wing Fat waved his hand at Little Min, dismissing him. 'You can go now. Be careful not to leave your wet tracks on the floor. I'll dock your pay a thousand *baht* for each misstep.'

· · · · · · · · · · · · · · ·
Chi-Time

San Francisco

'**N**ot *you* again, Sykes,' Harry Morgan, the tall Texan dressed in a matching armadillo-skin vest and jeans snapped at Paul Sykes. As though the British freelance writer was nothing but road-kill waiting to happen, to be added to Morgan's collection of voodoo *gris-gris* talismans.

'I thought I warned you to stay out of my face,' Morgan

hissed through the gap between his front teeth. 'You're not welcome at any of my events. Now *piss* off.'

Morgan was known for his hobby of crocheting fetish-skinwear. He even had a shop, *Ruined Skins*, full of the stuff at Fillmore and Haight. Born-again Deadheads wore the tie-dyed carcasses to the Full Moon Garcia Raves which Morgan organized at Limantour Beach in Marin County. He had Carlos Castanedas Nights, too, for the psychedelic crowd in Inverness, with D.J. *brujas*, Mexican shamans, playing acid house country & western ragas 'till the effervescent *chi* of Don Juan got channeled through the meta-patches they wore on their skulls.

Morgan had made his real fortune as the successful promoter of the 'Whole *Chi* Expo,' a three-day affair held annually in the vast exhibition concourse in one of the piers at Fisherman's Wharf.

It was the world's biggest convention of state-of-the art *chi* technology, complete with organic and post-organic product roll-outs, much bigger even than the rival *Chi* Comdex event held in Las Vegas in the fall.

Harry could have retired a million years ago, Paul Sykes thought to himself. He had it all – a 400-acre ranch in the mountains of Santa Cruz, an Olympic-pool-sized redwood hot tub filled with willing babes, buxom *chi*-groupies with their blond rasta locks and insatiable first *chakra* sexual centers, and more than enough toys to keep the bugger busy for the rest of his life.

So why did he hate Sykes so much? Was it that satirical piece he had written about him in *Aura Times* magazine?

Paul Sykes was hovering around the falafel stand when Morgan turned into the aisle and spotted him.

Sykes was hungry and a little more depressed than usual. He was in the process of deliberating whether he should splurge on a green algae burger, or whether he should save the money for the cable car fare – *or whether he should go ahead and eat one now and take a chance on sneaking a free ride up Russian Hill later . . .*

There were plenty of tourists in town, and thousands of *chi* conventioneers, and he could jump off at the corner of Union and Hyde *before* the conductor caught up with him, and *then* walk home to his dismal one-bedroom flat on Valencia Street in the Mission district, which was a good 45-minute walk, but what the fuck . . .

Now it was just his luck to run into Harry Morgan. Shit.

Paul Sykes *had* to file a story about the *Chi* Expo for *Primal Tube* magazine. *Big deal, right?* But he needed the bucks. He would sell his stuff in any medium where people would cough up the dosh. He could still hear the zine's editor Rita Volkov mouth off her editorial mantra, that old tired line about conception theology:

'*As people relive the experience of being a ripe egg in the ovary, they routinely report feelings ranging from an acute sense of regret at leaving the "sisterhood" to abject terror at "going into the void" or facing "certain death". We want you to cover the Expo from the point of view of the "ripe egg," Paul. Can you do that? In 2,500 words or fewer, but don't let that cramp your style, of course . . .*'

'*You bet,*' he had replied. '*Two hundred and fifty dollars – and the usual expenses?*'

Rita had given him a wan smile that said, '*Get to it.*' God knows why she liked him. Maybe she wanted to get laid, but wasn't sure which way he swung. He'd keep her guessing. She wasn't his type. Too much Gaia in her hips and she was always clopping about in her earth-shoes, which Paul thought were the un-sexiest form of footwear since man had invented the foot fetish. Still, he was grateful to her for the gig.

Survivors had to be grateful. Gratitude meant that you at least have something to be grateful for . . .

Paul Sykes was English, 32, not bad-looking, with good teeth for an Englishman, and a seemingly inexhaustible supply of wicked one-liners. 'Like Oscar Wilde on steroids,' one of his American editors had told him.

They expected 'British humor' — one of his country's last great exports — from him. It gave his freelance writing that little bit of edge over the home-grown competition. He had panache without being a pain in the ass. He was grateful for that gift too, as well as for all the other things he had going for him . . .

Sykes wore a buzzcut with a lavender-tinted Seminole tuft of hair. He was respectably tattooed, with a facsimile of the original frontispiece engraving from the first edition of The Pickwick Papers *on his left buttock. He had once had a genital piercing, a Prince Albert, but had to have it removed due to a flare-up of kidney stones.*

On Sykes' curriculum vitae: He had once been a theology student in a New Age abbey in Salisbury, near Stonehenge. But he had lost his faith after discovering that the Abbot and his kundalini weenies had a thing for molesting the auras of the younger students. A chance encounter with a Polish anarchist convinced him that they were all barking up the wrong tree anyway.

The next big religion was, of course, going to be Nazi occultism. And the next wave of devil-worshipping Crowleyism was already turning the corner as a backlash against the popular Gnostic suicide cults of the day . . .

After abandoning his dreams of entering the priesthood, Sykes worked for a while as a door-to-door salesman selling aura insurance. ('Insure six blue ones, get one green one covered free.') It was a dispiriting business, and he got laid off two months into the job for failing to meet the company's quota.

('Twelve new policies a week, Sykes, and that's the minimum,' Ajit Kirpalani, his sales manager at Poona Brother's Prana & After-Life Insurance Co. Ltd, rebuked him in their final face-off.)

Following that career setback, Sykes got his first taste of steady employment. He'd had the unique job experience of working for a couple of years as a grave-digger outside of London. He rather enjoyed the work – had buried himself in it, so to speak.

It gave him a chance to think, to ask all the deep questions he yearned to ask, and to realize the futility of it all. If there were no answers, then perhaps there were no questions either?

That was before he switched over to freelance journalism. Sykes had his younger brother Charles, 27, to thank for that. It was Charlie who had lured him to the States. Charlie had come out of the closet and was the lover of a famous English producer of a string of hit musicals ('Kundalini Girls,' 'Beach Blanket Shambhala,' Chakra Cabaret,' and his one box-office flop, 'Mondo Mandala').

Charlie was living in New York in splendid luxury, hob-nobbing it with the rich and famous, jetting to Bermuda and Beverly Hills with side trips to his lover's villa in Martinique. He had once flown Paul and his Mum to Martinique on an all-expenses-paid holiday.

Mum was an old raver, in her third decade of dropping Ecstasy. It had calcified at the base of her spine, and she was now permanently blissed out, but still a big trooper.

Paul was proud of her. She always seemed to have a vibrant interest in everything and anything that the world had to offer her. All the mysteries were still fresh for her, as fresh as they were when she was young. She had been at Tim Leary's beside when he had launched out into the bardos. She had even been there in the Canary Islands when the Pegasus rocket blasted off with Leary's ashes into orbit, along with the pranic remains of Star Trek's creator Gene Roddenberry.

Dad, by contrast, was a working-class brick-layer on the Old Internet, building fire-walls for hoary institutions like Lloyd's of London and the Bank of England. He hadn't even switched over to Omnispace yet.

'What's the point?' he would huff. 'They'll only replace that with something else . . . Tradition, my boy, there's something to be said for that.' And he would gaze at Paul's

Mum wonderingly. What was the secret that had kept them glued together for so many years?

Perhaps on some deep level, his Dad had honed in on the intrinsic conservatism of the universe. He was a right-wing vegetarian in his political beliefs, and always voted for the Tory Greens. ('Keep the foreign legumes out,' was another one of his favorite diatribes.) In fact, Dad was an enigma to Paul Sykes, much more so than his Mum who lived so exuberantly and openly and wildly. By contrast, Dad kept his third eye pretty much to himself. He was a staunch isolationist.

Anyway, during the Martinique trip, with its glorious sunsets and long cool tropical drinks on the veranda, Charlie had managed to talk Paul – *as if he really needed* any encouragement on that score – into trying his luck in America.

'Why don't you try your hand at writing? You've dug graves before. There's not much difference. It's just another demographic, that's all . . . Hadley' – that was the name of Charlie's lover – 'knows a publisher who's starting a brand-new magazine. Mondo 3000. They're looking for fresh talent. They want to do a cover on him, and you know *how* hard he is to get . . . Who knows, I could plant a word in Hadley's ear – and you'd come with the package? They wouldn't dare refuse. I would just trust you to balance the fluff with the proper amount of sycophantic adoration. I mean, I'm in a relationship *with* him, you know – Don't fuck it up. I'm just trying to do you a favor, that's all.'

'Charlie, brother of mine,' Paul replied, clapping him on the shoulder as their beaming Mum savored the moment. 'You can trust me not to bugger your boyfriend. It's a deal.'

Long story short: That's how Paul Sykes got transplanted to America. From one grave site to another, as it were, but with a better exchange rate for the living.

'What's the matter, Mr Sykes, sir? You didn't hear me the *first* time?' Harry Morgan taunted him. 'Get the *fuck* out of here.'

Morgan turned to the two security aides who had

materialized at his side, all brawn and walkie-talkies. 'Check his press credentials,' he ordered. 'I very much doubt whether they're current – *or* bona fide. I don't recall seeing his name on the press list, that's for sure. I think I would have remembered.'

Paul Sykes blinked at the realization of what was about to come down.

Shit, shit, and shit – and more tough shit!

This was bad news. He couldn't afford to lose the Primal Tube *assignment. He was a month behind in his rent, and Anne had moved out, and was through supporting him anyway. He couldn't pyramid-scheme his new room-mate into paying first and last month's rent because Zev was subletting for just one month anyway until he found his own digs.*

This was supposed to be his lucky year, goddammit. The Year of the Dog or the Rat or the Fucking Gopher, according to the Chinese Zodiac.

Sykes had gotten a free palm reading (the second palm reading available at a 50 per cent discount, so he'd opted for just one palm: his left, his yang male energy generator, i.e. his career hand).

The psychic from the Terra Linda Institute for the Transcendentally Impaired ('We Help Needy Ouijas,' was the slogan on her t-shirt) had dropped his palm like a burning coal.

'You're *hot, mister,' she told him with a startled expression on her face. 'Your chi is about to burst through all your pipes. Where've you been, meditating on Mount Kailas for ten years? Who's your master? It's hard to believe from the outside package, but you're a ten-degree* chi *adept. You're in it, man! What d'you need your palm read for? Checking my credentials? I can see where you're coming from, buzz off, buster . . .'*

So here he was, being told to fuck off again. This bad *chi* thing was haunting him like that supposedly good luck of his that had managed to turn sour.

At least, it *tasted* sour. Maybe good luck was just bad luck turned inside-out, which would make him the luckiest wanker this side of Serendipity Gulch . . .

'Morgan –' Sykes tried to reason with the man, which was a losing proposition to be sure. 'I think you're *overreacting* just a bit. If it's that article I wrote about you, I think—'

'You think *what*?' Harry Morgan's Apache chest-plate of coyote-bones rattled as he spun around to face his security guards. His grey-streaked pony-tail braided with little Zuni animal-shaped fetishes made a nasty little whipping sound.

'March this sorry pile of shit outta here on the double—' Morgan muttered in a strangled voice, his face turning a dangerous red. '*Mundo Kundaba Kun*, you son-of-a-bitch,' he swore at Sykes, who knew what the Amazonian curse meant. '*The witch-doctor wants your head . . .*'

Just in case Sykes didn't get the message, Morgan had his keychain out, the one with the tiny shrunken head attached at the end of it. He was twirling it around wickedly.

But before the security guards could react, Paul Sykes was on his hands and knees, scuttling like a beetle underneath the falafel stand. *Jeezus, what had come over him? He'd never had reflexes like this before . . . What was he thinking, for Chrissakes!?*

He had no idea where he was going. He was just moving fast. He had to get away from these guys. A scarab with a Honda engine under his butt. There he went – traveling in between people's legs, seeing their looks of amazement as they tried to avoid tripping over him.

Was he a fucking insect – or what!?

He scuttled under the flaps of the Cosmic Bodypainting Pavilion where they were levitating the Kirlian auras of paying customers and dipping them into the healing colors of a vat containing Kashmiri fetal *chi*. Then he was out of there, and into some dark place. It was like a long narrow entrance to an igloo that never quite led to the center.

It was just long, long, long and it went on for ever. There were membrane-like frames along the sides of the passage, and zipping comets of light – *Wait a minute! These were ecto-sperms!*

He must have somehow crawled into the Primal Pavilion that offered *chi*-seekers a simulated journey. '*From the soul to the cell to downtown,*' as the poster outside the booth proclaimed. There hadn't been much of a line at the entrance to this particular exhibit when Sykes had passed it by earlier.

'*Now you can learn how prenatal trauma can cause loss of passion in your most intimate relationships . . .*'

He listened to the taped voice of the moderator Jean Parvati Schaeffer drone on in the background. The Pavilion experience was an synaesthetic advertisement for one of her workshops on pre- and peri-natal regression. A scratch-'n'-sniff for the soul.

Pre-natal wannabes, Sykes thought to himself as he zoomed along on his hands and knees through the darkness of a seemingly endless Fallopian tube.

Then he saw the Light.

He was lying underneath a pile of crates, in a private showroom on the floor of the *Chi* Expo. There were cages filled with birds and monkeys and strange-looking creatures, all with sorrowful faces. One of them was a female Orang-utan.

Where the fuck was he?

He was just about to rise from his crouched position when the Orang-utan thrust her pink fingers at him through the cage and grabbed his wrist. Then she put one finger to her mouth, and said, '*Sssshhh—*' and shook her head dolefully.

This primate had *communicated* with him. It had *spoken* to him! Or was the *sssshhh* word some sort of a universal expression common to all primates? Paul Sykes wasn't up to date on the current state of Animal Berlitz. He was confused. And then he heard voices – human voices – and he froze behind one of the crates.

One of the voices, the harsher sounding of the two, came from a woman. What she said chilled him even more than the almost human expression in the Orang-utan's eyes when she warned him to be quiet.

The woman's voice said, 'Has Wing Fat gone mad? Is this his idea of a secure communications channel? This place is crawling with eighty thousand conventioneers and the press is here in full battle gear. VNN's got its nano-spondents buzzing through the rafters. We're practically live on the Net! Where the fuck *are* his people? There's no one here. Isn't this guy Chu – he's Wing Fat's representative, right? – supposed to meet us here? What time is it anyway?'

Another woman's voice replied. 'It's one-oh-five, Deedee. We're right on time. I don't know *where* Mr Chu is . . . I got a voice mail from him this morning confirming our appointment for one o'clock this afternoon . . .'

'It's *Ms* Chu,' another voice in the showroom replied. Sykes heard a gasp of surprise coming from the two Americans who remained out of view of the other side of the crates.

'A common enough mistake – it's a Chinese surname – and not one that is usually given to a primate. But I am only the messenger, and this is my master's prerogative.'

Sykes lay glued to the floor, unable to move a muscle. He was in shock. His eyes opened wide as he watched the female Orang-utan let herself out of her cage. She loped towards the center of the private animal exhibit, swinging her long hairy arms.

'I am your messenger – *and* your specimen,' Sykes heard her say carefully as she controlled the natural chattering of her teeth. 'Please listen carefully—'

Sykes heard the Americans gasp once again.

'I haven't much time,' Ms Chu said. 'I've been programmed to erase all my vital *chi* functions within three minutes. This is all the *chi* that my master can afford to send you right now.

You may perform an autopsy on me afterwards, if you like. Your own tests should corroborate the data that has been implanted beneath my left frontal lobe. You'll find a chip there with all of Wing Fat's test-results – as well as a recording of this conversation for your reference. Wing Fat wishes you to know he has uncovered a vast new resevoir of *chi*. The *real* thing,' the Orang-utan continued.

'Not the surrogate product that is synthetically produced in the labs of the *Chi* Triangle. People may become addicted to the various derivatives of that pseudo-life energy. And there are dangerous side-effects. O.D.ing on pure No. 7 *chi* can lead to permanent brain damage, even death, as you know. The more advanced esoteric studies conducted by our Taoist neurologists indicate that even *future* life-force may become depleted from the next installment of the contiguous life-form. That is, if you believe in reincarnation, which is, of course, not mandatory, nor even relevant in this case. As I said, Wing Fat has discovered a new strain of *chi*. Actually, it is the part of the original strain of *chi* that is being transmitted from the universal source into our physical dimension.'

'What the hell is this chimpanzee talking about?' the voice of the first American woman burst out impatiently. 'Is this some kind of a joke or what?'

'*Please*—' the Orang-utan interrupted. 'I have less than one minute of *chi*-time left . . . fifty-seven seconds, to be exact . . . Let me conclude Wing Fat's message to you: There is evidence of a new species of *Homo sapiens* that is taking its place on this earth. Just as the Neanderthal man was overtaken by the Cro-Magnon man in a giant evolutionary leap, you *Homo sapiens* have among you a new species. But they are wired in ways that you cannot possibly understand given your current state of human cognitive development. You are not even aware that they exist. Or to be more precise, that you *co-exist* . . . And that just as surely, they will overtake you and claim the earth as their own. Over time, your race will eventually become extinct, unless—'

'Unless *what*?' the first American demanded. 'You've got ten seconds left so spit it out, Cheeta.'

'Unless you agree to Wing Fat's terms of distribution and market share of this new strain . . .'

Ms Chu now began to gasp for air; her *prana* was leaving her body. She gave it an extra boost and continued.

Why did Sykes get the impression that she was speaking to him as well as to these two other strangers in the tent? But keeping that part of it secret from them – and probably from this unknown Wing Fat character as well. He'd seen that light in her eyes, and felt the current pass from her simian hand to his wrist.

Jeezus Maitreya Christ! She had shown him sympathy and compassion, as if she had known a great sadness of her own, and could read into his feelings of loss in his life . . . Definitely bizarre.

Sykes trembled as he felt that funny electrospastic feeling run spikily through his spine again. He'd been feeling flashes of it all day, and had attributed it to too much coffee, not enough sleep, burn-out over his going-nowhere-fast shitty career, and his recent break-up with Anne.

Now he wasn't so sure. It was all weird, and it was getting weirder by the moment. What if there had been a *reason* for his running into that asshole Harry Morgan at the show? And having to crawl like a baby on speed to get out of there fast – towards this? Towards this *what*?

Maybe *this* was the Big One for him – the Big Story that would land him in the major league. The one that would earn him the Neuro-Pulitzer for Consciousness Reporting on the Final Frontier?

Shut up your monkey mind and listen – listen *to what she's saying, it sounds so muffled now . . .*

The American's voice was much more conciliatory now

that her initial surprise had worn off, and her critical need for data began flashing its red warning light.

'Take a nice deep breath, there – go on. *Please* – what does Wing Fat mean when he says he can identify the source of this new strain of *chi*? Who *are* these new people? This new race of *Homo sapiens*?'

'Wing Fat calls them . . .' the breath of the Orang-utan rasped into the nether-register of ongoing brain-death. 'He calls them . . . "the children of *Chi*." They have the green eye and they see the black sun.'

* * * * * * * * * * * * * * * * * * * *

Brain Damage

There were a few moments of ponderous silence in the tent, with only the chattering of monkeys and the whistling of birds breaking the stillness. Then Paul Sykes heard the two women confer between themselves in subdued tones.

'Deedee, I think we should leave now,' the second woman urged in a rattled voice. 'We can demand an explanation from Wing Fat for this – for this *demonstration* – later. I don't know what to call it. It's all highly irregular, don't you think? Hardly a way in which to conduct business—'

'Hold your horses a sec, Mir—' the more strident voice of the two replied. 'Let's think about this for a moment. I mean, *you* saw it. *You* heard it. Wing Fat's a loony. He's way out there – he's definitely on the fringe. Just look at his lifestyle. He's a filthy degenerate. Remember when we first met him in Bangkok? They even think he's weird over there, and that's saying something. That's why he never comes to the States. He'd never be accepted in Sunnyvale.

Besides he's a *persona non grata* on the FDA's black list, we know that . . .'

She continued, 'But he's always delivered the goods to us in the past. He's one of our most reliable suppliers. And it's all untraceable. We don't ask questions, we don't want to know where he gets the stuff. It's *Chi* Town, right?'

'Yes, Deedee, but—'

Paul Sykes' curiosity got the better of him. He tried to position himself so he could take a better look at them. *Who were these people? Who was Wing Fat? He was based in Bangkok? That was a primary source for pirated prana – ka, ki, chi, manu, or whatever you wanted to call it – from the notorious* Chi Triangle.

Sykes shivered when he realized what these two American businesswomen were referring to.

The 'Chi Triangle' . . . Otherwise known as 'Chi Town' . . . Rumor was they mixed in the synthetic stuff with samples of the real thing that they sucked out of the human trade. There were unbelievable stories about the chi *lords trafficking in the living* prana *of children from the impoverished hill tribes of Burma, Laos, and Cambodia.*

Jackson Monroe, the Southeast Asian correspondent for the New York Times, *had written about it. He was one of the first to break the story, but it was largely based on legend and on unattributed sources. It was a sensational account, full of the most horrific anecdotes told by grieving families who had lost their kids to chi-traffickers.*

Monroe had suggested that some of the families actually sold their own children, and were hoping to get some additional revenue out of it, some sympathy money, from the international human rights organizations. Spiritual ecologists everywhere expressed outrage. But the Thai government disputed Monroe's article and officially dismissed it as being nothing more than Western propaganda and vicious rumor-mongering.

Then Monroe had crossed over the border from the

*north of Thailand into Laos, determined to document this
secret biotech vampire industry first-hand. Shortly
afterwards, he disappeared somewhere on the Mekong
River. He had met with an unfortunate accident during his
expedition, the Laotian Minister of the Interior Sieng Phang
solemnly declared after mounting a token rescue operation.
They discontinued the search after about a week of Royal
Air Lao helicopters buzzing the river and the outlying
reaches of the jungle.*

*It was more of a publicity stunt than anything, and the
press conference in the Laotian capital of Vientiane was a
suitably somber affair, with the smiles of the government
officials reflecting just the right amount of sadness and
sympathy at the loss of a distinguished foreign reporter.*

The Times *had mounted its own expedition, of course,
but Monroe was still missing, and presumed dead. A few
intrepid foreign journalists in the region tried to pick up the
trail of the story, but it always ended in the same place.
Nowhere.*

*'Chi Town' remained a closed myth. A legend for those
foolhardy enough to believe in the 20th-century
superstitition of Einstein. For them, science was the
ultimate fairy-tale that could be deconstructed down to its
minutest sub-atomic quarks. Rapunzel as the Cosmic
Geisha, letting down her hair into the black hole of the
universe . . . All you had to do was to grab a-hold of one
of her tresses – one of those strands of Big Bang DNA –
and keep climbing 'till you reached the top of the Tower.*

'Surely you don't intend to— No, Deedee, you're not
thinking of . . .' the woman who had been addressed as
Mir spluttered. 'You're not going to do as Wing Fat
suggested and have an autopsy performed on this Orang-
utan? She must weigh a couple of hundred pounds at least
. . . How do you expect to get her out of here and off the
grounds of the Expo?'

'Don't be stupid, *Mirabelle*,' her colleague sniggered. 'Of course I'm not going to drag this ape out in full public view, even assuming you were going to lend me a hand.' Her voice sounded condescending and full of irony. 'Which you're clearly not in any condition to do.'

'What's on your mind, Deedee? What do you want to do?' The woman sounded scared now as though she had already anticipated what was coming next.

'Wing Fat said there was a chip with all the data implanted in its front left lobe, didn't he?'

'Oh, God, Deedee – surely you're not . . .'

'Do you even *realize* what we might be sitting on here?' Deedee now unleashed her full scorn on her associate. 'Are you prepared just to walk away from it? Would you be able to live with yourself afterwards?'

'I'm sorry – I can't . . . I think I'm going to faint.'

'Scalpel—'

'Excuse me?'

'Where's that fancy blade of yours? Come on, now,' Deedee snapped at Mirabelle impatiently. 'You're always carrying that *gen-u-ine* carbon-steel-forged commando dagger that you ordered from *Angel of Fortune* magazine in your handbag, aren't you? You claim it's useful for a thousand and one things including self-defense. You even took a street-fighting class, learned how to slit the throat of any assailant who might be holding a knife to your throat . . . Get a grip on yourself, Mir! This is *war*.'

Mir groaned. 'We're talking about rapists in that event . . . Life or death situations. This is . . . this is . . . a dead monkey.'

'Goddammit, if you can't do it yourself, then hand over the fucking thing.'

There was the sound of fumbling. 'Where is it? Oh my God, Deedee . . .'

Deedee grabbed Mir's handbag and spilled its contents out on the floor. She rummaged through the pile. 'Condoms, mints – congratulations, Mir, your sex life must be improving . . . Ah, here it is! A real beauty, just as advertised . . . Billy Bushido, the all-purpose carving knife. Fits neatly into the palm of your hand like your boyfriend does. All right, let's snap it open, better get this over with. Who knows when they'll be reopening this zoo to the public?'

Paul Sykes heard the sound of Deedee clicking open the dagger, heard her whistle in appreciation, followed by a series of grunts. He peered over one of the crates at the spectacle. A short brown-haired woman in a tan pantsuit was bending over the dead Orang-utan, trying to turn it over so that it would be lying face-up on the floor.

'Come on, Mir, help me get this thing turned around – Jeezus Christ! It's fucking heavy!'

The strawberry blonde who stood cowering behind Deedee was dressed in a white silk *judo* outfit by Nisei Miyake, complete with a sequinned *judo* black belt, and Mother Teresa Love-A-Leper sandals. She was pretty good-looking, was Paul Sykes' guess, but she had her hand firmly clasped over her mouth as though she was going to be sick, so he couldn't be sure.

'I just can't . . .' she whimpered.

'Yes, you can,' Deedee ordered. 'Think of it as customer relations. Move your tush, honey, we haven't got all day.'

Mir shuddered, then took a step forward and helped Deedee flip the Orang-utan over. She covered her mouth again as she watched Deedee Delorean feel around the head of Ms Chu 'till she located the soft spot on her skull.

Paul Sykes stifled a gasp. *Deedee Delorean*. He could clearly make out the name on her *Chi* Expo name-tag, although that was an unnecessary corroboration of her identity. One glance at her was enough to know who she was. The woman with her was Mirabelle Myers. Sykes instantly recognized their faces from the industry trade-weeklies.

They were the two head honchos from *Chi* Memory Systems, the Sunnyvale company that specialized in the development of neural *chi* chips (*Chi*RAMs) for organic tele-networking systems.

Deedee (a.k.a. 'Digitella') Delorean was the firm's president and CEO, one of the most powerful women in the industry. And 'Mir' Myers was her VP of Product Development.

CMS, Inc. was *huge*. A $100-billion-dollar company worldwide. They supplied *everyone* with their neurals from the encrypted neural sets of the Pentagon's Psy-Forces Division ('Star Wars at the Blink of an Eye'), to the multi-national conglomerates with their pineal gland-networked communications systems, on down to the local Little Leaguers playing 'ball in their neighbourhood parks.

They were the leading consumer animism-providers of the Global Brain.

You could hold spirited conversations with your corn-flakes in the morning – on any topic specified on the back of the box – from Spinoza to the latest kiddie adventure of Sammy the Shaman in Disney's popular vitamin series ('A Fully Animated Psychotropic Cartoon Contained Within Each Fruit-Flavored Multi-Vitamin, the Kids Won't Want to Miss a Day of Healthy Fun'). Last Sykes had read they were planning an assault on the entertainment industry, to cut out the middle-media altogether.

Have a nice day, Paul Sykes thought to himself as he watched Deedee Delorean hack away at the Orang-utan's head with the serrated edge of Mir's Billy Bushido blade. She had rolled up her sleeve and was feeling around inside the cavity. Something grey and pink flopped out of the grapefruit-sized hole in Ms Chu's cranium.

'Squishy little bastard . . .' Deedee swore out loud, as she prodded the glop of brain-matter with the dagger. 'It's the left-lobe we want . . . *There!*'

She triumphantly held out a thin black wafer in her bloodstained fist. 'Mir, I do believe we've found the source of the Nile. This should tell us the entire story, assuming that Wing Fat's not full of it—'

As Deedee Delorean held out the Orang-utan's implanted bio-wafer for Mir to see, it suddenly shot out of her slippery fingers.

Paul Sykes caught his breath as it landed an inch away from his hiding place behind Ms Chu's cage.

'*Shit!*' he heard Deedee swear. 'Where'd it go . . .' And then she was there and looking into his eyes, as deeply as Anne had done when he had hurt her, before she had packed up all her feelings for him and moved out. It was a look that suggested the deepest kind of accusation, of betrayal, as if he were a condemned war criminal in the raw footage of her life.

'*Who* are *you? And what are you* doing *here?*' he heard Deedee Delorean hiss at him.

'Dunno, haven't figured that one out yet,' Sykes heard himself respond. He calmly picked up the wafer and slipped it into his jeans pocket before Deedee could react. If that wasn't pure instinct, what was it?

Then he began to crawl out of there as fast as he could, back under the flaps of the private animal showroom ('*Chi's Psychic Pets, By Appointment Only, Direct From Our Showroom in Kuala Lumpur*').

Now he was scuttling on his hands and knees once again, but backwards this time, through the long Fallopian tube of the Primal Pavilion where it had all started, where it had all begun, with no more inkling of what lay ahead for him than the confused embryo of an unborn mind.

. . . .

Damage Control

'**Y**ou really think you can do it? Break it all down, I mean? So that it makes some sense?' Paul Sykes asked the scraggly white-haired man who was seated at the long wooden work-table.

The surface of the table was cluttered with all the tools of Mort Wisenik's trade. There were different makes of *chi*-readers; a pile of protective mental-dams for entering the Net *bardos*, the after-life states of deceased avatars in Omnispace; and a vast array of sensitive instruments for sifting through the electronic compost of the world's orbiting satellites.

In short, all the gizmos for foraging among the wreckage of the Global Brain.

'What if it's booby-trapped?' Sykes asked nervously. He was aware of all the nasty security viruses that had a way of popping up when you least expected.

Like the 'Gulag' virus, for instance, which the Russians had perfected. Sykes had heard about the horrifying psychotropic mist that swept you away into the House of the Dead that lay buried deep in your psyche. You became the walking human labor camp, your own jailer and your own torturer. Then there was the Chinese variation known as 'Mad Mao Disease.' This was a hypnogogic water-torture that made each yactosecond seem like eons. A relentless *drip, drip, drip* of quotations from the Chairman's *Little Red Book* that splattered upon the convulsing ectoplasm of your brain . . .

Not even insanity could grant you political asylum from these mental tortures.

Mort Wisenik paused to brush away a few loose strands from the white Brillo-pad ensemble that constituted his wired toupee. A few greasy 'trodes had fallen into his eye.

'Don't worry, son. *Se hable techno-babble*.' He gave Sykes a reassuring thumbs-up sign. 'Have no fear. Fear is nothing but child-proof dogma. The root cause of all the wickedness in the world. Fear of failure. Fear of the boogeyman. Fear that one day all your hopes will be realized – and being afraid of where to go from there. Whatever poisons your soul, I call that fear. Let's have a look at this thing. *Hmm—*'

Wisenik held Ms Chu's bio-wafer with a pair of surgical

tweezers and studied it through the Mitsubishi *chi*-scope that was screwed into the socket of his right eye. He wore a fiberoptic face-mask. For all his seediness, Mort Wisenik looked like a Bond Street jeweler searching for a flaw in the Star of India ruby.

'Looks like it's a Hitachi Intel 9200 bio-ROM,' Wisenik remarked. 'Or rather, it's a pirated version of one. Yup. It's a clone, all right. Made in Kota Baru, Malaysia. No doubt about it. It's got a cheap casing. More chance of cranial seepage that way. Left-brain sludge. Don't know *what* you're going to pick-up. The odd daydream. Stream-of-consciousness sewage. Whatever. I can't promise you a clean transmission of the original document.'

He grinned. 'Hey, cheer up, Sykes. The prognosis is good. The psychosis is even better.'

He chuckled at his own joke. 'What's the matter with you, Sykes? You look like a ghost just bit you on the ass. What's eating you anyway?'

Ascetic and seemingly wiry in appearance, but with a paunch that his faded floral print Hawaiian shirt was unable to conceal, Wisenik looked like a Buddha who had joined the Rotary Club, instead of what he really was, a master of the black art of *chi*-dissection.

Sykes had come straight to him from the *Chi* Expo. If anyone could make this thing out, Wisenik could. Sykes had known him ever since he'd arrived in San Francisco. He used him as a background source for some of his more technical stories. In exchange, he helped Mort out by composing letters to his parole board.

Wisenik was a pro's pro – and an ex-con. He had served eight-to-ten in the Chico State Penitentiary for impersonating the home-page of Cardinal Wozniak of Chicago. His fund-raising drive for the digital lepers of Western Samoaspace had netted him fifty grand before the Om Police busted him. He was charged with extortion of consciousness, *fêng-shui* geomancy fraud, embezzlement of church funds, and the crossing of international ley-lines.

Paul Sykes shook his head. 'I don't know, Mort – I just have a bad feeling about this. I wonder if I've made a mistake sticking my nose into this business.'

Sykes sat reclining in a purple nagaldahyde easy-chair that Wisenik had salvaged from the junkyard. He had a worried look on his face. He had barely managed to get himself out of the *Chi* Expo in one piece. That she-devil Deedee Delorean had been on his tail. And he'd had to keep an eye out for Harry Morgan and his goon-squad. *Trouble times trouble equals more trouble.*

It was only when he had gotten lost among the bustling crowd on Fisherman's Wharf that he could let his guard down just a little, and breathe a huge sigh of relief. His adrenaline still pumping, he jumped aboard a cable car heading up Hyde Street and began to plot his next move.

Who did he know that could help him decipher this monkey-wafer thing he'd been crazy enough to pinch in the animal pavilion?

Sykes wracked his brain as he held on to the pole that was slick with the grease of a thousand palms. Tourists were smiling all around him. It was a warm spring day. The sky was blue. The old prison island of Alcatraz was clearly visible in the bay.

Alcatraz. Mort Wisenik. *Of course.*

Wisenik operated out of his second-floor walk-up flat on Powell Street. It was nice and anonymous, with the sound of the cable-cars clanging outside and a Chinese laundry on the ground floor that was the front for an illegal *fan-tan* betting-parlor. You could get a Starbucks algaeccinno at the corner, take out some Chinese food from the greasy spoon diner next door, and even bullshit with the transvestite hookers who pounded the pavement outside without getting hassled by anyone.

No one would find him here. Not Deedee Delorean. Not Harry Morgan. Not this mysterious Wing Fat character with his sinister menagerie from the Psychic Pets showroom at the *Chi* Expo. Not even Anne, should she have one last word, one final accusation, to levy against him.

You loser. You've lost the one single chance of happiness you will ever find. Someone who can put up with all your infantile vaccilations and all your childish infidelities and still be waiting there for you. You loser!

Paul Sykes gripped the arms of the purple nagaldahyde easy-chair and suppressed a shudder.

'Falling apart and turning into a total wreck must serve some higher evolutionary purpose, I suppose,' Wisenik said as he glanced at his young friend.

'Can't we just get on with it?'

'Whatever you say, old bean. Whatever you say.' Wisenik slipped the wafer into the Hitachi drive and began the vivisection of the stored cranial algorithms.

As he waited for the brain-wave recordings to digitally reconstitute themselves, he couldn't help add a few more words of advice. Sykes looked as if he needed it. He was a good candidate for some of Wisenik's perennial wisdom.

'One of nature's cruelest pranks is to make you want to pull the plug on hope. It's like a built-in, programmed obsolescence of man's faith in his own future. Damned if I know why. So that we decide to call it quits – and the next thing on the evolutionary ladder gets its turn at bat? Who knows? We're lemmings at heart. Looking for road-signs to guide us to the off-ramp that leads to the Apocalypse.'

Wisenik's eyes widened as the screen began to read out the alpha-and-delta bandwidth of the subject's bio-data dump. He tapped the screen pensively with his forefinger.

'All the archetypes are crumbling,' Wisenik continued, a frown beginning to crease his brow as he studied the screen. 'At first, all we aspired to was to fulfill ourselves as individuals. Individual liberties, individual rights, individual thoughts. Good old days, right? Then suddenly we all desperately wanted to become part of the interconnected whole. Now all our thoughts belong to this one vast commune – this Great Leap Forward into universal consciousness . . . In Singapore, they *cane* you if you have a guilty conscience. Did you know that?'

'What's going on, Mort? What's all that stuff coming through? Can you make it out?' Sykes asked as he rose from his easy-chair to stand behind the desktop philosopher. Wisenik was busy toggling switches. The colors on the screen were jumping through swirling concentric hoops.

'What *are* all those glyphs?'

Wisenik looked up at him solemnly. 'I told you there was bound to be some cranial seepage, didn't I? The primary data – the stuff you were after that was recorded on the chip. That's all gone. I'm sorry, Paul. I can't help you there, mate. It's Kota Baru product. Cheap *chi*. What you pay for is what you get.'

'*Shit!*' Sykes exclaimed with a bitterness that caught him by surprise with its force. 'All that for *nothing*! My fucking luck again, *my fucking luck*! I *had* something there! Now it's all fucking gone down the toilet . . .'

Fortune tellers, psychics, girlfriends with the 'second sight,' even his own mother who had told him he had been born under a lucky star . . . Poppycock propaganda, all of it, sugar-coating on the gristle of harsh reality. He *was* a loser, and damned good at being one . . . He felt completely deflated. He'd have to go back to grave-digging, if they still had a slot left open for him.

'Yeah, I can sympathize with that point of view, Paul,' Wisenik said softly. 'But this, I think, has got to be far more interesting than whatever it was they had originally imprinted on the Kota Baru chip.'

Paul Sykes cut his tirade short. That was enough self-flagellation for the moment. He was ready to move on again. His negativity had invigorated him. 'What do you mean by that? What have you got?'

'This is a monkey mnemonic, if I'm not mistaken. It's a cache of memories. Love letters sent through the monkey ether. *Communications*, in other words, from one primate to another. Some of them postmarked not that long ago, judging from the emotional time-stamp on this blob of color. From one side of the planet to another. See this green mango-shaped glyph?'

Sykes stared at the screen. He saw the stirring of a luminous green shape. 'Yes, but what does it *mean*?'

Mort Wisenik leaned back in his chair and rubbed his eyes. He suddenly felt very, very tired. He'd been there, done that, had shot the shit with the best of them. He had even coined a word for what it was he did so well. He was a *golemtologist*.

Wisenik could read the vital signs on a coconut and translate that into code. He could make the dead walk again in Omnispace. Some of his best clients were unscrupulous lawyers who hired him to transcribe the last thoughts of a dying person – perhaps even to get them to change their will at the final moment.

Not that any of this was admissible in court, mind you. Not in this day and age. Not yet. It was still an arcane technology, like lie-detectors had once been. But it still gave them some forensic leverage. '*Blackmail their fucking chakras*,' one of the attorneys had confided in him, derisively referring to some relative with a guilty conscience who'd been willing to re-negotiate a settlement on a joint-inheritance in favor of their client.

But this – this thing that was seeping through the heart chakra of a dead Orang-utan. What was it?

Mort Wisenik let out a deep sigh. 'This is a new one on me, bubba,' he said to Paul Sykes. 'Near as I can guess, this is the first documented record of a morphic communication – mind to mind, heart to heart – between two primates who have been kept apart at a great distance. Somehow it got recorded on this bullshit Kota Baru wafer. And it's a sad story, Sykes. Just like Romeo and Juliet. Of broken hearts and human cruelty. And it's not over yet. Care to have a look-see?'

mmm.gunung mulu.com

Paul Sykes gave Wisenik a dumbfounded look. 'How are you going to decode it, Mort?'

'Well, old chum, I'm not quite sure yet,' Wisenik replied as he rummaged around in a drawer. He found an old dented tin of Fisherman's Friend, and offered it up to Sykes.

'Rizlas,' he confided. 'Not cough-drops.'

'No thanks,' Sykes shook his head. 'I'll pass.'

'I'll just help myself then, it helps me think non-linearly,' Wisenik said as he withdrew a tightly rolled joint from the tin. He lit it, took a deep drag and stared up at the ceiling for a few moments absorbed in his own thoughts.

'You know, Sykes,' Wisenik finally spoke. 'I've been waiting all my life for something like this to break. Something so monumental. Something so awfully brand-new, yet so primeval, that it makes the Big Bang seem fresh again.'

Wisenik took another hit of the weed as he collected his thoughts. 'I feel like what's-his-name, that astronaut Neil Armstrong, the first man to ever set foot on the moon. And here I am, discovering an honest-to-God morphogram. Even if it's from a monkey.'

He tapped some of the Rizla's ashes into a potted plant, a leafy green philodendron that was perched on the windowsill soaking in the sunlight.

'Rupert Sheldrake, a fellow countryman of yours, was one of the first to get on to it,' Wisenik continued. 'Morphic resonance, he called it. He came pretty close to unraveling a lively correspondence between dung-beetles contained in specimen jars on opposite sides of the earth. From Cairo to Glasgow. He gathered they had some complaints about the food. Were pining for some home-cooking. But nothing like *this*, man.' Wisenik tapped a finger against the screen where the green mango glyph was whirling like a top.

'Nope,' he shook his head emphatically. '*This* –' Wisenik declared solemnly, '– is a neuro-historical document.'

Wisenik sighed. 'I wish an old buddy of mine, Frank Gobi, was here to share this with me. We were school chums at Berkeley. Graduating class of '11 . . . If anyone could make heads or tails of this, Frank could—'

'You knew Frank Gobi?' Sykes sounded genuinely surprised. 'I didn't know that.'

'Oh yeah, Frank and I go back a long way. Of course, he went on to bigger and better things. Got his doctorate in Omnispace para-psychology. Went deep-sea diving into Satori City 2.0 when it crashed in '26. Rescued a bunch of people from the VR-bends when he re-booted Virtuopolis. You know the story. Earned his spot in the Rim Hall of Fame, Frank did,' Wisenik reminisced as he sucked on the Rizla.

'His kid was one of 'em, you know.' Wisenik gave Sykes a strange look. 'One of the lost ones. A fine boy, Trevor. A real fire-walker. He's got asbestos soles just like his Dad. You'd dig him, Sykes. Anyway—'

Wisenik shrugged his shoulders. 'I went to the pen. And Frank's out there somewhere on some kind of an all-exenses paid lifetime sabbatical, looking into just these sorts of things. I could use his help now. What would Frank suggest, I wonder . . . Hmm, wait a minute.'

Wisenik sat straight up. He was staring at the philodendron. 'Fuck,' he said excitedly. 'I remember reading an article of Frank's once. On "Organic Cyberspace." The next big thing, he called it. It's like the morphic thing. But along the lines of interspecies communication. We've got all these morphic nodes all around us. We just don't know where they are. Nature is the perfect medium. *Nature*—' Wisenik's eyes brightened. 'Rocks, waterfalls, trees – plants!

'Plants, my boy!' Wisenik clapped his hands. 'Like Rodney here! Meet Rodney the Philodendron. Can't say he's had too much of an abused childhood. He gets watered regularly, has his favorite spot in front of the sun-telly. I

squirt him with the occasional vitamin like this fine
sensimillian ash. The original pot-head, Rodney is. Let's see
what he's got to say about this. How about it, Rod?'

Wisenik spun around on his chair, lifted the plant up
from the sill and deposited him gently on the work-table
beside the monitor. As Sykes watched without comment,
Wisenik busied himself wiring Rodney to his work-station
with a bristling array of electrodes.

'Plants – even common household plants – sorry, Rodney,
don't mean to be disrespectful – emit certain electro-
magnetic pulses. Now if we can just tap into them—'

Wisenik opened up a window on the screen, and ran his
fingers over the keyboard.

'Let me call up Frank's article. If memory serves, there
was an interesting footnote buried in there somewhere. An
algorithm for converting chlorophyll into an organic search-
engine . . . Are you still with me, Sykes?'

'Still with you, Mort,' Sykes replied as his mood lifted.
'All the way!'

*Maybe there was some hope, after all . . . Some inner
connection at work here that he hadn't quite grasped.
Wisenik knowing Gobi. Sykes' attending the Chi Expo.
Stumbling across the Orang-utan in the animal pavilion and
coming away with the chip. Sykes' knowing Wisenik . . .
God knows, perhaps even Rodney fit into the picture
somehow . . .*

'There it is.' Wisenik let out a manic laugh as Gobi's
algorithm flashed onto the screen. 'It was first published in
the *Interspecies Insider*, vol. 2, issue 8 . . . They folded after
vol. 4. Too far out for most conventional minds. Fringe
science, that's what they thought of Copernicus in his own
time.'

Sykes could see Rodney's brain-waves – was that what
you called a plant's *prana*-bandwidth? – hovering on the
screen in bright green colors. Ms Chu's morphic glyph was
still spiraling in its green mango envelope at the far corner
of the screen.

'Now we're going to bring these three components together. Make a little green tossed salad out of 'em. Hey, Sykes.' Wisenik nodded at him exuberantly.

'Put the dunce-cap on. There it is, at the end of the table. And get me one, too. There's an extra set around there somewhere. Great. Now, we're going in, my friend. If this little experiment works, Rodney's gonna channel us some real green wisdom. A plant's eyeball plugged into the mind of the Great Green Rain Forest in the Sky – *Shoosh!!!!*'

There was a crashing sound of vines and tendrils parting. A vortex of green that billowed to the limit, receded, then overflowed its banks again. There was a huge booming sound of giant pods falling to the jungle floor. Then a sonic bleedthrough of parrot bio-rhythms. A screech of a cloud leopard calling to its mate. Then the green, green silence that was filled with overpowering waves of luminous branches dripping with raw green data.

'Mort, you there?'

'Think so, mate. You okay?'

'Where are we?'

'Give me a sec to orient to this vector.'

More crackling green thunder and sudden sheets of rain ripped out of the sky. It was a tropical thunderstorm with a gift for pantomime. Sykes felt drenched to the skin, but he *couldn't* be.

He was sitting in Wisenik's flat on Powell Street, wasn't he? Wasn't he? Wearing this gizmo on his head? Get a grip, man . . .

He heard Wisenik's laughter lost somewhere in this dense green sonic jungle.

'Rodney's got the gift, man . . . He may be a small fry, but he's channeling Alpha Green big time.'

'Where *are* we, Mort?'

'Okay, near as I can tell – it's a web-site of some sort.'

'A *web*-site?'

'Not on-line. We're just patched into it courtesy of Rodney

and his chlorophyll search-engine. This is pure Mother
Nature e-mail, man.'

'Shit.'

'One small monkey turd for man. One giant elephant
dropping for mankind.'

'Be serious, Mort.'

'Okay, pal. I'm getting a reading on it now. I have to
translate all this stuff into human gibberish. "In the
Beginning there was Netscape . . ." Now there is . . . *This.*'

'Where *are* we, for Chrissakes?'

'Hold on to your pants, son. Okay, to be specific, I'm
reading the navigational charts now: Tree Number 17, Row
35, the Gunung Mulu National Park, somewhere in
northeast Sarawak. That's in Indonesia, in case you didn't
know. South of Brunei. It's got 1,500 species of flowering
plants, including ten species of the famous pitcher plant.
Most importantly, as far as we're concerned, it's got Tree
Number 17, Row 35.'

'What the hell is that?'

'It would appear to be a node for morphic communications. This particular tree is the hub for a vast natural
network of trans-species communications. It's sort of like an
organic satellite dish. Frank would be proud of me.'

'What do we do now?'

'You want to decode that Orang-utan's diary, don't you?
There's copies of everything that's ever been transmitted
stored in the data-base of this tree's root-system.'

'What the hell; now that we're here, let's give it a shot.'

'That's the spirit, Sykes. Okay, I gotta do a little more
conversion here. Get the human thing in sync with the
monkey mind. Ready?'

'Whenever you are.'

'Right.'

B-O-O-O-M!!!!!!

A green rush of light spun them around in a sentient
whirlpool of strange shapes, murmurings, fractals of
microscopic slides of faster-than-thought images.

'S-y-k-e-s?' Wisenik's voice sounded fragmented, wobbly, with an echo of an emerald-green rain forest behind it.

'Y-e-s?' Sykes wasn't feeling quite anchored himself in this Green No-Man's Land.

'C-o-n-g-r-a-t-u-l-a-t-i-o-n-s, m-a-t-e. I t-h-i-n-k w-e-'-v-e d-o-n-e i-t. W-e'-v-e b-r-o-k-e-n t-h-r-o-u-g-h t-h-e m-o-r-p-h-i-c r-e-z b-a-r-r-i-e-r.'

There was a crackling pause as they adjusted to the new tele-equilibrium.

'This is it. We're logging on to Tree Number 17, pardon the pun. *Jeezus Christ*, I can't believe it,' Wisenik spluttered. 'We've arrived in the storehouse of the Collective Primate Mind. The Alaya of the Apes. How d'you like that! It's even got its own morphic address: *mmm.gunung mulu.com.* I've got to save this address. Come back to the site later . . .'

Sykes heard the sound of Wisenik tapping on a tree-trunk like a woodpecker. 'Let the sap flow a little, collect it in these little buckets that I've brought along just for the occasion.'

Wisenik was talking to himself now as he busied himself with his task of data-tapping.

'Wow, there sure are a lot of files, man. Let's see now. What have we got ourselves here? Stacks and stacks of mail from moles, tree shrews, gymnures, moonrats, mongooses, otters, weasels, barking deer – *Jeez*, they're loud, man! – where are the primates? All right! *Pongo pygmaeus abelii* . . .' Wisenik babbled on.

'The Sumatran Orang-utan. In Malay, "*orang*" means "person" and "*utan*" means "forest." "*The person of the forest*." A beautiful description, really. Gentle as they come, but fierce if they're forced into it. They've been known to kill a croc by pulling open its jaws and ripping out its throat. Otherwise, they're primarily herbivorous. Young leaves, bark, flowers, insects, and birds' eggs is their main diet. That, and popcorn when they're held in captivity. Here we are, Sykes!' Wisenik announced.

'Green mango time! Our dear Ms Chu. Complete with
log-on dates and everything. Ms Chu a.k.a. "Nita." Most
of this stuff is between her and – hmm – an odd name for
an Orang-utan – Tommy. An unrequited love affair. I told
you it was going to be sad. Long-distance love affairs
usually are . . . Shall we take a peek then?'

'I'm right behind you,' Sykes replied hesitantly. He felt a
mixture of guilt and voyeuristic curiosity. Would this
constitute a violation of Ms Chu's personal privacy? They
were about to invade the records of her mind and heart. But
Sykes could still recall the pleading look in her eyes when
she sat in her cage in the animal pavilion at the *Chi* Expo.

And he could still feel the current of her life-force when
she clasped his hand with hers. She had been trying to tell
him something. What was it? Maybe that was all the
permission he needed, that light touch of her hand . . .

'Let's go in, Mort.'

'Aye-aye, mate,' Wisenik replied. 'Pick a grub, any grub
. . . This one's from Tommy . . .'

As they opened the first of Ms Chu's files, Sykes
discovered that he could read with eyes that he never knew
he possessed. Green as the jungle light that filtered through
the vast overhead canopy of vines.

>>> *The Gunung Mulu Memorandum* <<<

. . . .

Monkey See, Monkey Do

Pinang, Malaysia

Tommy Kok Lau stormed out of his parents' luxury
condo on Lebuh Chulia street in Georgetown, the
easy-going, sleepy capital of this mostly Chinese island
off the west coast of Malaysia. He was in a foul mood.

Tommy was at that awkward age that one particular segment of Malaysian and Malay-Chinese kids had great difficulty coping with.

There were strict but unwritten rules about their coming of age. Some of his pals were fatalistic about it. '*Inshallah*,' they said, shrugging their shoulders. 'Whatever will be, will be.'

Others in his position were more openly rebellious. 'We don't have to accept it. Fuck them. We didn't ask to be brought into this world. Times are changing. We don't have to stand for it any more. It's so fucking *barbaric*.'

'Tommy, where are you going?' his mother Leilah called out to him anxiously. She had been stretched out on the rattan couch in the living room, wearing her favorite peach-colored silk pajama outfit that she had bought at a boutique in Butterworth. She was painting her nails fire-engine red, cracking open anise-flavored watermelon-seeds with her teeth, and watching a Chinese soap on the combo-TV-air-conditioner.

Leilah knew that something was troubling Tommy. She could even guess at what it was. But it wasn't anything that mother and son could discuss together. She could barely bring herself to raise the painful subject with her husband, Samuel Lau.

Anyway, Sammy had already made up his mind. He had as much as told her so the other night. '*Leilah, be reasonable. He's going to be a young* adult *soon. Do you know what that* means?'

'Tommy, did you tell your father you were going out?' Leilah demanded feebly, as her son angrily slammed the door behind him without saying a word in reply.

She heard the sound of Tommy kick-starting his Kawasaki 500 c.c. motorcycle in the compound, heard the thunderous roar of the bike as it came to life. Then he was gone in a fury that she secretly knew was justified.

What would she tell Sammy? Her husband would never believe that she hadn't warned Tommy. Leilah suddenly caught herself thinking, '*And why* didn't *I? Why* didn't *I warn him?*'

She covered her eyes and wept as though a monsoon had sprung out of her face and was washing away each tear of motherhood that she had been saving for this day.

Leilah was thirty-eight, but could pass for twenty-six. Sammy was forty-eight, a prosperous man from an old distinguished Chinese family that had settled in peninsular Malaysia a century ago. He owned a chain of convenience stores on the island.

For years, Leilah had tried to bear him sons to carry on the family name. She had tried everything – fertility pills ground from rhinoceros horn and tiger testicles, Taoist incantations, in vitro fertilization at a Swiss clinic in Kuala Lumpur, everything. No luck.

She had to face the facts. She had as much chance of conceiving a baby as a wok-fried bat had of flying out of a bowl served at a roadside food-stall.

Things had gotten bad between her and Sammy after that. Apart from Leilah's loss of face – among her relatives, in-laws, ancestors, friends, business associates, even the servants, she shivered in shame at the thought – there was the strong possibility that Sammy would divorce her.

Or if not divorce her, take on a Number Two wife, a 'mee-uh noi' – which he had jokingly threatened to do. Only it was no joke. Leilah had her own intelligence network operating in the field. She knew that Sammy had his favorite girls, his young swallows, whom he would visit regularly in Chinatown.

She chose to turn a blind eye at that. That came with the territory with an important man like Sammy. 'Chinese husbands,' she shrugged to herself. 'What can you do?'

No, what alarmed Leilah the most was the news that Sammy had taken on a 'mee-uh noi,' a certain Mimi Fu, who came from a respectable family (they owned real estate in Melaka and several rubber plantations). Sammy had put her up in a beachfront duplex in Batu Ferringhi on the northwest-side of the island.

Leilah had to take drastic action. Desperate last measures were required. But Sammy would have to be talked into it. Adoption was not an option. 'Other people's babies, other people's ancestors . . .' The obligations would be too great, the commotion at the family's ancestral tablet would create havoc. And that would lead to bad joss, great misfortune, and Sammy's business would suffer. It would be the end of the world.

Still, nothing ventured, nothing gained. She had heard through the grapevine about this one other 'neutral' solution. 'Other people do it. You would be surprised if you knew who, some of them are your friends. Who would suspect?' it was whispered to her. 'If you *can't* tell the difference, who *can*?'

'It's a compromise, of course, but you can't have everything. The ancestors can be fooled – or at the very least, they don't need to be consulted or informed. It doesn't concern them as such. There IS another way, Leilah. But it's your choice. Take it or leave it.'

Leilah's choice of middleman – actually, her secret source of information on the subject – was Kitty Wong. Kitty had a beauty salon on Lebuh Campbell Street where Leilah had her hair done once a week. Leilah had beautiful gossamer hair that flowed down her back in waves like black silk.

She knew that she was still beautiful in Sammy's eyes. She knew that he still loved her, that he still desired her. If only . . .

Anyway, among Kitty Wong's various side-lines – she liked to dabble – was match-making. She specialized in arranged marriages. But she would branch out whenever she saw a fresh business opportunity arise. So when some of those arranged marriages failed to produce the necessary off-spring, she saw the writing on the wall. She had found another niche, another void to fill.

It was Kitty who had gotten Leilah in touch with the

broker in Kuala Lumpur. Putting on a brave face, Leilah
told Sammy she was going to attend a high-school reunion
of her old school chums from the Sacred Heart Convent
Girls' Academy in KL.

'Be back in a day,' she told him. 'Just girl talk. You
know – talk, talk, talk. Catch up on all the nuns' bad
karma. You can come along, if you want. The husbands
will be playing mah-jong at the hotel.'

Sammy had put on a demure expression of false regret.
'No can do, baby. Go ahead, have a good time. I've got too
much business to take care of here in Georgetown.'

Too much business, Leilah had thought to herself, a
sweet smile disguising her black heart. Business named
Mimi Fu . . .

Leilah took the air-conditioned mini-bus from the Malaysia
Hotel down to KL the following morning. It was a 10 mg
Valium trip, with the bus-driver wired on speed, eye-lids
propped open with toothpicks, one foot on the gas and one
on the brake, playing 'say-hello-to-your-ancestors' with the
oncoming traffic.

But she arrived safely, thank God and Sister Felicia, her
one good-luck nun from high school. Leilah relaxed as soon
as she spotted the gleaming white minaret of the Masjid
Negara Mosque that was the landmark monument of Kuala
Lumpur.

She had made it.

Leilah took a taxi to the address that Kitty Wong had
scribbled down for her on a piece of paper. It was for a
shop named Chi Enterprises, 17 Jelan Melayu, at the busy
corner of Jalan Tuanku Abdul Rahman and Jalan Tun
Perak.

Odd, it looked like some sort of pet shop. But discretion
was called for in this business, as Kitty Wong had assured
her. The tinkling sound of the bell as Leilah opened the
door was immediately drowned out by the horrendous
screeching of parakeets, whistles of mynah birds, the

rat-tat-tatting of woodpeckers, and the whosk-whosk-whosk of the hornbill.

It took Leilah a moment to orient herself in the murky gloom of the pet shop. Her hand was still on the doorknob when she saw a wall of tanks filled with snakes – pythons and cobras and shimmering green tree snakes. She was ready to turn around and leave right then when someone called to her.

'That's a pangolin,' came a soft-spoken voice from a well-dressed Indian gentleman who appeared out of nowhere to greet her. He was handsome, in his thirties, and dressed in a short-sleeved blue safari suit. A gold chain glittered around his brown-skinned neck. He was pointing at a tank containing a scaly-looking reptile with a long tapered head and tail.

'It feeds on termites and ants, and I'm teaching it to read the alphabet,' he said proudly. 'Bahasa Malaysian, of course, and a few words in English. Also, a little Sanskrit can't hurt.'

He bowed from the waist down. 'Do come in, please. My name is Mohandir Das. This is my shop. But I can tell from your demeanor that you're not interested in household pets. If you were, I'd show you a lovely tapir that's just come in from Sumatra. It's a cross between a pig and a hippo, so you'd need a nice large backyard for it with a swimming-pool. Do you have a swimming-pool?'

Leilah shook her head dumbly. 'I'm sorry – I think I must have come to the wrong place.'

'Not at all. Not at all. I'm sure I can help you with your needs. You were referred to us by—?' A thick black eyebrow climbed up his brow like a hairy caterpillar.

'Ah—ah.' Leilah was tongue-tied as she tried to think straight. 'By my friend Kitty Wong.'

'Of course,' the Indian beamed warmly. 'Kitty Wong. From Pinang. She's directed quite a few clients our way. A most excellent lady. I've been expecting you. You must be Mrs Leilah Lau, if I'm not mistaken? Did you have a good trip from Georgetown? Please excuse this – this cacophony. It's close to their feeding time. Why don't we step into my office in the back where it's much quieter, and we can discuss things without interruption. Watch that cage, please—' the Indian cautioned her. 'That's a civet.'

The creature had rings around its tail and neck and had a spotted coat. It had extended one of its paws through the bars of its cage and was trying to hook its claws on her hemline.

Mohandir Das smiled. 'It's sort of a cross between a possum and a cat. Very amusing at times. At times, quite naughty. It can be easily litter-box trained. The children love it. We all have a good laugh when it does tricks. This one can't be parted from its Gameboy.'

Leilah saw a half-chewed plastic box in the corner of its cage with a few discarded game cartridges floating in the water-bowl. She lowered her eyes. If this be the will of the gods, let it be the will of the gods.

Mohandir Das opened the door to his office. There was a bronze figure of Ganesh, the Indian elephant god, standing in an alcove with a garland of marigolds dangling from it and the sweet smell of rose incense rising from a small brass incense-burner.

'Please make yourself comfortable,' he told her, as he waved a hand in the direction of a plush black leather couch in the corner of the room.

Leilah sat down and waited in silence as she tried to compose her thoughts.

'Some tea? A cola?' Das inquired graciously. 'No? Then why don't we begin—' He sat down beside her on the couch. There was a marble table in front of the couch with a stack of photo albums on it. He casually opened one up and began to flip through the pictures.

'Let's see, not this one. We've already placed this one in Denmark. Brother and sister, these two. We don't normally like to separate them. They form deep emotional bonds just like people do, you know. This one, poor thing, is no *longer with us. Didn't last long, I'm afraid. It was a crude job capturing it—'*

Leilah gasped when she saw the frightened face of a young baby gibbon in the picture.

'So adorable . . . What a pity,' Mohandir Das sighed as he shook his head. 'We don't deal with those suppliers any longer. Would you believe, it had only one finger when they shipped it to us? They cut all its other digits off in order to pry it away from its mother's back. She'd been shot, of course, with a poison dart. The savages.'

Das' dark features brightened as he turned the page of the album. 'Here – I think this is the perfect candidate for you. You wanted a son, I believe? Did you not, Mrs Lau?'

He gazed at her with deep concern. She was already experiencing the first stages of shock. He had become accustomed to this phase, and tenderly placed one of his hands on her tightly clenched fists that were balled up on her lap.

It was the shock of knowing – of realizing – that they had crossed the line to the other side. That they had crossed the line, and were already preparing themselves for that first embrace . . .

'Mrs Lau – Mrs Lau . . .' Das' voice brought her back to the present. It was critical that he did not lose her at this point. This was the actual point of sale.

'I hasten to assure you, Mrs Lau. This is the wave of the future. More and more people are becoming infertile as time goes on. You are not alone in this. This fact is borne out in all the recent population studies that are being conducted around the world. We humans are not breeding as profusely as the experts have predicted. The population of the planet has peaked at 7.2 billion. The "Population Explosion," as they called it in the last century, is over. Look at India and China, all declining in birth-rates. At the rate we're going, deaths will overtake births in another fifty years. We must take steps now, Mrs Lau—'

Leilah's face was drained of all its color. 'But it looks like a human baby. A human baby . . . I don't understand . . .'

She shook her head again and again. 'I don't understand.'

'That's the service we provide,' Das said with a note of pride in his voice. 'That's why people like you come to us. I may be a small shop, Mrs Lau, but there is an organization behind me. A vast organization, let me assure you. We maintain the highest international standards.'

He began to tick off the main points on his fingers for her. 'To start with, there is a highly personalized interspecies compatibility training program. Then the selection of the prime candidates for the procedure begins. Then, once the final decision to go ahead with the operation has been made, there are neurolinguistic implants and social conditioning softwares inserted in the brain. Some of the world's leading neurosurgeons and social skills therapists are employed by us. For instance, the head of neurosurgery at the University of Geneva is—'

Leilah interrupted Das' check-list. 'You haven't answered my question. If I am to convince my husband to go along with this idea, I'll have to explain everything to him. Why does it look like a human baby – yet something about its features is blank? Something is missing. Something about it is not quite right.'

'Ah, madame,' he replied with a smile. He had been saving this tidbit for last. It was worth every ringgit of his 25,000 ringgit ($10,000) commission just to savor this precise moment when he clinched the deal.

'It is amazing what plastic surgery can do these days. Re-shaping an Orang-utan's face – even its body – this poses no problem. It is an extremely malleable physical structure. Well, the legs will be a little short, a little bowlegged perhaps, the arms will be on the long side. We're still working on improving the surgical procedures. It's mind-boggling how far we've come in just the past few years. But the beauty of it – Mrs Lau – the beauty of it . . . The blankness of its expression, which you so rightly detected – this is, in fact, a deliberate omission, pending, ah, the finalization of the foster-parent agreement.'

'A deliberate omission? The blankness? What do you mean by that?'

'Do you by chance have a photograph of your husband with you?' Das asked her. 'I believe that your friend Kitty Wong conveyed our request that you bring it along for the consultation.'

'Yes, but—?' Leilah frowned. 'What's that got to do with it?'

'Simply this – our plastic surgeons have purposely outlined a general blank area on the face of the – ah – child. You do want your son to bear a family resemblance, don't you? Father's nose, mother's eyes, chin, cheekbones, that sort of thing? We've left room for that final master-stroke. We are always eager to please our clients, Mrs Lau. In every respect. Customer – er – parental satisfaction guaranteed. We'll just prepare a mock-up baby picture for your husband. We know how Dads are. So proud, yet needing every assurance that Junior takes after them.'

Tommy

Tommy Kok Lau parked his Kawasaki next to the trishaw stand beside the brightly lit *pasar malam* night market in the center of Georgetown on Gurney Drive.

He climbed off his bike and sniffed at the air. The smell of spices wafted on the balmy evening breeze along with the sweet heady fragrance of jasmine and frangipani. It was a beautiful night. Twinkling clusters of stars dangled overhead like coconuts from the giant illuminated palm branch of the Aurora Borealis.

Tommy recognized one of the constellations, the slung hammock of stars that formed Gemini. The Twins. That was his astrological sign. *How appropriate*, he thought to himself. *Two heads, two minds, two hearts . . . Never more true than now.*

He saw the familiar bustle of native food-stalls offering skewers of mutton, chicken and beef *satay* dipped in peanut sauce, fiery curry prawns, Malaysian flat-noodles, and fragrant coconut rice dishes. A row of south Indian eateries nearby served customers little pastry *thali* snacks which they ate with their fingers off a green banana leaf.

The hubbub was unbelievable. Bootleg tapes of *gamelan* rap music from Kelantan blared from scratchy speakers, while strings of MTV fire-crackers popped with images of the Borneo Boys and the Fuji Fellinis performing their latest hits.

Beverly Bali, the heart-throb of *Plantation Place*, the on-going Southeast Asian serial, pouted her polygamous lips from the kinetic billboards. The voluptuous Beverly had long since shed her *chador* for the monokini veil between her legs, at least 80 outlawed episodes ago. But the soap was still being beamed in daily from the Free Zone archipelago of the highly fortified Spratly Islands.

Gunboat diplomacy had been replaced by gunboat show business, especially after the promised oil deposits under the Spratlies failed to materialize. Chinese, Filipino, and Vietnamese troops now jointly patrolled the waters of this new Hollywood in the South China Sea, keeping it safe from the region's *mullahs* and their suicide squads of censors. It was a cat-and-mouse game anyway.

It was rumored that the Sultan of Brunei had a controlling interest in the Spratly Studios – and in Beverly, as well. She had risen from a place in his *harem* to become the biggest celebrity in the South Rim.

Tommy took a last look around the night market. Everywhere he turned, there were stalls that sold everything from trained crickets that chirped 'Silent Night' to ladies' compacts that unfolded into 4 × 4 infants' playpens, to disposable cigarette lighter-pagers that printed out their messages in 13-programmable languages whose incandescent text flickered within each curlicue of flame.

Knick-knack city. Each season, there were new trinkets, new novelties, new games, and new illusions. But the magic had never worn off before.

It was all just as familiar to him as his own childhood. Now, it seemed just as foreign, like a badly dubbed Japanese *animé* cartoon whose soundtrack was out of sync with the kicks and punches. In that cartoon of his memory, Ma and Pa strolled with him on an evening just like this through the night market, a happy Chinese family on an outing together.

Little Tommy sitting proudly atop his father's shoulders, licking a mangosteen sno-cone as Ma dabbed at his sticky lips with a moistened towelette . . .

Toddlers in the tropics look like Caspar the Ghost. Tommy's face and arms and legs had been coated with a white talcum-paste against prickly heat. But the paste had done nothing to disguise what his parents sought to conceal, his unnaturally pale-pink complexion and the razor-burns that were the result of Ma having to shave his body every day.

Even as an infant, Tommy had drawn curious stares from passers-by as though they *knew* . . . Of course, they had known all along. Everyone had known. It was Tommy who had been slow in fathoming the mystery of his parents' secret shame. That no-name shame that burned within him now like this feeling of heart-burn in his soul.

So his childhood, too, had been nothing but a trinket . . . His life, a novelty-item. That's the way it was. That's the way it would always be. Until next season. If there was to be a next season . . . How much time did he have left?

'Nice machine. Watch your 'saki for you, *tuan*?' a Malay street-hustler approached Tommy on the curb. 'Five *ringgits*, and no one touches it.'

Then came the inevitable pause. 'Never mind . . .' The dark-skinned Malay grabbed at the crotch of the sarong that was wrapped around his hips and made a swift get-away when he saw Tommy's face. He knew an evil spirit when he saw one.

Tommy smiled grimly. Beads of perspiration streaked the pancake make-up that was plastered above his upper lip.

The mask was falling apart. It was time to get out.

Tommy never turned to look back. It was all behind him now. He roared down Lebuh Light Street, racing past the spotlit walls of old Fort Cornwallis with its massive 17th-century cannon that had been passed down first by the Dutch to the Sultan of Johor then to the Portuguese and then to the pirates before it ended up in the ramparts of this old British colonial outpost. Childless women still came to lay garlands of flowers on its rusted *lingam* barrel, hoping to be blessed by its procreative powers.

That's what Ma should have done, Tommy thought bitterly to himself as he put on more speed.

Then I would never have been created.

He scattered the slowly pedaling trishaw drivers and mopeds like so many *mah jong* tiles as he made a sudden sharp right turn on to Lebuh Pantai.

There was one more place he had to go. One final farewell he had to make.

His 'saki spluttered to a stop outside a colonnaded gallery that had been converted into a ghetto of pubs and bars where the outcasts hung out. There were some familiar figures standing in the shadows, and one of them waved at him.

'*Apa khabar*, Tommy, how's it scratching, man?' It was Roki, a freak of nature if there ever was one. His parents had gotten him cheap from some quack in Selangor. Part *ungka*, gibbon, part *monyet bulanda*, proboscis monkey, and part Orang-utan, not to mention a cocktail of human genes, Roki was never quite the sum of his parts.

There had been a bad sex-change operation thrown in as part of the bargain. His parents had wanted a boy, then they had changed their minds. They wanted a girl. Finally, inevitably, after the novelty had worn off, after puberty set in, they abandoned him to the life of the streets. Roki now eked out a sad living as a transsexual hooker catering to the more privileged primates.

With his pendulous nose, his tarted-up looks, and dressed in a slinky *cheong-sam* that showed a bit of hairy thigh through the slit in its side, Roki didn't have many takers.

He was a pathetic figure who survived mainly off the charity of the Church of Chimpanzees, a non-profit primate welfare program run by Donna Brooks, a crusty old Briton who had once worked as an animal handler for the Interspecies Communication Centre in Chiang Mai in the north of Thailand.

After her retirement at the age of seventy-one, Brooks moved to the island of Pinang where she had established the Church of C. Free meals, free sermons on animal liberation theology, and free lice checks was what she offered to any unfortunate trans-primates who crossed her threshold. Roki lived in a dorm on the premises, when he wasn't busy working the streets. Whatever money he made went into his habit of shooting up animal tranquilizers.

The irony was that the Malaysian government still hadn't figured out its drug laws concerning primates. They caned human offenders with a *rotan* switch. They hanged them for possession of minute quantities of *chack*, heroin mixed with *chi*. But they didn't want to acknowledge the drug problem among the trans-species segment of the population.

Because they didn't want to admit to the world that the final taboo had been broken. That the mixing of the species was a booming trade and was flourishing in Malaysia.

As far as the government was concerned, it was a question of morals – and of citizenship rights.

Do you grant a humanized Orang-utan the right to vote? What would happen to Malaysia's confederation of sultanates if, Allah forbid, an ape were elected to the Dewan Rakyat, the People's Council, or to the Dewan Negara, the States' Council?

So the government chose to cast a blind eye at this growing social problem. They ignored the new untouchable class. For the time being, the 'transes' were treated under an obscure provision of the flora and fauna laws of the country.

Roki was at the very bottom of the ladder. Roki was what Tommy never wanted to become. Roki was his nightmare vision of the future.

'Chill, Roki,' Tommy replied, slapping five.

'That's cool, Tommy.' Roki gave him a zany smile. Tommy saw his dilated puplils. Roki was high again.

'Later, Roki, keep them buzzing.'

'Yeah, later.' Roki shuffled back into the shadows, his eye on the figure of a German tourist, an old guy in his sixties, who seemed to be window-shopping at the far end of the arcade, but who was slowly but surely heading in Roki's direction.

Tommy had noticed him as well. *God, it was disgusting, these interspecies perverts who had mined-out the child langurs and the long-tailed macaques that were kept in filthy cages in the animal brothels of the red-light district. The Triads had moved in to control this lucrative new sex trade. Animal pedophiles, all of them . . .*

Tommy felt the bile rise in his throat. He had read in the paper about a world-famous zoologist who had been busted at the Semenggok Wildlife Rehabilitation Centre in Sarawak for molesting the langurs. What was the world coming to?

Tommy squared his sloping shoulders as best as he could, then stepped into the air-conditioned habitat of the No-Name Bar.

The No-Name Bar

'**N**o-Name' was really a misnomer, as the regulars who congregated there each night could attest. Everyone knew it as 'Pinky's.'

Pinky was the proprietor, a battle-scarred humanoid gorilla with a no-nonsense attitude about drawing the limits in rowdy behavior among his customers. His father was an Aussie, his mother a half-breed gorilla-Orang-utan mix cloned in a Sydney laboratory. He had arrived in Kuala Lumpur traveling business-class in a test-tube via Federal Express.

Needless to say, his mother's genes predominated. He wasn't bad-looking for a reconfigured primate. He had a hefty chest, bulging muscles, and a Mel Gibsonesque handsomeness to his facial features. He stood at about five-two, when erect. Most importantly, he could throw any drunk clear across the bar-room floor with a well-directed flick of his little finger.

Hence, his name, 'Pinky.'

Pinky was tending bar tonight as usual, dressed casually in a green khaki t-shirt, shorts, and a pair of flip-flops. He looked up from the counter when he saw Tommy walk in. He had a nostalgic fondness for Tommy. He had seen him grow up, had seen him struggle with his identity, and deal with the demons. If anyone *could* make it, if anyone *could* break out, Pinky believed that Tommy was the one. He just had that feeling about Tommy.

It wasn't going to be easy, it wasn't going to be a smooth ride, Pinky thought to himself. *If Tommy didn't fall apart in the process, the boy might actually come out all right. Swinging. From the top vine . . .*

'Hiya, Tom, what can I get you?' Pinky's voice growled affectionately at the young man. 'A Kloster's? Singha? Carlsberg?'

'Make it a Tiger beer, thanks, Pinky,' Tommy replied as

he glanced around the bar to see who was around.

Pinky had gone to considerable trouble to give his place the right ambience, to invoke it with a sense of primate pride and dignity. There were pictures of wildlife preserves from around the world. A framed commendation from the director of the San Diego Zoo. There were posters of celebrity primates on the wall as well – among them, King Kong (Hollywood had made KK out to be a giant African gorilla, but his home was an island off Java, which implied Orang-utan lineage). Then there was Kala, the she-ape that was Tarzan's foster-mother; and Koko, the first gorilla to break through the sign-language barrier. There was even a poster of Einstein.

When asked to explain, Pinky would say, *'Just look in his eyes, mate. He knew. He knew where it was all heading. Leakey had it all wrong. We're not descended from Lucy. We're descended from Desi Arnaz. We're the fucking toll-bridge, man. From one side to the other. This Homo sapiens shit is gonna hit the fan one day, sooner or later. They've reached their limit, and they don't know it yet. They think they're fucking with us. Bio-tech, bio-dreck . . . They don't know the half of it. We're fucking with them . . . Besides, look at all that hair Albert's got on him. He'd make a gorgeous gorilla. Now what'll it be?'*

Tommy accepted a frosted mug and a bottle of ice-cold Tiger beer from Pinky with a nod of thanks. Then he walked over to the table by the juke-box where a few of his pals were sitting. One of them had just fed the juke-box, and their theme song was playing: 'The lion sleeps tonight'.

'Jeezus, Carlo, you're regressing.' Tommy grinned at one of them as he sat down in a wicker chair. 'Hi, Mo – Peter, Sally.' They were all his classmates from school at Pinang Polyteknic High.

Carlo was smoking a Benson & Krakatoa cigarette which he held to his mouth with the thumb and big toe of his right foot. His eyes narrowed when he saw Tommy.

'Just coming out of the closet, man. That's what they expect us to do, right? Don't tell me you're not getting any flack at home. Any more of that bullshit, and I'm bringing out the *parong*. "Disgruntled student hacks parents to death in fit of angst. Flees the scene of the crime." That'll make the *Straits-Times*, all right.'

'You look like shit, man,' Mo said to Tommy. 'Your make-up's all runny and stuff. And what's this?' He leaned over to inspect Tommy's face up-close. 'You're letting it grow out, huh? I bet your Mama's real thrilled with that. They've tried everything – electrolysis and all that shit – and nothing's worked, right?'

Mo laughed bitterly. 'They call it "losing face." I call it making up for lost time. They're starting to treat me like a fucking animal at home, man. "Go and clean up your room. It's a real pig-sty." They got *that* part wrong, for sure—' He stared at the wall gloomily.

Sally had the tell-tale reddish tint of an Orang-utan in her silky brown hair that she wore down to her shoulders. She was cute and sexy, with an upturned nose. More gibbon than langur in her gene-pool. She had long graceful hands and nice legs. Her eyes were blue.

'It could be much worse, you guys,' she said as she brushed her hair back from her face. 'Like in the old days.'

'Like in the old days? Is this a history lesson or what?' Mo fixed his gaze on her. 'And this is supposed to be our Golden Age, right?'

'That's right,' Sally said defensively. 'I'm talking about back when it all started. The adoptions, I mean. Before the implants. Before the plastic surgery. Back in the last century when they used to pluck us right out of the rain forest, right off our mothers' backs. The poachers would sell us to these childless couples *au naturel*. Just as we were. Scared, frightened out of our minds, half-dead from shock. But we were still cute, weren't we? They'd shave our bodies and raise us like human babies. Make us wear clothes, nappies. Cuddle us. Give us their love. Until one day—'

'Until one day *what*?' Tommy found himself asking although he already knew the answer.

Things hadn't changed all that much, had they? He had seen the expression in Pa's eyes too many times, had seen a darkness there that he couldn't understand. Even Ma was helpless in the face of that anger. She had stopped trying to defend him from his father's rages. She even looked away when Pa went into one of his fits, when he slapped and kicked him and screamed: 'You're not one of mine. You're a monster . . .'

'Until one day,' Sally continued in her quiet voice, 'we got too big, too unruly . . . and too much of a hassle to raise. They couldn't take us out anymore, and then . . . ' She suddenly let out a high-pitched squeal of nervous laughter. 'And then they'd just kill us and eat us for supper. Just like that!' Sally snapped her fingers.

Everyone at the table looked horrified. Pinky stared at them from the bar across the room, wondering what the commotion was all about. *Teenagers . . .*

'All too true,' Peter said. Peter Wong was the poet in their group. He had long wavy black hair, and wrote classical Chinese verse in the style of Rimbaud. He was introverted, experimental, and intuitive in ways that most of the trans-kids just couldn't grok. He listened to things on a different wave-length. He had insights that scared them, but they paid attention to what he said anyway. It was partly out of fear, partly out of grudging respect for the loner that he was, but mainly it was because they were just superstitious. That was the Chinese side to their simian nature.

Peter had sworn off Omnispace altogether. He still 'surfed,' as he confided to them, but on a more Primal Net, off-line in the untouched rain forest depths of the psyche.

'*I can hear them coming/like the rain that falls,*' Peter began to recite one of his impromptu poems. '*I can see their green eyes and the mist of love/blinded by the black sun that sustains us all.*'

'That's really beautiful, Peter,' Tommy said. 'Where did that come from?'

Tommy suddenly felt clear-headed and unafraid. He had been wrapped in his fear and uncertainty for so long that his own heart had become frozen. He had been bumping into walls in his psyche that he knew didn't really exist.

Those walls were part of the old programming that had begun to self destruct. Perhaps this was what his parents feared the most. They feared it more than the cosmetic decay that was setting in. The original human glitch was coming unstuck. The dam was about to burst and there was nothing that his parents – or anyone – could do about it.

Tommy's generation of trans-sapiens that had been 'born' out of the original Primate Boom of the twenties was *doomed*.

Doomed, on one hand, because the bio-tech paradox of their creation had imploded. *Homo sapiens* could put the *mind* of man into the primate, but they couldn't replace its *soul*. Primates had souls, too, but on a much grander scale. They didn't have the baggage of *karma* to contend with, for one thing. There was no expiration date to their innocence. No need for any Judgment Day to be pre-set on their species calendar.

The trans-sapes were *saved*, on the other hand, because they were *more* than human, and *more* than ape. And because they could see and hear the New Ones who welcomed them on the other side of all this pain and disillusionment. They were just one short step away – just one transparent riddle to solve – before they could cross the abyss into the rain shower of light.

'Where did that poem come from, Tommy?' Peter smiled at him with a sly twinkle in his eye. 'Why, it came from *you*. I just borrowed it from you, right this instant. You've been hearing them, too, haven't you? But you're still carrying that heavy heart. Let her go, Tommy. Let her go, and then you'll be able to be with her again. She's over there, Tommy. Waiting for you. Just like she's always been. There are no goodbyes. Not ever. That's why you came here tonight, isn't it? To say goodbye?' Peter grinned.

'So why don't you get your ass out of here – your sorry no-name ass – and go and find her like you're supposed to? They're calling you, Tommy. It's time for you to go home. To your *real* home . . .'

>>> *end of first transmission, mmm.gunung mulu.com* <<<

. . . .
B.S., I Love You

San Francisco

'**A**nyone home?' Paul Sykes called out, as he stuck his head warily through the open front door of his apartment.

He couldn't be sure it was safe to tip-toe in as though nothing had happened. As though it were just another routine day in Paul Sykes' bachelor-bullshit-freelance existence. As though he had never gone to the *Chi* Expo, and had never stopped off at Wisenik's with the Kota Baru chip.

He felt dizzy and a little nauseated. The long walk home to Valencia Street in the Mission hadn't done him much good. His inner ear was still twanging from the ride on Wisenik's morphic roller-coaster.

Thundering heebie-jeebies . . .

Sykes shivered when he thought about his unreal experience of being on-line in an off-line world.

Of actually being *there* . . .

Coming back hadn't been any easier than going in. There had been that unscheduled stop at the Philadelphia Zoo,

*where he and Wisenik found themselves inadvertently
logging in at the Primate Center and delivering some junk
mail to a group of eight stump-tailed macaques. At first,
the group had regarded them with hostile indifference.
Finally, after interrupting his grooming session, an elder
macaque approached them. A younger female had been
giving his coat a thorough going-over as he sat on a branch
scratching his rear end.*

Lice Check No. 30,015. *He kept the days of his captivity
numbered in this manner as though he had been busy all
these years marking Xs on the wall of a jail cell.*

*The old guy's face was a naked pinkish-brown, his fur
was dull brown with lighter underparts, and he had long
white cheek whiskers.* 'Do I know you guys?' *he asked,
baring his incisors.*

'Umm, not exactly,' *Wisenik had replied. They were still
in Gunung Mulu mode. Wisenik had been working out the
exact coordinates to get them back to home-base but they
had been routed here by mistake.*

'I believe these are for you,' *Wisenik said as he handed
the old macaque a sheaf of mail wrapped in a bundle of
green tree-leaves. The geezer blinked as he accepted the
package and began to read through it. Chattering his teeth
with disappointment, he tossed the material over his
shoulder without glancing back.*

*The leaves of data dissipated as they blew into the
concrete moat encircling their monkey-island.*

'Sheet, *this is just another one of those sweepstakes
things they keep on sending us! I told them to take our
names off the list! But no – they won't listen. What on
earth do we want to win a million bananas for? Or, for
that matter, an all-expenses-paid two-week vacation to the
Bukit Lagong Forest Reserve? Just get us out of here . . .
Can you do that for us, mister?'*

*The old macaque was just about to fling a fresh pile of
monkey dung in their faces when Rodney the Philodendron
kicked in. Good old Rodney, he was worthy enough to*

navigate for Magellan, if house-plants had only charted the seas back then . . .

'Phew,' Wisenik remarked as they jacked back in to the sound of San Francisco cable-cars clanging in the street below.

'Terra firma once again. Feet to the ground. That was a close call, eh, Sykes? Monkey VR. There are parallels after all. No wonder we're related.'

First, they removed their head-gear. They stared at each other for a moment in an awkward silence. Then they began to grin. Then Wisenik broke out into a whoop-whoop-whoop of a victory dance, scratching under his armpits with exaggerated motions, making out like a chimp, and they both began to laugh uproariously.

'We did it, Sykes! We did it! We broke on through to the other side!' Wisenik spun around as he studied the monitor. 'What's more, it appears that we brought the file back with us intact.' He squinted at the screen. ' "The Gunung Mulu Memorandum." '

'Congratulations, Mort. I don't know what to say – I've never taken part in anything like this before.'

'Who says that the Age of Discovery is over, eh?' Wisenik clapped Sykes on the back enthusiastically. 'I'll make a back-up copy for you. You don't mind if I – er – retain the original for research purposes? Anything comes out of it, we'll both share in the credits. Even Rodney here will get a by-line.'

He poured a half-finished cup of cold Starbucks mocha java into Rodney's pot. 'My treat, Rodney, a little caffeine to give your tendrils a boost. A job well done!'

'Uh, Mort,' Sykes said nervously. 'I'd appreciate it if you – uh – sat on this for a little while. It's still, uh, sensitive information at this point. I don't know if it's cool to—'

Wisenik lowered himself down on his stool, his arm still embracing Rodney in his brown earthenware pot.

'What do you plan to do, Paul?' he asked Sykes in a quiet voice. 'Are you planning on going in? I mean, in to

*the real thing? Like in, in, in? You're going to try to
connect with him? Do the intercept? You know where he's
heading, don't you?'*

*Sykes paused for a moment before replying. 'I'm giving it
some thought.'*

*Wisenik scratched his chin. 'I suppose you could do it.
Of course, he won't know that you've read his file. And he
won't be expecting you. It might be dangerous. He's a
hybrid. They've tinkered with him genetically. You can't
predict how he might react. He's at that age – at that
point,' Wisenik corrected himself, 'when their original
programming is beginning to deconstruct. He might not
even make it in time.'*

*'It's a chance that might be worth taking,' Sykes replied
cautiously.*

'And one more thing—'

'What's that?'

*'We may have gone in. Done the green thing. Returned
with the download. But whoever implanted Ms Chu with
this Kota Baru job – the test-data that we lost – can trace
the cranial seepage back to the original source themselves.
Then they'll come looking for you. For him, too, most
likely. He's going to lead them to it just like he's leading
you, Sykes. And the poor devil doesn't even know it.'*

*'Like I said, that's a chance that I may have to take.
Now can you sit quietly on all this? Give me a few weeks,
Mort,' Sykes pleaded. 'Besides, you know this stuff is hot.
You might even end up getting hurt if you get mixed up
in it.'*

*Mort Wisenik gave Sykes a puzzled frown, then winked
at him. 'Well, it's not exactly like I've never dealt with
"hot" merchandise before, mate. But I tell you what – you
go on right ahead. Keep me in the loop. Who knows, with
all this "Children of Chi" business, you might just stumble
across King Solomon's Mines . . . Now, wouldn't that be a
hoot? Sure, why not? I'll sit on it. But don't take any
unnecessary chances, all right? Promise? There are a lot of*

unscrupulous characters running around out there, just
waiting to take advantage of innocents such as yourself . . .'

'Hu-ll-o-o?' Sykes reiterated tentatively, then stepped inside
the hallway. The Omtron was on in the living-room. Had
he left it switched on? Mail. Unpaid bills. Flashing red
copies of copies of unpaid bills. His hand on the remote,
Sykes instinctively dragged the unsightly pile over to the
trash-hole to dump it.

Shit. The collections agency had frozen his trash icon.

'You got a call from your agent.'

Sykes did a double-take as Zev, his room-mate, raised his
frizzy brown Jewish-Afro up from behind the couch.

Zev rubbed his eyes. 'I was taking a nap. Didn't hear
you come in. What's the matter with you, man? You look
freaked out.'

'What did you just say?'

'I was taking a nap—'

'No, I mean something about my agent calling?'

'Yeah, your agent called a little while ago.'

'I don't *have* an agent, Zev,' Sykes said as he moved
across the living-room floor to his bedroom.

Zev occupied the front of the apartment. His gear was
stowed against the walls. He was a musician. His groove
was old stringed instruments – North African ouks, Celtic
zithers, Japanese kotos, Okinawan samisens. He was 23,
good-looking, with Mediterranean features, a gold ring in
his ear, and an easy manner. All the girls liked him.

Even Anne dug him. That was a burr in his butt, even
though they weren't together anymore. Sykes still felt
jealous when he thought about her with other guys. The
other day, when she stopped by to pick up the rest of her
stuff, he had introduced her to Zev and the old paranoia
set in when she began to flirt with his new room-mate.
Even though he knew she was doing that on purpose, just
to get on his case.

Zev was watching him go through his closet. Sykes

pulled out his backpack and began stuffing it with clothes. *Keep it light*, Sykes told himself as he packed.

T-shirts. Shorts. Sandals. You won't be needing much. He had done a travel scan at Mort's place. *It was going to be fucking hot down there this time of year. Even the red ants were running around wearing sun screen . . .*

Sykes had withdrawn his last $800 and had gone ahead and booked a cheap Pyongyang Air Lines charter to Bangkok with about a dozen stops en route, one of them being Lima, Peru. The Super Shuttle to take him to the airport was already on its way.

'You planning on going somewhere, man?' Zev asked him from the couch. Zev was sitting up now and doing that thing he did when he splayed his toes. Zev played with his toes a lot. He said he was training himself to play a new ancient instrument he'd recently discovered, a pigmy butterfly harp from Ougadougoo.

Sykes turned around to face him. 'Umm, yeah, I'm gonna be gone for about a week or so. Don't forget to take out the garbage, okay? Tuesday night's recycling night.'

'What do you want me to say if your agent calls again?'

'Tell him anything you want. I've gone out of town. I'm sick. I'm not available.'

'It was a chick, man.'

Sykes stopped his packing, and laid his backpack on the floor. He walked over to where Zev was practicing his atonal scales with a string of twine stretched between the toes of both feet.

Ping, ping, ping, ping, ping . . .

'Did she leave her name by any chance?'

'Yeah, she left a name and a number where you can reach her. She said she met you today. Said she was real impressed with your work. She wants to represent you. She says she has a buyer for your manuscript.'

A buyer for his manuscript? Sykes' mind churned. What *manuscript? Not that half-assed novel he'd been trying to get going for the past two years?*

Sykes had a bad feeling about this. Another bad feeling on what was turning out to be a bad-feeling day.

Ping, ping, ping, ping, ping . . .

'Fucking scales, can't get this thing to work right—' Zev swore to himself. 'Oh, I'm sorry—' He looked up at Sykes who hovered above him, an intense expression on his face.

'She said it was Deedee Something. Deedee Delorean. That's right. She said she had an offer you couldn't refuse.'

Zev gave him a puzzled look. 'Hey, you should be happy, man. What's with the death mask on your face? Someone wants to buy your book. Deedee said to tell you that channeled animal stories for the kiddies were the big thing right now. I didn't know you wrote for that market, Sykes. You're a strange bird, all right . . . Hey, where are you going?'

Paul Sykes hoisted his backpack on to his shoulders and headed out the door, slamming it shut behind him.

Fuck Mort Wisenik, he thought to himself. He should have known better than to trust him.

Once a con, always a con . . .

Green Thumb Alley

The Super Shuttle driver told Sykes, 'This is an unscheduled stop, mister. It's going to cost you an extra fare.'

Sykes fished in his pocket and pulled out a twenty-dollar chip. 'Five minutes. That's all I'm asking, is that okay?'

The driver glared at him and looked around at the rest of the passengers.

'It's fine with me,' the wispish thin brunette in the back seat of the van declared. She might have been attractive in a Salvador Dali lithograph, Sykes thought. She was in her forties and was wearing a skin-tight black jumpsuit with enough cleavage to suckle an entire camp of malnourished Rwandan refugee children. All she needed was a leopard on a leash.

'My flight to Detroit's at 6:30 anyway.' The brunette batted her orgone-flecked eyelashes. She had taken to Sykes' British accent and his boyish good looks. They had rubbed knees together like urban Eskimos. Sykes, out of nervousness. The brunette, because her boyfriend Bruno had run away with her ex-best girlfriend and she needed consolation. Lots of desperate amounts of it.

The Chinese dude in the Manchu ponytail with the pockmarked face, who had been picked up at the last stop, didn't look happy. The Russian couple flying to Las Vegas grumbled loudly, '*Eta na prasna.* This is unnecessary.'

The Manila-bound Filipino businessman travelling with his 100-pound *balikbayan* box filled with reverse-engineered *chi* chips, remained silent. That was always the best policy in a crowd. He was practicing Deep Pockets Chapstick Mind Control in order to get through Customs at the airport without a hitch. The chips converted into 45 caliber-strength bad vibes that would be used to assassinate the mayor of Quezon City from the distance of a mile away from his office.

The shuttle driver grabbed at Sykes' twenty-dollar chip and barked at him, 'If you're not back in five minutes, I'm leaving. I'm not triple-parking in Chinatown.'

Sykes waited for the clanging cable-car to pass along its tracks, then dashed across Powell Street to Mort Wisenik's crumbling mustard-colored stucco apartment building.

The fucking asshole, Sykes thought. *He'd have to find out how much damage Mort had done. How much they knew. If they knew where he was heading . . .*

A Chinese family was leaving the building and Sykes caught the front door a second before it locked shut. They gave him a startled look, then stepped away. They didn't want trouble from any crazies today. Not today or any day.

'*Shay-shay*,' Sykes muttered under his breath at them. '*Thank you*.' Those were the only words Sykes knew in Chinese and they sounded vaguely Irish to him.

Like O'Shea. Ridiculous. He'd been living in San Francisco for two-and-a-half years and he could barely order Chinese dim-sum from an illustrated menu. Languages were definitely not his forté. Especially not primate dialects, but then somehow the 'Gunung Mulu Memorandum' was different . . .

Sykes had downloaded the whole story without a hitch, all the nuances coming to him as smoothly as though they were puréed through his psyche.

And just in case, he had the back-up disk, all the glyphs neatly subtitled in English.

He had to hand Mort that much. *The bastard was a natural when it came to deciphering and transcribing monkey talk . . .*

Sykes bounded up the stairs to the second floor and pounded on the door marked 2-B, Wisenik's official residence when he wasn't serving time in prison.

'Wisenik, open up, I know you're in there.' Sykes heard the radio playing in the background. Wisenik had hacked into the Kenny G. Mausoleum Home-Page. Wisenkik loved to listen to elevator music from the grave. He had an ear for the macabre.

'You don't have to break the door down, sweetheart,' Sykes heard a silky smooth voice call to him from behind. He turned around. It was one of the transvestite hookers who worked the street below. Cherry, a Puerto Rican mulatto, was a neighbor of Mort's. He had his hand cocked on his Versace-model hip as he gave Sykes a pouty look.

'There are *other* ways to effect a forced entry, y'know,' Cherry declared. 'Mort hasn't been out *all* day. And frankly I'm worried. He promised to walk Sugar, and he hasn't. Now Sugar's been a bad girl . . .'

Sykes stared at a fluffy white Yorkshire terrier with black-velvet eyes who lay cowering between Cherry's legs.

Cherry looked down at her dog in disgust.

'I'm beginning to suspect that he's a lesbian. He's got some sort of a grudge against me. He's just been doing it everywhere . . . Aren't you a naughty, naughty boy . . .'

Cherry lifted Sugar in his arms and cooed into his ear. 'Say hello to the nice man.'

'Um, do you mind if I use your fire-escape?' Sykes asked. 'I've got an urgent message for Mort and he hasn't been answering the phone.'

'Go right ahead, I just love cat burglars, I think they're s-o-o-o sexy.' Cherry gave him an inviting smile. 'You can do my place too while you're at it.'

Cherry stood aside as Sykes entered her tiny apartment. There was a fish-tank on the kitchen counter filled with goldfish. It was a shrine dedicated to her regulars – 'Bruce' from Sunnyvale, 'Hank' from Alameda, 'Jerry' from Pacific Heights, 'Richard' from the Sunset district. The fish were all named after her favorite tricks.

Sykes noticed their carefully inscribed names written in violet ink on the little labels that were pasted on the side of the tank.

He walked over to the window that led to the fire-escape, opened it and climbed out on to the landing. He saw the Super Shuttle driver in the street below looking up at him, scratching his head.

Mort's window was half open. Rodney the philodendron wasn't in his usual place on the window-sill. *Either Mort hadn't returned him to his roost, or he was using him to surf the Green Net again . . .*

Sykes peered in through the grimy window. He couldn't make out very much of the interior. He tried to force the window up, but it refused to budge. He looked down into the street again. The shuttle driver was tapping on his wristwatch. The asshole was getting ready to split.

Shit . . . Sykes put his shoulder beneath the warped window-frame and gave it a powerful shove. Crusts of paint and chips of wood flew into the air as the window yanked open. He climbed into the apartment and brushed the debris off his pants.

'Mort . . . ? You in there? No use hiding. Come on out. You owe me an explanation . . .'

Sykes stopped in his tracks. He felt an icy shiver run down his spine. The radio was still playing Kenny G. from the Grave. But there was another sound, too, muffled in the background. It came from Mort Wisenik's open mouth.

Correction: Mort's mouth had been forced open. The sound was coming from Rodney who was stuffed into Mort's mouth. Someone had shoved the entire plant down Wisenik's throat. Mort was sitting up on the floor, his legs apart. He was leaning against the wall like a human plant-box.

Rodney's green marbled leaves covered Mort's face and eyes. But Sykes could see the plant's roots and the clumps of dirt that had crumbled from the yawning grimace of Mort's open mouth. The front of Wisenik's Hawaiian shirt was caked with a mixture of saliva and dirt.

Sykes knelt beside the body and reached over to tentatively touch one of the muddy streaks on Mort's chest. *It was still wet . . .*

Sykes felt another icy thunderbolt of adrenaline zap through him. He spun around. *What if they were still here, waiting for him to show up?*

He rose to his feet quickly. But he sensed the emptiness in the apartment, the emptiness and the feeling of dread. There hadn't been much of a struggle, as far as Sykes could tell. No furniture had been knocked over. Mort looked as peaceful in death as if he were a still-life. *Nature morte . . .* The poor guy. Whatever he had done, he didn't deserve this.

Sykes slowly approached the work-table. The Hitachi system was still switched on and running. He scanned the files. A bunch of stuff. But the green mango glyph that had been Ms Chu's last will and testament was missing from the screen. So was Frank Gobi's bio-algorithm for the chlorophyll search-engine. And the Gunung Mulu Memorandum that had been plucked from Gaiaspace – that was nowhere to be seen.

It was a safe assumption that whoever had done this to Mort was now in possession of the data.

More importantly, they must have obtained the location of Tree Number 17, Row 35, the organic node for all that interspecies morphic communication.

If they could decipher it, that is . . .

Then another thought hit him. They must know that he had the back-up. The only copy with the coordinates for mmm.gunung mulu.com.

The key that would lead them to the Children of *Chi* through Tommy who was on his way to them now.

Fuck, what was *that sound!?*

Sykes spun around again. There *was* some sort of a garbled buzz coming from Rodney.

Jeezus, was the philodendron still on-line? To Green Time?

Sykes approached Mort's body. He could hear the sound more distinctly now. Overcoming his sense of horror, he brought his ear over to Mort's gaping mouth. It was definitely the source of the staticky noise.

No good, it was still too muffled.

Shit . . . Here goes . . .

Sykes grabbed a-hold of one of Rodney's roots and yanked the whole potted mess out of Mort's face. He could make it out now. As he held Rodney's tangled root-system to his ear, he heard the plant's murmuring like a chant from another time and place.

'*To-mmy . . . To-mmy . . .*'

It was another transmission. But Mort Wisenik would never hear it. And perhaps neither would Tommy. Wherever the hell Tommy was. Sykes laid the philodendron gently down on Mort's lap.

'Have to go now,' he said to no one in particular. He left the apartment.

Next door at Cherry's, he heard Sugar's whiny yapping as Cherry scolded him. 'Bad girl . . . bad boy . . . bad girl . . . bad boy.'

'Sure took you for ever, mister,' the Super Shuttle driver bitched at Sykes as he climbed into the back of the van beside the wispy brunette. She giggled as she made room for him, thigh to thigh.

'I was just about to take off. This must be your lucky day,' the driver groused as he gunned the engine and pulled away from the curb.

'Sorry about that,' Sykes apologized. 'It took me a little longer than I expected.'

The brunette giggled again as she brushed away the dirt from Sykes' sleeves. 'Been doing a little gardening, have we? Watering the lawn? I like a man who's got a green thumb.'

The Chinese dude with the Manchu ponytail and the pockmarked face continued to look on impassively. Sykes noticed that he had some traces of dirt on his cuffs, too.

>>> *beginning next transmission, mmm.gunung mulu.com* <<<

• • • • • •
Nita

'**T**o-mmy . . . To-mmy . . .'
    Tommy Kok Lau heard the voice echoing inside his head again. He had stepped out of the No-Name Bar into the damp furnace of the night. The sweat was already beginning to pour from his armpits. It streamed down his sides, drenching both his front and his back. His t-shirt was plastered against his chest like a living membrane with a logo.

He was wearing the '*I Hate Bali*' t-shirt that Ma and Pa

had given him as a joke souvenir after they returned from their last vacation. Of course, he hadn't been invited to join them. There had been some minor technicality concerning his Malaysian passport.

He had none.

Tommy smiled grimly. He had one now. It hadn't been that difficult to fix Pa's passport. There was a one-stop grafix shop in a back-alley off Lorong Salamat Road. It was operated by a sympathetic mixed-breed – a part langur-angutan, part Indian untouchable from Madras. Why someone would want to generate that particular combination was anyone's guess. Must have been the karmic spin of that particular DNA sequencing, Tommy guessed. *A double untouchable. The closest thing to animal karma.*

Samir was a whizz at desktop gymnastics. He had expertly encoded the sentient passport with all the necessary particulars down to the voice recognition patterns.

'Passport *karaoke*,' Samir told him proudly as he handed him the travel document. 'It ain't *bhangra*, but it ought to get you across the Thai border.'

Tommy was now Samuel Lau – 16 years old, born in Georgetown, Pulau Pinang State, Malaysia, May 23, 2023. That was in human terms, of course. In Orang-utan time, Tommy had just turned eight. He had actually been born in 2031.

He was old enough to have developed cheek pads and a sac on his throat, and to have sprouted a ginger-colored mustache on his diamond-shaped face. Old enough to know better. Old enough to have fallen in love . . .

'To-mmy . . . To-mmy . . .'

Tommy climbed on to his 'saki and sat there thinking for a moment. He glanced vacantly around the colonnaded gallery, wrapped in his thoughts. There was no one around. Roki had gone. Presumably with his German tourist trick to some short-time hotel.

The street was quiet. The shops had been shuttered for the night. Through the metal grille-gate of a Chinese herbal shop, he saw rose-tinted shadows cast from an illuminated red-lacquered shrine placed high on a shelf. The protective deities on the altar's icon-screen had been activated.

Menacing phantoms of Chinese gods with spears and long black beards patrolled the premises.

Door Gods, Tommy thought to himself. *Just what I need to get me through . . .*

'To-mmy . . . To-mmy . . .' He heard it again. He knew who it was. It was Nita calling to him.

'Ni-ta . . . Ni-ta . . .' Tommy groaned to himself, but inwardly reaching out for her. There was no response. Sometimes it took a little while for their connection to synchronize. Lately, her voice had been growing weaker, as if she were becoming weary from all the effort.

Strange. It wasn't like her . . .

Tommy closed his eyes. *Nita*. His first love. He could still picture her clearly. He would *always* picture her clearly. Somewhere in his memory, despite the Belgian-manufactured cranial implant, a meandering stream of images had begun to flow. It was a recent phenomenon. How long ago did it start? Not more than a few months ago . . .

At first, these images seeped through his dreams like a sluggish current, gradually building up their momentum as his REMs approached the rapids of his sleep-cycle. Then they began to trickle into his ordinary waking consciousness as flashes of green light and sound. Demanding his attention . . .

His *heart* was the medium for this traffic of picture-feelings, as Tommy soon discovered. The tug-and-pull of his growing heart-ache actually helped generate the flow. The pain of separation – his separation from his beloved – was the necessary lubricant for these early communications.

His loneliness had more strength than will-power or determination could give him. His loneliness knew no rest.

It did not suffer from lethargy – nor from forgetfulness.

Tommy's next big discovery was that the flow worked *both* ways . . .

He now could send as well as receive.

Tommy was growing up.

>>> mmm.gunung mulu.com transmission cont'd <<<

An aerial view of the freshwater swamp forest near the Kinabatangan River in Eastern Sabah. Tommy could identify it now: His first home.

As if bridging his two worlds, Tommy studied the canopied panorama in real-time on SabahNet's 'Conservation Watch' satellite channel on the Omtron set in his room.

'Just finishing my home-work, Ma,' he would reply to his human mother Leilah who called to him from downstairs, demanding to know what was keeping him from the dinner-table.

It was all just a channel-switch of a lifetime away.

Alone in his room, Tommy would peer down at the Orang-utan nests in the tall trees of the dark green dipterocarp forests that cloaked this vast island wilderness.

He foraged freely among his memories as his real mother had once foraged for fruit among the bountiful fruiting trees in the forest . . .

Clinging to her chest and side, with one hand grasping her upper back, and his other foot gripping her lower back, they traveled together as she swung from one climbing liana vine to another.

Whenever they came to an awkward gap between the trees, she would rock the liana to and fro in increasing oscillations until she could reach for the next branch with her outstretched hand.

Then they would move on.

As Tommy suckled at her breast, his mother would stop

here and there for a snack of tender young liana leaves. Or she might pluck at a few choice juicy figs dangling from a nearby strangling fig tree, as she checked on the progress of trees that would bear their crop in the coming month.

The sweet juicy part of the hairy rambutan fruit, the cheesy-garlicky flesh of the spiky durian, even the bitter-tasting, toxic strychnine seeds of the woody climbing plant which she would crack open and then spit out, these were all his natural mother's favorite foods . . .

Not like the stewed pigs' feet, bok choy greens, congee rice porridge, sweet-and-sour prawns, or the curried Pinang chicken dishes that Leilah prepared for him at home in Georgetown.

Some days, Tommy's Orang-utan mother would consume hundreds or even thousands of fruits, pausing to scoop up a handful of rainwater in the fork of a tree-branch to quench her thirst.

Something inside Tommy thrilled when he recalled how she would find the cardboard-like nest of some tree ants, pull off a chunk and hold it to her lips, pouring a steady stream of ants into her mouth as she ignored the ant bites to her lips. She only got annoyed when any stray ants got into her hair, and then she would brush them off quickly.

Big trees, small trees, woody climbing lianas, shrubs, herbs, ferns, palms, orchids, mosses, the buzzing of insects, the chirping of birds, the hooting of gibbons, the mist rising from the canopy of forest in the early morning, the swift darkness falling at night as they nested in the towering safety of a forked tree-trunk among the saplings . . .

These were some of the vivid images that comforted Tommy in the darkest moments of his human existence in Georgetown.

These were his earliest memories. Like the memory of the day that he first met Nita . . .

The forest is vast, vaster than any green imaginings. As dense as it is, rain forest animals like the Orang-utans will

*not stray within a few kilometers of their habitual foraging
grounds. They will avoid each other, especially if they meet
in the same fruiting tree. They might recognize each other —
relatives, uncles, aunts, grown-up offspring, siblings, in-laws
— but they will choose to silently ignore the incoming
traffic.*

*Unless the Orang-utan is an intruder, an outsider from
another clan that has wandered into their territory. Then
the home-'tans will move back and forth along the bough
like an angry 'mpongo,' exposing their bulk, and make
noises that sound like loud hisses and grumphs from the
depths of their throats.*

*Occasionally, two mother Orang-utans will find
themselves sharing the same fruiting tree as their youngsters
cavort and play together. The mothers, of course, will pay
no attention to each other.*

*On this one particular morning, Tommy's mother
stopped to rest at a favorite spot, a strangling fig tree by
the river. Tommy, two-and-a-half years old, was in a
boisterous mood, full of pranks and shenanigans. His
mother pushed him away from her furry chest as he tackled
her, swinging upside-down from a vine.*

*Suddenly, she stiffened and grabbed a-hold of him
tightly. They had unexpected company. Another Orang-
utan female had arrived, her hairy infant in tow. They were
strangers. Tommy's clan hailed from the forest reserves of
the middle Kinabatangan River. These newcomers were
from the lower Kinabatangan, the other side of the tracks.*

*Tommy's mother bared her teeth, and rose from the
bough to claim her branch. But Tommy was too fast for
her, too reckless and heedless. He made his way straight
towards his new playmate.*

*She was a delicate brown with pale markings around her
eyes and mouth, and shy at first. Tommy wrapped his long
thin arm around her neck and opened his mouth wide,
proudly displaying his first complete set of twenty milk-
teeth. She showed him hers.*

Chattering with excitement, they scampered up the tree together and dangled from a vine, each with a mouthful of leaves in a chewing-contest.

Their mothers sat beneath them on the bough, at first tensely observing each other, then gradually relaxing into a wary indifference as they let the 'maias kesa,' the young ones, enjoy their playtime.

Then something happened that would change the world of the rain forest for ever. Not just the vast green forest, but the world of the 'hantus,' the ghosts that walked on two legs on the ground. Those who sent up pillars of smoke from clearings in the jungle, and who spoke angrily to the animals with sticks that barked loudly in their hands . . .

That outside world would be changed too, but neither of the watchful Orang-utan mothers could have possibly known the precise moment when the seed of this coming transformation was planted.

Microscopically small fungi will coat the roots of the tallest trees, stealing the trees' energy, until one day, in the distant future, those mighty giants inevitably toppled, leaving room in the forest canopy for new species of plants to colonize and repeat the struggle for life.

It was a moment like this, a green nanosecond of time uttered within a syllable of space, that signaled the particular shift in evolution. Tommy saw something in Nita's eye. He reached out to touch her face and their lips met.

It was their first kiss, and it, too, would evolve into new forms and pass through as yet unimaginable new incarnations.

Tommy should have recognized the next omen.

Cigarette smoke.

He had already observed 'hantus' on several occasions from the safety of a tree-top. Mother had told them they had once been Orang-utans, but that was a long, long time ago when the forest was still young. They lost all their faculties when they began to live on the ground and walk on both legs.

Usually, these exchanges between 'hantus' and the 'tans was brief. The 'hantus' might make strange noises, taunting the tree-dwellers, perhaps even throw a stone or a coconut up into their tree in order to provoke them into some action. They were jealous that they could no longer climb the steps of the trees.

Eventually, they would tire of their rude sport and move on.

But these two ghosts were standing still, very still. They had appeared out nowhere, climbing up from the bank of the dried riverbed. Now they began to walk slowly towards them.

Tommy's mother had stopped earlier that afternoon at a strangling fig tree to eat some fruit and to take a little siesta. It was Tommy who had spotted them first. He had been napping, but the sweet acrid smell of burning clove alerted him. He let out a little whimpering cry of alarm.

His mother immediately leapt to her feet from her springboard of liana vines. Clutching Tommy closely to her side, she issued the usual 'Do Not Disturb' signals, garumphing and blowing what sounded like loud intimidating kisses at the forest-ghosts.

For a moment, this ruse succeeded in halting the 'hantus'. Then they began to approach the tree again, moving slowly and deliberately. What happened next would be etched on Tommy's reawakened memory for ever.

One of the ghosts held what looked like a stick of bamboo in his hand. He brought it to his mouth as if he were going to chew on it. Food thought Tommy.

Then he heard a light whistling sound and the impact of the dart as it pierced his mother's neck. It stuck in her skin like an angry wasp as she slapped at it in pain and confusion.

Tommy had never known his mother to lose her balance

before. There were plenty of slippery surfaces on the trees. Nothing ever really dries out in the forest. And the Orang-utans were at constant risk of a bad fall from the towering canopy of the forest ceiling. Tommy had seen some of these fallen hulks, their skulls smashed, lying lifelessly on the ground, their matted fur swarming with flies, an invitation that the flesh-eaters could not resist. The cats would come, the 'harimau dahan,' the clouded leopard, and the civet, and drag the bodies into the brush.

Groaning from the pain of the sting, Tommy's mother sagged to her knees. She attempted to hold on tight to a branch for support. But it was no use. His mother's strength emptied out of her body just as swiftly as the ants'-nests that she used to siphon out with her lips.

All the rest – the motions of his mother's spiraling fall and the crisp darkness of the jungle floor as they hit the ground – was a blank in his mind.

Tommy never saw his mother again, although he thought he recognized her head among the collection of Orang-utan skulls and other rotting carcasses that the 'hantus' kept in their camp.

That was the occasion of Tommy's second encounter with Nita. The 'hantus' had separated the living from the dead, the crying ones from those that remained silent.

The young Orang-utans – there were five of them in all – had been crammed inside a small animal-crate. The forest had never seemed so small to Tommy. It had shrunk to his size in the time it usually took to swing from the strangling fig to the ironwood trees by the river bank. The cage was stifling inside. The stench of Orang-utan feces mixed with the scent of their blood and urine.

There was nowhere to escape to. No one to turn to.
Except for Nita.

Tommy and Nita recognized each other instantly inside the cramped cage. They huddled together in misery, as they *both rode the long waves of shock. Nita had been badly injured; her left arm hung limply at her side like a broken twig. Tommy cradled her in his arms. The other Orang-utans were in much worse shape.*

One of them died within the first hour, although the 'hantus' did not come to remove its broken body until nightfall.

The other two lay motionless, the sound of their short rapid breathing rasping from their chests like the creaking of brittle vines.

That night, when the 'hantus' came to check on them, they shone the light of a thousand fire-flies into the crate, blinding them. Tommy and Nita shivered in fear in the corner of the cage beside the body of the dead one.

'One dead "mawa,"' one of the 'hantus' said to the other in a strange dialect. 'Dog's piss. Those two are goners, too, for sure. Open the crate, Rahman. Let's have a look at the others.'

There was the sound of a bolt sliding as the cage-door swung open. The fire-flies froze in a single column as they fixed their beam on Tommy and Nita.

'Look, her arm is broken, Sakar—'

The fire-flies danced over Nita's form. 'You're right. Another useless catch. Not worth a rat's shit. Add her to the skull-pile. At least we'll get a few rupiahs for her. Grind up the bone, mix it with a little deer antler, they'll never know the difference. They'll still get a hard-on.'

Both 'hantus' laughed bitterly.

'Too bad,' Rahman said to Sakar. 'The "tuan" says he is paying good money for any "mawas" that we deliver in one piece. He said the more intelligent they are, the higher the price. Piss on our luck. All right, let's clean up this mess. Separate 'em. We've got one "mawa" out of five. That's something—'

Tommy did not understand the words, but he felt the energy of a green snake uncoil at the base of his spine. He understood them. What they were about to do. And somehow he had to prevent them from doing it. Tommy grabbed at the dancing column of fire-flies that one of the 'hantus' was holding in his hand.

'What the fuck—?' Sakar recoiled in surprise. 'This bastard is a little devil. You're not going anywhere, "mawa." Hand the flash-light back.'

Sakar leaned into the cage with a stick that had a wire-noose dangling at the end of it. 'I'll teach you to play tricks. Come on, give it up—'

'Wait a moment, Sakar – what's he doing?' Rahman restrained his partner. 'Check it out.'

Quickly, Tommy chattered to Nita. Take this in your good hand. I'll show you. I've seen how they do it. Move this up, move it down. The fire-flies go to sleep, then they wake up. Like this. Quickly, Nita . . . Quickly, show them you can do it . . . Show them . . . Show them . . . Show them the light . . .

Nita's eyes widened as Tommy forced the flash-light into her open hand.

Now DO it . . . Tommy hissed at her. Do it or you will die . . .

'I'll be damned, Rahman,' Sakar began to laugh. 'We've got two "mawas" here with brains. They know how to work an electric torch. Maybe we can sell them to the Public Works in Sabah. They can put them in charge of the power-plant in Kota Kinabalu. I think the "tuan" will pay extra for these two . . .' He laughed again. 'I think we've got something here.'

'What about her arm?' Rahman asked dubiously. 'She's going to be a cripple . . . He wants them in perfect condition.'

'So put a cast on her, you dog's brain. Or do you want her little "mawa" friend to do it for you?' Sakar snapped. 'Give it some time. She should heal all right.'

Rahman grabbed the flash-light away from Nita and shone it directly into Tommy's eyes. 'You think you're smart, don't you? You saved her life. But you don't know *where you two are going. And you don't know what it is you've saved. You'll find out soon enough.'*

Rahman laughed again. He was in an excellent mood. He would soon have enough money to wear out the mattress in that flea-bag of a whorehouse with his favorite whore. A three-day binge in that piss-hole port town of Lahad Datu would suit him just fine. But first he'd have to get these two hairy moneybags aboard one of the speedboats that the dog-faced pirates used to shuttle their precious cargo up the coast to the Sulu Sea where the transfer would be made.

Then the two wildlife poachers removed the dead baby Orang-utan and the other two border-line cases from the cage and slammed the door shut behind Tommy and Nita. The night-sounds of the forest soon enveloped them with the buzzing of insects, the random call of the hornbill, and the occasional crashing sound of a wild pig as it trampled its way through the underbrush.

The *Pattaya Queen*

Chatchai lowered his high-powered binoculars that had been focused on the approaching speedboat that was still a speck on the horizon.

'The duty-free package is on its way,' he announced to the dour-faced European passenger who stood beside him on the bridge of the Pattaya Queen.

They had been cruising aboard the gleaming white 80-foot luxury yacht for three days on the South China Sea. They had entered the slate-grey waters of the Sulu Sea this morning.

It was already noon. The sky was overcast. The waters were perfectly calm. There was no breeze, and the heat

hammered at them as if the sea were an overheated engine
with its radiator ready to burst.

Chatchai studied the pattern of cirrus clouds in the sky.
He could practically read them blind-folded like a fortune-
teller's easy reading of a tell-tale palm. 'Whores had hands
like this sky,' he thought to himself. You always knew
what their destiny was, no matter how many times they
offered their palms up to fresh interpretation . . .

'No, this sky had the canvas texture of a shroud,'
Chatchai thought. The kind you wrapped the bodies of the
dead in before you pushed them overboard to be cremated
in the fires of the deep.

'Not a good fêng-shui, this sea . . . Full of bad omens
today.'

Chatchai spat overboard to ward off the evil joss.

The Herr Doktor Klaus Wörringschafft, whatever his
unpronounceable dog's name was, was wiping the sweat off
his brow with a sopping wet handkerchief that he clenched
tightly in his right fist.

The farang peered into the empty horizon and shook his
head skeptically.

'I can see nothing,' he declared. 'Are you quite sure?'

Wörringschafft's white-fringed bald head was lobster-red,
his thin neck was branded with angry red furrows from the
sun. He was tall and gangly, in his mid-sixties, and dressed
in what the older European farangs took for tropical wear
– a long-sleeved white shirt open at the collar, knee-length
length white stockings that reached up to his bony knees,
leaving a gap of a few hairy centimeters between his
kneecaps and the seams of his white Bermuda shorts. He
wore a pair of open-toed brown leather sandals on his feet.

Chatchai sneered inwardly when he looked at the farang.
With his flakes of pink skin peeling like rust from his sun-
burned nose, with his watery-blue myopic eyes and his
sparse white goatee, the Herr Doktor looked more like a
parrot-fish that had been garrotted by a squid than the
human figure of a man.

Piss on his jai tahm *black heart. The* farang *had been in a foul mood ever since they had set sail from Singapore five days ago . . .*

'They're late. They should have been here hours ago,' Wörringschafft complained as he wiped his brow again. 'What's keeping them?'

Chatchai grunted. 'They here. I think you get ready now soon.'

Wörringschafft heard the loud mosquito-like buzzing of a speedboat as it came into view on the leeward side. It looked like a sewing-machine with hover-craft wings as it stitched the grey elephant-hide sheets of the waves together.

Where were its tusks? Wörringschafft wondered. That pair of 50-caliber machine-guns mounted on its bow?

Pirates, that's what they were, like this dark-skinned Thai skipper with the blue Khmer tattoo on his chest, who smiled grimly as he lifted his binoculars to his eyes to study the markings of the incoming craft.

Not exactly the kind of colleagues he had in mind when he left his practice in Europe to work for the man in Bangkok.

'Them arrive,' Chatchai declared. He did little to conceal the note of contempt in his voice.

'Very good, Chatchai,' Wörringschafft spoke in a truncated English with a clipped German accent. 'You must make sure they are transferred on board as gently as possible, *ja*? They will be suffering from exhaustion, dehydration, and most likely severe trauma. We do not want to lose any more than we already have . . .'

Wörringschafft paused for effect. 'Otherwise your bossman will not be pleased. And we might have some explaining to do, *ja*?'

Chatchai did not remove the binoculars from his face. To do so would have revealed the smoldering rage in his eyes. And that would mean a loss of face.

If this *farang* didn't have the chao phor's protection, if the godfather hadn't given Chatchai this responsibility *personally when he came aboard for a brief consultation in Bangkok, then there was no question about it, the sharks would have choked on his foul-tasting putrid bones by now . . .*

Wörringschafft paused, and nodded curtly. 'I shall be waiting in the surgery down below.'

Then he went downstairs to scrub himself down and to make sure that everything was ready for the preliminary evaluation.

The *Pattaya Queen was registered in Bangkok. It could make more than 100-knots when set loose on the high seas. It did not need any guns to protect it. No pirate in the South China Sea, the Celebes, the Sulu Sea, the Andaman Sea, or the Melaka Straits would have dared assault its colors.*

They knew its flag, the flag of the chao phor, *the devil-lord of the Chi Triangle. No* maw pii *witch-doctor or shaman could protect them in this lifetime – or their next – if they risked his wrath.*

Besides, the rumors and legends – one and the same really – had already rippled across the bandwidth of the shipping-lanes and the myriad island-coves in the region where the pirates would lie low.

Here, in little camps hidden by an overgrowth of jungle, they would rest up, replenish their supplies, and wait for the heat from the Regional Piracy Center in Kuala Lumpur to die down. This was their usual practice after conducting one of their lightning-fast raids on an unprotected freighter that had the misfortune of carrying a rich cargo in these largely unpatrolled waters of the Southeast Rim.

Drinking and whoring to pass the time – generations of kidnapped Vietnamese women boat-people provided the whores' stock – the talk around the camp-fires would inevitably turn to the devil-ship that flew the flag of the Pattaya Queen . . .

In its previous incarnation, the vessel had been known as

the Atlantis Mermaid, *and it had been registered in the*
Bahamas to a wealthy American businesswoman whose
plan called for sailing it around the world. At least, that
was her dream until she rounded the eastern cape of Sabah,
once known as North Borneo. She was never heard from
again.

Now strange things were known to happen wherever the
Pattaya Queen *appeared . . . Strange things that made even*
the most hardened of the Malay, Filipino, Indonesian,
Chinese and Thai pirates reach for their lucky talismans
and press them against their racing hearts. There was the
story of Hai the Sting-Ray to be told and re-told . . .

A young, emboldened fisherman-turned-pirate, Hai was
known for his hot temper and his merciless treatment of
prisoners whenever he hijacked a ship. He would line up
his captives on deck and give them a choice – it was either
a bullet in the head, or one of them – just *one of them, it*
would have to be a volunteer – would be offered a flask of
water and a little food.

And a life-jacket.

The catch was the life-jacket was fashioned from the still
writhing body of a wounded string-ray. The volunteer
would have to willingly slip his arms into the sleeves of the
jacket – it would be locked in the front securely, and
impossible to escape from. Sewn into the back of the jacket
was the crazed sting-ray . . .

Given the choice, most men and women opted for the
bullet, but there was always one person among them who
was foolhardy and desperate enough to try their luck with
Hai's life-jacket.

Watching their performance in the sea as the sting-ray
perforated the skin of their backs with its venomous spiny
tail was said to be the real reason why Hai had taken to
piracy . . .

One day, Hai's band of pirates came across the beautiful
white vision of the Pattaya Queen *cruising off the Turtle*
Islands, northeast of the port of Sandakan in the Sulu Sea.

*They had heard of the taboo, of course, but Hai could
not be dissuaded.*

*He ordered it boarded. 'Refuse to obey –' he warned his
reluctant crew '– and you'll be wearing the sting-ray as a
loin-cloth.'*

*They had not counted on the spirit-house on the bow of
the vessel with its immobilizing rays. It was the invisible
sting-ray that Hai had feared all his life . . . The one that
drained the* chi *out of your body without leaving a single
mark.*

*Kra was only sixteen, but he had already participated
in more than a dozen acts of piracy on the high seas
under Hai's command. He watched as Hai was led down
below. He heard the screams, the silence, and then the
screams that started up again. At first, they were
coherent. Hai begging for mercy, Hai swearing that he
had made a mistake, Hai pledging eternal loyalty to the*
chao phor.

*Then the screams began to transform until they became
an inhuman sound altogether, although Kra swore that he
still could hear Hai's cries trapped within the jibbering of
an ape-like lament.*

Two days later, the Pattaya Queen *cast its anchor off the
largely uninhabited island of Pulau Cagayan Sulu, one
hundred-fifty kilometers east of Pulau Jambongan, the
island closest to the Sabah mainland. Two life-rafts were
lowered, both of them attached to each other by rope.*

*Kra could not believe that he was to be released, much
less that he would be spared. He was placed inside the first
life-raft. He kept his head lowered, not wishing to
antagonize his captors. But when he saw them place the
bundle into the life-raft that was tethered to his own
dinghy, he could not suppress a scream.*

'Now paddle to shore,' the skipper of the Pattaya Queen
*ordered Kra. The skipper was a dark-skinned Thai with a
blue Khmer incantation tattooed to his chest, its Pali spell
visible through his open Lahu hill-tribe vest. He wore green*

pantaloons and he stood barefoot on deck with his legs spread apart.

'Get going,' the Thai skipper growled.

Kra began to paddle, manically and automatically. He cast one fearful eye backwards at the Pattaya Queen, and another more horrified glance at the inhuman cargo he was bringing ashore.

He would become a monk if he survived, Kra swore to himself. Anything to gain merit, and to put distance between himself and this nightmare. He soon reached shore, and his bare feet felt the cool wash of the surf and the smooth sand of the beach. Kra was going to make a run for it, when the Thai skipper on board the yacht called to him through a loudspeaker.

'Pull the other raft up on shore. Now.'

Kra hesitated, then did as he was told. This was his punishment for all his evil deeds. Perhaps it was worse than dying. Dying was letting go, rejoining the gene pool of the ancestors, emerging as a fresh face from the mirror of karma. But this – this was surely beyond the threshold of acceptance.

It was beyond the grace of the Lord Buddha. Beyond the pee, the spirits that populated all living things, from the stones in the ground to the clouds in the sky to the desiccated tail of the langur served up in the gris-gris stew of the fetish market.

This was an abomination.

Kra reeled in the raft that contained the remains of Hai the pirate. He was still alive, but his head had been grafted onto the body of an Orang-utan. Hai's eyes, which had been closed, suddenly opened. Kra found himself staring into the dilated pupils of Hai's face. There was a look of horror in them that Kra would never forget. Then Hai spoke to him in a cracked whisper. 'Help me, Kra – please – you must help me . . .'

Kra shook his head and backed away slowly, then turned and fled into the jungle.

The Pattaya Queen *remained within fifty yards of shore for another twenty minutes, blew its whistle two or three times, then with its engines rumbling headed back out to sea.*

Kra remained on the island for three days and nights until some passing fishermen rescued him in their fishing-boat. Hai's raft was still on the beach beside Kra's, but it was empty. There were tracks on the sand as though an ape had dragged itself on its hands and knees into the jungle.

Somewhere on that island, as the legend of the Sulu Sea had it, Hai was living out the rest of his tormented existence in the form of a hairy Orang-utan ghost with the head of a Thai pirate.

'Is everything in order, Rosarita?' Doktor Wörringschafft asked his Filipina assistant in his kind professional voice. He was already scrubbed down and had donned his lime-green surgeon's smock and surgical-mask.

'Yes, Herr Doktor,' Rosarita replied as she handed him a box of fiberoptic-threaded latex gloves. He pulled out a pair, then slipped them onto his hands. He stretched out his long bony fingers until the gloves fit snugly.

She was similarly garbed in a gown, and Wörringschafft's eyes met hers for an instant. They were soft and brown, almost doe-like. He could not see the tiny asterisk-shaped birthmark on her chin, as she was wearing her surgical-mask. But it gave him a certain reassurance to know that he was familiar with everything about her, her completely dependable professionalism as well as her intimate flaws.

Rosarita Fernandez had been with Wörringschafft for twelve years, through thick and thin – through all the ups and downs of his career as a maverick neurosurgeon. Rosarita was 32, and unmarried. She had consciously chosen the curve of her life, much in the same way that Wörringschafft would select a scalpel from the tray she presented him in surgery.

She had a family back home in Mindanao to support, an RN degree with honors from the University of the Philippines and, most importantly in Wörringschafft's eyes, she was entirely dependable and loyal.

'Loyalty,' Wörringschafft sighed to himself as he gave his latex gloves a reflective snap. Loyalty was a lost art, as faint as the prehistoric rubbings in the Neanderthal caves of Lascaux . . .

Rosarita had stood by him through his darkest times, even after he had been forced to leave the University of Geneva Medical School under a cloud of disgrace. Wörringschafft subsequently attempted to reestablish his practice – and his private research – at the University of Leipzig, but the ugly allegations about his past caught up with him there.

Once again, he was forced to abandon his life's most important work.

Next, he had a brief stint as head of the newly established 'para-neurosurgery' department at the Belgrade Institute of Medicine in the Serbian Peoples Progressive Democratic Republik.

There, he had finally come out of the closet. He could now be appreciated for what he really *was*, a pioneer in this radical new field of para-psychological brain-surgery. He was an alchemist really, as much as he was a neuro-surgeon, and like all great geniuses of the past, he had to suffer persecution for his craft and his beliefs.

The virulent paparazzi had hounded him even in his Belgrade sanctuary. Somehow a picture had appeared in one of the 'Neuro-Euro' tabloids. It showed Wörringschafft implanting an 'elemental' during one of his brain-surgeries. The 'elemental' was a genie that the Swiss doctor had hatched on-line in one of his encrypted Omnispace nurseries. In the photograph, it resembled an oblique shaft of light more than anything else.

But even Wörringschafft had to concede you could clearly make out the whorl of a chin, a pair of perfectly formed eyes, intelligent yet piercing, and the ethereal curve of its leering grin . . .

A perfect delivery, in other words. A successful birth transfer of one life-energy form to another. Designed to empower the enfeebled patient who was lacking the necessary prana required to lead a dynamic life. All of Wörringschafft's cutting-edge work had been cruelly mocked by the hypocritical press with their jeering headline: Faust-Food Comes to Belgrade.

Wörringschafft resigned his post to avoid causing further embarrassment to his employers in Belgrade. Black-listed in Europe, unable to continue his outlawed brand of research anywhere else in the West, Wörringschafft succumbed to the deepest melancholia.

What was thwarting him? Was it possible that there had been some seepage from his handling of 'elementals' during his operations? Had his Odic force-field been contaminated by some toxic prana? Had he inadvertently hexed himself?

Swallowing his pride, Wörringschafft consulted with a former colleague of his, Dr Hans Konnig, a para-psychologist in Vienna, who combined the holotropic breathwork of Stanislav and Cristina Grof with the latest cell psychotherapy techniques adapted from ancient shamanic trance rituals of Lapland.

'Yours is a most unusual syndrome, Klaus,' Konnig advised him after giving him a thorough examination.

Wörringschafft had checked into the Kundalinipunkt Klinik for a three-day stay under the assumed name of Mr Dieter Petersen from Copenhagen.

'What is it, Hans? Am I just having an old-fashioned nervous breakdown or what?' Wörringschafft inquired anxiously.

Konnig suppressed a smile. He was familiar with his colleague's unorthodox reputation. 'I wish that it were so, Klaus. Then we'd have you out of here in no time, nicht wahr? Fit as a fiddle and without climbing the walls. No, Klaus, this is something new for me, too.'

Konnig cleared his throat as he pronounced his formal diagnosis. 'It has hitherto been unheard of in the annals of Western psychiatry for a single individual to exhibit the symptoms of mass-psychosis.'

Wörringschafft stared at him for a moment without blinking. Then he asked quietly, 'So what in your professional opinion should I do about it?' He paused. 'If anything?'

Konnig pursed his lips and frowned. 'That would be extremely difficult for me to say without further study. It might be an occupational hazard, of course, considering your – er – rather specialized field of research.'

Then Konnig brightened up as an idea came to him. 'Perhaps you can work with it. Use it to your advantage instead of trying to suppress it. Why don't you get a life, Klaus? Get many lives. Get as many lives as you can. In your line, that shouldn't prove too difficult, should it?'

He gave Wörringschafft an inquiring glance. 'You just need to spread it all out – this mania of yours – until you become more even-tempered . . . That might do the trick. What do you say?'

As Wörringschafft let this thought sink in, a tear came to his eye. He wiped it away with his sleeve and shook his friend's hand. 'Thank you, Hans. Thank you. I knew I could rely on you. You were always the brightest lad in the class.'

When the offer came from Bangkok to join the organization, Wörringschafft snapped it up eagerly. It was more than just the money. He had never been offered so much money before in his life. No, it was something very Asian, yet intrinsically German as well, that appealed to him. It was a question of 'face.' Of honor.

Of steadfastness in the face of the unknown. And it was his destiny, Wörringschafft was certain of this now, to give the face of the unknown a proper nose-job . . .

'Herr Doktor . . .' Rosarita's voice interrupted Wörringschafft's thoughts. 'Channel One is receiving. Channel Two is on-line as well.'

'Thank you, my dear.' Dr Wörringschafft smiled. 'Let's see what our friend Chatchai has fished out of the Sulu Sea today.'

The clear plastic chutes of the twin-elevator chambers were misted with the vapor of the Orang-utans' breath. Nita was huddled inside one capsule, Tommy stood upright in the other.

Dr Wörringschafft and Rosarita approached the capsules. 'Subject A appears to have suffered damage to its left arm,' he spoke into a VDO device. 'In my opinion, a broken femur,' he ventured, with a bit more hesitation than he would have preferred.

Wörringschafft was not a veterinarian, but his employers in Bangkok had not made that qualification a part of his job description. As long as he could make the neural implants connect with the organism's synapses within the matrix of the neo-cortex and not produce a jibbering idiot in the process, he was on solid ground.

The finer details of cosmetic surgery and social skills conditioning were left to other teams of technicians further down the assembly-line.

For now, Wörringschafft was to conduct the initial examination to determine if these Orang-utans were worthy candidates for the trans-speciesization procedure.

If not, he would signal Rosarita to press the red button on the control-panel. The blue button signified Phase Two of the evaluation procedure – the L-unit phase. The red button would turn the chutes into incinerators.

This was always a sensitive moment for Rosarita, Wörringschafft realized.

He had to admit it was never a pleasant sight to see the flames erupt and the beasts turn into cinders before their very eyes. He found it much more rewarding to detect signs of an acceptable level of H.S.C.Q. (Homo Sapiens Chi Quotient) within the primates' Tachydon Field.

That meant he could work with them. That they could be 'up-graded.' Wörringschafft appreciated the wisdom of *that old Thai proverb, 'Not all coconuts make good curry.'*

'Subject B has no apparent injuries, and appears to be alert despite the rigors of transshipment,' Dr Wörringschafft continued. He pressed his hand against the clear plastic surface of Tommy's chute. He felt a true connection with these creatures at this stage of the proceedings. It was the mystery of creation wrestling with the paradox of potential. He could identify with them. His own life, too, had its red and blue buttons.

Nita looked at Tommy through her capsule. Their eyes touched across the distance of a thousand clear plastic rain forests. Tommy was alarmed by the expression on her face. She was fading on him.

Nita . . . He tried with all his will to reach her. Nita . . . We'll get through this. Don't give up on me now . . .

'Und so . . .' Dr Wörringschafft lapsed into his native German. 'Now comes the moment of truth? Do they have the makings of a Wagner? Of a Schiller? Or a Werner von Braun? Henry Kissinger? Or is the wit of the village idiot going to be lost on them?'

He turned to Rosarita and addressed her in English. 'Which button will it be today – the red one or the blue? What do you think?'

Rosarita knew that he was teasing her and declined to answer. She had no stated opinion about anything. She had feelings, it was true. But not opinions. In her years with Dr Wörringschafft, she had witnessed a great many things that had forced her to revise her views on the world. What was normal? What was paranormal? Too often, the lines were blurred. It was better not to see them too clearly.

'Rosarita?' Dr Wörringschafft inquired solicitously. 'Is something wrong?'

'I'm sorry, Herr Doktor. I think it's the ventilation in here. The air-conditionining has been bogging down all morning . . . I'll just go and get the L-unit . . .'

Rosarita stepped away from the capsules and crossed over to the other side of Wörringschafft's floating laboratory. She rolled a trolley carrying the L-unit back to the operating console. She plugged the connections into the control panel and checked the gauge on the machine.

The L-unit was Wörringschafft's own invention. It was his personal contribution to the new science of telemorphosis and neurosurgery. He was an alchemist, he thought as he flushed with pride. An alchemist who transmuted the living 'prana' of one living creature into the re-engineered form of another . . .

The L-unit was an advanced model of the unorthodox bio-telemorphic device that had been the main cause of Wörringschafft's expulsion from the University of Geneva Medical School, from Leipzig, and his final retreat from Belgrade.

He had perfected it here, aboard the Pattaya Queen, as it sailed from one shark-infested sea to another, always operating in international waters, where he could not possibly be found guilty of violating any international medical conventions concerning an undefined branch of neurosurgery on the high seas.

'Call it a legal loophole into the cranium,' the chao phor had told Wörringschafft during their first interview in Bangkok just before he got the job. 'Do you have any qualms about the nature of your assignment?'

Wörringschafft shook his head emphatically. 'Nein, mein Herr. For me this represents the opportunity of a lifetime, and I thank you from the bottom of my heart.'

The Asian godfather had impressed Wörringschafft from the first moment he met him. This was not a man to be monkeyed with. He knew all about Wörringschafft's expertise in the field. His knowledge did not appear to be technical, but none of the nuances was lost on him. Wörringschafft was proud to work for such a man. He was a true leader.

'L' stood for 'Larvae.' It was the next bio-telemorphic step up from Wörringschafft's use of psychic 'elementals' – those

Web-generated 'genies' – which he had incorporated into his controversial para-neurosurgical procedures.

The difference between an 'elemental' and a 'larva' was basically the fact that an 'elemental' was implanted deliberately by the neurosurgeon into the psyche of the subject. They had passive-aggressive tendencies both on-line and off.

The 'larvae' formed themselves involuntarily in the subject's mental sphere. They were self-generated projections of the subject's own worst nightmare, caught in an endless loop of despair and dementia.

Bottom-line: The resulting mental struggle between the subject and their own self-generated 'larvae' tested the resiliency of their psyche in all the known dimensions. Crossing, of course, the interspecies boundaries . . .

The L-unit experience strengthened the subject. It made them that much more resilient.

So that when Wörringschafft finally implanted the subject with the commercially programmed bio-RAM, they were much less likely to reject it. They were less inclined to break down and devolve back into their original form.

In effect, they would be inoculated against their original nature. And be forced to embrace their new identity whole-heartedly. Whole-mindedly . . .

'Ready when you are, Doktor,' Rosarita announced.

Tommy and Nita gave each other a final look. They could already sense the stirring of the vibrations in the tubes that had been connected to their capsules.

This thing, whatever it was, smelled like dead snails, millions of them, and they were already beginning to crawl through the fiber-optic piping in their noxious slithering race to reach them.

'Achtung!' Dr Wörringschafft gave the order and Rosarita switched on the L-unit.

'Now let the games begin,' he said as he folded his arms to watch in rapt attention.

Crossroads

Pinang Island, Malaysia

Still parked outside the No-Name Bar in Georgetown, Tommy Kok Lau hesitated before kick-starting his 'saki. He had to consider his next move carefully. He wondered if he should ditch the bike somewhere. Find an alternative route from Pinang to the mainland, then up north to Hatyai on the other side of the Thai-Malaysian border.

There, in Thailand, he would be safe. At least for the time being.

Should he take the car-ferry across to the mainland and head up north from Butterworth? Or should he risk the long span of the Pinang bridge which linked the island with the north–south highway on the other side of the channel?

What if his parents had already put the alert out on him? What if Pa had discovered his passport was missing, and had put two-and-two together?

Pa and Ma would probably have figured it out by now. Maybe they'd be happy just to see him go. Maybe they'd be relieved that they wouldn't have to send him away on that 'Happy Islands' cruise . . .

Pa had brought the brochure home one night, and left it on the coffee-table. Tommy hadn't paid much attention to it at first. They never took him anywhere, and lately Pa's rages had been getting out of control. So who would have imagined that the '4-days, 3-nights All-in-One Coconut Fun Cruise' tour package had been meant for him?

'You've been stressed lately, Tommy,' his mother Leilah told him when she presented him with the slick brochure. 'Pa's been worried. And so have I . . .'

'Pa's been *worried*? That's a new one!' Tommy gave her a dark grin, deliberately flopping his wrist against his forehead to smear the white pancake make-up. Leilah shuddered. Tommy knew just how to get to her. He knew how to punch her buttons, at least the ones that counted . . . He knew she knew that he knew . . .

It was all a game anyway, and it was winding down to the end-point fast.

Leilah entered his room unannounced one night when he'd been scanning SabahNet's 'Conservation Watch' live-feed channel on the Omtron. He'd seen the look of shock on her face when he pulled a fast zoom out of the freshwater swamp forest of the East Kinabatangan River.

'I didn't know you were so interested in wildlife, Tommy,' Leilah had said dumbly.

'What'd you think I was, Ma? Tame? *Me?*' He scratched himself under his arms for effect.

'You're nothing but a hairy delinquent,' Pa declared as he appeared in the doorway behind Ma.

'I'm just doing my home-work, my *real* home-work,' Tommy smirked as Pa stepped forward and smacked him across the face. His cheek stinging from the blow, Tommy hung his head as the tears began to flow. He didn't want them to see him crying. He didn't want them to see what his *real* tears looked like.

'That's enough, Samuel,' Leilah insisted. 'I'll speak to Tommy myself. Why don't you go on downstairs?'

'You talk to the freak then,' Pa said as he left the room, slamming the door behind him.

'Tommy . . .' Leilah laid her hand on his shoulder gently. Still sobbing, with his head bowed, he angrily shrugged her hand away.

'Tommy, I need to speak to you about something—'

'About *what*, Ma?' Tommy lifted his tear-streaked face to hers. There, she was shocked again. She looked pale. 'About *me*? About what I'm *becoming*?'

'Tommy . . .' Leilah had an anguished look on her face. She brought out the brochure and laid it on his desk. 'This is a special program, Tommy,' she said in a quiet voice.

'It's a . . . a workshop. There will be other boys and girls your own . . . your own *age* . . . on-board. You won't be alone. It'll be fun . . .'

'And what is this workshop supposed to *accomplish*, Ma?' Tommy saw through her ploy. He picked up the brochure and held it up to her as though it were damning evidence.

Which it *was*.

Tommy had already heard the scuttle-butt from his no-name club at school. From Carlo, Mo, Peter, Sally, and the others who were like him. This was their last ride-out. It was supposed to set them straight. To get them re-integrated, squared-away, cleaned-up, looking *human* again . . .

But they all knew about the glitch. Their programming was coming apart at the seams.

For some, the glitch had manifested itself sooner than for the others. Look at Elmer Wong, a total retard. He was completely dysfunctional except when it came to climbing trees. His parents had been forced to withdraw him from school when his physical structure began to deteriorate rapidly at the onset of puberty. Elmer had been one of the kids that had gone on this 'Happy Islands' cruise.

Except that he never came back. Quite a few of them never did . . .

'Listen, Tommy,' Leilah said as though she was reading his mind. 'It's a free trip. Your Pa and I won it in a . . . in a magazine sweepstakes. It's for gifted kids, it's designed to give you the opportunity to . . . learn and see new things.'

'A free trip?' Tommy stared her straight in the eye. He knew all about that, too. 'You mean it's covered by the *warranty*, right?'

Leilah's face flushed in anger. 'That's enough out of you, Tommy. You're *going* – and that's final. The cruise is in two weeks, just after the spring break starts. You'll be sailing on the *Pattaya Queen*. It's a dream vacation, Tommy. You'll be cruising in the Melaka Straits, and you'll have all kinds of exciting activities to keep you busy.'

'I am *not* going.'

Leilah crossed her arms across her chest defiantly. 'Tommy,' she said in a quiet determined voice. 'I don't know how to get through to you anymore. Believe me, I've tried and tried. But it's just not happening. This trip will be good for you – and I hope and pray that it will be good for us, too. As a *family*, Tommy. I hope it brings us together again.'

'I am *not* going, Ma,' Tommy repeated firmly. 'Get that through your head.'

'That's too bad, then—' Leilah snapped at him harshly as she turned to leave the room. 'Because for *your* information, your *girlfriend* Anita Chu *is* going . . . I talked to her mother about it today. They've already booked passage for her. So you won't know what you'll be missing . . . Who knows, you've heard all about shipboard romances, maybe she'll find herself another more suitable boyfriend, nah?'

After his mother stalked out, Tommy shook his head in disbelief. He hadn't heard this news yet. It was just like Leilah to save this bomb-shell for last.

He buried his face in his hands. *It couldn't be true* . . . It just *couldn't* be true . . . And yet he knew it was. He had this feeling that Anita Chu had broken his heart before. Who knows when, in some past life? They were sweethearts at Pinang High. They hung out together at the No-Name Bar. They had kissed and made out in the movies. They had even come close to making love on more than one occasion. It was just a matter of time for them.

But Anita was one of those who had been turning. Turning fast . . . He knew that her parents were worried about her. It would make sense that they'd send her on the trip. But why hadn't *she* told him anything about it? Why was she keeping it a secret from him? She knew that he was in love with her. She had told him she loved him, too. That they were *special*.

Tommy rocked his head in his arms and cried his real tears. He didn't want to lose her again. Not again.

Not ever again.

>>> *mmm.gunung mulu.com transmission interrupted* <<<

Paul Sykes traced his finger on the frosted grime that coated the oval window of his cheap Pyongyang Air Lines charter flight to Bangkok. He sighed. He was traveling in *kim chee* class, all right. Even the coffee tasted like fiery fermented Korean cabbage.

The North Korean stewardesses all had black-belts in *tae kwon do*, wore Kim Jong II bouffant hair-dos, and prowled the aisles like sentries on the look-out for defectors.

There was one clogged loo for the 200-or-so backpackers who were crammed in the rear of the ageing Ilyushin 627 airbus. A few of the more daring Friendly Planeteers had tried slipping through the DMZ curtain to reach the one working lavatory in the 'Five Year Plan' (Modified Economy class) section, but the cadre-detectors had given them away.

They had been forced to sit in hastily organized 're-education centers' on the aisle floor, with their hands clasped on top of their heads, for periods of up to two hours.

Still, cheap is cheap, Paul Sykes thought to himself through his haze of mental fatigue. *What you pay for is what you get.* It seemed as if they'd been flying for more than thirty-two hours since their flight had departed San Francisco, but they had yet to reach Seattle.

Not that he'd been idle exactly. Sykes had been dipping into 'The Gunung Mulu Memorandum' from time to time. He had downloaded Mort Wisenik's neuro-ROM catridge into his Hitachisoft eye-mask. Settling back in his seat,

Sykes pretended to doze as he scrolled through the synaesthetic collage of primate tele-memory.

It was an absorbing account all right, Sykes thought as he tiredly rubbed his eyes. He was taking a little break from the material. He had pulled his eye-mask up to his brow, and was staring out the window.

Mort was right. Poor Mort. Poor dead Mort . . . What a way to go, Sykes shivered. *With his philodendron Rodney shoved halfway down his throat . . . Who could have done that to him? But Mort was right . . . It was a tragic love story, like that of Romeo and Juliet . . . Tommy and Nita . . . Of broken hearts and human cruelty . . . And it wasn't over yet . . .*

Sykes stole a glance behind him. Three rows back, roughly in the middle of the row, about seventeen seats away from the aisle (there were twenty-four seats in each row), sat the stony-faced young Chinese guy with the ponytail. It was the same dude who had traveled on the Super Shuttle to the SFO Airport with him.

Funny, Sykes wouldn't have made him out to be a native backpacker, with his Nokia-Rolex platinum-plated satellite watch and his patent leather Armani k'ung fu slippers . . .

Chalk one up to 'you-never-can-tell' . . .

Their eyes met for a brief instant.

Sykes felt as if he was staring into one of the cracks in a brick wall that was covered with thick ivy. He felt that even if he could climb that wall and peer over to the other side, he would find nothing there. An abandoned backyard with sorry-looking poured-over concrete for a lawn, broken bottles, and some withered vines choking the drain-pipe.

That was the image he got from the Chinese dude's eyes. They were blank, impenetrable.

Not bad for 'No subtitle-land,' Sykes thought. The guy was giving him negative ESP. *And fuck you too, gizmo-head*, he added for good measure.

Neither of them blinked. Then Sykes pulled the Hitachisoft

eye-mask down over his eyes again, and re-entered the jungle book. He switched on the static-filter just in case anyone might be tempted over his shoulder.

>>> *mmm.gunung mulu.com transmission cont'd* <<<

. . . .
Pinang Hill

'It's happening to you, too, isn't it?' Tommy confronted Anita Chu when they were finally alone together. She had been avoiding him for nearly two weeks, but had finally relented and agreed to see him.

It was Saturday afternoon, the day before Anita left on her 'Happy Islands' cruise aboard the *Pattaya Queen*. The 80-foot white luxury yacht had already docked at the Pinang Marina in the shadow of Fort Cornwallis.

Tommy and Anita could see the yacht from their vantage point high up on Pinang Hill where the old former English colonial governor's villa once stood. There was a coolness to the air at this higher elevation that the stifling settlement of Georgetown would never know.

Up here, 830-meters above sea-level, the crimson bougainvillea had a fresher fragrance, and the orange flame-trees flickered their fire-tongued leaves more brightly. There were pine trees that made the green fringed elephant-eared palms seem out of place.

Peacocks wandered the lawns of the stone-flagged Crag Hotel where Tommy and Anita sat sipping their lemonades on the terrace. It was easy to pretend that there was nothing to pretend about except this false sense of serenity.

At a lower elevation, gimlet clouds of haze slowly unfurled like tattered lace-curtains in a cheap Chinese hotel in Georgetown.

Tommy and Anita had been tempted once to go into one. They had entered the white-gravelled courtyard of the Cathay Hotel, a ramshackle Victorian boarding-house built in the nineteenth century, but had decided at the last moment not to go through with it. 'It feels haunted.' Anita had squirmed uneasily.

'Haunted by ghosts?' Tommy had asked, disappointed.

'No, it's haunted by *people*,' Anita said as she made a face. 'I don't want to make love where these people pretend to make love. Do you?' she challenged him.

'I'm not sure what you mean by that,' Tommy had replied, caught off-guard. His longing for her in that way had been growing. But he didn't want to press her into a corner. He wanted it to happen naturally. At the right time, and in the right place. He just wasn't sure when or where that would be. If ever . . .

'Don't take it personally, you baboon.' Anita attempted to reassure him with a hug. 'It's just that you and I are different. Not like them. Or hadn't you noticed?' She gave him a playful jab in his ribs with her elbow.

'*Ouch!* Okay, Anita, but sometimes you drive me crazy, you know that?' Tommy exclaimed.

She *did* drive him crazy. *Like today* . . .

Like today when they both knew that this would be the last time they would probably see each other again. Only they didn't know how to say it – *their next goodbye* . . .

Their next goodbye in their long series of goodbyes . . .

Tommy and Anita had taken the funicular tram clear up to the top. It had been a slow ride, an hour of painful silence as Tommy tried to fathom what was on Anita's mind.

They held hands as the cable-pulled carriage trundled up the steep rock face of Pinang Hill.

Once they reached the peak, they strolled together in silence, still holding hands. They stopped outside the mosque and lit some incense at the old Hindu temple. They had eaten a couple of Magnum ice-cream bars, and finally arrived at the Crag Hotel where the Indian waiter had brought them their lemonades.

Anita excused herself to use the ladies' room, then rejoined him on the terrace a few minutes later.

'I said, *it's happening to you, too, isn't it, Anita?*' Tommy repeated angrily. 'You're just in a state of denial about it.'

Anita let Tommy's moment of frustration pass. Then she said quietly, as she touched his cheek gently with her hand, 'There are some things which I could *never* deny, Tommy.'

'Such as?' Tommy demanded to know.

'When we first met—' Anita reminded him. She had told him this story before, but he didn't know what to make of it. Whether to believe it or not. Anita was an odd-ball. A strange one. But that was one of the things that had attracted him to her in the first place.

Sure, she was cute. She was a *fox* . . . She had this cute caramel complexion, this upturned nose, full sensual lips, with sexy peach-fuzz on her cheeks, and long waves of thick curly brown hair. *Nice legs. Thighs. Her ass. Her bust. Umm* . . .

Tommy got hot just thinking about her. And her *eyes* . . . There was something magical about them. Like delicate brown chestnuts with a sparkle of sunlight in them.

'I was the new girl in school, right?' Anita continued as she sipped her lemonade. 'And all the guys were coming on to me. But I wasn't interested in any of them. Only in you. Right away—'

'That's right,' Tommy agreed. 'You certainly didn't beat around the bush.'

'Oh, *Mr Cool* . . . Just look at you,' Anita jived him. 'But you never stopped to think about it? Why I singled you out. You never wondered *why?*'

'This is your *Tales of the Supernatural* again, isn't it?' Tommy raised his eyebrows.

If every guy listened to every girl that fed him that line, and *bought* it, where would the mystery of romance go?

Tommy wondered. The randomness – the blind chance – of the mystery?

Anita looked as if she had been hurt by his remark. She composed herself and continued. 'All right, a moment ago you asked me "if it was happening to me," too? You mean these changes that we're going through? These physical changes . . .'

'Emotional changes, too,' Tommy said defensively. 'It's much more than the physical . . .'

'*Exactly.*' Anita nodded her head. 'We're in agreement about that, at least. But . . .'

'But *what*, Anita?'

'There are *some* emotions that run a lot deeper than the ones *you're* talking about, Tommy. And I am *not* referring to all that horrible shit we have to put up with every day from our families and friends – our so-called "friends" . . . Of course, it's painful. But that's only the tip of the iceberg.'

'Only the *tip* of the iceberg?' Tommy asked incredulously. 'You mean that's not bad enough?'

'No, Tommy.' Anita shook her head. 'Some of us are the "chosen ones" . . . We have to endure the unendurable . . . Like you and me, for instance . . . It can't get any worse really. It can only get better.'

Tommy sat up in his wicker chair and gripped the railing on the terrace. He scowled darkly as he leaned over and looked down the side of the craggy cliff. It was a sheer drop into a granite ravine below.

'Is *that* why you're leaving on that ship tomorrow? Because you have some kind of a crazy compulsion to "endure the unendurable" . . . ? That sounds pretty sick to me, Anita. I mean it, it really does. You've *got* to know that you're not coming back,' Tommy tried to reason with her one last time. 'It's a one-way ticket. But you're still set on going . . . *Why?*'

'Don't you understand, I *have* to go,' Anita said, as tears began to well in her eyes. 'I *have* to face them again. By *myself*. Not like the last time, Tommy, when *you* were there to fight them off . . . Otherwise, I will never be free of them. They're *still* inside me, Tommy.'

Tommy shook his head helplessly. They had discussed this all before. Endlessly. Anita had her own name for them. She referred to them as '*that slithering army of snails*' . . . As far as Tommy was concerned, it was just one of her old recurring nightmares.

One that she'd been having since childhood. One that she kept trying to foist on *him* for some reason. '*If only you would begin to remember them yourself, Tommy, that would be the first step . . .*'

Remember what? *First step towards* what? Tommy wondered. *Millions of decaying snails that slithered towards them through a tube that smelled like the rotting entrails of an elephant carcass in the jungle?* He didn't share the same memory.

Didn't want to, in fact . . .

But there was a familiar queasiness inside him that Tommy couldn't quite shake. *These days people had a nostalgia for all the old diseases that had been successfully eradicated – yellow fever, hepatitis, polio, malaria, typhoid, tetanus, diphtheria, AIDS . . .* Tommy reflected.

They were all tame has-beens, ex-prize fighters, compared to the newly hatched bio-tech viruses that ravaged the earth today. Shit, there were even fan-clubs devoted to the common cold . . .

Some of these new-fangled things didn't even have names, let alone numbers . . . he mused. *No wonder the population of the world was shrinking.*

What if Anita's nightmare was the equivalent of some spectral mosquito that had buzzed through the protective-netting around his psyche and infected him with its toxin?

Tommy didn't want to admit this to Anita, but he had been getting the shakes himself lately. Pretty bad. Fevers and hallucinations. But the snails were *larvae*, and they had been incubating in his eyes. Growing ripe and full and juicy until his eye-balls would burst open, and he would find himself lying in his bed in the middle of the night, awake and drenched in sweat and shivering.

'Seems to me that *you're* the one who's in denial, Tommy,' Anita chided him gently as she read the worry in his face.

'You're really beginning to sound like a broken record, Anita,' Tommy retorted. Somehow she had managed to turn the rock over and expose all the fears that were festering underneath.

'Let's face it,' Tommy groused. 'You're just a martyr to the cause. To those deeper, darker feelings of yours. Whatever the hell they are. Whatever the hell you *think* they are.'

'Do you want me to *show* them to you, Tommy?' Anita asked him with wide eyes. Then she reached over and kissed him softly on his mouth. He felt her warm lips on his like a salve that took the sting out of his wound. But his feelings still smarted.

'Show them to me? *How?* Either you've got these feelings or you don't. Isn't that how it works? Either you believe in them or you don't. Thunder doesn't just happen—' Tommy said, as he heard the beginnings of a rumble in the swiftly gathering storm clouds. Georgetown was going to be drenched in a tropical downpour at any moment.

He felt some raindrops splatter on his face and wiped them away.

'Do you remember, Tommy, when we wanted to go to that awful place, to that grungy Chinese hotel, and get a room there and make love?'

Tommy gave her a quizzical look. He nodded.

'And I didn't want to. I said it was haunted by living people, not by ghosts. That wasn't what really bothered me. That wasn't the real reason.'

'What was it then?' He wondered where this was leading.

'The real reason I wasn't ready to make love to you,

Tommy, was that we were still too much like *them* at the time. Like those people. It was too soon for us. I wanted the real *you* to make love to the real *me*.'

Tommy sat there, dangling his legs. Unconsciously, he leaned back in his chair and gripped the railing with his feet. 'Ooops,' he grinned apologetically as he caught her staring at him. He lowered his feet to the ground.

'No, *don't* do that, Tommy,' Anita said. 'Don't change what comes to you instinctively. That is exactly what I'm talking about. This is the real *you* . . . This is the real *me*. We must never *ever* forget that. The best thing for us to do is to remember as much of it – of what we *really* are – as we can . . .'

'How do you propose that we do that – 'Nita?' Tommy asked her, confused.

'I took the liberty of reserving a room for us here, Tommy,' Anita announced to him in a matter-of-fact voice, as though she were swatting a fly away from her glass of lemonade.

Tommy was shocked. *Anita was making the first move?* He studied her face to see if she was putting him on. She wasn't. Her brown eyes never once left his with their clear level gaze. He hadn't been expecting this development. Anita was always full of surprises. Tommy, the wild one, was always getting caught in one of her innocent snares.

Trying to put on his cool look, but losing it, Tommy blurted out, 'For real? At the *Crag*? But rooms here must cost a fortune . . . How can you afford it?'

He babbled on with his small talk. 'Did you know that Buckminster Fuller stayed here once? There's even a geodesic suite named after him . . .'

Anita snapped open her purse and showed him the room-key. 'I charged this to Daddy's card. I may not be a rebel like you are, Thomas Kok Lau. But after I'm gone, I'd like my dear father Mr Albert Chu to know that I was more than just *Daddy's* little girl. Or his darling little ape. Come on, now—'

Anita stood up as she took Tommy's hand and led him inside the dim Alpine interior of the hotel.

'The rain's starting to come down. And we've got something that we need to show each other. Something that I suspect we already may know.'

≫ mmm.gunung mulu.com transmission interrupted ≪

Paul Sykes heard the buzzing sound of a mosquito close to his ear. Still wearing his Hitachisoft eye-mask, leaning back in his seat, he brushed at his cheek unconsciously.

≫ mmm.gunung mulu.com transmission cont'd ≪

Paul Sykes now followed Tommy and Nita into their hunting-lodge suite in the Crag Hotel. He heard their footsteps as they entered the room. As they posted the 'Do Not Disturb' sign on the doorknob outside and double-locked the door with a resounding 'click.'

Tommy and Nita paused in the hallway for a moment. They turned to each other grinning as their eyes adjusted to the 'Das Niebelunenlied' decor designed by the venerable ethnoclectic design team of Chu & Li & Wong & Kruger of Singapore.

There were framed pictures of Alpine scenery on the walls. A Dürer engraving. A photograph of an old Scottish manor above the writing desk with its old-fashioned ink-pot and quill pen. Pale blue chintz curtains embroidered with tiny yellow corn-flowers hung from the large bay windows.

A rocking-chair was wired into CNN, BBC and Star TV for the old geezer trade. This was a strictly non-Omnispace room. Mozart's 'Symphony No. 22 in C' played softly in the background.

The air-conditioning unit hissed quietly from the neatly piled Panasonic logs in the large stone fireplace, the high-rez flame-optics casting off a cheerful glow amidst the gushing air of Alpine coolness.

In the middle of the room stood the centerpiece, a king-size bed with a rustic wood frame constructed of gnarled branches from the Black Forest. It was covered with a colorful marzipan-patchwork quilt. There was soft white goosedown bedding, the kind you could get lost in unless you laid a trail of bread-crumbs from the center of the bed to the fluffy Matterhorn-size pillows at the headboard.

Tommy and Nita both walked up to the bed, gave the goosedown bed a rectal exam up to their elbows, then plopped into it together. The sound of their laughter was muffled as they began to wrestle each other in the downy depths.

Sykes felt the sweat grow on his brow as, a few moments later, he saw Tommy's t-shirt tossed to the floor, followed by his jeans, then Nita's blouse, skirt, bra and panties . . .

Sykes brushed his hand against his cheek brusquely. *Damn this mosquito* . . . It was buzzing his ear again.

'Tommy?' Sykes heard Nita's voice call. She sat up in bed. Tommy had his arms wrapped around her. She covered her breasts as she looked up at the ceiling.

'What is it?' Tommy inquired, his hair tousled as his gaze followed hers up towards the ceiling.

'I don't know. I just have this creepy feeling that we're being watched,' she replied.

Shit, Sykes was beginning to feel like a damn voyeur again . . . Was this where anthropology and pornography intersected? Was he simply an anthro-pornographer? Was 'research' some kind of academic version of foreplay? He had the Gunung Mulu file loaded in his Hitachisoft eye-mask. He was reading it – 'receiving' it – now. They were transmissions.

The Gunung Mulu file contained priceless information. The implications of an organic interspecies network were staggering. Mort Wisenik had been killed because of it. Sykes was flying to Thailand, for God's sake, to try and connect with Tommy. He already knew where Tommy was heading. He'd seen the preview . . .

Jeezus Christ, he was planning to give Tommy the last recorded message from the girl he was watching Tommy make love to right now, *at this* very *moment . . .*

Had real-time become as twisted as that? Was there some sort of a real-time/post-time/future-time bleed-through in the Gunung Mulu site that Sykes had failed to consider?

Sykes felt that he knew them – that he was becoming engrossed in Tommy and Nita's story – but was it right *for him to become so intimately involved in the personal details of their love?*

Maybe he should just pull this Hitachisoft mask off his face right now, and leave them alone to enjoy these few precious moment of privacy to themselves . . .

Shit, this buzzing mosquito . . . Sykes slapped at his neck. A mosquito? On Pyongyang Air Lines? Maybe bed-bugs or lice on the head-rests, he wondered. But a mosquito . . . ?

Sykes heard Tommy say to Nita, 'That's just a bug on the ceiling. And see – that gecko on the wall? It's moving in fast. Looks like the gecko's going for it, honey. It's just the food-chain. The food-chain's the room-service of the natural world . . .'

Nita shivered, still covering her breasts. 'It feels evil to me. I don't like it.'

Then she added. 'It feels like we're on TV . . .'

>>> *mmm.gunung mulu.com transmission interrupted* <<<

Sykes tore off his Hitachisoft eye-mask. The Pakistani exchange-student sitting next to him seemed to be sleeping. His head was slumped against Sykes' head-rest. There was blood on his neck where the mosquito had mistakenly landed and spiked him first.

Wait a minute, his seat-mate appeared to be asleep. But he wasn't breathing. Then the realization hit Sykes. *The mosquito.*

Now the fucking thing had finally found him . . .

From the corner of his eye, Sykes could make out the mosquito's ultra-finely wrought natureplex wings, its long legs bowed on his cheek. Its delicate stinger was retracting into its belly.

It was in the process of refueling its delivery-mechanism . . . How much time did he have left before it sucked up enough toxin and plunged its stinger into him?

All of Sykes' reflexes went into overdrive. *He had to get it off fast.* Then he caught himself. *Slow down, take a deep breath . . .* He couldn't risk slapping it. If he crushed it, the toxin would be quickly absorbed into the pores of his face.

Bad idea. He would just be doing its job for it . . .

No, if he could just . . . If he could just bend his face, ever so slightly . . .

Careful now . . . Don't disturb the little bastard.

Nice mosquito, nice little mosquito . . . Whoever raised you must have an advanced degree in toxicology and nano-hang-gliding, maybe even doing laundry . . . You leave nasty little blood stains, you know that . . . Someone like that son-of-a-bitch three rows back fiddling with the navigational controls of his Nokia-Rolex, probably . . .

Steady, boy, you're almost there . . .

Fuck, its stinger was coming down . . .

It's now or never. Paul Sykes brought his cheek in direct contact with the Arctic Gulag flow of air from the Pyongyang Air Lines panel overhead. The reading-light didn't work, but the air-socket shot enough air out of it to give your neck permanent whip-lash. The infra-red guidance system that flew this ninja bug wasn't powerful enough to maintain its position. The pre-fab mosquito tipped on one set of legs as it was blown off his face by the current of air. It nose-dived onto the floor.

Sykes quickly put his foot down on it and crushed it. When he turned around to give the Chinese dude with the ponytail an angry challenging look, Sykes found him immersed in reading a magazine. It was one of those trashy tabloids that covered the new entertainment media springing up in Asia. The title on the masthead read *Mischief Reef*. That was the name of the atoll in the South China Sea where the Spratly Studios, the new mega-Hollywood of the Rim, was located.

The Chinese dude looked up from his paper. For the first time since they'd been playing the cat-and-mouse game with their eyes, he gave Sykes a smile. A big, broad movie-star smile.

Phase 2

. . . .

Pupa

·········
Thorax

Kho Samui, Thailand

Kroon had Butterfly pinned artfully to the
operating-table. The Thai *katoey* lay spreadeagled,
leather-straps securing his arms and legs. His eyes were
open, but Butterfly was a million miles away, the whites
of his eyes rolling upwards into his head.

The needle for siphoning the *chi* had already been
inserted into Butterfly's abdomen beneath his flattened
katoey breasts. A frothy pale blue light bubbled in the
transparent tube that fed into the collections reservoir.

Kroon, the Boss Bitch of the Rasta Palace, glanced at the
chi-emissions chart. Pouting his curvaceous full lips with an
air of mock disappointment, he *tsk-tsked* loudly.

Tan and Krik – Kroon's underlings – looked on
impassively from the side of the table. They'd been
working on Butterfly for hours, milking him of his pranic
colors.

Two containers-worth, refrigerated, glowed on the
counter like a tropical sunset captured in a capsule. An
earlier sample had already been shipped to Wing Fat in
Bangkok. *How much more pranic silk could this human
cocoon produce anyway?*

'Butterfly, Butterfly – can you hear me?' Kroon whispered
as he grasped the *katoey*'s chin, squeezing it hard.
'Sweetness and light, where are those colors, those *bright,
bright* colors that we want? As bright as a million fucks,
goddamit! Not *this* shit!'

Kroon suddenly exploded in a rage as he whirled around
to face his men with an angry expression his face. He
turned to Tan, his chief technician. 'His colors are fading,
can't you do something?'

Tan was wearing a tie-dyed 'Rasta Palace' Bob Marley
t-shirt over a faded pair of black jeans. He shifted on the

flip-flop soles on his ex-Thai kick-boxer's feet and gave his boss a wary look.

Tan was brawny and solidly built compared to the coiled snake-like figure of Kroon who loomed over him on his high-heels. Kroon was dressed in his usual thigh-revealing red Spandex micro-skirt and fuzzy-plastic see-through halter-top.

Sometimes it was hard to believe the Boss Bitch was really sixty years old. With his shoulder-length platinum blond hair tied back in a pony-tail, his high-cheekbones delicately etched on his face, a stormy expression his eyes, and a body defined by curvy hips and full breasts, he looked more like a young Thai joy-girl than an old fart *katoey*.

Shit, he looked cute, but watch out – Kroon was perfectly capable of scratching your eyes out and making you swallow them, one eyeball at a time. You didn't want to get in his way when he flew off the handle.

Tan swallowed hard before he replied tactfully, 'Maybe he just needs a rest, sir. We've gotten excellent results from him so far. First-class *chi*. The best we've ever harvested—'

Tan had been a kick-boxer, whose brain had been flattened in the ring. But that was before he'd gotten his degree in neuro-media science from the Media Lab, courtesy of a *farang* who had been led astray at the Rasta Palace and divested of his doctoral implant. Kroon never let Tan forget that he owed his educational windfall to his forceps.

Now Kroon smiled sweetly, which was a dangerous sign. 'I *know* how good it is. You don't have to tell me.'

His mouth opened slightly and the tip of his tongue played with the ink-jet palette of his upper lip. He was wearing that high-rez chameleon gloss that changed lipstick colors like a mood-ring whenever he played with his lips. They were turning a vivid banana-leaf green.

He turned to look down at the supine figure of Butterfly on the table. 'Who would have ever figured that our own little queen here was full of such sweet honey? Where did she *get* it from anyway?'

Tan made the mistake of replying. 'That blond *farang* gave her the charge, sir. For sure. He began the process. Her DNA is already almost completely altered. I don't know what he did to her. But we have that picture of him crossing the bridge to the Rasta Palace. If we can find him, we'll locate the source. He can't be far, sir. He must be somewhere around here. One of the islands where the *farangs* go perhaps. We know he's not on Kho Samui.'

Kroon grimaced at him. 'I *know* that, too, angel of mine. But our sweet little Butterfly here has not been exactly communicative on that point, *has* she?'

Kroon traced Butterfly's rib-cage which was criss-crossed with the finely wrought red slash marks of his sharp fingernails. 'Our *farang* friend, the mysterious Dr *Chi*.' Kroon scowled contemplatively. 'And his Traveling Free *Chi* Clinic . . .'

He drummed his fingers on Butterfly's inert torso. 'No, we can't have that . . . We can't have a *farang* dispensing free samples. Of the *real* thing, no less. That would be bad for business. Bad for Kroon. Bad for Wing Fat. Bad for many, many people who rely on us. No, we must find the original supply, of course. But meanwhile—' Kroon glowered at Tan again.

'What can we do with this freak? You say he's mutating. But his colors are getting thinner. Is he dying or what? How much more can we pump out of him? Check his condition again.'

Tan stepped up to the operating-table and peered down at Butterfly. He ran a hand-held *chi*-meter across his body, holding it above his navel where the needle had been inserted into Butterfly's *hara*. A staticky buzzing sound registered loudly on the device.

'Well?' Kroon demanded. 'Are we still in business or what?'

Tan checked the life-support implant reading on the

monitor. He looked puzzled. 'Butterfly,' he said to Kroon, 'is still in his body so far as I can tell. But he's multi-processing his *chi*. We're picking up strong signals of another flow somewhere else. On a much higher frequency than we're used to. It's weird . . . These colors, sir—' Tan waved his hand at the canisters on the counter. 'Are the feedback of his *chi*. Almost like echoes, if you think of them as soundwaves.'

'Feedback?' Kroon brought his ear to Butterfly's face. He could feel the faint mist of Butterfly's breath tickling his mascara. He gave Tan a hard look. 'Are you bullshitting me?'

Tan winced. 'My guess is that he's bypassing us, sir. I don't think that our equipment is nearly sophisticated enough to intercept his main supply. He's producing high-end *chi* at a rapid rate, no question about it, but he's disseminating it elsewhere—' Tan said thoughtfully. 'Some place we can't tap into easily . . .'

'Some place *else*?' Kroon looked startled. 'But he's right *here*, isn't he?' He placed his hand on Butterfly's rib-cage again. 'I can feel his heart beating plain as day. Where *else* can he be . . . ?'

'I don't know, sir. I really can't say . . . These phenomena aren't truly localized,' Tan replied apologetically. 'They can manifest in different forms in different places.' He braced himself for the storm, and sure enough Kroon's claw was at his throat gingerly squeezing it.

'Try,' Kroon said as he pinched Tan's carotid artery, shooting a wave of black-out ripples through his head. 'Why don't you try and make an educated guess?' Kroon repeated softly.

Tan gasped for air as Kroon released his hold. He coughed as he steadied himself against the table where Butterfly lay pinned.

'Very well, sir—' Tan croaked hoarsely as he hobbled over to the main console. He inputted the data from the hand-held reader into the Omni *Chi* system. 'I've never seen anything like this spectrum of *chi* before. These are the fractals of his Tachydon Field . . . See, these colors all massed together here?'

Tan pointed out a jetstream of colors that pulsed on the screen in the shape of a thorax. 'It's like he's sending this big cloud of *chi* out into the atmosphere. Let's see if I can pinpoint these vectors. It's sort of like tracing an echo back to its source.'

The vortex of colors began to spin and rotate against the grid of global ley-lines that Tan called up on the screen. 'These are the four quadrants,' he tapped on the screen. 'North, south, east, and west—'

'Never mind that,' Kroon snapped at him. 'What the fuck is that!?' He pointed at the screen. 'If those are clouds, that looks like an ocean to me.'

Tan raised his face from the monitor. 'That's correct, sir. It *is* a body of water, as a matter of fact . . . According to the charts, this would be the South China Sea.'

Tan paused as he stared at the immobile form of Butterfly on the operating table. 'That's where Butterfly's cloud of *chi* is at the moment. Or rather, that's where his force-field is merging into the overall weather-pattern of organic *chi* that's drifting over the planet . . .'

Kroon was speechless for a moment. 'The South China Sea!?' he finally exclaimed. 'But what the hell is he doing there?'

Tan studied the moving cloud of colors that was now taking on a more definite shape. The thorax had been joined by an abdomen and a head on the screen. There were six legs and three body segments in total, with eyes, antennae, and a slowly unfolding proboscis. 'It's beginning to resemble a butterfly, isn't it?' he mused to himself. Then he looked up at Kroon with an odd expression on his face.

'Why, sir, I think he's pollinating Xiang Gang with his *chi*.'

···············
Download

Orientation. Registration. Contact.

In that single fluttering instant, chrysalis turned into butterfly. It had broken through to the other side and was now Queen Rim. Thousands of hexagonally shaped eyes studied this sparkling new world with intense curiosity and interest. A kaleidoscopic burst of color and light — a sudden uplifting thrust — and its wings snapped open like twin-sails in the breeze.

It was free at last.

The vertigo of caterpillar was a thing of the past. The Queen Rim floated, hovered, danced, meandered, and flitted through the rainbow spectrum of morning sunshine, reading each mote as if it were a fragment of ancient scripture engraved upon the ambrosia of light.

Butterfly adrenaline pumped through the tube of its heart from its abdomen to its head as Queen Rim spiraled upwards, downwards, forwards, backwards, left and right.

Now the Queen Rim floated joyfully like a kite on its iridescent gossamer wings.

It rippled in the air like the hoisted square sails of the Chinese junks that darted like busy dragonflies in the harbor far, far below.

Then it began its descent . . .

It was time for the download to begin.

It took a massive amount of will for the Queen Rim to manifest itself in each of the 5.2 million minds of the people of Xiang Gang. Each one of those minds fused with the vision of the butterfly at precisely the same moment.

They saw it, it saw them.

For a brief moment, although they did not realize it on a conscious level, they recognized something of their own higher selves in that fluttering scroll of light.

Breathing in the Butterfly teachings made the process that much easier for them to assimilate through their bloodstream.

• •

The Queen Rim Affair

Special Autonomous Region of Xiang Gang

Frank Gobi sat on the Ming dynasty rosewood divan in his suite at the Panda Hotel in Kowloon. He was staring spellbound at the brilliantly hued image of the butterfly on the Omtron set.

It was the hottest news topic in all of Xiang Gang. Three days after the butterfly's appearance, its picture was being played and replayed on every Chinese channel all day long.

Queen Rim – the public had seized on the name given to it by one of the Chinese tabloids in the Special Autonomous Region.

What was it really? Gobi reflected. He tinkled the ice in his glass of club soda and took a sip. He leaned back in the divan and stretched his long legs out on the coffee table, careful not to topple the stacks of press clippings and special editions of the *South China Morning Post* that he was compiling on the subject.

The killing fields of research. Gobi grimaced as a pile of papers slid to the floor.

Maybe there was a clue buried in all that material somewhere. A 'smoking archetype' perhaps . . .

Gobi loved paper the way some people loved Omnispace. He was an 'old-school futurist,' as his wife Tara liked to tease him. *Well, you can't recycle Omnispace the way you can paper,* he usually replied. *Once it's gone, it's gone, and*

*we all know it's going fast. The whole creaking structure is
about to collapse any day soon.*

Gobi glanced at his watch. *Where* was *Tara anyway?*

He wondered if she was having any luck locating Terry
Jordan. Terry Jordan was their young American ethno-
botanist friend. Brilliant, but definitely eccentric, a fact
which endeared him to both Frank and Tara. Their paths
had kept crossing during their Asian travels.

Terry Jordan had shown up suddenly in Xiang Gang –
out of the blue – about a week ago. If anyone would have
a clue about this business, it would be Jordan.

At least, that was Tara's theory. *That, and a whole lot
more . . .*

Gobi's eyes returned to the image of the butterfly on the
screen as he listened to the patter of an endless stream of
commentators. They were like army ants trying to decipher
the Morse code of a rice-field that had suddenly landed on
their ant-hill.

It was all the same thing really. The telling and the re-
telling of the story was a form of collective therapy, he
realized that. An entomologist's version of the 'Stockholm
Syndrome.'

The public was slowly coming to terms with the fact that
their minds had been held hostage by this consensually
imagined insect.

The only question in Gobi's mind was: *Who was it that
had written this particular script? Kafka or Confucius?*

The Xiang Gang media was full of personal eye-witness
accounts and reports about the sighting.

Commuters on their way to work in the MRT subway saw
the butterfly as they hung on to the hand-straps in the railway
carriage. Those who had been crossing Deng Xiaoping
Harbor on the Star Ferry from Kowloon to Xiang Gang
island witnessed it hovering above the gangway at the ferry
terminal. They had mistaken it for a candy-bar wrapper
blowing in the wind until it opened its wings and flew away.

Students on their way to school observed it, so did office workers stopping for a quick bowl of *congee* rice porridge on their way to work. Stockbrokers saw it flashing on the trading-board, tycoons visualized it in their villas on Chairman Mao Peak, bus-drivers, clerks in shops, police officers, old-time bird-fanciers with their fancy caged birds out for a morning stroll in the park, coolies working in the container-shipyards, airtraffic control officers at Chep Lap Kok Airport, lorry drivers in the New Territories with their live cargos of ducks and chickens and pigs, addicts glimpsed it as they chased the dragon, lovers in short-time hotels embraced it as they woke up in each other's arms . . .

Gobi tinkled the ice in his glass again. *Think, man, think . . . Where was all this leading?*

There were the inevitable supernatural spins to the story, of course. The sensational tabloid *Ming Po Daily* featured a poignant account of the death-bed testimony of the eighty-three-year-old matriarch, Wong Yee-shing, late resident of Kwan Shing West Estate in Tuen Mun.

Wong Yee-shing had just been officially pronounced dead of causes due to respiratory failure by Dr Hsieh Chu at the Fung Lin Hospital in Wanchai. To the astonishment of the medical staff attending her, the deceased opened her eyes for a brief instant, then pointed her trembling finger at the corner of the room where the apparition of the butterfly was plainly visible to all those present.

Her last words were: 'On what do you feed and where do you come from, dear butterfly?'

Then she expired, and was pronounced dead a second and final time.

Hmm, Gobi mused as he stared at the butterfly on the Omtron screen. The more you looked at the image, the more of a sense of inner peace you derived from it. You could almost *breathe* it into your system.

Which fit in neatly with Tara's theory, of course . . .

The Queen Rim incited people to acts of *peace*. Of course, there was a natural resistance to it among certain types of people, especially those who derived their power from the use of brute force.

Look at what's happening in the Chinese underworld, Gobi reflected as he picked up a news clipping from the *New Shenzhen Courier*. He scanned the item.

> Triad members have been dropping out from their gangs at an alarming rate causing Leung Tai, the godfather of the notorious '14K' syndicate, to issue a stern warning to his followers: 'From today, it is not allowed to mention the Poisonous Butterfly. Otherwise, bullets will have no eyes and knives and guns will have no feelings. Be forewarned.'

Gobi adjusted the vision on his horn-rimmed Canon bifocals with a tweak of the zoom control, then flipped through the pages of the *Tsimshatsui Tatler*. This was a thick glossy society magazine full of ticking Bulgari ads and old-style quicktime photo montages of black-tie galas chronicling the lives of the expatriate community in Xiang Gang.

> The so-called 'Queen Rim' phenomenon occurred in Xiang Gang on April 6, 2039, at precisely 8:32:01 a.m. It lasted for exactly one minute and fifteen seconds.
>
> At 8:33:16 a.m., the butterfly vanished from sight with a spectral fluttering of its heavily ornamented wings, like an ancient Rolls-Royce of the insect world pulling out of the posh driveway of the old British colonial-era Peninsula Hotel in Kowloon, before heading down the ghost of Nathan Road . . .
>
> And *no*, contrary to reactionary rumors – shades of Nury Vittachi of the *South China Morning Post* – this beast was definitely *not* a stunt perpetrated by that running-dog clique of *avant-bored* artists belonging to the pro-gerontocracy ranks of the Multi-Maodia Movement . . . Remember their last prank? They set off a motorized wax effigy of the Chairman swimming in the waters of Aberdeen with a little red book of 'Quotations' clenched between his teeth, causing some minor damage to the passenger jetty of the Jumbo Floating Restaurant in the harbour.

Now for our final item: Our Official Queen Rim Contest. Send us your entry describing what YOU were doing at that precise moment of *lepidoptera interruptus*. The most tantalizing accounts will be published in these pages in our next issue. First prize is a weekend for two at The Peak Health Spa including a complete series of *chi* mud-pack treatments, with the second and third prizes being, respectively, dinner for two at Deng Xiao-Spago's, and a bottle of Comrade Camus V.X.O.P. Cognac. All entries must be accompanied by a self-addressed stamped coolie (just kidding, we're all equal-opportunists here), no later than by . . .

What retro-colonial clap-trap! Gobi thought with disgust, as he tossed the *Tatler* onto the coffee-table along with the rest of the documentary evidence he was amassing about the 'Queen Rim Affair.'

He'd like to send the *Tatler* an entry, all right. *Where had HE been when the butterfly appeared? How could he ever forget?*

And goddamnit, he wondered as he glanced at his watch again. Where *was* Tara? Was she any closer to finding Terry Jordan? Maybe she was right about him. Maybe he had something to do with all this. Jordan – Terry Jordan, the bio-morphic boy wonder – and his pheromones.

· · · · · · · · · · · · · · · · · ·
Pheromones

What had *he* been doing when it happened? Frank Gobi cast his mind back for a moment.

It *had* been precisely 8:32:01 a.m. And it *had* lasted for exactly one minute and fifteen seconds. The *Tatler* had gotten *that* fact right, at least . . .

'Stroke #86, this shave begun 8:32:01 a.m., 6/4/37, 512 strokes remaining . . .'

DiGillette in hand (the razor recorded the units of shaving-time remaining), Frank Gobi brought his face up close to the magnified orb of the shaving-mirror in the bathroom.

He was just about to tackle that tricky spot on the curve of his chin, when he suddenly snapped his head back as though someone had just landed him a punch.

'What the—?' he swore out loud as he nicked himself. A crimson smear blotted the white foam on his face.

Gobi peered into the mirror again, then backed away a step. '*Holy Kwan Yin!*' he exclaimed. He laid the razor down on the marble sink and blinked. No mistake about it. 'There's a BUTTERFLY in the mirror!' he exclaimed.

There, he could clearly make it out now. *All of its parts* . . . The giant quivering knobs of its antennae. The *samurai* armor of its thorax. Six legs and four brightly colored wings like elaborately painted Chinese screens reflected in the mirror.

'*Tara!*' Gobi called out to his wife. 'I want you to see something! Hurry!'

At that hour, Tara O'Shaughnessy Evans-Wentz Gobi was still in bed. She was enjoying her first cup of morning coffee, while reading the freshly pressed copy of the *South China Morning Post* that room-service had delivered along with a basket of croissants.

'*Frank!*' Gobi heard Tara's reply. And then he *knew*. He absolutely, positively *knew*.

Holding a towel to his chin to staunch the trickle of blood, Gobi rushed into the master-bedroom.

Tara was sitting up in bed, her honey-golden hair draped against the pillows that were arranged behind her, her silk kimono open to reveal her full breasts. Her magnetic green eyes were fixed on him with more than their usual degree of intensity.

There was a triumphant look on her face as she held the newspaper open for him. 'Is *this* what you wanted me to see?'

Gobi sat down beside her on the bed and watched as the butterfly flew up from the mid-section of the *South China Morning Post*. It was the same one he had just observed in the bathroom-mirror.

It fluttered above the crisp white sheets of their bed, flapping its wings in steady measured beats like a procession of miniature Chinese paper lanterns aglow during the Moon Festival.

'What do you think of our little winged visitor, Frank?' Tara asked him. 'Pretty, isn't she?'

Frank Gobi held out his hand under the fluttering butterfly as though he were cupping a velvet hologram with wings. 'It's beginning to dissolve.'

He closed his hand over it. When he opened his hand again, his palm was empty.

'Sayonara,' he said. 'It's gone. 'Bye 'bye, butterfly.'

'It'll be back,' Tara replied as her green eyes flashed at him. 'This is just the beginning. You realize that, don't you, Frank? It's all just starting to happen now.'

Tara switched on the Omtron set in the recessed alcove on the opposite wall. 'See, it's already making the news. It isn't just us . . .'

The special bulletins were pouring in from all over the SAR of Xiang Gang. Butterfly sightings in Mong Kok, in Lantau – then another special news-break to announce further sightings in Shatin, in Wanchai, and in the New Territories.

'A butterfly typhoon,' Gobi gesticulated. 'I get the picture.' He picked up the remote and switched the Omtron off.

In the dozen years that he and Tara had been together, they'd seen a lot of strange things. They had sifted through the lost-and-found department of the Collective Unconscious. They had broken through the taboos of Omnispace, and challenged many of its archetypes. Venturing into the crashed world of Satori City and resuscitating the ghosts of dead avatars had been just a first step for Frank Gobi. Their journey was still unfolding.

Now he and Tara were traveling in Asia. *In Conradian Cyberspace as it were*, Gobi mused. *Where anything was possible.* Psychic typhoons included. Where else in the world could you join an organization like Mutants Anonymous and not feel like an outcast?

Sometimes it seemed to Gobi that human evolution was pumped up on steroids. You gotta carry that weight or else it will all come crashing down on you . . . The weight of the stage and the weight of all the personas who strutted their stuff across it.

Out here on the Rim, there was no such thing as boundaries anymore. Only priorities.

The question was, *Whose were they?*

'So what do you make of it?' Gobi asked Tara. 'Is it just more seepage from Omnispace? Consensual hallucination No. 19? What if it's a new form of subliminal advertising? I've heard Saatchi & Saatchi has been experimenting with *kundalini* billboards. Scratch 'n' sniff Kali. But that was in Bhutan, and the campaign never quite got off the ground—'

Tara sniffed in the air. 'Do you smell that, Frank? That faint aroma? What is it? It's like jasmine, but it's got sort of a muskyish tang to it.'

Gobi took a whiff. 'You're right. I noticed it in the bathroom when I was shaving.'

He sat down on the bed beside Tara and sniffed again. 'Now what does that remind me of?'

Gobi had a nose like a Roto-Rooter in an aromatherapy shop. 'Okay, now I've got it,' he declared. 'It's an aftershave. What's it called? "Old Official." You know the brand, it's quite popular out here. They've got a catchy little jingle. "*It's our theme to present these wifty fine drops for the chase of your pleasure . . .*" You know the one I mean, Tara. Christian Dior puts it out in a joint venture with Tiger Balm.'

Tara shook her head. 'No, Frank. I don't think it's a commercial scent at all.'

'You don't?' As a couple, Frank and Tara sometimes went nose to nose on these matters. It was a little fifth *chakra* olfactory game they enjoyed playing. Trying to identify the source of the myriad-and-one reeking odors that Asia was justly famous for. Was it birds' nests adulterated with cicada droppings, raw sewage (easy), civet-sweat marmalade, gall-stones from cow or water buffalo (a fine distinction), pigeon bile, ass-hide glue, bad poetry, or just plain old graft?

'No Frank, I think it's *pheromones*,' Tara said as she wrinkled her nose.

'Pheromones? Now, why didn't I think of that!? I think you've got something there, Tara!'

'Thank you,' she said. 'But you were right, too. It *is* someone's aftershave. Now who do we know that's into using pheromones as an aftershave?'

'You don't mean . . . Jeezus.'

'That's right,' Tara's green eyes flashed. 'Our curious new friend. The one we keep bumping into wherever we go, it seems. In all the oddest corners of the Rim. *And* when we least expect it. Terry Jordan.'

Frank Gobi whistled. 'This *is* Jordan's brand, all right. What a strange coincidence.'

'Is it? I wonder.' Tara breathed in deeply again. 'Uh-huh, this scent definitely has Jordan's signature written on the molecules. We both know he's got a tropical rain forest supply of the stuff. *Pheromones*, Frank. They really *are* like aftershave on a man, but they come from the deepest part of his soul. A woman knows these things. Trust me.'

•••••••••••
Jordan

'**D**o you remember when we first met Terry Jordan, Frank?' Tara asked Frank Gobi.

She had slipped out of bed and had drawn the heavy drapes, flooding the room with sunshine. Behind her in the distance, the green mountains of China snaked between the towering grey highrises of the Tsuen Wan district.

Tara turned to face him, cocking her hand on her hip as if she were Venus de Milo posing as a gunslinger. The sunlight caught her golden hair, as golden as the spires on a Thai temple. She was a beautiful woman, Gobi thought to himself as he looked at her admiringly.

'That must be, what? About six months ago?' he replied. 'That's when we were on our Cambodian junket recording those trance-mediums at Angkor.'

'That's right. Do you remember what you said about him at the time?'

'Remind me.' Gobi's eyes met hers with a meditative look. He was feeling a rush of dark adrenaline. There was something about Terry Jordan that was troubling him. Something terribly familiar about Jordan, yet so strange at the same time. He couldn't quite put his finger on it.

Tara O'Shaughnessy Evans-Wentz Gobi folded her arms under her full breasts. She gazed fondly at Frank who was still sitting on the bed in his dark blue Japanese *kimono*, his feet placed firmly on the floor. She always thought that her husband looked sexy when he was brooding.

With his curly brown hair still wet from the shower, his grey alert eyes, aquiline nose, and handsome features – he had a smattering of Central Asian genes mixed in with his French Huguenot ancestry – Frank Gobi had an exotic air about him, like a fiery Russian dancer seeking to defect from some troubled past life.

Maybe that was why they complemented each other so well. They were both natural-born gypsies. Tara had been born in Tibet. Her parents had been Microsoft missionaries in Yarlung Valley. Frank Gobi looked as if he might have been born anywhere, at least once. He was an old soul.

'I remember *distinctly* what you said,' Tara said as she faced him squarely. 'You said that he looked like an insect of some kind . . . Or a butterfly in *Homo sapiens* drag. Something like that—'

'I did not!' Frank laughed. 'You're making this up . . .'

'Okay then.' Tara tossed back her hair and smiled as she revealed her white teeth. 'What was it? That's right! You said that he reminded you of some kind of an urban Yeti. What do the tabloids call them? The "Children of *Chi*"? What if you were right, Frank? What if he *is* one of them? Let's just say?'

Gobi frowned. *The Children of* Chi . . . He was familiar with those travelers' tales. He had read the chats posted in the lively 'coconut press,' those backpacker 'zines that floated down the MekongNet in the middle of the night like uprooted trees.

'I believe I said he had a kind of other-worldly quality to him,' Frank ruminated. 'Almost as though he'd served time in Atlantis. As if he had escaped from some terrible prison and was free at last to do what he pleased. Not recklessly, but with some higher purpose in mind.'

'Tell me about those "Children of *Chi*" again, Frank,' Tara asked as she approached the bed and put her arms around him. He hugged her back.

'First of all, don't forget that this is only an unsubstantiated legend, okay?' Frank replied. 'It's myth, like the Big Foot.'

'I'll keep that in mind,' Tara nodded. 'But hey, you've delved into some pretty esoteric stuff yourself, Dr Gobi. Like that chlorophyll-search engine idea of yours to jack into Organic Omnispace . . .'

'Nothing ever came of that. I ran out of research funds—'

'As far as *you* know nothing ever came of it. But I still think it's a brilliant idea. I mean, that's one reason you took such a shine to Terry Jordan, isn't it? You guys related very well to each other. Almost as if you were brothers or twin souls. He's a – what do you call it?'

'Terry's an ethno-botanist by training, but with leanings towards morpho-biology. He said he was primarily interested in studying the vanishing species of intelligent flora and fauna in the region. Organic networking, that's his specialty.'

'That's right, a morpho-biologist,' Tara nodded. 'That's pretty close to your own field. Para-psychology. I'd say you guys were really compatible.'

'Morpho-biologists are not held in such high repute in the academic world. And neither are para-psychologists, by the way. We're the next thing to quantum quacks.'

'Bully for them. What do they know?'

'Hmm,' Gobi laughed. 'You've got a point there.'

'So come on, Frank.' Tara wrapped her arms around his neck again. 'About those "children of *Chi*" of yours.'

'They're not *my* children.'

'Well, maybe we can adopt.'

Gobi laughed again. 'Give me a break – okay, here goes . . . And this is all *I* positively know about the subject—'

Tara gave him a kiss. 'I love you, honey.'

'Teacher's pet. All right – to begin with: There've been various so-called "sightings" of them. Initially, the reports came from isolated outposts in eastern Borneo, in places like Tanjung Selor and Tanjung Redeb, along the Berau and Bulungan rivers . . . That's deepest, darkest Kalimantan and Sarawak. B-O-R-N-E-O to you, baby.'

'You can't get any deeper or darker than that, right?'

'Oh, well—' Gobi smiled. 'If you *try*, you might. You're pretty deep and dark yourself at times.' He cupped her breast in his hand, but Tara brushed his hand away.

'Later, if you're very, very good. Go on, please—'

Gobi continued. 'Supposedly, they're a new breed of *Homo sapiens*. But on a much higher wave-length than we are. They can communicate naturally – "telemorphically," so to speak – with all of nature. Trees, rocks, animals, insects, marine life, planetary weather systems, you name it. They're more advanced than we are. More jacked in to the natural *chi* of the planet. Which gives them a homeochromatic ability to mime nature. They can morph right into the landscape. Or even into people. They can mimic your DNA. Then presto, we've got Tara the Second!'

He stroked her hair. 'Then I'd have two of you. Sounds nice, doesn't it? What a threesome that would be!'

'Mmm,' Tara said. 'I still think I'd be jealous. But tell me, why would they inhabit those remote places? To be close to what's left of nature?'

'Apparently,' Frank said. 'But hold on, honey. There's more to the story. Recent sightings have them showing up in more populated areas. In busy megapolises like Singapore, for instance. Striding down Orchard Road with its highrise malls, mixing it up with the crowds, acting as "natural" as you please. As if they were jetting in from the future for the weekend, to pack in a little bit of shopping and to do a bit of sightseeing . . .'

'Which brings us to Terry Jordan,' Tara said after they'd been quiet for a few minutes. They were both leaning up against the Qing dynasty headboard of their bed.

Tara had turned on the Omtron again, but in silent mode. They were watching the Queen Rim news-bulletins as they continued to stream in.

'Ah, yes, Terry Jordan. The enigmatic Terry Jordan. Mr Child of *Chi* himself.'

'I think he fits the general profile, don't you?' Tara replied. 'Look how he popped out of the wood-work in Xiang Gang. And besides, he does like to shop.'

Tara and Frank had run into Jordan just the other day in Xiang Gang. That was twice in two weeks. The week before, they'd seen him in Macau. This last time, he had

been standing in the corner of the lobby of the Mandarin
Oriental. Looking tanned and fit as ever, dressed in khakis,
and carrying a leather case, the young American beamed at
them happily as they approached him.

'Hi, guys, fancy running into you globe-trotters again,'
he flashed his white teeth at them. 'Where will it be next,
I wonder? Central Asia? Are you following me around or
what?'

'We're with the CIA. The Chlorophyll Intelligence
Agency,' Gobi ribbed him. 'What have you got inside that
case, eh? What's left of Borneo?'

'Specimens!' Jordan laughed. 'I've got Borneo in my breast-
pocket right here.' He patted the front of his khaki shirt.

'Seriously, what are you doing here?' Tara inquired.

'What am I doing in Xiang Gang?' Jordan sounded
evasive. They were standing by a large potted palm in the
corner of the crowded Mandarin lobby. 'Oh, I was visiting
Old Ming here,' he said as he rubbed one of the palm's
jade-green fronds.

'This old fellow's a survivor and a veteran. His
capillaries have been bothering him lately. It's all that cigar
smoke and negativity. He's got lots of war stories to tell.'

'Oh, I bet that what you're really doing is secretly
trafficking in tiger-testicles.' Tara poked Jordan in the arm.
'I've always suspected that you actually lead some sort of a
secret double life. There's big money in that sort of thing in
Xiang Gang. Why, go to any old Chinese herbal shop on
Temple Street, and—'

'Please, Tara.' Jordan sounded genuinely shocked. 'Don't
even joke like that! I was in Sarawak when they were
cutting the last of the trees down in the Bako nature
reserve. Nature reserve, what a laugh! As if nature needs to
make a reservation. "Be there at eight, table for two trees."
Only they're the table. Do you know, I actually heard the
tigers come out at night and scratch their nails against the
bark of the trees that were going to be cut down the next
day? That was the loneliest sound in the world, believe me.

They were saying goodbye to the forest. They knew.'

'I'm sorry, Terry,' Tara apologized instantly. *'I hear what you're saying. It was a bad joke.'*

'Oh, I know. You guys wouldn't hurt a philodendron. But people who would hurt a philodendron are just as easily capable of hurting other people as well. Even of killing them sometimes.'

Then Jordan looked at Gobi with a sad expression in his eyes. Gobi couldn't help but wonder what he meant by that look. He just had a funny feeling about it. Seeing Jordan standing there in the lobby beside Old Ming, as if he and Tara had just interrupted a conversation they'd been having. Gobi felt like an intruder at a wake.

'Bad news, huh?' Gobi asked him, nodding at Old Ming in his fine Chinese porcelain pot. *'Death in the family or something?'*

'A distant relative of Old Ming's, I'm afraid,' Jordan replied with a sweet yet ironic smile. *'Sometimes you don't even know when an old friend of yours has passed away. And sometimes—'* He gave Gobi that sympathetic look again. *'It's better not to know . . .'*

That was the last time that Frank and Tara had seen Terry Jordan. He said he was late for an appointment and walked out of the lobby and into the street.

'And the first time we met him, Frank, remember that night?' Tara nudged Gobi gently in the ribs. They had switched off the Omtron and were busy piecing together everything they knew about Jordan.

It was like a ritual of getting reacquainted with a mask. They had kept running into Jordan since that first time in Phnom Penh – in Bangkok, Rangoon, Kuala Lumpur, Surabaya, Toli-Toli, Macau, Xiang Gang . . .

'Yeah, how can I forget?' Frank replied.

So there they were, Frank and Tara, sitting at this rickety bamboo table in this backpackers' hang-out, which was a combination café-bungalow-hammock community, on the outskirts of Phnom Penh.

The sun was setting against the dark green backdrop of jungle, the batik shadows were deepening, and a little boy with the smiling face of a serene Khmer Buddha was lighting the smoky kerosene lamps that hung from the eaves of the open-air café.

It was hot and humid and happy hour for the mosquitoes.

A group of young backpackers had gathered on the verandah, Friendly Planeteers from the looks of them. Judging from their smorgasbord of accents, they were mostly Scandinavians and Swedes, in their late teens and twenties, almost the same age as Frank's son Trevor, who was also backpacking somewhere in these regions.

The aroma of clove cigarettes wafted in the air along with the tell-tale smell of ganja.

With his sun-tanned face and his Nordic blond hair, Gobi and Tara had almost mistaken Terry Jordan for one of the Swedish crew.

But Jordan was a natural mimic. That was one of his shticks, too. The next time they saw him, in the company of some olive-complexioned Italians in Bangkok, he had more of a Latin look about him. Much more Italiano, with all the emphatic hand-gestures and flourishes that go with it.

Yet, with all that mimicry going for him, Terry Jordan was a true original, all right.

'Watch how he's focusing on that Swedish chick,' Tara whispered to Gobi excitedly. It was a little game that she played. She liked to peep into people's secret nature with the tuning-fork of her sixth or seventh sense.

They had just finished their awful green curries, the flies were thanking them for it, and Gobi was working on his second Carlsberg. The sweat was pouring down his back like one of those trick rapids that the Mekong is notorious for.

*Gobi loved the tropics. He just couldn't bear the heat.
He was feeling particularly worn out this evening. He
preferred looking at ancient ruins to feeling like one.*

'What did you say, honey?' he asked wearily.

*'She's under the impression that he's attracted to her,'
Tara provided Gobi with a running patter of commentary.*

*He took a sip of his ice-cold beer, felt immediately
revived, and replied cheerfully, 'Well, isn't he?'*

*'Don't be silly,' Tara responded. 'Well, yes and no. See –
she's responding to him on a sexual level – uh-oh, second
chakra alert! And he keeps leaning in towards her, his
knees are even touching hers. But he's not coming through
on the same channel as she is, Frank. He's no Mr Second
Chakra. Let me see now – Jeezus, Frank, he's turning our
way! Wave nicely and smile! He's noticed us. "Hello there!
Ja, ja, willkommen!"'*

*Tara gave him a friendly little wave, and Jordan smiled
back their way. He looked slightly amused.*

*'I wonder if he realizes that he's got a professional
chakra-voyeur seated in the audience,' Gobi thought as he
washed some more Carlsberg down.*

*The Swedish girl gave them an indifferent glance, then
started up her conversation with Jordan again.*

*'Wow, Frank,' Tara whispered to him. 'I think our boy
just picked up on our vibes.'*

*'You mean, he picked up on your vibe,' Gobi teased her
as he sipped his beer. 'You couldn't be more obvious if you
were looking at him through field-glasses.'*

*'Oh, come on,' Tara retorted. 'I'm really being quite
discreet, believe me.' Then she turned to him with a
concerned look on her face. 'I'm not embarrassing you, am
I, Frank? Because if I am, I promise to stop.'*

*'Who, me? No such thing. Go ahead, peep away—' He
grinned. 'So what's happening now?'*

*'As I was saying, Frank,' Tara continued. 'He's not even
remotely interested in her sexual signals. He's much more
intrigued by stuff she's got inside that she's probably not*

*even aware of. I doubt that her parents gave her any
cautionary advice about being picked up on an astral level
. . . No, see, he's coming at her through his sixth chakra –
my God, he is so s-m-o-o-o-o-th! This is the proverbial
foreplay of the third-eye, Frank. He's doing it with his eyelashes. Watch—'*

'Uh-huh.' Gobi was picking up on the interplay himself.
'That does seem rather unusual . . . He seems to be sniffing
at her, too.'

Tara leaned back in her wobbly rattan chair and gave
Gobi a radiant smile. 'Exactly,' she said. 'That's exactly
what he's doing. He's inhaling her essence as though he
were smelling some sort of rare species of orchid. She's his
flower-child. Literally, Frank. His flower-child.'

'So what does that make him, then?' Gobi challenged
her. 'A Casanova of higher-consciousness? A kundalini
vampire?'

Tara thought about it for a moment before replying
carefully. 'I think that makes him a gardener, Frank,' she
said quietly. 'But any garden that he's interested in has got
to be natural. And otherwise untouched by human hands.
Even if they are his own.'

'If we knew then what we know now,' Tara said to Gobi.
She was getting dressed, slipping into her baggy cotton
Tibetan pants and putting on a loose grey coat with rose-
colored Vajrayana-style thunderbolts embroidered on its
sleeves.

'Where are you going?' Gobi asked her. He was sitting at
the Omtron console downloading images of the Queen Rim
butterfly in order to study them. He had a little research
project in mind.

'I'm going to see if I can locate him,' Tara said. 'Check
out his usual haunts. Mainly, I want to look him in the
eye. I'll be able to tell right away if he's got something to
do with any of this.'

'That's going to take some schlepping around,' Gobi

remarked, a frown appearing on his forehead as he studied the screen.

'I know. I'm going to have to hit every taxidermist's shop and herbal emporium in Xiang Gang,' Tara said with a shrug of her shoulders.

'What's the matter, honey?' she asked, noticing the expression on his face.

'I don't know exactly,' Gobi said. 'I thought I'd access that article I wrote a long time ago. For the *Interspecies Insider*. You know the one. It's got that hypothetical algorithm I cooked up—'

'For your chlorophyll-driven search engine?'

'Right.'

'What's the problem?' Tara stood behind him, her hand on his shoulder. 'Won't it come up?'

'No. It's pretty strange. That entire volume – that entire series of monographs – it looks like someone's been in there and deleted them. According to this database, the *Insider* ceased publication prior to the issue my piece appeared in. That's just not possible. There must be some mistake. It's going to take some work to dig it up, I think—'

'Nothing like dusting Omnispace for fingerprints, eh, Frank?' She squeezed his shoulder. 'Who would do a thing like that?'

'I'm not sure.' Gobi sat there with a puzzled look on his face. Then something began to dawn on him, something devious, something sad.

'What are you going to do about it, sweetie?'

'Maybe I should ask Old Ming about it.'

'Old Ming?'

'Remember that potted palm in the lobby of the Mandarin Oriental. Jordan's pal? The one with all the hard luck stories?'

'Oh,' Tara said. 'Him.'

'Never mind. I'll look into it later. Good luck, Tara. Finding Jordan.'

'And you, too,' she said as she kissed him goodbye. 'Good luck to you, too. I'll see you later.'

'Right. We'll compare notes later.'

She slipped out of the room quietly and Gobi was left with all these images of the Queen Rim and a very bad feeling in the pit of his *hara*.

154

Made in Thailand

Kho Samui, Gulf of Thailand

'**O**ne minute and fifteen seconds,' Butterfly heard Kroon's voice saying in the background. 'Is that a milestone or what? He's a regular *chi*-stronaut, this guy. Good work, Tan, bringing him back. I think he's coming around now.'

Then Butterfly heard Tan – *or was it Krik?* – laugh. It was a low, guttural sound like the hoarse whisper of gravel being shoveled slowly into a shallow pit.

Butterfly wanted to bury his pain in that hole. What were they *doing* to him? They had been torturing him for hours. Draining him. And now they had managed to reel him back in like a broken paper-kite. It had been a struggle tearing himself away from the sky . . .

That beautiful transparent sky. And the wind, with its beautiful natural skin, its shimmering complexion. The wind needed no operation to transform its being, *or* its sex. What sex *was* the wind?

Even as they dragged him back down, Butterfly, the *katoey* she-man of Chaweng, could still taste that magical flight on his lips. Those androgynous clouds, and the secret caress of that one single magnificent beating heart.

Beating in so many places at the same time.

What had the Master told him? He hadn't actually *told* him. He had given it to him to *feel*. It had dawned on him in stages:

'When you fly, you must think of them, of those who remain below. And give them back what they have never given to themselves . . .'

'Which is . . . ?' The butterfly whisked its wings briskly, softening their laminated hardness in the brilliant warmth of the sunshine.

'The free-flight of your love, Butterfly.'

For a brief instant, Butterfly was Queen Rim again. *Had he really been out there? In that OTHER world, undoing all its millions of blindfolds? Making them SEE? Had that really been HIM?*

It was an irresistible impulse. To shine for a moment, to give them a vision. One that could never be blindfolded again. All those hearts in disarray. They were in much more pain than he was, truly, because they could not feel the pain themselves. They had to be reminded of it constantly.

They had to feed its hungry moth's head. So the Queen Rim fluttered its butterfly teachings for them like a prayer-flag, as a reminder and as a signal.

'If the wind has no sex, if the clouds never age, and if the colors never fade on the gossamer spool of time, then you have no need of your tongue to taste the nectar. Or the bitterness. You can just fly to your knowing . . .'

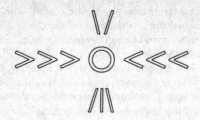

The first thing the *katoey* saw when he opened his eyes was Kroon hovering over him with a smile like the curved blade of a *parang*. A *parang* in a short skirt with a hand swivelled on its hip.

'Welcome back! We've just been worried *sick* about you.' Kroon beamed at him with pleasure, as he patted Butterfly on the cheek. 'You'll have to tell us *all* about your latest adventures. *Everything* . . .' he tittered. 'You're our little treasure, don't you know that? Isn't he, boys?'

Behind him, Tan and Krik nodded their heads. Stupid Krik with his wired eyes and his torn t-shirt that read 'So *many stupid people, not enough comets.*' And Tan, the ex-Thai kick-boxer turned neuro-spastic paramedic, holding something in his hand, a glistening tube to connect Butterfly back to the *chi*-siphoning machine.

Butterfly tried to close his eyes, but felt the vise of Kroon's hand tighten on his brow forcing him to re-focus his vision. 'One more thing, Butterfly, in case I need to remind you. You're back in Thailand now – back at the Rasta Palace, honey, in Chaweng Beach, on the beautiful island of Kho Samui. And, honey, remember this *good*. In Thailand, you *never* change your mind. You can only change your heart. And your heart belongs to Kroon. *Bplee-un jai!*' the Boss Bitch swore at Butterfly.

'You're *still* working for me,' Kroon reminded him. 'Not for Dr *Chi*. Got that straight? Any more questions? No? Good.' Then Kroon turned to Tan and said, 'He's all yours. Fill 'er up.'

'Shu Fong' and the Monkey

Kowloon Tong and Macau

Tara Gobi adjusted her black beret in the grimy reflection of the store window before she entered the Chinese herbalist's shop. She had found it in one of the side alleys off Temple Street in Kowloon Tong. The spluttering pink and green neon sign outside the decaying building read: 'Long Life Herb and Fungus Co.'

She checked the name one more time before she tried pushing the door open. It was stuck. She tried ringing the bell, but couldn't find one on the peeling lime-green-painted doorway.

God, had anyone even entered *this place in the past hundred years? Tara wondered. Except perhaps for Terry Jordan?* It didn't look as if it was doing a land-office business.

The Long Life Herb and Fungus Co. was just one establishment on Tara's list of herbal emporiums to check out. She was hoping to come up with some lead that might help her locate the elusive young American ethno-botanist.

So far, the impression Tara had received, after visiting more than a dozen such places in Xiang Gang and in Kowloon, was that Jordan had left town suddenly, a couple of days prior to the 'Queen Rim' visitation. She didn't know where his boarding-house was. And she didn't have his number. Jordan never gave his number out. 'Synchronicity, that's my number,' he liked to joke.

'You're just too cheap to own a phone,' Tara told him on more than one occasion.

'Too cheap,' he would readily agree. 'And much too quiet.'

Still, Tara hoped to come up with something – *anything*, really. She had been pounding the pavement for the past two days without any luck.

Tara peered through the dirty window-pane and tapped on the glass. 'Hello? Anyone in? *Nei hou?*'

There was no reply, although she could hear some tinny Peking Opera playing on a radio somewhere inside the shop. She wrinkled her nose, as she tried to identify the reeking musty odors that wafted through the chinks of the door-frame. What *was* that? Mugwort? Moxa weed? Tiger thistle?

She saw a light on inside in the back-room where the Chinese herbal remedies were stored. She tapped on the glass again, more loudly this time. Still no response.

Tara tried pressing her shoulder against the warped door. It wouldn't budge, even though it didn't appear to be locked. She would have given up, and turned back in the direction of the more brightly lit section of Yaumatei where the Night Market was already in full swing.

'Jeez—' she muttered as she gave the door one more go.

I should have come here earlier, Tara berated herself. This was one of Jordan's regular stops whenever he visited Xiang Gang. If anyone could get in touch with the man, it would be Mr Chin, the herbalist. Jordan had admitted as much to them. He'd even made a point of it, hadn't he?

Jordan had told Frank and Tara about the Long Life Herb and Fungus Co. when they had run into him in one of the casinos in Macau.

Frank and Tara were doing some field-work on collective out-of-body-experiences in first *chakra* 'survival' environments. Gambling dens fit the bill nicely.

And Jordan – he was up to something secretive, as usual. Something secretive – and if Tara didn't feel she knew him better than that – almost sinister.

As Tara reflected now, it had been another one of their strangely choreographed, synchronicitous appointments.

Yes, Jordan had a knack for synchronicity, all right. He would never ever need a secretary, that's for sure. So if he was hiding out somewhere right now, it was certainly no accident.

'The Long Life Herb and Fungus Co. is Mr Chin's place,' Jordan told them over drinks at the Lisboa Casino where their paths had joined.

'Now Mr Chin is a unique individual,' Jordan confided. 'He's an old-timer, which means that he still has this thing for rhino horns and snake galls and all that tripe. They're synthesizing the stuff these days, but he's too traditional for that.'

Jordan's eyes wandered around the casino. 'Mr Chin's even got potions to help gamblers win at the tables – like some of these jokers here.'

'You mean he deals in Taoist spells on the side, don't you?' Tara asked him directly. She'd had this strange intuition since she spotted Jordan standing behind one of the fan-tan tables.

'Mmm,' Jordan nodded as he sipped his Campari and soda. 'A little "Ku" magic, some work with "Mao Shan" talismans, a bit of "Chia" ritual. You're familiar with some of the old Chinese occult traditions, Tara?'

'It's black magic, isn't it?' Tara insisted.

'So is riding in elevators,' Jordan laughed. 'It's all open to interpretation, don't you think? Like the definition of "good" vs. "evil." "Right" and "wrong."' He gave Frank and Tara a penetrating look. 'Some people believe in karma. You reap what you sow.'

'So some black magic is justified?' Gobi pressed him. He was still bothered by the vibes in the casino, by what he had seen.

Jordan sighed. 'Some people believe that the ancient magic wars of the gods against the demons are still being fought today. Am I right, Frank?'

'You might say that,' Gobi replied cautiously. 'According to some schools of thought, Zeus is still engaged in his struggle against the Titans. Indra is still battling Vritra the

Demon Serpent King. And the Hittite Storm God Teshub is still warring against the Illukummi Serpent . . .'

'With a little help from his lover, the goddess Inara, I believe,' Jordan added as he gave Tara a smile. 'Anyway,' Jordan continued, 'Mr Chin's a blast from the past, a really old codger. But he knows his bee's whiskers, and he's sort of been keeping an eye out for me for some rare and unusual spores of mushrooms that I need for my research.'

'Oh, are you into mushrooms, too?' Tara asked him innocently.

'It all depends,' Jordan had replied. 'Some of them, yes. Some of them, no. Mr Chin, he's one of the few traders in the business who's even heard of the "Shu Fong" mushroom. That's the one I'd dearly love to get my hands on, if I could.'

'What's so special about this "Shu Fong" 'shroom, Terry?' Frank inquired.

'Well, for one thing,' Jordan laughed. 'It's ancient and it's practically extinct. The "Shu Fong" was originally used as a treatment against piles and gout and various gastrointestinal disorders. I mean, it really was effective against those ailments, don't get me wrong. But it's been almost entirely harvested out since around the middle of the last century, thanks to all those assholes.'

'You sound bitter,' Tara observed.

'Oh, you know, Chinese medicine—' Jordan shrugged. 'There's a lot of bitterness there. It's built in, you might say.'

'I thought you were interested in the "morphic" angle.' Gobi raised an eyebrow. 'Not in hemorrhoids, eh?'

'Very funny, Frank. Are there any proctologists practicing in Omnispace? Or is it all strictly "para-psychology," as you fellows put it? That's your field, isn't it? Para-para-para-psychology?' Jordan made a little fluttering gesture with his hands.

'Hmm, I was just wondering, that's all.'

'As a matter of fact . . .' Jordan continued. 'There is a "morphic" connection—'

'I knew it.' Tara clapped her hands, in an attempt to break the tension.

Jordan glanced at her. 'I'm sorry that I sound so tense. It's a sore subject for me. The "Shu Fong" is virtually unobtainable these days because it's been used up for all the wrong reasons.'

'So what are the real benefits of the "Shu Fong" in your opinion?' Gobi slipped into the conversation again. Jordan really fascinated him. He was a new breed of scientist. If he'd been twenty years younger, Gobi probably would be hunting for the mushroom and working himself up into a lather over it, too.

'It's kinda funny to be discussing this in a casino, wouldn't you say?' Jordan said with an impish grin on his face. 'Or maybe it is an appropriate setting, who knows?'

'Everything you do seems to be equally weighed in the direction of being "appropriate" as well as "inappropriate,"' Tara joked. 'Which side are you really on?'

'Your wife has a good eye for drama, Frank.' Jordan winked at Gobi. 'And a good nose, too, I think.' He gave Tara a knowing look. 'You're a lucky man,' he said to Gobi. 'You've got a real winner here.'

'Thanks,' Gobi quipped. 'And this being a casino, I can safely assume, at least at this table, that each of us is gambling on the inherent goodness of the world. Am I right?'

Jordan grinned. 'Save your compliments for the footnotes section of your next monograph, Frank. You want to know about the "Shu Fong," right? I was going to tell you about it anyway—'

'If it's not prying too much.'

'No, no. I trust you guys with my "Shu Fong." You'll never find it anyway – it's quite the desiccated fungi.'

Terry Jordan set his glass on the table. 'Okay, listen

close. The deal is this: This mushroom, which to all intents and purposes no longer exists — except maybe inside some ancient Central Asian mummy's asshole, if I strike it rich, that is; they cremate here, as you know — contains a potential blue-print for a highly advanced telemorphic communications system that would put all of the world's satellites out of business for good. How does that strike you?'

'You're a big roller, Jordan,' Gobi said quietly. 'But you're not in this for the money, are you?'

'Money?' Jordan replied without hesitation. 'Take a look around, Frank. Just look at this place. Money kills. That's how money communicates. I'll bet ninety percent of these people here would be willing to stab each other in the back just to win a bucket of chips at baccarat or "pai gow." No, they're the real losers here, Frank.'

Jordan suddenly looked tired and depressed. 'It's a real horse-race, you guys. You can't imagine. And anyway, the "Shu Fong" is just a pipe-dream. It's not "Taipan's Pants" or "Golden Lotus" or whatever they happen to call their high-strung Arabians at the Shatin race-track.'

'You're an idealist, Terry,' Gobi said gently to soothe his young friend's angst.

'Am I?' Jordan smirked. 'I know what you're probably thinking. This guy's got a case of "mushroomitis" real bad, right? I mean, does it sound crazy or what? Mushroom satellites growing all over the world in the wild. You don't even have to launch them off the ground! Well, I happen to agree with you, my friends. It does sound loony.'

'Not any more than anything else does,' Tara offered. 'All new ideas at first sound a bit—'

'Far-fetched?' Jordan interjected. 'The poor extinct "Shu Fong" . . . Let me put it this way, guys.' The young American had gotten his steam up again.

'Imagine what would have happened to the world if all the early personal computers had been hunted down by high-tech poachers, trashed, then recycled into tiny little

Mattel matchbox-cars . . . Where would we be today? We're talking about the same thing here.'

Tara was ready to call it quits for the night. It certainly looked like the Long Life Herb and Fungus Co. was permanently sealed off from the rest of the world. She peered through the window one last time. The interior was wrapped in a murky darkness except for the bit of light showing in the store-room in the back.

Maybe the old guy, Mr Chin, was hard of hearing. Or maybe – she scoffed to herself, maybe he was on-line right now, at this very moment, logging on to his 'Shu Fong' mushroom. Maybe one had come in with his latest shipment, from what, a couple of hundred years ago? Maybe it was still fresh in the box . . .

Tara smirked. Her nerves were frazzled. She dug into her little pouch for a little pinch of Marlboro Zinger. She rolled a cigarette. *Time for a little tobacco offering*, she sighed. *The last 'Shu Fong' in the world*, she mused to herself. *What would it sell for, I wonder?*

As she lit up and inhaled, Tara thought about what Jordan had told them in that Macau casino that night. *You couldn't take anything for granted with that fellow.*

She blew out a lungful of smoke.

And he was right. People would kill for money. Maybe even for a mushroom that would almost certainly put the entire world's commercial space program out of business, if it were for real, that is . . .

Tara eased herself down on an empty crate that was stacked against the store-front to the herbalist's shop. The crate was marked with huge black Chinese ideograms. They always looked so mysterious and so beautiful to her. She could barely make out the characters for the port of origin.

Hey, it's stenciled in English, you dork! she laughed to herself. 'Shanghai . . .' Tara read. *'Destination Oakland, California, USA.' Hmm, this must be some sort of a transshipment point. Oh, well* . . . she blew out another wreath of smoke. *Maybe this is where they cut the rhino horn with the water buffalo horn or something—*

It was so pretty sitting here, she mused. A mess of signs in Chinese, closed shops, just an old Chinese lady, bowed almost in half – *was she impaled on her cane, or what?* – shuffling towards her.

The street was so quiet, except for that scratchy Peking Opera that was playing on the radio inside . . . So unlike the hustle and bustle of the rest of Xiang Gang.

Mr Chin had found himself a real out-of-the-way spot in which to conduct business.

Tara stretched her legs out on the pavement and massaged her thighs. She had done a lot of walking in the past two days. Enough to qualify her for a trek in the foothills of the Himalayas.

Hmm, she took another drag from her tobacco offering and sent the butt spinning into the air. Xiang Gang was the only place in the world where Tara permitted herself the luxury of being a litter-bug.

Really, she was just contributing to the economy. There was so much trash everywhere. Someone had to collect it. Maybe that old lady there, she looked like she was carrying a sack of flattened cans on her back.

Jeezus, Mom, do you have to do that?

She sighed again as she thought of Terry Jordan. She wondered what Frank was up to. Whether he was getting anywhere on *his* end, trying to get to the bottom of this mystery—

Terry Jordan. No, nothing with him was ever just a coincidence. Mr Synchronicity himself.

Not even meeting him in Macau. Which was *why*, in fact, she was sitting outside an old Chinese herbalist's shop at this very moment in a deserted quarter of North Tsimshatsui.

Terry, you're a real card, all right . . . Tara thought to herself. *But I think I'm beginning to see your hand behind*

*all this. Really, what you are, you're just a card-shark from
Shambhala . . .*

That night in Macau, Frank and Tara had wandered into
the Lisboa Hotel Casino off the waterfront of the former
Portuguese territory. It was four crumbling stories of
gambling halls that never shut down, not even when the
worst typhoon signal No. 8 was hoisted.

They had been astonished to find Jordan in the bank-
vault-like hull of the 'fan tan' hall.

In hindsight, if Tara was right about him, their meeting
was beginning to look like a typical Jordan set-up . . .

There were hundreds of frantic Chinese pressed up
against the tables in a small enclosed area, happily betting
their lives away in a clamor of excitement.

They saw Jordan standing off to the side of one of the
fan tan tables. He was part of the group, but not in the
same way that everyone else was. He was playing a very
different sort of game.

Very calculated, very Terry.

Frank and Tara observed him for a couple of minutes
before elbowing their way through the crowd to greet him.
'He's not playing, Frank,' Tara had remarked to Gobi. 'But
look – he's got that same intense expression on his face
that he had when we first saw him that night in Phnom
Penh.'

'I can see that,' Frank replied. 'But that's no Swedish
babe he's got his eye on. Not this time. Our friend has
eclectic tastes.'

Gobi followed Jordan's gaze. There was a beautiful
Chinese girl in a salmon-pink cheongsam, with a slit that
ran up the side of the skirt. She was clutching a pile of
chips to her breast with lacquered-red nails. With her
classically cut black bangs on her ivory face, her black
lipstick, her sensual almond-shaped eyes, and her 24k gold
bracelets and jade ear-rings, she could easily have been a
No. 2 or No. 3 wife to some Chinese big-shot. He was

playing upstairs in the serious room with the serious boys.

'She's got Jordan's full attention,' Frank whispered to her.

Tara shook her head. 'He's not looking at her, Frank. You *are*. No, see, he's focusing on somebody else. That man over there. The one who looks like he's going to pass out if this game doesn't pan out for him. See, that skinny guy next to Lily Wong . . .'

Gobi frowned. 'You're right, honey. This guy is sweating razor-blades.' He'd never seen such palpable despair in a human being. Not even in the slums of Calcutta. The Chinese man was in his thirties or forties, you couldn't tell. His entire expression – his whole being – was on the verge of exploding through the hollows of his eyes. He was dressed in a cheap 'rich' sort of way. A shiny gray Shantung silk suit, a fake Rolex on a wrist that was as skeletal as the rest of his body. Hair brushed back over his skull like a poster warning about the use of illicit substances.

'He's a junkie,' Gobi observed.

'A junkie with the face-lift of a gangster,' Tara exchanged observations. 'Let's see. Let me tune in a little – I'm sure he won't mind. He's beyond caring what the world thinks. He's probably being hunted right now. There's too much money involved. He's ripped someone off. Someone who's very, very angry at him, and who wouldn't mind seeing him dead. And that's putting it very mildly.'

Tara paused to take in the rest of the reading. 'Okay, see his dwindling pile of chips – he's down to the wire. Major ESP flash, huh? You impressed yet, Frank?'

'Go on, I'm with you. I'm sure you're absolutely right—'

'There's a slight chance. What are the odds?'

'A thousand to one?'

'Okay, I'll go with that. There's a thousand-to-one chance that if he wins, he might be able to beg and grovel and plead – not for his life – because he knows they're going to kill him anyway. They've got to make a lesson of *him, right? Send the message out to the troops. No, he's going to beg and plead that they make it quick, and, shall we say, relatively painless. This is it, Frank – this is the moment of truth.'*

The 'fan tan' dealer, a short fat Chinese guy in a white open-collared shirt and a black casino vest, was holding an inverted silver cup in his hand. With a brisk motion of his wrist, he plunged it into a pile of porcelain buttons that were lying on the green-baize table-top. He moved the cup over to one side. Then he began to repeat the process over and over again, faster and faster, as if he were chopping bok choy greens for the dinner table.

The crowd at the table held their breaths as the pile of buttons dwindled.

The skinny Chinese gangster's face was turning purple, an amazing contrast to his pale twitching hands.

Gobi was familiar with the rudimentary basics of 'fan tan.' After all the bets were placed, the buttons would be counted out in groups of four. You had to bet on how many buttons would remain after the last set of four had been taken out. The players could bet on numbers one, two, three or four, as well as odd or even.

'Does he die fast – or slow?' Gobi whispered under his breath to Tara. 'Is it going to be a thousand slices – or a quick bullet in his head?'

Tara's face clouded. 'It's going to be slow, I'm afraid, Frank—'

Gobi turned to her, startled. 'Wh—?'

She nodded in Jordan's direction. Jordan was standing barely two feet away from the anguished Chinese gambler. 'He's playing through him, Frank. Terry's the dealer here.'

The crowd shrieked. Some in despair, some burst into insane laughter. Those were the winners. The beautiful Chinese girl had lost, but her composure remained the same as it had been earlier. Still cool, still distant, even in her loss. She was the plaything. So she was allowed to play.

Gobi sought out the cadaver in the fake silk suit. The mobster with the curse of all the wrathful Chinese deities on his head. But he was gone.

He had disappeared the instant the game was over. There was no reason for him to stay. His hand had played out, and he was in a hurry to get it over with, whatever was waiting for him on the outside. He was already dead anyway. In that space, where Gobi had sought the Chinese gambler, he saw Jordan.

Jordan was looking at both of them soberly, as though a sentence had just been carried out. He looked supremely peaceful at that moment. The verdict was 'guilty.' And the punishment would follow as sure as the sun would rise and the sun would set. It had already set for that Triad member.

'My God,' Gobi whispered to Tara as Jordan waved a greeting to them. 'What could that guy have done to deserve what's coming to him?'

'I don't know, Frank,' Tara replied with a deep sigh of compassion. 'But he's hurt a lot of people – no – yes, he's hurt a lot of people. But he's also hurt a lot of other living things. Animals, Frank. I think that was the deciding straw. Whatever it was. A little puppy. An elephant. A snow leopard. A monkey of some sort. That's it. It was the monkey on his back that nailed him in the end.'

● ●

The Golden Caterpillars

Tara was still taking a breather as she sat on the crate outside the Long Life Herb and Fungus Co. Her rubber-soled *k'ung fu* shoes planted squarely on the ground, she ran through a quick *yin-yang* breathing exercise to recharge her *chi*-batteries.

Poor grandma, she thought as she watched the old Chinese woman shuffle her way down the alley with the oversized load on her back.

The old woman was bent over almost doubled, her frail hand shifting gears on her walking cane as she carefully navigated each snail-like step of her gnarled root-shaped feet. Tara's eyes registered surprise as she took in this geriatric tightrope act.

Unbelievable, Tara thought to herself as she shook her head. *She's got bound feet! When did they outlaw that barbaric Chinese custom? She must be ancient, she's got to be over a hundred years old at least, and poor thing, she's still hustling for a living . . .*

The old woman would pause every few paces as if to adjust the weight of the sack of recyclables that was slung over her hunched back. From under her floppy black velvet hat, a pair of rheumy eyes studied Tara's figure from the distance of a dozen meters away.

Then she shuffled forward again in her black baggy pants and high-collared quilted black coat, until she paused at the sidewalk where Tara was sitting. Tottering at the curb, huffing with labored breaths, it looked as if she was contemplating a final obstacle.

'*Nei hou*, Grandmother.' Tara rose from the crate. 'Can I help you make it up to the sidewalk? You really shouldn't be out by yourself this late, or even carrying that heavy load . . .' she chided her gently. 'Don't you have anyone to help you? Here, take my arm—'

Tara extended her arm for the old woman to grasp onto, and was about to reach for the bag on her back, when a vise-like talon descended on her forearm and made Tara gasp from the sudden pressure.

'The foreign missy's too kind, *shay-shay*, thank you . . .' the old Chinese grandma addressed her in a husky sing-song voice.

My God! Tara recoiled on her feet. *This was no crippled old lady, much less a woman! It was a Chinese man, with an Hour of the Rooster shadow clearly visible on his chin under the cheap make-up. He looked to be in his mid-to-late sixties at the most, but what was this bizarre get-up?*

Tara tried to back away, but his iron grip restrained her. 'You've been waiting outside the shop long?' he inquired.

'Excuse me—' Tara began. 'But who—?'

'The front door's stuck, have to go around . . .' he apologized. 'Not much foot-traffic these days, don't like visitors anyway. You can take the bag, if you wish, missy. But you'll have to be very, very careful handling it . . . Too many vibrations will damage the contents. Then I'll have to go and make the rounds again, collecting. Always collecting. Follow me this way, please—'

With a sudden vigorous stride, the old guy stepped onto the sidewalk and handed Tara the sack. It wasn't as heavy as it appeared, but Tara felt the pull of its magnetic-field immediately. As if it contained the gravity of the Great Wall of China in some condensed form.

The old Chinese guy didn't wait for Tara to answer. She followed him obediently down a narrow passageway that ran like a shaft of shadows between the Long Life Herb and Fungus Co. and its adjoining building of old flats with barred windows. He unlocked a side-door, and the light suddenly illuminated his face as he stood in the doorway, waiting for her to enter.

He pointed at a spot on the floor for her to lay the bag down. 'Be careful,' he cautioned her once again as she gingerly set it down.

Tara pursed her lips and frowned at him. 'I expect you must be Mr Chin, the owner of this shop.'

He leaned against the wall, lowered himself down onto a wooden stool, and kicked off his tulip-bulb-sized black slippers. He sighed deeply and wiggled his white-stockinged toes as his feet resumed their non-constricted shape.

Then he looked up at her curiously as if he were trying to place her somewhere in his memory.

'I'm a friend of Terry Jordan's,' Tara explained, sensing

his hesitation. 'You know, Terry Jordan, the young American who's interested in the study of Chinese herbal medicine—'

Still the blank stare.

'The one who's interested in the "Shu Fong"—'

As if she had said the magic words, he nodded at her with a bright animated smile. 'Yes, yes, of course. *Jor-Dan*. I am Mr Chin. Tell *Jor-Dan* I've got what he wants if he's still interested. It just came in. Have to run a few more tests. Been doing that all day today. Those golden caterpillars are driving me crazy. They're such beauties, but they think they're such big stars already. They think they're ready for the Peking Opera themselves—'

He turned down the volume on an antique surround-sound Aiwa digital CD player. 'They love this opera so much. It is very moving, don't you think? "The Great Oppressor Landlord Is Ground Under the Heel of the Victorious Proletariat." But it makes me too sad to listen to it all day and all night long.'

Tara couldn't believe her ears. 'Mr Chin,' she exclaimed. 'You've got *the* "Shu Fong"?'

'Missy—' Mr Chin interrupted her. 'I'm so glad you came. Sorry to have kept you waiting. You must tell *Jor-Dan* he will be most happy with this particular "Shu Fong." It looks very, very good for its age. *Shuah!* Eight-hundred-and-seventy years old. It was not so easy to obtain. I had to personally go to Shanghai and exchange my professional services for it. The girl was close to death by the time I got there. Only when the family was certain she had fully recovered, were they willing to part with their precious fungus.'

Mr Chin fanned himself with a paper fan that bore the logo of the 'Monkey Holding a Peach' camphor balm.

'I spent *hours* in their store-room – what a catalog of rare treasures they have! It's a very, very old family. Almost as old as the mushroom. But the girl survived.' Mr Chin waved his hand weakly as he recounted his ordeal.

'I gave her some thunder pills – three *t'siens'* worth – mixed in with a little alum to stabilize her. But first, of course, I had to use a gold pin to pierce the *ku*. Then I fed her some soup made from *jang ho* root, very nice ginger flavor, and some minced stalks of orange tree. It was really just an old curse placed on the family a few centuries ago by some *tao nai-nai* witch that one of their enemies had hired.

'I told them, "*When wolves block the road, why bother to examine foxes?*" Let's get to the point. Each time you lose twenty taels of gold, which family is it that *gains* twenty taels? They were so grateful. They tracked down the perpetrators, or rather their descendants. Of course, I had to reverse that ancient curse. Now they will become prosperous again. Now I,' Mr Chin said proudly, 'have *two* new clients, including the family that it was my unfortunate duty to jinx. *And* I brought back *Jor-Dan* what he has been seeking.'

Mr Chin cleared his throat. 'I am certain it was the last "Shu Fong" in all of China.'

He eyed Tara warily. 'Of course, you must tell *Jor-Dan* there were extra expenses.'

Then he paused before asking her, 'Do you think that you are ready for the audition?'

'The *audition*?' Tara asked, perplexed. She wasn't sure where this was leading.

Mr Chin got up from his wooden stool. 'I'll make some tea for us.' He hobbled over to an electric-plate in the corner of the room. Swishing a tea-kettle in his hand to make sure it contained enough water, he placed it on one of the glowing coils to boil.

'You're not in a big hurry, are you?' He turned to Tara as he opened a tin of tea and added a few pinches of fragrant yellow buds to a tiny Ming-style ceramic pot with blue butterfly designs.

'Chrysanthemum tea all right for you?' He threw in a few more tea-buds and sighed again. 'They're eating me out of house and home. Must get some more tea soon now.'

Keeping a straight face, Tara nodded. 'Chrysanthemum tea's just fine with me.'

Mr Chin removed the velvet hat from his head and slipped a greasy-looking old lady's wig off his bald head. He rubbed his scalp. 'They ate my other wig this morning.'

'They *did*?' Her eyes widened.

'Yes, that's why I told *Jor-Dan* to send a girl. Very good.' Mr Chin appraised Tara. 'With yellow hair like yours. They like yellow. Not an old fellow like me—' he chortled. 'I must dress like a woman just to get near them. The "Shu Fong" is like that. I warned him. "Only women. Or else eunuchs." That's what I told him. And the golden caterpillars are very, very difficult, moody and complicated creatures. The larvae are very demanding. If you don't meet their standards, they become quite withdrawn. Practically useless then. They will refuse to perform. But they'll like *you*—' he said as he eyed Tara again. 'They will dance to your *chi*.'

Mr Chin rubbed his bald head again as he waited for the water to boil, then poured it into the tea-pot.

'Yes,' he laughed. 'There are the *yins* and the *yangs* – the female and the male energies. And then there are the "curried noodles." Like myself. Cross-dressing is essential in my line of work, you know. How else to reach my inner-shamaness? Witches cast the best spells. The fact can't be denied. So I can't be too prissy about it. So—' Mr Chin asked Tara again, as he poured some tea into a cup and handed it to her. 'Shall we begin?'

Tara accepted the cup and felt the warmth in her hand. *Okay, Terry Jordan*, she thought. *You brought me this far. If I'm to be the courier for your 'Shu Fong' mushroom – your Chi Web Mistress – I may as well get the show off the ground. Learn some more about your little scheme—*

'I'm ready when you are, Mr Chin,' she said as she took a sip of the delicately flavored brew.

'Excellent,' the dowager drag-queen replied. 'Why don't you get it out yourself? It's in the bag. I've been giving the "Shu Fong" a tour of Xiang Gang. The butterfly fireworks were only the beginning. It will get more interesting as time goes on. *Shuah*. The golden caterpillars are next. Imagine, a rain of golden caterpillars! From now on, I must carry an umbrella with me everywhere I go.'

He wrinkled his brow in thought. 'They're quite persistent little things. Much more persistent than the Queen Rim. How *Jor-Dan* ever came up with that one, I don't know. He's certainly improving his style. But I don't believe she was locally produced. My guess is she was an import. Prices are much cheaper abroad.'

'It's in the *bag*, Mr Chin?'

'Oh, call me Mei-Li, everyone does. Go on then. Let's get started.'

Tara stood over the duffel-bag, her hand poised over the zipper. This thing was radiating even more powerfully now. 'It senses your presence,' Mr Chin encouraged her. 'Feel the change of energy in the room. The "Shu Fong" is probing you. Ha! Ha!' he laughed. 'If you weren't half the American *tao nai-nai* that *Jor-Dan* said you were, you'd be dead by now. Ha, ha, ha!'

Tara took a deep breath. She felt a hot-and-cold electrical current shoot up from the balls of her feet, up to her shins, then all the way up her thighs, into her groin—

Oh, Frank! Tara swooned. *Wait 'till you feel this, honey, because I'm going to bring this home to you, this feeling, when you hold me . . . It's like a million orgasms you never felt before, each one purer and more ecstatic than the other . . .*

From the corner of her eye, as she steadied herself, she could see that Mr Chin was clearly enjoying the spectacle.

'I wish I were you,' he told her from the distance of a

thousand leagues away. 'A *real* woman. A real *tao nai-nai*
. . . You get the most bang from this! I'm *so* jealous!'

Tara swooned again as the energy uncoiled throughout
her chest and shot up through the top of her skull.

*Zig-zagging green and blue thunderbolts pierced her
crown 'chakra,' and spiraled out into the Void where
Jordan was observing her with the patience of a Super-Cray
Mencius . . .*

What was Jordan? Man or woman? Tara gasped. *Neither
man nor woman . . . and* neither *was he the 'neither,'
either . . .*

Catching her breath and flexing her fingers, Tara
unzipped the bag. Then with both hands she lifted up the
"Shu Fong."

It was the definitely the ugliest and the most beautiful
thing that she had ever seen in her life.

Mr Chin approached Tara and stood behind her as she
rotated the mushroom in her hands. It was the size of a
small palm tree, or of a large bonsai. In fact, it had
emerald-green palm fronds growing out of its hideously
shaped giant wart-like brain. Brown-and-black furrows
braided its misshapen head like a collection of clumped-
together water-buffalo patties. It was porous and it oozed
through her fingers – and it stank.

'The future,' Mr Chin said, 'is not pretty. But you have
to admit, it's much better looking than the past.'

'What am I supposed to do with it?' Tara asked him, still
feeling her dizziness that was rooted somewhere beyond her
sixth *chakra*.

Beyond her consciousness. Am I going to faint? she
wondered.

'*Well*,' Mr Chin said reassuringly. 'I think you've got it
well in hand. It's just a question of the golden caterpillars
now.'

'The golden caterpillars?' Tara regained her equilibrium.
'What on earth are *those*?'

'Our little show. Tonight, after the Queen Rim vision-gram, which *Jor-Dan* arranged, we present yet another spectacle for the benefit of the public.'

Still holding the 'Shu Fong' in her hands, Tara turned and watched as Mr Chin stepped across the room and walked over to a tall cabinet. It looked like one of those old Chinese herbalist's cabinets with hundreds of little drawers in it, each one containing some herb or powdered potion. But Mr Chin didn't pull any of the individual drawers out.

With a smile on his face, and holding a finger to his lips, as though he were committing her to an oath of secrecy, he pressed one of the carved panels. The front of the entire cabinet swung open on a hinge. There was a hidden storage space behind the drawers. It was deep enough – and had enough shelves across it – to house a thousand crawling golden caterpillars.

Tara almost dropped the 'Shu Fong' when she saw them. The caterpillars had been feeding on anything and everything that Mr Chin had thrown to them – packages of instant *ramen*, rolls of fiber-optic wiring, old Chinese scrolls, TDK diskettes from the curio shops on Hollywood Road, Chairman Mao buttons, tea-bags, a tattered wig, and, of course, their favorite food, the piped-in music from a Peking Opera.

'Oh, my God!' Tara exclaimed. 'I don't believe I'm seeing this!'

'You *are* seeing this, missy,' Mr Chin reassured her. 'Now bring the "Shu Fong" closer. I can't do it myself. I can only deceive them up to a certain point. They need the "Shu Fong" to launch themselves. Hold it up to them – and you will see what happens . . .'

'I can't. I mean . . . I just *can't*. They're swarming all over the place.'

Mr Chin put a grave expression on his face. 'You must. You've come this far. You *must* do this – you *must* be brave. It's all up to you now.'

Tara took a deep breath and stepped up to the cabinet,

and held the "Shu Fong" up as close as she could bring it without coming into actual contact with the slithering swarm of yellow caterpillars.

'Ugh – mmm.' Tara sank down to her knees, the 'Shu Fong' vibrating like a temple gong in her hands.

Mr Chin ran over to the window, then clapped his hands. 'It's working, missy! It's working! That's enough for now. Come see—' He led her to the front of his herbalist's shop, then wiped the grimy window with his sleeve to show her. Tara was all heat now. Sweat was pouring from her body, from every pore, like an unfathomable tidal wave. She couldn't bear it any longer. She dropped the 'Shu Fong' to the floor, and kicked the front door open. She ran outside for air.

She stood in the alley and looked up at the rain of golden caterpillars that was falling from the sky all over Xiang Gang. As each drop fell, the caterpillars molted on the ground for one brief second, then flew up into the air like a thunderstorm of tropical butterflies flapping their golden wings. Each pair of wings that fluttered sounded like other-worldly wind-chimes ringing through the ether from the other side of the universe.

Ting-ting-ting-ting-ting . . .

Tears began to stream down Tara's face as the light tinkling became a drone like a Tibetan sky-horn rupturing the membrane between the *Aum* and the human soul. '*Jordan!*' she cried out, her face raised up to the rain of golden grubs and the whirlwind of a trillion fantastically colored lepidoptera.

'*What have you done? And why did you make me do it for you?*'

Slo-Mo

'Jeezus Maitreya Christ,' Frank Gobi said to Tara. 'Jordan's got a lot of nerve putting you through all that! I'd like to get my hands on him.'

'Jordan's gone, Frank,' Tara said quietly. 'He's left Xiang Gang.'

'That's just great!' Gobi exclaimed. He was pacing the floor of their living room in their suite at the Panda. He was angry, his nerves were doing push-ups in his fourth *chakra* heart center. He was trying to blow off steam.

'Jordan set us up from the very beginning, didn't he?' Frank reflected. 'He had us tagged as easy marks just to facilitate his little experiment in tele-morphing the collective consciousness of Xiang Gang.' He looked at her. 'Especially *you*, Tara.'

Frank Gobi paused on the peach-colored Tianjin carpet as he studied the coiled dragon design on the plush rug for a moment. It was so soft, Gobi felt he could launch off the carpet in his stockinged feet. He was ready to do that, too. All he had to do was log on to ShanghaiNet which was wired into the fiberoptic double-knots in the weave.

Log on and start hunting for Jordan. Maybe he was hiding out in some mulberry-patch somewhere, blast his caterpillar hide.

Frank looked straight at Tara. 'You were just right for the part, of course. Out of all the people Jordan must have 'scoped out on his travels, you were the medium he chose for the job. His designated pitcher. Child of *chi*, huh? Son of a centipede is more like it . . .'

He stopped his pacing and looked at Tara. 'I'm sorry, I'm getting all worked up. How are you feeling, honey?'

'I'm okay,' Tara shrugged as she ran her fingers through her wild tangle of blond hair. She looked as though she had run through a wind-tunnel. Her face was pale and drawn. 'I'm a little tired. It would have been nice if Jordan had asked me first. I honestly didn't know what I was walking into.'

Tara was sitting cross-legged on the divan, taking sips from a mug of medicinal tea that Frank had brewed for her. Mr Chin had given her a small packet of *zingiber mioga* – red ginger – to take home. The *jang ho* potion was Mr Chin's house-blend to counter any negative *ku* energies Tara might have absorbed during her caterpillar rain-dance.

She was collecting all her scattered *chi* synapses, sorting them out by color as if they were socks in a drawer.

'How did it look to you, Frank?' Tara asked Gobi curiously. 'What was it like on your end? I was caught in the middle of it while it was happening. I couldn't really tell – it felt like a tremendous wind though. A thunderstorm of glow-worms.'

Gobi shook his head and gave her a manic laugh. 'Incredible. What a light show! Naturally, the fire-alarm went off. These things were coming through the ceiling, fast and furious, shooting through the walls, pouring through the sprinklers . . . Like flames. But they weren't, thank God. They *might've* been. The electrical circuits blew out all over the city.'

He lowered himself down on the horseshoe-shaped Ming chair beside the divan and grasped the curved rosewood arms.

'First thing I did was to grab a fire-extinguisher. I didn't know *what* the hell was going on . . . It's all over the news again, of course. "Golden caterpillar rain," they're calling it. Isn't that a lovely name for a mass-induced hallucination of grubs and butterflies? The Chinese have a long history of unexplained supernatural phenomena. Now they're getting to televise it all for posterity. "The Annals of Xiang Gang," or whatever file they choose to put it in.'

Gobi shook his head again. 'Where does Jordan *come up* with this stuff? Not at Princeton, that's for sure. They're still bending spoons with a conscience over there. This guy's a maniac. He's a serial shaman . . .'

'It's Chinese *ku* magic,' Tara sighed as she took another sip of her *jang ho* tea. 'Mr Chin explained it to me. It's an ancient form of insect sorcery.'

She traced some Chinese characters in the air. 'The word *ku* is formed from the Chinese ideogram for "pot" which appears beneath the ideogram for "crawling animals." If that gives you some idea—'

Gobi whistled. 'I'll be damned, the Chinese equivalent to the European witches' brew . . . But any way you slice it, it's black magic, Tara. Black, black, black—'

'Exactly,' Tara nodded. 'But do you remember what Jordan told us in Macau? One person's notion of black magic is someone else's idea of a major scientific breakthrough. The ancient Taoist alchemists believed that magic was merely natural wisdom, Frank. That it represents the highest as yet undiscovered – or at the very least, the most misunderstood – levels of natural science.'

'Right,' Gobi scoffed. 'Tell me about it. "*A naturalist is a spiritualist working under an assumed name.*" I don't remember who said that, and I can buy it to a certain point. But Jordan's a charlatan in my book. A high-class act maybe, but he's *still* playing with people's heads without their permission. Karmically speaking, Tara, it's just *not* kosher. Come on—'

'He felt justified. The world's on the wrong path, as he sees it. There's not going to be much left to save when Omnispace goes, and we're going to be left with just the cinders of the Gaia when we're through with fucking things up.'

Gobi stared at Tara. 'I can't believe I'm hearing this! Are you suddenly taking *his* side? After what *you've* been through? You're telling me that poor Jordan is simply a misunderstood guy with noble intentions?'

Tara shook her head. 'No, Frank, I'm just trying to understand his motivations, that's all. He definitely should have explained his intentions to me – to us – before pulling this stunt. He should have trusted us that much. I'm very disappointed in him about that. And I'm going to tell him that the next time I see him.'

'Oh?' Gobi blinked at Tara. 'And when do you suppose that will be?'

'Hopefully soon, Frank.' She leaned over and patted him on the knee. 'You want some of this tea? It'll help calm you down. You're acting like some kind of an irate father.'

'I'm not sure what effect it's having on you, frankly. Maybe I'm missing something? You know something that I don't?' Frank *was* seriously pissed.

Tara shifted on her divan. 'I'm thinking about something Mr Chin told me about the Queen Rim – Jordan's "debut" butterfly.'

'What was that?'

'He said she wasn't locally produced. She was an import. So we've got to trace the source. We can't do that with the golden caterpillars. I channeled those. But I think the dynamic principle – or whatever the triggering mechanism was – remains the same in both cases.'

Tara closed her eyes. Okay, she was satisfied. The *jang ho* had done its work. She had worked the last kinks of irresoluteness out of her neck and shoulders. She sprang up from the divan with a sudden movement that surprised Gobi.

Now Tara was the one doing the pacing, but it was a slow and measured walk as though the peach-colored Tianjin rug were a meditation-station in some misty mountain retreat painted in the corner of a Sung picture-scroll.

Gobi watched his wife go through her energy transitions. Sometimes reading Tara was like reading tea-leaves. He picked up her mug of herbal *cha* and studied it for a moment. He could smell the red ginger of Mr Chin's *jang ho* blend, but the leaves were unfathomably clumped together.

'According to Mr Chin,' Tara continued, 'the *ku* magic dates back to the days when the barbarian tribes dwelled in ancient China. That was before the dynastic periods began. Chinese pre-history, in other words. The leaders would control powerful figures in their tribes by forcing them to drink these insect concoctions. The original "gold caterpillar" was a sort of venomous little snake, or a viper, a worm, or a larva of a very bright color. Luminiferous or phosphorescent in its nature . . .'

Tara paused to put her hand on Frank's shoulder. 'Are you following this, sweetie?'

He kissed her hand. 'Perfectly. Golden caterpillars. Barbarian tribes. Say no more.'

'Okay, Frank, bear with me – I'm trying hard myself,' Tara replied. 'I'm trying to see this from the original perspective of the *ku* masters. Obviously, Jordan's been doing his home-work, and it would help to understand his methodology, if not the premise itself. So, to go on . . . Only the old tribal leaders had the antidotes to the so-called mental 'poisons' of the *ku*. The kicker is, these antidotes had to be administered *before* the year was out if the illusion was to have its desired permanent effect. The victims had to take fresh doses of the *ku*-induced vision and await the following year's infusion of the antidotes . . .'

'He's going to do this again.'

'That's right.'

'And he's going to *keep on* doing it . . .'

Tara nodded. 'At least until it becomes fully integrated into the exisiting program. Until everyone is naturally tuned in to the same frequency.'

'What do you think he's planning to do next? "Son of Queen Rim and the Golden Caterpillars?"'

'I'm not sure, Frank. He'll think of something.'

'Our boy should be in show-business. He should be producing soap-operas for the Spratly Studios.'

'He already *is*, Frank. Xiang Gang was just the pilot for the series. It was the test-market. Don't you *get* it?'

'I do,' Gobi said morosely as he cupped his chin in both hands and stared straight ahead at the wall where the Omtron set was sitting in its alcove.

'That's the trouble, honey. I *do* get it.'

Tara let Frank mope for a minute. It was his unique form of 'mopitation.' Part-moping, part-meditation. Gobi came up with some of his moodiest, most brilliant ideas while he was engaged in this Russian yoga of sulking.

'Okay,' he said as he swiveled in his chair to face her. 'You said this original butterfly *ku* projection was an import? Which means that it was transmitted from somewhere else.'

'Right.'

'And it was his *first* production – I mean, we haven't heard reports of any luminous maggots showing up on the airwaves anywhere else in the world, have we?'

'Correct.'

'Fine then. So he's still finessing his directorial style, I guess you'd say. But if his second and most recent spectacle is any indication of how he works, then my guess is he must have picked someone else to do the honors for the 'Queen Rim' show. Just like he picked *you* to do the sequel.'

'You're probably right,' Tara said. She could still feel the adrenaline rush of colors that pumped through her system when she held the 'Shu Fong' mushroom-satellite up to Mr Chin's chorus-lines of karaoke caterpillars. They were still vibrating in her solar plexus.

Gobi watched Tara shift into the channel-mode again. 'Drink some more of Mr Chin's tea, honey, if you think it's doing you any good.'

Tara shivered, then picked up her mug of *jang ho*. 'Thanks, I will.'

Gobi poured her some more tea. 'Take it easy, honey,' he said. 'Flashbacks, you know—'

'I know.' Tara straightened her back and exhaled. 'I'll be all right.'

'Is there anything else I can get you?'

She laughed. 'Mr Chin said that eating the ashes of old silk with flowered designs also does the trick of restoring the system to equilibrium. It's an old *tao nai-nai* remedy that *ku* shamanesses would resort to.'

'You want me to get your silk *kimono* for you? We can barbecue it, if you want. Or we can stir-fry it.'

'No, thanks,' Tara laughed again. 'I'll live. Besides, I'm not very hungry—'

'Can't say I blame you. Your Mr Chin is full of useful advice on the subject. Steeped in the lore, is he? No wonder Jordan studied under him.'

'Mr Chin has a frog in his head.'

'I beg your pardon?'

'He actually acquired his *ku* from first-hand experience, Frank, not just from studying the classics,' Tara told him. 'He told me that when he was first apprenticing in *ku*, he went on a drinking spree one night with his friends. It was a hot summer evening. When he took his hat off, there was this big frog on his head. His friends – they were Chinese sorcerers, too – they knocked it off. Then they went back to their drinking, but some time later that night the frog reappeared on Mr Chin's head. When he finally retired to his room, he felt an ulcer form on his head. The next morning when he woke up, he found that all his hair had fallen out and there was a red swelling there. A blister. When the blister finally broke, the frog peeped out. His friends tried to pull it out, but it was too painful for him so they stopped. One of them read up on the subject in some arcane scroll. They decided it was *ku* magic gone awry, and that it had to be killed with a gold hair-pin.'

'Wonderful—' Gobi said. 'So Mr Chin's got a gold pin in his head. This is all beginning to make sense now.'

'They pierced the frog with the pin, and managed to kill it. Mr Chin got over his frog-migraine, but he's as bald as a billiard-ball. And he's got a sunken spot in his skull-bone where the frog was embedded. He wears wigs.'

'Do you think Jordan might have a frog in his head, too?' Gobi inquired.

'Not a frog, Frank. A butterfly, maybe. But definitely not a frog.'

'What are you doing, Frank?' Tara asked Gobi as he fussed with the remote to the Omtron.

'Pulling sathe frog out of Mr Chin's head has given me an idea,' Gobi said to her as he settled back into his chair. 'Let's see if we can do the same thing with Jordan's "Queen Rim." Let's do a little Kirlian biopsy on the critter, see what it tells us. It's worth a try anyway.'

Gobi froze the brilliant image of the Queen Rim into a slo-mo on the Omtron.

'Okay, you gorgeous butterfly you,' Gobi spoke out loud to himself as he played with the controls. 'A nano-zoom, let's go for that . . . Wow, she's beautiful, isn't she, Tara?'

'It's not the least bit malevolent, is it, Frank?' Tara commented. She was curled up on the divan under a comforter, still sipping Mr Chin's brew as she watched the color display.

'I get your point,' Gobi acknowledged. He felt the serenity seep into the room again just as it had that morning when the Queen Rim first appeared. 'But that still doesn't make it right. People have to *want* to feel the light . . .'

'Maybe Jordan was just helping them cut through all the crap.'

'Maybe, maybe – lots of maybes. Let's keep on going, however—' He scanned the panorama of the butterfly's wings. 'From this angle, it looks almost like a cross between a Rajah Brooke's Birdwing and a Moroccan Orange Tip, doesn't it?' he said admiringly. 'I'm no expert on butterflies, but—'

'It's got the vibes of a Kwan Yin,' Tara interjected. 'How can it be bad?'

'It's *not* bad, Tara!' Gobi protested. 'It *is* beautiful. And it *does* invoke a sense of compassion. Maybe it's got some sort of a compassion algorithm built into it. I don't know. I just happen to think that the truth – *whatever* its form might be – shouldn't be shoved down people's throats. Or through their pineal glands, or whatever, okay? So call me old fashioned, if you like.'

'Okay, Frank.'

'Okay, *what*?' Gobi threw a quizzical glance at her. 'Okay, I'm old fashioned? Or, okay, you agree with me?'

'Okay, Frank. Just, *okay* . . .'

'Okay, okay, it's the okay *mantra* . . . Just a minute, let's have a closer look.' Gobi zoomed in on the tip of its forewing to the inside edge of its hindwing, and entered the calligraphic scalloping of its wing margins. Then he ran a series of close-up diagnostics on the Queen Rim's venation and eye-spot patterns.

'Look!' he exclaimed triumphantly. 'Look at that script!'

'What's the label say? It looks like it's printed in Thai . . .'

'Hah! This Queen Rim's a *pirated* bug! It's a Chrysalis clone!'

'I'm picking up two sexes out of this thing,' Tara said. 'It's, what, a *transsexual* butterfly?'

'They call them *katoeys* over there in Thailand. They're "cross-overs."'

'This is a spiritual cross-over, Frank. From one plane to another.'

'Whatever . . .' Gobi zoomed-in closer. He focused on an eye-spot, then popped through the painted butterfly-pupil and did a free-fall through the flowing currents of butterfly colors. 'Plastic surgery of the soul, wouldn't you say?'

'I'd say it evolved on its own.'

'With some help. Electroplastic surgery then. With a *chi*-knife. That's what our friend Jordan is, Tara. He's Dr *Chi*

with a scalpel, scraping away at the insides until they glow
. . . Wow – and wow again and again! What is *that*!?'

The symbol was as plain as the face of the man on the moon, as clearly delineated as the irrigation-canals on Mars. As unmistakable as a Pepsi logo.

Gobi left the blow-up on the screen and stepped back to take in the full sweep of it.

There were two major eye-spots on the Queen Rim's wings. Two pairs of spiraling, revolving *yin*-and-*yang* symbols, like two halves of another dimension that were fusing together in a compressed crescent of blindingly iridescent colors.

Then they saw *his* face. The face of the *katoey*. And they heard a voice laughing in the background like a roll of dice being broadsided by destiny or karma or remembrance or by the mimicry of love. Somehow it had seeped through into the image.

'*One more thing, BUTTERFLY.*' Frank and Tara both heard the enhanced drone of the whisper resound from the Omtron's speaker system. '*You're back in Thailand now – back at the Rasta Palace, honey, in Chaweng Beach, on the beautiful island of Kho Samui. And, honey, remember this good. In Thailand, you can never change your mind. You can only change your heart. And your heart belongs to Kroon. Bplee-un jai!*'

Tara looked at Frank Gobi. 'At least we know where the Butterfly comes from,' she said.

As Gobi downloaded the clip, he said, 'That's right. Pack your bags, honey. I think we're going to Thailand.'

'Thailand—' Tara mused.

'Yes, Thailand. The Land of Smiles, the Emerald Buddha, and the Queen Rim butterfly. It's going to be hot, hot, hot, honey. But we've gotten used to it by now, haven't we?'

Phase 3
. . . .
Chrysalis

Khao San Road

Bangkok

'**K**hao San Road,' the Thai taxi driver announced to his passenger as he pulled up at the curbside. *The touts await your lordship*, Paul Sykes thought to himself as he gazed at the bustling scene outside. Grinning Thai men appeared out of nowhere on the sidewalk as they thrust cards bearing names of guest-houses at Sykes' face through the glass: The Peachy Guest House, Yin & Yang Hotel, Smile House, Shanti Lodge, Marco Polo Hostel, Katmandu West . . .

'Are you sure?' Sykes asked the driver as he shrank back from the window. He felt certain they'd been driving around the same district for the past half-hour. He could have sworn he'd seen the sign for the Peachy Guest House earlier. *How many Peachy Guest Houses* were *there in Bangkok anyway?*

The narrow street was filled with clusters of young foreigners dressed in shorts, tie-dyed t-shirts, Thai fishermen's pants tied at the ankles, ornately embroidered Nepalese vests, and blowsy print-tops with dreamy Sanskrit lettering and images of Lord Shiva holding his trident. They carried backpacks with sleeping rolls on their backs, and clutched copies of the Friendly Planet guide to Thailand in their hands like articles of faith.

Paul Sykes watched in fascination as they streamed in single and double file towards a nearby bus-stop on the street corner where the signs on the waiting buses proclaimed their destinations: 'Chiang Mai,' 'Chiang Rai,' 'Phuket,' 'Krabi,' and 'Surathani.'

Damn! The taxi from Bangkok International Airport into the city had almost bankrupted him. The ride cost Paul Sykes one-eighth of the total value of his traveler's chips. And he hadn't even set foot on Khao San Road yet, the budget district for his sort of traveler.

Broke, hungry, and disillusioned, that's how he personally felt. Dis-*something* anyway. Sykes was reasonably sure that he was the only one in Bangkok with this particular monkey on his back.

Tommy and Nita's 'Gunung Mulu Memorandum' was like a psychic bookmark in his private album of hell. It was part of his internal archives by now, well thumbed, read through and through and memorized, a rare and frightening volume in the library of his subconscious. And it was overdue. He had to return it to the original owner soon.

He had been getting nasty monkey flashbacks from his Hitachisoft eye-mask during his entire flight aboard Pyongyang Air Lines from San Francisco to Bangkok. *Jeezus*, when he thought about it, it must've taken the explorer Thor Heyerdahl less time to reach his Polynesian destination on his outrigger Kon-Tiki canoe than it had taken for Sykes to fly from SFO to BGK aboard the North Korean charter-flight.

Next time, he'd take the Bullet Express that crossed the Pacific Chunnel from the Golden Gate Bridge terminus to Yokohama, then zip through the tunneled-through trough that ran along the Ring of Fire, transfer in Xiang Gang, then take the sub-hydrofoil connection to Chao Phraya Central in Bangkok. *Right*.

Next time, he'd stay at home where he belonged, or where at least he *knew* he didn't belong.

Sykes had to find Tommy somehow. Tommy Kok Lau. And Tommy would lead him to the 'children of *Chi*.' But that was in the south of Thailand on some island named Kho Samui. And that was somewhere in the Gulf of Thailand, wasn't it?

Right-o, then— Sykes sniffed and coughed as he braced himself for his next major mental and physical exertion, that of actually getting out of the cab. Sykes shook off his fatigue as he struggled with his personal 'move-your-ass' demons.

It was amazing how quickly he became attached to things. This despicable taxi was already like a second home to him. He was loathe to leave it.

The Thai driver watched Sykes impassively in the rear-view mirror as the *farang* squirmed in the backseat. The truth was, Sykes was afraid to step outside.

God knows what awaited him out *there* in the Bangkok night.

'Khao San Road,' the driver repeated brusquely, pointing at the sidewalk. *The surly devil*, Sykes thought to himself. You'd think the bloke hadn't received his commissions from all the toll-booths on the aerial skyway that his cab had kiss-assed to . . . It was all a massive conspiracy to turn him into a penniless vagrant on his first night in the Thai capital.

So this was Bangkok. Traffic like a bad acid trip, three-wheeler *tuk-tuk* passenger vehicles spewing exhaust and fumes, shops selling discounted coffins and Buddhist memorabilia, malls that went nowhere but sold everything, street stalls with weird smells, and the heat, the relentless heat . . .

Sykes was soaked through with layers of grime, sweat, and grease. He had a blast-furnace of a migraine pounding in the top of his head, and it was growing by the minute like the self-replicating spires of a Thai *stupa* in a frenzy of reconstruction. That was it. This city was cancerous and he had six months left to live, if he was lucky.

'Are you sure this is *the* Khao San Road?' Sykes hesitated. 'Cheap, cheap? Not like your taxi? Your taxi more expensive than the Oriental Hotel . . .'

The Thai driver gave him that sedated smile again as he turned on the ignition. 'No, wait – I believe you!' Sykes exclaimed. 'Let me out here, please. Khao San Road! Khao San Road!'

He climbed out of the cab, wrenched his backpack onto his shoulders, and stepped through the crowd like a tightrope-walker with vertigo. He felt as if he was being swallowed by a python with bad breath. There was no squeezing out of it now. He was here. In the belly of the beast. And it was all too familiar to him, like the story of Tommy and Nita.

With both hands gripping the front-straps of his backpack, Sykes paused on the crowded sidewalk to absorb his new environment. Despite his throbbing migraine, he could see that Khao San Road was happening all around him. It was hopping with energy. *What a scene!*

Thais squatted on the curb smoking Marlboro Krakatoas as they eyed the parade of *farangs*, and chatted amongst themselves. The Thais that were working stood behind stalls selling bronze Jerry Garcia figurines with smiling Krishna eyes, racks of pre-empowered talismans ranging from Celtic crosses to Buddhist swastikas and Japanese Shinto nature-spirit *kami* amulets, tantric Dick-and-Jane *yoni-lingam* night lights, *nag champa* incense-scented mosquito-coils, carved Buddha-head cigarette lighters that ignited through the third-eye, bootleg *chi* beads that gave you a mild orgone rush, and tons of colorful clothes including those blowsy Indian-looking things.

Sykes made a mental note to buy a gauzy purple shirt with the Lord Shiva motif printed on its sleeves after he'd done a bit of on-the-road accounting. They were cheap enough, no doubt. He could stand upgrading his wardrobe from his once-white, now grimy grey Fruit of the Loom t-shirt to something more festive and less sweat-absorbent. Those colorful Thai fishermen's pantaloons looked quite appealing, too.

Sykes' damp jeans were chafing his thighs like wet sandpaper. He could feel the heat rash burn through the denim of his 501s like a brushfire moving on his skin. He had to keep in mind that he suffered from a male strain of Candida. There was a *yang* excess of yeast in his system.

Fuck, he was getting that *tsunami* itch again.

Climate dictates fashion all right, Sykes thought to

himself as he scratched his chest and arms. May as well dress like a happy gecko and enjoy it. Be a proper *farang*. That's what they were called here, wasn't it? *Farangs*. Ambassadors from American Express, JTB, Visa, and Mastercard. Or in Sykes' case – his traveler's chip being rather low on octane – he held the rank of a cultural attaché or at the very least a second secretary at the chancellery of capitalism.

He felt the relative affluence of his Western debt-ridden social class. He could go far here, but he'd have to be sure to stay out of those damned money-sucking cabs and not dine out more than once a week. It was a good time to practice being a vegetarian again. His own Friendly Planeteer guide had warned about the water buffalo steaks and the dog-meat *satays* served to unsuspecting budget travelers.

If it was going to be meat-protein, he'd have his Fed Ex or DHL steak cooked medium, thank you very much.

No, he'd definitely have to banana pancake-it and eat lots of local fruits and the official grub of the FPs, lovely bowlfuls of yogurt and muesli. *Food*, that was number one. *Number two*: bedbugs . . .

Sykes didn't want a repeat of that Chinese dude's pet mosquito buzzing him on that sorry North Korean excuse for a plane. No wonder he still had shakes and his head was pounding like a howitzer. He stole a glance behind nervously. They *all* looked like Chinese guys . . .

Okay, they weren't. But he still had to be careful. Look what they did to poor Mort Wisenik. They iced him with a philodendron. And that Pakistani exchange student who had been sitting beside Sykes on the plane, he'd never see Karachi again, that's for sure.

What the fuck. Khao San Road, eh? He had arrived in fabled Muesliville at last.

Sykes' head swiveled as he took in the fellow *farangs* sitting at the outdoor restaurants and cafés, drinking their beers, eating their banana pancakes, watching their VDOs,

looking all sun-tanned and wind-surfed. He observed a
wide assortment of body, mind, and soul-types.

Let's see, some were cute, sexy, indifferent-looking,
average, plain, plain-with-potential, open, closed, blasé,
world-wise, or world-stupid. They congregated outside
tattoo parlors in the side-streets, they sat on stools at cut-
rate travel agencies, they leaned against the counters at the
currency exchanges booths with serious expressions on their
faces. *I'm from Basle, please don't cheat me.*

That sort of look.

Sykes noticed the bodies of prone *farangs* lying on mats
in outdoor massage-kiosks, getting their 'Wat Po' Ancient
Thai massages (so the signs said) at a discount. He'd like to
get one of those. Maybe later. *Shit, you're already over-
spending, you dummy,* Sykes warned himself. Better learn
to pace your desires, pal. *Desires, huh?*

As Sykes glanced into the labyrinth of guest-houses and
hostels, he supposed that some *farangs* were probably
getting laid and/or stoned at this very moment. The Big
Time. When was the last time *he* had gotten laid or stoned?
Without being in love? *Think about something else,* Sykes
told himself bitterly. Anne's five thousand miles away and
ancient history. You don't want to conjure her up now.

Besides, you got laid the night before last, inside one of
those twin-size capsule-motel rooms in the terminal lounge
at San Francisco International. Remember? With that
insatiable fortyish brunette you met on the Super Shuttle.
Anything to throw the buggers off the track.

An hour of frenzied anonymity with a total stranger at
an airport . . . *Jeezus, how could you!?* Sykes berated
himself. What *was* her name anyway? Gloria something.
She must be in Detroit by now. Doing drive-by blowjobs
probably.

You crude bastard! Okay, think positive. You helped her
get over that what's-his-name, Bruno or whoever, that jilted
her. And you helped her regain some of her orgasmic self-
esteem.

Hey, what are you talking about, you pathetic guilt-tripping jerk!? She seduced you! Forget it!

Sykes stretched his arms out to get the kink out of his back, and began to walk down the street. Then he stopped. There was something whirring at the base of his head. A feeling like a Cuisinart blade dicing his medulla oblongata. Dizziness. *Christ, this heat!* You're not used to it. You're going to faint . . .

'*Paulie,*' Sykes heard his mother calling to him from some vast distance. '*Have you seen my tab of E anywhere, dear?*' '*No, Mother, I haven't . . .*' '*Oh, what a pity.*'

That whirring sound again, now a roar of thunder. Sykes felt his knees go limp, the weight of his backpack pressing him down like Annapurna rising from the crust of the Himalayas when it was still an amoebic corn-field in Kansas. The earth was shifting rapidly on its axis. Was he really falling through this long black tunnel? *Would someone help him up, please?*

The Khao San Road suddenly exploded in Paul Sykes' head. It exploded again and again. Each time it exploded, he saw a black sun spewing magna-like rays from the center of his forehead. Then he felt the drizzle of a green light that cooled him down just as abruptly as he had heated up. He let himself float into the deepest sensation of equilibrium he had ever known.

When Sykes opened his eyes again, it was all somehow quite different. It was still Khao San Road. He hadn't fallen down. But he knew that his eyes had turned green. They were still blue, as blue as the day he was born. But they were also *green* now. That was the main difference. That, and all the things he could now see—

••••••••••••••
Chi Eyes

He saw the shadows differently. And the things that moved inside the shadows.

Oh, the Friendly Planeteers were still fluttering their wings like humming-birds as they moved from one flower of sensation to another. The Thais in the street were still busy peddling their wares at their curbside stalls. The noise, the heat, the music blasting from the cafés and bars, the neon signs of the guest-houses – P-E-A-C-H-Y, P-E-A-C-H-Y, S-M-I-L-E H-O-U-S-E, S-M-I-L-E H-O-U-S-E – continued to flicker as they did before.

So *what* was different then? It was the line of back-packers that Sykes *hadn't* noticed earlier.

It wasn't the same group of *farangs* he had seen decked out in their tropical spirit-house fashions. All Bhagavad Gita'd up in their colorful *saris*, Krishna blouses, Thai fishermen's pants, and Tibetan Wheel of Life-print Bermuda shorts.

These weren't the backpackers who were streaming towards the bus-stop where the buses were rumbling their engines, ready to carry them off north, south, east and west of Bangkok.

No, it was a different sort of traveler altogether. Paul Sykes blinked his new pair of green eyes as he adjusted his vision to the sight. He had to focus on the exact shade of the substratum of light. They moved more slowly than these other *farangs*. *More than that* – Sykes blinked again to be certain – *they looked like a strangely flowing mosaic of moving human parts*. A subtle mixture of contrasting patterns of similar color made them appear almost invisible.

Incredible. They were so homeochromatic that they blended into the background! They mimicked the landscape like stereoscopic particles of kinetic wallpaper. Sykes watched with amusement as these masters of camouflage took on the visual texture of the trinkets on display at the stalls. A moving fragment of *batik* paused to avoid a collision with a *farang* backpacker who was hurrying towards his waiting bus. *Jeez*, these guys were like Japanese Butoh dancers performing energy forms!

Sykes was so absorbed in the spectacle that he forgot he was watching it.

He counted maybe half-a-dozen of these chameleon specters, but it was hard to be sure. How many of them was he actually seeing? How many was he missing? They were very, very good at mimicking the art of invisibility.

Sykes caught his breath as he stared at them. *Hey, they're naked!* Their taut, muscular bodies were dusted with chalk-white powder, and except for some loin-cloths which blended into their private parts, they were as nude as albino butterflies . . .

Like an instant connoisseur, he couldn't help admiring the gracefully flowing sequence of their energy forms. He could even identify their *kata*, their primordial energy templates. For a moment, Sykes' consciousness yo-yoed back to his original sight. He startled himself with the sudden realization. *Shit! How* could *he possibly distinguish one kata from another?* But his appreciation was definitely rooted in some strange new knowing.

That female Butoh, for instance, she was doing something called 'The Worm.' That other one, a male, he was doing 'Jogs' – that was way funny and cool! What sophistication and subtle irony! He was a great artist!

Sykes then recognized the *kata* for 'Leaping Across A River,' followed by the *kata* for 'Picking Flowers.'

What the HELL! They were Butoh Backpackers!? Or *what!?* Precisely. That was the point. Who or what *were* they? And where on earth were they headed in this weird street procession of theirs?

Catch these moves, Sykes reflected admiringly: *Tilting pelvis up on intake of breath and down on out-take. Lower ribs up on intake and down on out-take. Hands on shoulders – twist to right on intake, left on out-take . . .*

That's odd, Sykes thought as he looked around. No one on the street seemed to notice the Butohs as they made their way down the sidewalk. The Butohs, in turn, ignored the external traffic. The Butohs did not notice that Sykes was noticing them. They were so intent on maintaining the level of their inconspicuous energy. Or perhaps they took their art too seriously . . .

And yet . . . And yet . . .

Paul Sykes began to feel another sort of energy present. A certainty that someone was watching *him* watch *them*. Someone who was standing outside the entire picture-show, yet remaining part of it at the same time. He felt that energy trickling towards him like an icy stream of observation. As though an alien Hubble telescope was observing life on earth. He wanted to turn and confront it, but he began to feel that old fear again. It was that same fear he had felt when he started this trip when he wondered if he had bitten off more than he could chew.

Back in the animal pavilion at the *Chi* Expo in San Francisco when the Orang-utan touched his hand and lit the fuse that led to the evolutionary powder-keg of the 'Gunung Mulu Memorandum.'

He felt Tommy's fear of losing Nita. He felt Tommy's fear of falling apart into a mess of confused primate logic. He felt Nita's fear seep into him now . . . Her fear of whatever it was that she had to confront in the hell of her own transformation. Millions of decaying snails that slithered towards her in a tube like the cyanide of consciousness dropping into the bucket of her deepest soul.

Enough of this shit.

Paul Sykes turned around to catch the secret observer in the act. It was not human. Not as he knew it. It was even less human than these Butoh backpackers who moved in such painstakingly glacial frames of light. They didn't see her watching them. They were oblivious. Was it a woman? No, but she had the female form. She was an incubus of some sort. Or was possessed by one.

She stood on the opposite side of the street. A *farang* woman with brilliant plumage on her head like parrot feathers. Shocking red, green, blue, and yellow. She was smiling at Paul Sykes now. She knew that he knew. Slowly, she raised her hand up to her shoulder and fed something – *what the* fuck *was it, bird-seed?* – to the two parrots that were grafted onto each shoulder. She shrugged as if to say, '*What can I do? They just won't shut up otherwise . . .*'

My God! Paul Sykes barely suppressed a shudder when he realized that they *fucking were* grafted to her body.

Two huge Amazon parrots that were as much a part of her body as her hands and feet were! They were as much a part of her total expression as that icy smile on her face.

The parrots both flapped their wings at the same time. He could feel the ripples of cold air reach him from across the street. As cold as the woman-bird-creature's laughter.

Sykes shook his head. *I'm fucking outta here, man.* Then he turned away and ducked down the first alleyway that was open to him. Wouldn't you know it? It was the Peachy Guest House, and there was a register for him to sign at the counter. He didn't even ask how much it was for the night, but the young Thai girl whispered it to his back as he took the stairs to Room 208 on the second floor. 'Hundred *baht* a night, mister!' she called out softly. That was about four dollars. Paul Sykes could afford that. That, and a good long sleep.

Fly Patpong Airways

Frank Gobi looked down at the city of Bangkok that was spread out beneath them like one of those ornate Thai tapestries, all gilt-embroidered and embossed with the shapes of mythical animals. 'Look at the Chao

Phraya River,' he pointed out to Tara. She was sitting across the table from Frank in the main cocktail lounge of the S.S. *Kinnari*, a massive entertainment dirigible that was the maiden-ship of Patpong Airways.

'That bend in the Chao Phraya always reminds me of a cobra that's poised to strike,' Gobi reflected. 'And all the river craft zipping along, the longboats, ferries, barges. It's quite a sight.'

'Beautiful, isn't it?' Tara agreed as she glanced out of the floor-to-ceiling window. 'See the Grand Palace with all the spires lit up? And that latticework of lights? That's the New Bangkok Skyway.'

'Hmm,' Gobi remarked thoughtfully. 'I wonder where Trevor is right now. Down there somewhere, I suppose.'

'He said he was backpacking it, didn't he?' Tara replied as she gave Frank an inquiring glance. Her step-son Trevor was always a sensitive subject with Gobi. 'So my guess is that he's somewhere in the Banglamphu district. That's where all the cheaper guest-houses are located. Which means – see those lights just east of the Democracy Monument, that monolith-looking structure with all the spot-lit flags? – he must be down in there somewhere. Having a good time, I would hope.'

Gobi winced when he thought about his son. He dabbed his napkin to his lips. The peanuts that the waiter had brought them on a plate were natural, unsalted, and oily. 'He's broken up with Nelly again. This time it's for good. Or so he says.'

'Well, they were both too headstrong for each other,' Tara said sympathetically. 'Don't worry about him so much, Frank. Trevor's a big boy. How old is he now anyway?'

'He's what – twenty-five or twenty-six?' Gobi shrugged. 'He's on his way to Katmandu, then he's off to India. He says he wants to live in Goa for a while. Be a *kundalini* beach bum . . .'

Tara sighed. 'He'll find himself. It's just part of the

natural process of healing. He's got plenty of time. Thank God he's gotten rid of all those horrible tattoos. I don't think they were a good influence. They were running interference with his life, weren't they?'

'That's the trouble with this whole concept of *sentient* tattoos,' said Gobi as he drummed his fingers on the table. 'They're too smart for most people. Just one bug in their epidermal programming and they can take over the body's neurotransmitters and start issuing their own orders. Those tattoos wear *you*, not the other way around. It's quite diabolical, really.'

'Well, I hope we get a chance to see him,' Tara said as she studied the cocktail menu.

Frank Gobi popped a few more peanuts into his mouth. 'Did you want to order some drinks?'

Gobi stirred in his seat uncomfortably as he took in the scene in the cocktail lounge. There were Rim businessmen seated at little tables holding hands with their young Thai girl-companions. A Filipino torch-singer was karaoking it on-stage. It all looked rather harmless really, drinks and dinner on a blimp that hovered 500-metres above the city of Bangkok. But both he and Tara knew what the S.S. *Kinnari* was really about.

It was a high-rise air-ship with twelve-stories of casinos, sex clubs, saunas, massage parlors, a warren of dope-dens, short-time hotel rooms, and God knows what else.

In short, it was a floating vice den filled with helium, owned and operated by Wing Fat Enterprises. Gobi knew about Wing Fat. That's why he and Tara had come aboard for the evening cruise.

Tara squinted at the menu. 'I'm not sure about these drinks. What's a "Slippery Nipple"?'

'Bailey's and Sambucca.'

'And an "Orgasm," wait don't tell me, let me guess—'

'Cointreau and Bailey's.' Gobi gave her a deadpan look. 'Read the fine print underneath. Personally, it's not to my taste. But why don't you try a "Lovely Jubbly" or a

"Dance on the Beach" or a "Sex on the Beach," if you want?'

Tara laid the menu down on the table and frowned. 'I don't think so. Why don't we just go and do what we came aboard to do, Frank? I just have to see it for myself. I've heard about it, but it does sound too unbelievable even for me.'

'I don't much care for Bangkok,' Gobi remarked sourly. 'Armpits have more charm. Why couldn't we have just flown south directly to Kho Samui?'

'Because it might be important, Frank. Come on—' She rose from the table and offered her arm to her husband. Tara had dressed up for the evening. She was wearing a slinky gold lamé dress that showed off her figure to its best advantage. It was low-cut in front, revealing her buxom cleavage, with a micro-mini hemline that clung to her thighs like spray-painted golden flakes.

Frank looked handsome in a white silk t-shirt and black silk drainpipe pants. He complained that they were too tight in his crotch, but Tara had insisted he wear them anyway.

That evening Frank and Tara Gobi were Mr and Mrs Emmanuelle, a decadent Western couple bent on tasting the forbidden fruit of Bangkok. They had even booked a threesome – or was it a foursome? – at the Misty Sauna on the eighth level of the *Kinnari* for 10 p.m.

'Was that two guys, two girls, or a couple?' Frank had asked Tara after she had phoned in the reservations earlier that evening from their suite at the Oriental Hotel.

'Oh, I can't remember, honey. What difference does it make?'

'Huh? I guess none,' Gobi replied with a sulking note in his voice. 'We're not actually going to go through with it, right?'

'Hey.' Tara had jabbed him in the ribs playfully. 'I thought you were a regular firewalker, Dr Gobi.'

'On the ground, honey. On the *ground* . . . Not in a helium-filled *balloon*.'

'Don't worry,' Tara reassured him. 'It's just for appearances' sake. Otherwise, someone might question our real motives for coming on board. Monogamy is just too kinky for some people to accept these days. In fact, it's a dead give-away.'

'That's just the trouble, Tara,' Frank had cautioned her. 'The dead aren't exactly known for giving things away. This could be dangerous, you know.'

'I *know* what Wing Fat is capable of. Believe me, you don't have to explain it to me,' Tara reminded Frank. 'Wing Fat's a notorious *chi* dealer, Frank. They say he siphons off *prana* from young children and mixes it up with his synthesized rejuvenation drugs in the Golden Triangle. They've never been able to bust him because he's got too many corrupt politicians and big-shots in his pocket. Not to mention the fact that he's been supplying the international neuro-software industry with questionable *chi* algorithms.'

'I don't doubt any of it. So why do we have to patronize his fleet of *chi* whorehouses? It doesn't go down too well with me.'

'Because,' Tara replied as she focused her magnetic green eyes on Gobi, 'Wing Fat is offering something new these days. I hope they nail his ass for ever for what he's done to damage people already. But this may be the beginning of a whole new era, Frank. If the rumors are true – and Mr Chin believes they are – Wing Fat is going to be doing much worse than blood-sucking *prana*. He's supposedly test-marketing this new stuff aboard his fleet of dirigible junks.'

The Thai pimp in the elevator was getting on Gobi's nerves, the way he kept ogling Tara and trying to whisper something in her ear. 'Hey, you,' Gobi snapped at him. 'What do you want?'

There were four of them in the elevator, Frank, Tara, the

short Thai pimp who was dressed in red satin kick-boxing sweats, and a *katoey* transsexual elevator operator who was wearing a one-piece swimming suit and high-heels.

A photo gallery of joy-boys and girls with I.D. call-numbers pinned to their outfits was mounted on the rear-panel of the gleaming mirrored walls of the elevator. You could press the touch-screen and book them en route to the steam-room on the eleventh floor.

The Thai pimp gave Gobi a dismissive smile and kept on whispering something in a squeaky-raspy voice to Tara. Tara shrugged at Gobi with a look of incomprehension. Gobi tapped the man on the shoulder impatiently.

'I *said*, what do you *want*? That's my *wife* you're talking to.'

The *katoey* elevator operator attempted to translate for the pimp. The she-he gave Frank and Tara a warm smile and explained the situation to Tara. The pimp beamed at Tara. 'He asking you if it's *irrelevant*.' The *katoey* blushed.

'Is *what* irrelevant?' Gobi demanded.

'No, *no*, he ask *missus*.' The katoey blushed again. 'He ask missus if it's "your elephant." He mean *you*, mister . . . He wonder if you are bull to her. Or if she free to roam, he has good business for her right away on twelfth floor, special hospitality room.'

'That's it, we're getting off on the next floor.' Gobi scowled at Tara. 'And *you*, I'm going to punch you out if you don't watch it,' he addressed the Thai pimp who sensed the menace in Gobi's voice. The Thai took a step towards Gobi, his grin suddenly settling to the corner of his face as it hardened into a stone challenge. One hand disappeared into the waistband of his sweats.

'No, Frank, wait—' Tara said as she stepped between the two men. She turned her back to Frank and aimed her cleavage at the pimp's face and began to speak to him softly.

'Tara, what are you doing?' Gobi asked in stunned disbelief.

She turned around to face him. Tara and the pimp and the *katoey* were now smiling broad smiles. 'No harm done, Frank.' She gave him a nod as the elevator door opened onto the tenth floor. She pulled Frank out of the elevator by the arm and called out, '*Sawat dii*, thank you!' to the pimp.

'Bye, bye, see you later,' the pimp replied as the elevator door closed.

'What on earth was all that about!? You'd better explain, Tara,' Gobi complained. 'What the hell did you do with that guy? Did he cop a feel or what?'

They were standing at the entrance of a long dingy corridor with scuffed-up floors and litter spilling out of the trash-receptacle. Loud disco music came from a row of Patpong girlie bars. They could see an aquarium-glass wall outside the Mermaid Bar where nude girls with goggles dived for credit-chips that customers tossed into the water.

Gobi blinked. The girls had beautiful brown-skinned bodies with patches of black pubic hair and nipples that were hardened from the cold water.

'That's enough, Frank,' Tara said as she steered him down the narrow passage-way. 'We're not going fishing, you know.'

'The hell we aren't! What just happened back there? Do you mind telling me?'

'Frank, Frank – listen to me.' Tara suddenly pushed Gobi against the wall and gave him a deep squirming kiss as she pulled him tight against her body. From the corner of his eye, Gobi saw a group of three tough Thais eyeing them with curiosity. The men were standing outside the doorway to a Japanese *sushi* bar. There was no name identifying it in either English or Japanese.

Nothing except for a paper lantern that was decorated with the calligraphic brushstroke-image of a butterfly.

He kissed her back. 'Honey, what the—?' he muttered through their embrace.

'Okay, Frank,' Tara breathed into his ear. 'I'll give it to

you straight. He wanted to fuck me. So I let him play his little game—'

'What!'

'Shush—' Tara brought her hand to his mouth and pinched his lips shut with her fingers.

'Gmm—, but— gmmm, Tara—' Gobi mumbled as he struggled to speak.

'Shut *up*, Frank! Just listen – you see that Japanese *sushi* bar? Don't be so obvious! Those men are still watching us.'

Gobi calmed down. 'What about it?' he asked.

'That's where Wing Fat's doing his little test-marketing of his new product, Frank. Of the new line of *chi*. It's not open to the general public yet. You can't get in without *this*—' She unclenched her palm and showed him a token with a butterfly logo on it. 'I got this from that idiot in the elevator, all right? Wing Fat's been passing them around to the locals. It's good for one Butterfly Roll.'

Tara paused so Gobi could sync into her reasoning. 'You got that token from *him*, that *pimp* in the elevator?'

'Yes, Frank!' Tara nodded. 'I asked him if he knew where the butterfly place was, the one that was going to be opening up soon. He said he had a token. I told him – well, I promised him actually – that I'd have a drink with him later on to discuss his business proposition if he'd let me have the complimentary token.'

'You *did*?' Gobi raised his eyebrow skeptically. 'You promised to *see* him?'

'Come on, now, I'm not going to actually show up, am I? Of course not! Don't be so jealous. In the meantime, we get to go inside and check the place out. All in a day's work, Frank.'

Tara put her arm around Gobi's waist, and strolled him in the direction of the no-name *sushi* bar. The three bouncers at the door tensed up as Gobi and Tara approached the establishment. A blue *noren* half-curtain hung in the doorway.

'What kind of a *sushi* bar is it?' Frank whispered to Tara.

The bouncers stood in their way. Tara smiled at them and handed over the token. The three men stepped aside and allowed them to enter.

'That's just the thing, Frank,' Tara whispered back to him. 'It's got to be some kind of a strange coincidence. But this is a butterfly *sushi* bar. The first of its kind anywhere. *Butterflies*, Frank – remember Terry Jordan and the Queen Rim? They serve butterflies here. Fresh. And full of nectar.'

Butterfly *Sushi*

The first thing that struck Frank Gobi as they stepped inside was the fine-mesh netting that encircled the interior of the restaurant. A young Thai girl dressed in an elegant Japanese *kimono* and brocade *obi* sash gave them a deep bow. She held one corner of the netting up for them so they could enter quickly.

'Don't let butterfly out,' the young hostess smiled. 'Only in memory or in photo album.'

'Don't worry,' Gobi answered grimly as he followed Tara under the net.

He had never seen anything like it. It certainly wasn't like any *sushi* restaurant that he was accustomed to. Not even the interactive *sushi* joints in Neo-Tokyo could hold a candle to this place.

Gobi's eyes couldn't keep still. They followed a colorful flurry of butterflies that roamed the air above the *sushi* counter like waves of pink, red, gold, blue, ochre, yellow, and dazzling violet light. They were everywhere at the same time, settling on artfully placed potted plants and flowering shrubs. The decor was that of a tropical garden gone ga-ga in a New Nippon that had been transplanted to Bangkok.

Miniature *bonsai* palm trees lined the zig-zag stone path

that led to the main dining area. A pair of Thai classical dancers stood on a small stage and performed their exaggerated steps to the sound of a Japanese stringed *koto* instrument. Their fingers were splayed like the wings of a butterfly in the throes of insect passion.

The *sushi* chef was a Thai dressed in a *happi*-coat. He held a butterfly net in one hand, and scooped the air-borne butterflies into another enclosed working-area where he filleted the butterfly wings. The chef laughed gaily as the customers seated at the counter amused themselves by trying to capture the passing lepidoptera with their raised chop-sticks.

The next thing Gobi and Tara noticed was the human mountain who was seated in the corner by the counter. He was a huge Chinese – he looked as if he could weigh 600 pounds at least. He was dressed in a diaphanous black silk robe, and was tended to by his manservant who fed the dainty butterfly *sashimis* to him from a pair of ivory chopsticks. 'It's Wing Fat,' whispered Tara to Frank. 'This place is his brain-child.'

Wing Fat had been observing them from his enormous wheel-chair that was designed like a collapsible Ming-dynasty sedan-chair. It looked as if he was entertaining a pair of guests. They were American women. They looked out of place among the other diners in their Silicon Valley Brooks Sisters suits.

Wing Fat's multiple chins wobbled on his ocean-liner deck of a chest. His eyes were like carved ebony billiard-balls and they rolled in his tiny eye-sockets like eggs that were too large for their shells. His mouth was full. He opened it and several butterflies flew out.

He mumbled something to his manservant, who listened carefully, looked in Frank and Tara's direction, nodded, then approached them with a deferential bow of his head.

'My master invites you to join his party, Mr and Mrs Gobi. Please come this way—'

Frank and Tara exchanged glances. How on earth did

this Himalayan-sized Chinese know who they were – much less be expecting them?

The two American women sitting at the *sushi* counter opposite from Wing Fat did not appear to be pleased to have Frank and Tara crash their party. 'Deedee—' Tara heard the strawberry blonde with the anxious face remark to her companion.

'Not *now*, Mir,' came the abrupt reply from her stern colleague. The second woman had short brown hair, was slightly built, but she exuded a sense of self-importance and power that sprang from her deep conviction of her own superiority.

She's a winner, Tara observed to herself, *but only because she knows the secret of making others lose more than she needs to give up herself. A know-it-all in the art of aggressive compromise.*

Tara gave Deedee a quick secondary reading as the brown-haired business exec sized her up for her boardroom smarts and her panty-size. Tara flinched. *So she likes women, especially strong women . . . The one with her is her alter-ego, smart but servile – only really herself in the bedroom, not in the office.*

Deedee now gave Tara a sympathetic smile. That was their first intimate communication, but it would get no further than that, Tara sensed.

Deedee, whoever Deedee was, had a fire-wall built around her throat chakra, *the energy center that governed the emotive stream of data that translated into self-expression. This woman would keep all her cards to herself, all right. Even from this mountain that she happens to be doing business with. Not that he trusts her either . . .* Tara mused as she gave Wing Fat a polite nod.

Now this Wing Fat character – He looked like a landslide just waiting to happen . . . Watch out for him. He's a volcano that's lost its hard-on but is still spewing its magma out of habit and poor bladder control . . .

Strange, Tara hesitated a moment. *His* chi *is blocked.*

Oh, the haze around his eyes. Of course. The billboard sign that he's an addict. That figures. The master of commercial chi is a slave to it.

'Let's go and meet the nice folks, Frank,' Tara said as she gripped Gobi's hand. They both strolled down the zig-zag path towards Wing Fat and his guests.

Wing Fat's automatic headrest rose to elevate his oversized head. His manservant Little Min stood behind him and fanned his hands over his master's face as though he were slinging pizza dough. Wing Fat was now smiling at them like a broken doll with a hollowed-out grin.

How weird, Tara and Gobi communicated to each other with a squeeze of their hands. As though it were the most natural thing in the world to do, Little Min had his fingers in both corners of Wing Fat's mouth and was aiming his master's smile their way.

'You must excuse my servant's disability,' Wing Fat addressed Gobi and Tara in a husky whisper. 'He is dependent upon my smiles – he thinks they are an endangered species – and he will do anything to coax them out of me.'

Wing Fat's blubbery hand flicked its fingertips from the crater of his lap. 'Thank you for joining us. And welcome to Bangkok. That's enough now, Min.' Wing Fat's eyes slowly rolled their dismissal of his servant. Little Min released his smile-hold and the wave of Wing Fat's facial fat settled into a bleak mutton-like stare.

Gobi raised an eyebrow by a nano-hair. *So this was Wing Fat. It was difficult to imagine that he controlled anything. He was a Baby Huey wearing a silk bib the size of the Great Wall of China. Something was out of sync here. This wasn't the whole hockey-team . . . It couldn't be.*

Tara squeezed Frank's hand as she concurred with his own reading of the situation.

'I'm sure we're interrupting something here,' Gobi said as he gave the group a bow.

'Not at all, not at all,' Wing Fat insisted. 'Please join us for a moment. It's not every day that we receive a visit from such distinguished guests—' His right hand did its deep-knee bend on his belly again. 'Present company included, of course—'

There was a rumble as the gears shifted in Wing Fat's abdomen. 'I apologize for not introducing myself and my friends – I'm Wing Fat. The captain of this air-ship, you might say. Patpong Airways is one of my business ventures. And this is—'

Deedee and Mir hesitated. Finally, Deedee extended her hand to Tara and said, 'Hi, I'm Deedee Delorean and this is my associate Mirabelle Myers. We're from California. We were discussing a little business with Mr Wing Fat.'

Mir bit her lip and waved her hand at them feebly. 'Hi there.'

Deedee continued, 'I didn't realize that he was expecting company.' She gave the Chinese a puzzled look. The giant ignored her. His headrest swivelled his head as he studied the Gobis up-close. *Their* chi *was very fine. Very fine indeed . . .*

'I wasn't really expecting them, but here they are,' Wing Fat answered Deedee with a rasp as his headrest swivelled to the side again.

'How fortunate for us,' Deedee replied cautiously. 'A chance to get acquainted. Any friends of Mr Wing Fat's—'

'Actually, we're *not* friends of Mr Fat's,' Gobi piped in. 'We haven't had the pleasure of making his acquaintance. In fact, I was wondering how—'

'I'm sorry, we should introduce ourselves,' Tara said as she gave Gobi her 'chill-out, honey' look. 'I'm Tara Gobi, and this is my husband Frank Gobi. We were just passing through Bangkok and we thought we'd get a bird's eye-view of the city. It's very beautiful from the air, and much less congested.'

'I was wondering,' Frank persisted as he addressed Wing Fat, 'how you happened to know who we were.'

Deedee Delorean and Mir Myers turned to Wing Fat to

see what his response would be. This impromptu meeting wasn't on their agenda, that much was obvious.

'There are very few secrets in Bangkok, Mr Gobi,' Wing Fat replied sardonically. 'Your reputation precedes you, as I'm sure you know. It's an honor to meet the great man who resurrected Satori City. *And* his beautiful wife, too, of course.' The Chinese blinked blithely at Tara. 'Who is every bit as accomplished in her own way. You *do* make a perfect couple. I would be so pleased to count you among my friends and come to know you better.'

Wing Fat's mirth was irrepressible. 'But rest assured, I am the very soul of discretion. I can appreciate that your visit aboard the *Kinnari* is a private one, and that what you do on board is your own business.' He gave them a knowing wink.

'Everyone needs recreation,' Wing Fat continued. 'That's the very nature of life. The Patpong asks no questions. It welcomes all visitors with open arms – and an open libido, *Mr and Mrs Emmanuelle* . . .'

Frank Gobi stared at Wing Fat for a moment. 'Oh, I see—' He wondered how this mountain of human *dim-sum* had blown their cover so easily. 'We were – ah – just checking the scene out,' he explained. 'When in Bangkok – and all that. Strictly from a sociological perspective, of course. Mustn't overlook the dark side, eh?'

'Of course.' Wing Fat nodded sagely. 'As the saying goes, translated roughly from the Chinese: "Those who control their desires often do so not because of strong control, but because of weak desires."'

'You certainly do know your classics, Mr Fat,' Gobi said. 'That's very astute. *And* you are very well informed about current events. I mean, you know who's coming and going.'

'I make it a point, yes. My customers come first. That's one of the rules in the – ah – pleasure-business.'

Deedee slipped Tara a glance of intimate condescension. *Oh, I get it, you're a party-girl*, she broadcast a smile at her. But Tara ignored the overture.

'What Mr Wing Fat means, Frank,' Tara explained to Gobi, 'is that he's obviously been briefed about our arrival.' She turned to Wing Fat. 'Very recently. Am I right? Since we came aboard?'

'Oh, please!' Wing Fat clapped his beached whale-hands together. 'There are far more interesting mysteries to preoccupy us all. We have the same passions. Perhaps we can share them together. After all, you've come to see the butterflies, haven't you? Surely you have developed a taste for them in Xiang Gang?' He contained a snigger. 'Would you like to try some of our papillons? *Chef—*' Wing Fat's voice now boomed loudly across the room. 'What are your specials tonight?'

The wiry Thai *sushi* chef in the *happi*-coat behind the counter snapped to attention. 'Yes, sir!' He lowered his butterfly net. 'We have an excellent Leopard Lacewing *sashimi*. The Red-Spot Sawtooth is delicious also. Or if you prefer, we can prepare a *hibachi* steak with the Jewelled Nawab, it's got a very delicate flavor that goes well with a Nymphalidae *miso* . . .'

'You see,' Wing Fat beamed at Fank and Tara. 'The pleasures of the flesh extend to the wings as well. You must join us for a bite. You'll be my guests, of course.'

Just then a gauze curtain of brilliant butterflies swept across the counter and into the Thai chef's net. Tara and Frank watched him deposit his catch in a holding tank. The butterflies clung to a branch and began to feast on what looked like little balls of white fruit that were strung together on a string.

'I think I've just lost my appetite.' Tara blanched.

Wing Fat followed her gaze to the holding tank, then his expression hardened on her face like a layer of sticky lacquer. 'You object to butterflies nourishing themselves before their final metamorphosis into the human system? It's too epicurean for you?'

'To tell you the truth, we're really not that crazy about the idea of butterfly *sushi*,' Tara replied in a cold level voice. 'We were more interested in observing the phenomenon. But I think we've seen enough, and we're ready to go. Aren't we, Frank?'

Gobi's wide eyes signaled his agreement. Tara squeezed his hand to absorb his shock. There was no mistaking what they had just witnessed.

'It was nice meeting everyone,' Gobi said as he and Tara turned to leave. 'Good night.'

'Are you sure?' Wing Fat protested. 'But you've only just arrived! Oh, well,' he called after them as they slipped through the netting. 'Enjoy the rest of your stay—'

Wing Fat, Deedee and Mir watched the couple leave the restaurant. Then Deedee asked Wing Fat ominously, 'You're not going to let them go just like that, are you?'

'Of course, not,' Wing Fat answered. 'Now, shall we continue our discussion about the terms of the technology transfer?'

Deedee stared at the butterfly holding-tank, then looked up at Wing Fat.

'You're one sick fuck, Wing Fat, did you know that? But, all right. Mir – you keeping notes?'

' "*One . . . sick . . . fuck*," ' Mir scribbled in her PDA compact. She looked up. 'Yes, I got that.' One way or another, she'd get her two cents into the record. 'Anything else?'

'You Americans are much too squeamish,' Wing Fat said dimissively.

'If we were, we wouldn't be dealing with you,' Deedee Delorean retorted. 'Would we?'

Little Min stepped up to his master with a hand-towel and mopped up the spittle mixed with butterfly remains from the corner of his mouth. These were precious treasures which he would analyze later on in the spirit-house at home. He wondered how much cholesterol the butterfly *chi* was generating in the heart of the mountain.

'Min,' Wing Fat murmured.

'Yes, master?'

'Get to it.'

'Yes, master.' The servant bowed and withdrew discreetly to make the necessary arrangements.

••••••••••••••••••••
Helium Cheese

Frank and Tara turned in the corridor, away from the row of Patpong girlie bars and Wing Fat's unholy *sushi* restaurant.

'Did you see that?' Tara swore under her breath. 'What those poor butterflies were feeding on?'

'Those things on the branch that looked like they might be grapes, or lychees? Those were *eyeballs*, weren't they?' Gobi shivered. 'Suffering glaucoma! I wanted to puke right on his fat face.'

'Hello!' A Thai tout approached them from the doorway of a darkened sex club. 'Want to see massage show? Monkey massage dog . . . Cat massage rat . . .'

'No, thanks!' Gobi glowered at him. '*Beat it!*' The tout retreated back into the shadows.

'What do we do now?' Gobi asked Tara. They were standing at the bank of elevators. Tara pressed the button. She pursed her lips as they waited for the lift to arrive, thinking hard. 'I don't know.'

'I think we should leave as soon as possible.'

Tara looked at him. 'Frank, we're on board an air-ship, remember? Patpong Airways? This is a dirigible. I don't think it's scheduled to touch down at the Lumpini Air Field for another four or five hours yet. It heads back down at two o'clock.'

'Just our luck. How did he know we were coming? I don't like it. I don't like it at all.'

'I agree with you, Frank,' Tara reflected. 'Wing Fat's got this place wired.'

The elevator door opened and they stepped inside. There was another *katoey* elevator-operator at his or her post. Gobi knew what their racket was. They were there to perform quickies on customers who were traveling between floors. It was another Patpong side-line of the S.S. *Kinnari*.

'What floor please?' the *katoey* inquired in a sing-song voice.

'Can you take us down to Rama IV Road?' Gobi joked darkly.

'Ha?' The *katoey* grinned. 'No can do. This elevator not go down that far.'

'Misty Sauna,' Tara said as she gave Frank a penetrating look. 'We may as well kill some time there. Make ourselves as scarce as possible.'

'Misty Sauna.' The *katoey* pressed a button. 'Eight flo-a.' They began to descend.

The cell phone clipped to the *katoey*'s belt began to purr. Frank and Tara both stared at it at the same time. '*Sawat dii?*' the *katoey* answered the phone as he/she looked at both of them with a new curiosity. '*Ao.*' Then the *katoey* extended the cell phone to Gobi. 'This call for you, sir.'

But Gobi grabbed the *katoey*'s wrist and twisted the cell phone away. 'No, it isn't,' he muttered as he shoved the guy-girl against the wall of the elevator. 'I think it's for *you . . .*'

He'd seen the *katoey* press the last digit on the display, the one that released the stiletto from the base of the hand-set. 'Oh, my God!' Tara exclaimed. The *katoey* went at them with full fury, trying to knee Gobi in his groin and scratching at his face with his free hand.

Little Min listened on the other end. Then when the line went dead, he dialed another number.

'Are you hurt, honey?' Tara touched the rip in Gobi's white silk t-shirt with concern.

'Just a scratch,' he said when her hand came away with a daub of blood. 'The bastard. I mean, the bitch . . . It wasn't the blade, it was one of her high-heels that grazed me. Are we on eight?'

'I . . . I think so,' Tara replied. They had sent the elevator back up with the *katoey* that Tara had disabled with a rabbit-punch to the fire-kidney. It was a 'Niann' technique – one of the methods of 'stopping thought' – which she had learned in a *chi kung* street-fighting class in Berkeley.

'Look, there's the Misty Sauna over there.' She pointed down the corridor. The sign was barely visible among the swirling barber-shop poles and other massage parlors.

Frank Gobi felt his ribs and groaned. 'I don't know, Tara – I think this whole scene is bad news. I think Wing Fat's got the elevators wired, and everything else, too.'

'You're right,' Tara agreed. 'Let's go for pot-luck. Any of these places will do.'

They were already beginning to attract attention in the corridor. Thais, *farangs*, joy-girls and boys were giving them strange looks. 'Oh, oh,' Gobi said as he grabbed Tara's arm. 'The Patpong militia has arrived.'

Four or five Thai gangsters were pushing their way through the crowd, heading in their direction. They were wearing wraparound shades, Japanese *yakuza* shirts unbuttoned at the collar and steel-tipped cowboy boots.

Frank and Tara ran into the New Hong Haw Tora Massage Center. The sign read, 'The Heaven's In Bangkok.'

'Can I help you?' The mama-san at the counter smiled at them, then froze the welcome when she saw the hub-bub in the corridor outside. The door swung shut.

'How much for an Ancient Thai Massage?' Gobi asked, but didn't wait for an answer as he and Tara ran through the foyer into a labyrinth of cubicles with fogged-up glass doors.

'We busy tonight, stop!' they heard the mama-san call, then they heard her scream as the goons crashed through the front door.

They ran through a sauna that was thick with steam and couples in the middle of a group grope. 'Hi!' A Thai cutey addressed them. She was dressed in nothing but a hand-held loofah that covered her jade gate. 'Watch you want, ha?'

'Where's the coffee shop?' Frank replied, as he led Tara through the sauna and out the door into a dressing-room.

'Where are we going, Frank!' Tara asked him breathlessly.

'Through here, honey – then anywhere where our *karma* still works.' He paused in the locker-room as he listened for the sounds of pursuit coming from behind them. The Thai gangsters were now running through the sauna, stepping on toes as they ran. There were screams of protest and pain. 'That's them,' Gobi said as he pondered the next move.

'Frank, hurry!' Tara pleaded.

'Wait a second,' Gobi replied, then rose on the balls of his feet and plucked a string from a socket on the wall. 'Retractable clothes-line,' he explained as he hooked the end of it to the slot on the opposite wall. Okay, honey, let's split.'

As they exited the locker-room, they heard the sauna door swing open and the thudding sound of bodies getting snagged at the Adam's apple and falling backwards.

'What the fuck—' a *farang* customer yelled at them.

'Sorry to bust in on you like this,' Gobi apologized as he and Tara ran through a cubicle where the *farang* lay like a soap-sudded statue on an air-mattress. A Thai joy-girl was slipping and sliding up and down his front with a bored expression her face.

'Shit!' The *farang* was now addressing the next delegation that was violating his soap-play. 'I'm not paying for this! Shit!'

Frank and Tara ran through several more cubicles, stepping over buckets of water and other bodies engaged in various forms of coitus, ancient and modern.

'You know your way around here?' Tara asked dubiously.

'No, but I know where we're going!' Gobi replied. 'Down those stairs, baby, wherever they lead us is all right with me.'

'I'm right behind you.'

They took three stairs at a time, holding on to the hand-rail. They heard the commotion at the top of the stairs as the goons picked up the trail.

Gobi studied a lever on an emergency exit door on the landing. Tara looked out the window. 'You can't be serious, Frank. We must be a thousand meters above the ground!'

'You're probably right.' Gobi bit his lip. The blimp was sailing somewhere above the Chao Phraya River. He could see the lights of the Grand Palace through the haze. He opened a closet door that had a sign that read 'Staff Only.' 'Hello, what's this?'

'A life-boat?'

Gobi ignored the thudding steps of the Thai gangsters as they crashed down the stairwell with excited shouts. He glanced up. One of them had his head over the railing and was pointing at them.

Gobi yanked the contraption out of the closet. 'That's right, it's a life-boat, Tara. We've got no choice. You game?'

Tara looked at the device and shook her head. 'We'll never make it.'

'This is the Thai *Hindenburg*, Tara,' Gobi said to her in a serious voice as he unsnapped the frame and turned the handle on the emergency door. A blast of wet, warm tropical air blew in their faces. They stood there for a split-second, before he said to Tara, 'We're going down in flames otherwise.'

'Okay, I'm with you. You're the pilot.'

Gobi kissed her cheek, then slipped into the straps of the emergency hang-glider. 'Put this on, honey.'

'I don't need a helmet.'

'It's not a helmet. It's a parachute. And you're going to hold on to me. Slip your hands under my straps and hold on to me. Hold on tight.'

'*Farangs!* Stop!' There were three goons barely six steps

away. But they were hesitating because the door was open and the wind was roaring up the stairway.

'I'm sorry, but there's only room for two on this rig,' Gobi called out to them. 'Talk to your travel agent.' Then he gave them the thumbs-up sign, and he and Tara nose-dived out of the dirigible until the wind caught them in its hammock of air, bouncing them up and down on the cross-currents, and they began to glide towards the lights that were moving on the river.

They saw the Wat Arun, the Temple of Dawn, on the other side of the Chao Phraya, the spire of its *stupa* like a landing strip for some half-man, half-bird that was crazy or devout enough to try to land on it without getting speared by the prayers of the gilt Thai Buddhas that ringed its circumference.

Gobi heard Tara laughing like a banshee as she clung to his back and they soared through the night. 'This is better than sex, Frank!' she shouted in his ear.

'It is *not*!' he shouted back. 'We'll catch a cab back to the hotel as soon as we touch down. Then I'll be happy to prove it to you.'

Peachy's

'I wouldn't do that, if I were you,' the voice behind him advised.

Paul Sykes spun around in his tiny airless room to see who it was that addressed him. He had set his backpack down on the floor beside the thin foam mattress and was trying to get the window open, but it was stuck in its frame.

The door was open, and a young blond American was leaning against the doorway watching Sykes work up a sweat.

'I beg your pardon?' Sykes answered bleary-eyed. He was ready to drop from exhaustion, but he was afraid that he might suffocate first if he didn't get some air into this meagerly furnished coffin they called a room.

'It's not advisable,' the stranger repeated. 'Even if you *did* manage to pry it open, which I doubt, it still wouldn't be a good idea.'

Sykes looked him over. The fellow was tanned, about five ten, had blond hair, blue eyes with a greenish tint, and wore a 'Dr Zog's Sex Wax' t-shirt over a pair of faded blue shorts. He was standing barefoot in the hallway, holding a plastic bottle of mineral water in his hand.

'The fan doesn't work.' Sykes frowned as he whacked the side of the window frame with the back of his hand again.

'Now why am I not surprised to hear that?' the blond *farang* replied as he took a swig of water from his bottle and scratched behind his ear.

Sykes let a sigh of exhaustion escape his lips. He sat down on the only stool in the otherwise bare room and studied the hole in his right sock. Even his big toe, which was sticking out, seemed to be oxygen-deprived. He looked up at the young American wearily. 'How's a chap supposed to breathe in here?'

'Try calling room service,' the Yank replied. 'I mean, why don't you inquire at the front desk? They'll be happy to rent you a set of air-tanks for about a hundred *baht* or so per day. They get them used from the dive-shops. Since the reefs in Thailand have all gone to hell anyway, the diving business has moved upstairs, so to speak. All you have to do is leave a valve open on an aqualung and you'll get enough oxygen to sleep comfortably through the night, provided it's not defective. Watch out for the bends when you get up in the morning. You have to take it real slow. Let your system adjust.'

Sykes sighed again and shook his head. Since his head had exploded on Khao San Road, he had gone from worrying about his mind to becoming concerned about his heart. It seemed to be beating quite fast, with an irregular rhythm.

'Are you some kind of a diving instructor, or what?' he finally asked the American.

'Who, me?' Mr 'Dr Zog's Sex Wax' replied. 'Oh, nothing like that! I'm sorry I startled you. My room's just across the hall from yours. We're neighbors. You looked like you were new to Bangkok, so I thought I'd warn you about the windows. I mean, *window*. Hi, my name's Gobi. Trevor Gobi. Just a word of caution. Well, goodnight—'

'Wait a second.' Paul Sykes rose from the stool and walked across the floor over to the doorway. He watched as the Yank fiddled with the lock to his door. 'Gobi, that's an unusual name, isn't it? I'm Paul Sykes.' He extended his hand. 'Glad to meet you.'

'Oh.' Trevor turned and shook Sykes' hand. 'Yeah. I guess it is somewhat unusual. Oh, well,' he shrugged. 'Goodnight again.'

Gobi's door swung open and Sykes saw a similar-looking foam mattress on the floor, with sheets on it, and a pair of aqualungs placed strategically at the head of the mattress within the mosquito net.

'Wait, *wait* just another second.' Sykes crossed the hallway. 'I don't mean to disturb you, but are you – where are you from?'

'San Francisco,' Trevor Gobi replied.

'No shit,' Sykes responded with a sudden exuberance. 'That's where *I'm* from. I just flew in this evening.'

'So I gathered,' Trevor said as he began to rummage through a pile of clothes and clutter of objects that were lying on the floor by the bed. He found a wrench, gave Sykes a grin, then turned one of the valves on his air-tank.

As the air hissed out of the tank, Trevor cooled his face with it. 'That's better,' he said. 'The next best thing to air-conditioning.' He picked up a mask-and-snorkel and tossed it back into the pile. 'I tried sleeping with one of these hoses connected to the tank, but it was more of a nuisance than anything. Just old-fashioned canned air, that's the ticket.'

Sykes lingered at Trevor's doorway, puzzled. 'What's with not opening the windows? Is the air supposed to be toxic in Bangkok?'

'What?' Trevor slipped off his t-shirt and scratched himself under his arms. 'It's shitty, but no, otherwise it's not toxic. No, it's a question of taking basic security measures, that's all. I guess you haven't been reading the newspapers. I take that back. It's not in the regular newspapers, that's the point. They never print that kind of news, especially not in Bangkok. It's bad for tourism, and all that bullshit. But it's been all over the backpacker 'zines . . . The coconut press.'

'What's the trouble then?' Sykes asked, feeling the anxiety return.

Trevor tossed his sweaty t-shirt into another pile of clothes in the corner. 'What color are your eyes?' he asked suddenly.

'Blue, blue-grey,' Sykes replied. 'What's that got to do with anything?'

Trevor rose to his feet and walked over to where Paul Sykes was standing at the doorway. He looked into his face. 'They're green, I'd say. Yup, definitely green. Greenish-hued.'

'No, they're not,' Sykes blurted out but he felt a constriction in his throat. 'Anyhow, you didn't answer my question—'

'Look, I'm very, very sorry about this,' Trevor said quietly. 'But you're going to have to be extremely careful. I don't mean to alarm you. But I think you need to be properly advised about the situation.'

'What bloody situation? What are you talking about, for Chrissakes! Listen, I've got jet lag, the bleeding window's stuck, I don't feel very well, and you're warning me about something, I have no idea what it is . . . What am I supposed to be careful about? Is there some kind of a crime-wave being directed against green-eyed foreigners or something as exotic as that?'

'Okay.' Trevor raised both hands in the air. 'My fault, my fault. Sorry. No more forked-tongue. Plain speak, then. Let's see, how shall I explain this to you?' He paced a few steps, then stopped. 'Okay, fine, Sykes. Sykes, is it?'

Sykes nodded. 'That's right, I'm Sykes and I've got about three minutes left before I crash. So please be brief.'

Trevor clasped his hands together in front of him and pursed his lips thoughtfully. 'It's like this, Sykes. There's some kind of weird black-market thing going on involving hijacking organs. Apparently, it first got started in Cambodia, around Phnom Penh. Young *farang* backpackers have been the target of this ring. They gouge out people's eyes, Sykes. Don't ask me why. They drug 'em, gouge 'em, and sell their eyes to someone who's in the market for green eyes. They've got to be green, or some shade of green. That's the scoop.'

Paul Sykes felt waves of adrenalized disbelief whiplash the center of his solar plexus.

'You've got to be kidding.'

'I wish I were. Not only that. But it's been happening in Bangkok, too. On Khao San Road. There've been flyers put up in the cafés warning people not to accept drinks from strangers. You'll see them when you go out. Not bad avice. If I were you—' Trevor peered into Sykes' face again. 'I'd sleep with an eye-mask padlocked to your head. Funny, Sykes, you don't know what color your eyes are. They look green to me.'

'Green? They used to be blue – oh, fuck, I don't know *what* I'm talking about. It's been a very hectic past couple of days. And it's not getting any easier. I'm just waiting for the tide to change. Fuck. All right.' Sykes turned to leave. 'I'll just get out of your way. Thanks for all the advice.'

'No problem,' Trevor said thoughtfully. 'Paul Sykes, huh? From San Francisco? Your name's kind of familiar. Are you a writer or something? I may have read your stuff somewhere.'

Sykes stood in his doorway facing Trevor across the hall. A wry smile appeared on his face. 'Yeah, I'm a freelance. But your name's familiar, too. *Gobi*. Any relation to—?'

'To Frank Gobi?' Trevor interrupted his new acquaintance. 'You've heard of him? He's my Dad. That's cool, Sykes. We've only just met and we already know each other. Where are you heading anyway? Up north to the Triangle? Or down south?'

'Down south. To the Gulf of Thailand,' Sykes replied.

'No kidding!' Trevor grinned. 'Son of a gun! So am I. I'm bound for an island called Kho Samui, then to Kho Phangan, to a place called Hat Rin. It's got a beach like no other. And every full moon, there's a Full Moon party, it's the archetypal rave of all raves. The place is happening. People come from all over the world to find God and get laid.'

Sykes laughed. 'Sounds all right to me.'

'So where you are going in the Gulf of Thailand?'

Sykes smiled for the first time, relaxing. Mort Wisenik had told him about Trevor, and here he was across the hall from him in a flea-bag guest-house on the Khao San Road. *If he only knew—*

'Same place, mate. I'm Kho Samui-bound myself. I've never heard of Kho Phangan, though. Maybe I'll check it out. When are you going?'

'The Full Moon thing's three days away. I was thinking of leaving tomorrow.'

'How are you getting down there?'

'Oh, the VIP bus. It's cheap. It's air-conditioned. And it's an overnight trip. They drive you down the mainland to a place called Surathani, then it's a two-hour car-ferry-ride to Nathon, which is the main port of Samui. Kho Phangan's only forty-five minutes away by ferry from a pier on Big Buddha Beach on the north side of Samui.'

'Big Buddha Beach, huh? Sounds fascinating. Mind if I

tag along, seeing that we're both heading in the same direction?'

'Cool, Sykes. We'll talk in the morning, okay? We can have breakfast, if you like. They serve some mean banana pancakes here. And meanwhile, I suggest you sleep with a pot over your head. You can never be too careful.'

'Right-o, then, see you in the morning,' Sykes said as he shut the door to his room. He stared at the jammed window and felt the heat rise in the stifling chamber. No air. No fan. No luck. Oh, well. Never mind. Something would break soon for him. If it didn't, what difference would it make? He was fucked anyway. And his eyes were green, goddammit! No, he meant blue. No, they were green. Green like the light that flickered through the window.

He stepped over to the window and looked out into the alley. Carefree *farangs* on the prowl for a good time, Sykes saw their heads bobbing down below as they poured into the street. Khao San Road never slept apparently. And neither did *she*. She was still standing across the street. How could he miss her? That weird woman with tropical plumage for hair and the two parrots grafted onto her shoulders. She was standing very still, practically motionless, looking into the alley where the Peachy Guest House opened onto Khao San Road. What was she looking for?

The Amazons seemed to be studying the faces of the passers-by. Opening and stretching their wings, and craning their necks as they followed the action on the street. What on earth were *they* looking for?

He took it back. Sykes didn't really want to know.

The Heart Sutra Hoe-Down

Trevor chuckled as he leaned back in his rattan chair and wiped his mouth with a napkin. He nodded at the stream of young *farang* backpackers who were hurrying to the bus-stop at the crossroads. 'I call it the "Heart Sutra Hoe-down,"' he told Paul Sykes.

'When the spirit moves them, it *really* moves them. It's the whole heart-thing that you get into in Thailand. It's endemic really, like earth-shoes.'

'I see what you mean,' Sykes said as he took another bite of his banana pancake and washed it down with a cup of hot Thai coffee. Not bad. It was served black with dollops of sweetened condensed milk. The pancakes, stuffed with whole bananas, were pretty good too, Sykes thought. For $1, they were terrific. And a price tag of only 50 cents for the fruit salad – for fresh slices of watermelon, papaya, pineapple, mango, and yes, more bananas!

You could technically live like a mandarin here, Sykes mused. A cheap mandarin perhaps, but a mandarin nonetheless. And not the orange variety either. But the kind that swished around in silk robes and got carried about in a palanquin. Affordable luxuries, that's what Sykes wanted. He wasn't going to be a pig about it, but he was tired of feeling like a hamster running around a wheel in a Western cage.

The Rim, the Pacific Rim, give him the Rim, and you could even keep the silver platter, boy-o . . .

Sykes was having breakfast with Trevor Gobi at one of the outdoor cafés on Khao San Road. He was feeling a little bit better this morning. His mood had improved. He didn't feel as oppressed as he had the night before, arriving in a strange Southeast Asian country with little or no money and probably a price on his head.

The closest that Sykes had ever gotten to Asia was to the Japanese Garden in Golden Gate Park in San Francisco. It had a funny little steep hunch-backed bridge that you had to shimmy up on your hands and knees in order to cross over, and the red maple leaves were brilliant in the late fall, but who was anyone kidding?

That wasn't Asia, any more than San Francisco's Chinatown was China. Now Thailand, that was something else to get used to. It was like some kind of a baroque burlesque – but of what exactly? A 1,001 Arabian Nights' Dream, but without the Arabians. The Thais themselves were sweet, good-natured people, laid-back, and totally not into their heads, but thinking everything through their emotions. Their brains were wired into their hearts.

Sykes was glad to have met Trevor. The chap was friendly, intelligent, well informed, and definitely an asset. Over breakfast, Trevor had been lecturing him – *like father, like son?* Sykes wondered – about all the different heart dimensions that the Thais instinctively operated out of. It made a lot of sense to Sykes. He could see it. Feel it.

'Let's see, there's "*jai dee*," which means "good heart,"' Trevor explained. 'Then, there's "*jai tahm*," which refers to a "black heart." That's someone who's really got what you would call a mean spirit. And one of the most popular expressions here, it's practically a cliché really, I mean it's in all the guide-books, is when you tell someone "*Jai yen*." Have a "cool heart." It's like saying "chill out, man." It's about the patience of the heart.'

The patience of the heart. Sykes let that one sink in. It had a nice weight to it. His heart felt a whole new kind of patience. One that he didn't have to strive so hard for. He wasn't gritting his teeth. He knew it was happening. There were no accidents. There was just the Flow, and he was feeling a little taste of it. It was a trickle, true. But it held a lot of promise.

God, it was a beautiful sunny day even in the shithole of Bangkok!

'Go on,' Sykes smiled at Trevor. 'It sounds like all the

different sex positions. The missionary position of the heart. Rear-entry. Side-to-side . . .'

'Ha, ha, ha,' Trevor laughed. 'Exactly. There are even Thai terms for hearts that *rape* other hearts . . .'

'Jeezus,' Sykes remarked. 'That's terrible.'

'That's reality though, isn't it?' Trevor said as he spooned some muesli with yogurt into his mouth. ' "*Jai rawn*," that's the kind of heart that terrorizes other hearts. No pity. No mercy. Just the dagger that goes in and twists hard. Killers are "*jai rawn*," and there are lots of them in Thailand, too. You want to rub somebody out. Someone who insulted you, made a pass at your girl, screwed you, made you lose face. It'll cost you $150 to hire an assassin. More, if you want it done face to face. A bit more if you want it videotaped—'

'Good God!'

'Yup.' Trevor folded his copy of *The Bangkok Post* on his lap and glanced at a young *farang* couple walking hand in hand. 'Then there's love, right? "*Jep! Jai!*" The hurt, aching heart of the jilted lover. You know what that's like, I suppose?' He studied Sykes' face. 'Did you jilt or were you jilted? I don't mean to pry. But we're all traveling for some reason . . .'

'Both,' Sykes answered, surprising himself with his level-heartedness. 'I jilted and I was jilted.'

'Hey, you're a natural Thai!' Trevor grinned. 'Not bad, Paul. You're getting the idea. What goes around, comes around. That's the Rim, too . . . And, for that matter,' Trevor's expression darkened somewhat, 'that's the Rim *three*, as well.'

'A threesome, huh?' Paul intuited some personal subtext in Trevor's tone. 'Is that why *you're* running? Er, excuse me, I mean backpacking?'

'It's a long story. And it's already been told. I'm just trying to forget all about it now. Move on, you know. Literally.'

'Yeah, I can dig that.'

'Hmm, I wonder—' Trevor's eyes held a sad light in them, but he brightened. 'Then, to continue in the heart-catalog of things, there's *"Bplack jai!"*'

'You're sure that's not a card-game?' Sykes laughed gently. He could feel the hurt in his new friend, and shit, whatever he could do – he could tell Trevor was still on trial somewhere in his heart. Just like he was himself. With Anne, and with the others. The same old song. But funny, strange, odd, peculiar, even freshly astounding – *this* morning, it *did* feel like an *old* song, one that didn't necessarily have to get repeated like the chorus of some moronic pop-song. '*Pop-art. Pop-heart.*' There. He *was* feeling rather Thai today.

'Bplack jack?' Trevor chuckled. 'Right. *"Bplack jai!"* That refers to the *surprise* of the heart . . . Something that blows your mind so much that it transforms your heart . . .'

'That's pretty far out,' Sykes concurred. 'Something that blows your mind so much that it changes how you feel entirely.'

'Yeah, something that intense,' Trevor agreed. 'Something that you will never, ever forget.'

'What could that be, I wonder?' Sykes pondered. 'I mean, does it have to be something shocking that's negative, or something stunning that's positive.'

'Oh, they don't make any distinctions like that over here.' Trevor took a sip of his orange juice. 'That's a Western concept. Neither good, nor bad, man. It just is what it is, and fuck the duality.'

'I see.'

'And last, but not least – before we amble over to The Lucky Travel Agency down the street to get our tickets to Kho Samui on the VIP bus – there's *"Tuean jai!"*'

'Which means what?' Sykes asked as he reached for his bill. *Wow*, $1.95. He could afford to leave a 5 cent tip and still feel generous.

' *"Tuean jai!"* is a reminder that it's *not* in the head, that it *is* in the heart . . .'

'*What* is not in the head?' Sykes inquired.

'*Nothing* is in the head. In the head is emptiness. In the heart is fullness. Come on, Paul. Time to hootenanny. Those are the dance steps to the "Heart Sutra Hoe-Down" square-in-the-circle dance. The sooner we learn *that* lesson, the less baggage we have to carry with us.'

Trevor stroked his chin. 'Say, you're not planning on bringing all *that* with you, are you?' He pointed at Sykes' backpack which resembled one of the smaller pyramids in Egypt. 'That's quite a load you've got there.'

'Why? What are you carrying in *your* backpack, Trevor?' Sykes asked as he peered under the table. Sykes believed that he was carrying just the bare essentials in his own pack, which happened to include a folding ironing-table, an inflatable satellite-dish and his pet rock trilobyte hard-drive for wind-surfing Omnispace. Thirty-five kilos of commandeered jungle survival goodies.

Trevor Gobi smiled as he patted his own small valise-sized backpack. 'There's a lost city inside here, Paul. An entire lost civilization. All packed up and ready to go, along with a tooth-brush.'

'You're kidding, right?' Sykes rose from the table and heaved his own heavy pack on to his shoulders. It was almost as heavy as his past. 'A lost city? That's a cool metaphor for personal luggage.'

'Maybe.' Trevor grinned. 'Maybe not. Only time will tell. But don't mind me, I'm just acting out. Being enigmatic, y'know. Like *you* are.'

'*Me?*' Sykes was genuinely surprised. 'What do you mean? Why am *I* being so enigmatic? I'm just a humble Brit with delusions of even greater humility to come. I really *do* want to do the heart-thing, Trevor. Chuck the past *karma*. Make a fresh start of the heart. If I knew God existed, I would give him a second chance. Him, her, it, *shit* . . . Whatever.'

He scowled when he saw a *farang* at a nearby table light up a Rizla and blow the *ganja* fumes into the air. 'But

God's obviously a creation junkie, and a lot of that creation seems like pure bunkum to me. Just tooting his own horn, that's all. PR, nothing more . . .'

Trevor pushed his chair back. 'Yeah, I know what you mean. Each new galaxy that God creates is like one big cosmic press release. "Look at me, I'm all powerful. The CEO of All Existence."' He stood up. 'But I don't think that's really *God*, Paul. That's just Big Bro, the Spin-Doctor of the Void. I don't think God gives a shit about all his notoriety and people's self-serving praise-giving. For them, the name of God is greater than God itself.' He tossed some *baht* on the table. 'Which is, in a way *true*, I suppose,' Trevor added as he continued his Sermon of the Banana Pancake. 'The name of God *is* greater than God. But not in the way that most people might think. God is just selfless-consciousness, is my own opinion. Let's get going, shall we?'

They navigated past the tables where the *farangs* were bull-shitting about the merits of Goa over Bali. They stepped out on to the street. 'You know what Krishna said to Arjuna in the *Gita*?' Trevor asked as he slipped on his shades. ' "*And when he sees me in all and sees all in me, then I never leave him and he never leaves me. . . .*" We're birds of a feather, Paul,' Trevor said softly as he placed a hand on Sykes' shoulder. 'More than you realize.'

'Oh?' What did he mean by that? Sykes wondered as he shifted the weight of his backpack. The damn thing *was* heavy.

'You and me and God and yes, all the idiots and tyrants of the world, too. We're all in the same stew together. "*Jap chai,*" the Thais call this dish. It's got everything conceivable cooked in it. Yup, we're birds of a feather, all right. But things like world religion, institutionalized faith . . . Those are just bird-droppings on the windowsill of eternity, eh?' Trevor grinned.

'You certainly have a way with words,' Sykes said warily. His head was beginning to spin again. He closed his eyes. In the middle of his brow, when he squinted, he saw that tiny black orb again. That black sun just waiting to explode in his head, if he let it. He knew what would happen then.

It would grow in size from nothing to *nothing-else-but . . . One gigantic black sun.* Then *boom!* Sykes would be off and tumbling again, on some roller-coaster ride through his brain, past his brain, and beyond it . . . *Shit, he would never get used to it.* It was overpowering. He had to try and keep a lid on it. It must be some quirky jet-lag thing.

Trevor and Sykes began to walk down the sidewalk together, past the early-morning stalls that were still in the process of being put together. The head of a Jerry Garcia Krishna peeped out at them from under a tarp.

Trevor stopped at a fruit-stand, and bought some waxy-looking yellow star-fruit and some fuzzy-haired *rambutan* fruit which the Thai wrapped for him in a plastic bag.

Trevor turned to Sykes slowly with a question in his eyes. There was a shyness there that Sykes wasn't expecting. He felt as if he was suddenly being confronted, but by a gentle interrogator. He guessed what was coming next, especially when he realized that Trevor had caught him studying the subtle shapes that were moving along the Khao San Road.

'Your eyes are green, Paul,' Trevor said. 'Why don't you want to admit that? You *know* what's going on, don't you?'

Sykes stopped in his tracks. 'You mean, you see them too!?'

'See *whom*, Paul? Whom do you see?'

'Them,' Sykes said as he pointed across the street. 'Those invisible backpackers. Not these guys who're hurrying and scurrying to catch their rides. But those slow guys, the ones who are in no rush at all, but who seem to move at the speed of light. Can't you see them? There they are, Trevor. Right now.' Sykes was now revealing his secret. 'I see four of them, at least. I don't know how many others there are that I *can't* see . . . But I can sense their presence. I don't know *where* they're going or *why*. I thought I was losing my mind. But this morning – guess what? I couldn't give a shit.'

Trevor looked across the street, then turned to Sykes with a bemused expression.

'You're not losing your mind, Paul. Remember what we talked about earlier? "*Bplee-un jai!*" You don't change your mind, pal. You just change your heart.'

'So you see them, too, Trevor? Tell me.' Then he paused. 'The black sun, is that part of it? Do you see that too? It's some kind of a triggering mechanism, isn't it?'

Trevor nodded and looked at Sykes carefully. He took off his shades and Sykes noticed for the first time that Gobi had the same green tint in his own blue eyes.

'Uh-huh,' Trevor chuckled. 'It's kind of neat, isn't it? It's just part of the "Heart Sutra Hoe-down," Paul. Same–same. And it's coming down soon. That's why I'm heading down to Hat Rin. And that's why, I reckon, you're coming with me.'

Black Sun Interactive

Bangkok-Kho Samui

The 14-hour ride on the overnight VIP air-conditioned bus from Bangkok down south to Surathani was the nicest part of the trip for Paul Sykes. It was a double-decker bus with comfortable seats that reclined all the way back just like first-class seats on a plane, with padded foot-rests, reading-lights, and air-con controls.

To a frugally minded Sykes, for a paltry $20 bus-ticket,

the experience felt as if he was embarking on a luxury cruise aboard the QE5.

Once on board, Trevor Gobi and Sykes each received a bottle of water, sandwiches, cookies, blankets, pillows, and a chance to leisurely observe the passing Thai countryside through the bus's tinted windows.

There weren't many passengers. The bus was less than a quarter full. The silence was peaceful and soothing, the freeway smooth. The driver's entire family, his wife and two little kids, sat in the front of the bus beside Khun Papa at the wheel, keeping him company as he shifted gears and sped through the night.

It was a homey touch, thought Sykes. Imagine a United Airlines pilot with his entire brood and missus camped out in the cockpit of a plane during an international flight. Who knows, he wondered, there might even be fewer accidents as a result of all that mobile cocooning . . .

It felt as if the driver of the bus was connected to the highway through his heart, Sykes mused as he drifted off to sleep. He didn't need a road-map to drive his love-bus.

That's how it should be . . . how I want to be connected to things and people and places . . .

Outside Bangkok, in sporadic waking moments, Sykes caught fleeting glimpses of office highrises, crumbling housing projects, pyramids of gravel heaped outside bleak cement factories, and brightly lit Japanese car-dealerships with their latest model Toyota Pagoda XLs.

Further along the route, he stared at long dark stretches of palm-studded coconut plantations. Opening the window and looking up, he saw inky-black skies sparkling with bright stars and the occasional blinking satellite.

There were meandering green hills, rivers that flowed through deep jungle ravines, Thai temple-compounds with white-and-gold spired *stupas*, roadside food-stalls, truck-stops, and isolated night-clubs that appeared out of nowhere, decorated with fairy-tale strings of green lights advertising the sexual services being offered on the premises.

Getting *to* the VIP bus had been another story altogether. Trevor Gobi and Paul Sykes had been shuttled from one Bangkok travel agent to another, each one a middleman. At each stop, they waited over forty-five minutes for a mini-bus to deliver them to their next drop-off point, before finally arriving at the VIP bus-depot.

The bus-depot itself turned out to be just a five-minute walk from their initial starting point on Khao San Road.

Their last travel agent, a smiling Chinese in a tiny office located in a back-alley behind the railroad station, offered them tea and a complimentary packet of Ziffy, a cheap buzz to take the edge off their waiting.

'*Farang* medication for impatient hearts,' he explained to the two weary travelers who declined his generous offer.

At first, Sykes suspected it might be a knock-out drug and instinctively felt for his money-belt. But Gobi assured him the L-Dopa-based Ziffy was just a feel-good powder.

'As far as most Thais are concerned, *farangs* are tea-bags steeped in boiling pots of neuroses,' Trevor remarked. 'They obviously feel that we can benefit from a little mellowing out. So when they jerk you around a bit, they're actually giving you a healing.'

'But a two-hour commute to get to a destination that's only five minutes away!' Sykes marveled to Trevor as he flopped into his seat and covered himself up with a wool blanket.

'That's Thailand,' Trevor explained to Sykes. 'It's never in front of you, it's always around the corner. Which is actually quite a useful paradigm to remember. Because what seems to be around the corner is frequently right under your nose. It's all a question of perception. And of patience. This is a great place to test your resolve and your vision, Paul. In a thousand easy lessons . . .'

Sykes and Trevor Gobi were stretched out in two adjoining seat-nooks. Trevor was nibbling on some sesame-seed crackers he had bought at the marketplace.

'What was it like for you when it first happened?' Sykes asked him a few moments later.

'The "black sun," you mean?' Trevor gave him a questioning glance.

'That's right, the black sun,' Sykes repeated. 'What was it like?'

'That's a good question. I guess it happens differently for each individual,' Trevor reflected. 'For me, it felt like an effortless breakthrough of sorts. You know, I spent years trying to meditate. Doing the *mantras*, doing the *yantras*, getting up at four a.m., taking cold showers, reading, studying. I guess even praying . . . I sent the entire pantheon of gods – Hindu, Greek, Tibetan, Babylonian, pagan, you name it – little flares signaling my distress. I gave up meat, I gave up vegetables. I *became* a meat-head vegetable. I did affirmations, cancellations, I took espresso enemas, enzyme baths, I had my aura tattooed . . . I bought every Ziffy-laced best-selling paperback by what's-his-name, the current Dr Feel Good, that Indian guy, Deep Pockets Chapstick. I ordered *shaktipats* through the direct energy transmission catalogs – you know, toe-nail clippings from the enlightened Himalayan sages. Rub the relic, get instantly blissed. And the result was – predictably: Zilch. *Nada*.'

'Uh-huh, I can relate to that,' Paul Sykes nodded. 'I used to earn a living back in the UK digging graves. That was by choice. To converse with Death face-to-face about the meaning of life. "Alas, poor Yorick," I thought to myself. Then it hit me. I wasn't Yorick. I wasn't even *related* to him. "Fuck Yorick. Get a life . . ." I told myself. So what happened next?' Sykes asked Trevor. 'What was the final breakthrough like for you?'

Trevor was very quiet. Then he spoke. 'You know who my dad is, right? Frank Gobi. You've heard of him.'

Sykes nodded. 'Of course, I have. I wonder what it was like growing up with him as your father . . .'

'Oh, he was present and absent at the same time,' Trevor replied. 'Sometimes he was absent when we were together. Other times he was present when we weren't even in the same space. The wave-and-particle school of parent–child relationship, I suppose . . . When I was about ten years old, I spent a lot of time isolating myself on-line. I think it was the normal thing to do at my age. I was exercising my right to feel alienated from the world by trashing parallel universes . . . Anyway, I was in Gametime when Satori City crashed—' Trevor paused, his eyes assuming a blank expression as he focused on that distant memory.

'Yeah, that must have been tough,' Sykes commiserated. 'I guess a lot of kids got stranded in that terrible time–space warp. Being caught off-line in an on-line environment. Like being wired to nothingness. You were damned lucky to get out in one piece, Trevor. I'd say you were freaking lucky that your father was able to jack in and re-boot the whole thing again before it turned into the Tomb of the Unknown Hacker . . .'

Trevor Gobi smiled. 'Yeah. But I have to admit something to you, Paul. I don't know if you're going to understand this or not. There've been times since then when I really *wanted* to go *back* there. Into the Hole. I know I was only ten years old at the time. What did I know about anything?' Trevor shrugged. 'I was just a kid. But *now* – now that I'm older – there are things I miss about that feeling of being marooned out there. It wasn't that bad, you know. It's like being dead, but *more* so, in a way . . . There was a certain freedom of movement in that world that I've never been able to duplicate in *this* meat-dimension, y'know? Until . . .'

'Until what?'

'Until one day it happened. I *did* go back. I revisited Satori City, Paul. *Not* the new and improved Satori City 2.0 which my Dad got up and running . . . but the *dead* one. The one that crashed originally. Satori City 1.0. RIP City.'

Trevor gave Sykes a quirky grin. 'Guess what, it's *still* there, Paul. I can revisit it anytime I want. And I *do*.'

Sykes felt a shiver run through him. He bundled up in his blanket, but the feeling of cold swept over him like the breath of an encroaching ice-floe. He waited for Trevor to go on with his story. He didn't know what to think. What was this guy's big secret?

'I finally found the opening, Paul,' Trevor continued. 'It was there all the time, buried deep inside me. I just didn't know how to access it. And I'm not the only one who knows the route. There are lots of others like me, others who were trapped in Gametime, who've found the same pathway.'

'The black sun.'

'That's right. The black sun. I see it in my head, Paul. It's the essence of pure *chi*. The most concentrated form of energy there is. Once you become accustomed to it, there's nothing to it really. It's just an icon. You picture it. It appears like a black dot, a black sphere. Then you click on it mentally. And then you're *there* – on the Other Side.' Trevor laughed. 'It's as simple as pie.'

Sykes shook his head. 'Something about this escapes me, Trevor. It happened to me, *too*, the first night that I arrived in Bangkok. When I got to Khao San Road. I saw the black sun, too. It exploded in *my* head. I tripped out. I saw things. And I'm still getting these flashbacks. At least, that's what I *think* they are . . . But I can't say that I ever was trapped in Gametime or in Satori City, for that matter . . . I never went through that same trauma. So how could it be happening to *me*?'

Trevor blinked at Sykes before replying. 'I don't know how to answer that, Paul. Except to say that perhaps it's a form of cosmological natural selection. The intersection between mental gravity and quantum physics. I suppose there's some sort of a scientific explanation for it. Or a para-scientific explanation. It goes beyond anything we understand. But this is something that I *do* believe to be true: Satori City is *still* crashing . . . In fact, it has never *stopped* crashing. My Dad may have gotten me and all the others out of Satori City. But he never got Satori City out of *us*. It's still happening, man. It's become like a spiral that's taken a higher turn. We're going around the bend now, the whole planet is . . . You're a perfect example of that. You weren't there. You didn't experience the event itself. Yet you can tune in to the black sun. You can fly, too, Paul. You're a "child of *chi*," too, whether you buy into it or not. It doesn't seem to make any difference, apparently.'

Paul Sykes closed his eyes. The black sun was throbbing deep in his inner vision like a chess-piece waiting to be moved on a cosmic chess-board. He opened his eyes again abruptly. 'Tell me one more thing, Trevor,' he asked with a wondering look.

'What is it?'

'Does your father know about this – about what's been happening to you? About the black sun? About your going back to this black hole of Satori City?'

Trevor looked out the window at the shadowed landscape of a rice-paddy with the dark shapes of water buffalos standing still on an embankment.

'To answer your question, Paul, no, he doesn't.'

'Why not, if I may ask?'

'Because he has to discover the pathway back himself. Only this time, he's not going to be rescuing me like he did the first time around. He got us out. Now he has to go back in through another door. That's how it is, and that's how it has to be. Part of my father is still there in the lost ruins of Satori City. I've seen him. He's even seen *me*, but he hasn't recognized me. His own son! Does the father of the caterpillar recognize the butterfly?' Trevor laughed ironically. 'And he *won't*, until the black sun sheds its black petals on the ground-zero of his memory.'

'No more questions, Trevor,' Paul Sykes sighed as he stared out the window into the glistening river of the rice-fields. The black light was sliding on the ice of the night.

'That's good because there *are* no more answers, Paul,' Trevor replied. 'The Q & A is over. The rest is just picking up the pieces and putting them in the right order. The universe is a jigsaw puzzle that never stays still, so we'll be doing that for a long, long time. But the Shift has already started and it can't be stopped. The process is only going to accelerate, and the rest of the world needs to catch up. It *has* to catch up. Or else it *will* get caught. Otherwise, just like some butterfly that gets snagged in a net of its own device, it'll end up as a specimen on display inside its own case, the memory of its flight and the beauty of its freedom pierced by its own pin.'

•••••••••••••••
White Saga

Chaweng, Kho Samui

The indoor stadium looked more like a corral than it did a kick-boxing ring. It was Kroon's idea. Kroon, the Boss Bitch of the Rasta Palace, chief of police of Chaweng, and purveyor of bootleg *chi*, was a fight promoter at heart.

Kroon had the old kick-boxing ring refurbished. First of all, he had it enlarged to three or four times the size of a regular boxing ring. Next, he did away with the ropes and had bamboo poles laid out on all four sides to create an appropriate corral-style enclosure. As a final touch, he had the floor packed with brown dirt to give it a gritty, realistic touch reminiscent of the outdoor water buffalo fight arenas.

The seating arrangements remained the same. Kroon was a visionary, but a cheapskate. The fold-up chairs surrounding the ring were the same beat-up metal chairs, and the seating in the upper-rows of the gallery were the same uncomfortable wooden planks. But he quadrupled the ticket-prices. And the ticket scalpers, who were on the take by Kroon, were asking three times the going price of a regular ticket. He was making a killing all around.

This event was something new – a brand-new sport, a hybrid of Thai kick-boxing and water buffalo fighting. Kroon even came up with a nifty name for the match: "*The World's First* Human–Kerbau *Kick-Boxing Fight. Never Seen Before Anywhere Except Chaweng.*"

It was the chance of a lifetime to witness the coming fight on Saturday night at the Chaweng Stadium. Gambling madness swept the entire island at fever pitch. Kroon's bookies were working night and day taking wagers, but they could barely keep up with the onslaught of betting. The odds were given as 3 to 1, with the water buffalo favored to win, despite the savage unpredictability of the kick-boxer. Still, the 500 pounds of the *kerbau* – not to mention the awesome curvature of its massive awl-sharp horns – made the water buffalo the odds-on favorite.

It was going to be a big night, a big fight. A Las Vegas show-girl with Thai cleavage. The match was between 'Stone Age Steak,' the undisputed water buffalo champion of the island's fighting *kerbaus*, and the contender, that ferocious, powerful, maniacally vicious, and hitherto unbeaten kick-boxing sensation known far and wide as 'The White Saga.'

The White Saga . . . A human monster if there ever was one. Hard-core kick-boxing fans and ordinary citizens alike shivered when they heard his name. He was a fright to see in the ring. An overnight legend, he had dispatched every single kick-boxer who faced him, however briefly they lasted in the ring.

The White Saga's signature 'whiplash' left kick was known to be deadly. Mon, the former Thai champion who had held the title for two years straight, had been knocked out in 45 seconds. His neck had been broken, snapped like a reed. Mon lingered in the ward of the Chaweng Hospital for three days in a coma and died without knowing he had lost the fight.

On one of White Saga's biggest nights – the one that established his reputation as Thai kick-boxing's biggest sensation – he had taken on Samui's finest kick-boxers in ten consecutive matches. Not a single opponent lasted longer than three rounds, and those who endured the punishment did so only because the White Saga was bored and enjoyed prolonging the agony of his prey.

He would toy with them cruelly as though he hated the idea of what they represented. To White Saga, they were not so much 'fighters' as they were *men*. To Thai kick-boxing aficionados, it appeared that White Saga hated human beings more than anything else in the world, the way he trampled on the sacred traditions that made man tremble in the face of the gods.

With his horrendous appearance – his white-pancake-smeared make-up running down his sweating face, and with his hairy arms and hairy torso and hairy legs, he looked more like an ape than a man. By comparison, the Thai kick-boxers who faced him had smooth hairless bodies, and muscles that rippled gracefully when they moved.

White Saga was short and clunky, and he ran in circles around the ring, bouncing off one rope to the other, before landing in the center of the ring. His dark-ringed brown eyes blazed with challenge and inhuman irony.

More than that, the White Saga steadfastly refused to participate in the elaborate pre-fight rituals that the Thai fighters religiously observed. While they prostrated themselves in each of the four directions, mumbling secret incantations, rubbing their protective tattoos, and expressing obeissance to their *khruu*, their guru-trainer, the White Saga would smirk at their useless folly.

He laughed into the air, and made monkey-like sounds deep in his throat. He would mock their prayers and spiritual exhortations by pulling down his red satin kick-boxing trunks and displaying his hairy behind to the shocked public. Who *was* the master that had taught him this outrageous defilement of the time-honored Thai kick-boxing tradition?

Where did White Saga come from? And what was his real name? No one had any idea. Some said he was from Borneo, others believed he had come up from Malaysia.

All that was known for certain was that White Saga showed up one day on Kho Samui island, having arrived by ferry from Surathani like anyone else crossing the Gulf of Thailand. One of Kroon's talent scouts spotted him in a bar-room fight in Chaweng. He was surrounded by a group of taunting Thai youths who thought his appearance was comical. One of the punks had a knife, and the other waved a pistol in the air. White Saga made a breakfast ritual out of them in a split second.

Swiveling with an unexpected swiftness from the bar he was leaning against, his fabled left kick connected with three chins in one fell swoop. It was a triple knock-out.

'How would you like to make some real money?' Kroon's man asked after the punks' remaining buddies had fled the scene.

'For doing what?' White Saga asked.

'Fighting,' the Thai replied. 'Here's five hundred *baht* just for you to consider the proposition,' he added as he peeled off a note and laid it on the bar-counter.

White Saga was a man of few words, and of even fewer emotions. Wiping his bare foot clean on the shirt of one of the unconscious toughs, he pocketed the purple-colored bank-note, downed his shot of Mekong whiskey, and stared the Thai in the eye.

'When do I begin?' he asked.

'I'd say you've already begun,' Kroon's man laughed. 'But starting Friday night at the Chaweng Stadium. You'll be the surprise challenger of the evening. You're a natural born kick-boxer. How about it?'

White Saga smirked as he replied, 'You believe in *karma*?'

The Thai's eyes narrowed shrewdly. He was not so much a judge of character as he was of brutality. He guessed that there was some hidden subtext here that was not sociopathic in the usual sense. He chose to make a qualified response. He did not want to lose this fighting devil before he had the opportunity to deliver him to Kroon.

'Do you mean dispensing or receiving *karma*?' he asked evasively. This hairy freak with the white make-up on his face could not possibly be concerned with gaining merit according to the Buddhist precepts. In his mind's eye, the Thai could already see White Saga standing outside the ring of *karma*, while kicking the shit out of anyone who challenged him within the accepted boundaries of the conventional violence of the sport. There was no referee who could possibly interfere with this freak's own rules of the game.

White Saga laughed menacingly. 'You're a real fuck-head, but I like your style. Where do I sign?'

The Thai understood the joke right away. He didn't press the point. He glanced at the bloodied faces on the floor. 'Your signature on them is good enough for me.'

White Saga laughed again. He was now the 'property' of Kroon. And he would work for him, not for the money, but for the joy of the kill.

The word spread that White Saga had never trained to be a kick-boxer. That he had learned his fighting techniques from some evil *maw pii*, some witch-doctor with a grudge against the world.

White Saga did not use any of the classical kick-boxing techniques that might have identified the school where he had trained. His own unique fighting style sprang from a natural aggression that was imbued with an evil speed, a frightening display of hellish *chi* in eye-blurring motion.

When the White Saga released his trademark left kick as

a *coup de grâce*, you could see the blood and the sweat of his opponents splatter three rows deep into the audience. The spectators who were splashed by the effluvia became instant collectors of White Saga's blood-lust. There was even a black market of sorts selling counterfeit blood-stained t-shirts with labels that brazenly proclaimed 'So-and-so [fighter's name] Knocked Out By White Saga, DNA tested and guaranteed.'

Kroon took his percentage from the souvenir stalls that sold the merchandise.

Kroon had flyers announcing the Big Fight put up all over the honky-tonk main streets of Kho Samui. Vans with loudspeakers drove through the *farang* tourist-traps in Lamai where the Germans congregated in their Thai Hofbrau girlie-bars; through Bhoput where the French did their laissez-faire beach-slumming during the day and their drinking at The Exotica bar at night; along Big Buddha Beach where the laid-back backpackers smoked and snorkeled (sometimes both at the same time, wearing bong-modified masks that got them stoned underwater); and through the main commercial and administrative center of Nathon, the island's port-town where the car-ferries and speedboat limos unloaded their passengers at the central pier.

'Watch White Saga Confront Stone Age Steak! The fight of the century at Chaweng Stadium on Saturday night!' the loudspeakers harangued as they drove slowly through the resort villages.

In his private office upstairs at the Rasta Palace, Kroon felt a sexual thrill as he put on his make-up. Two joy-boys were sprawled naked on his leather couch performing on each other for his amusement. He could feel the *boom-boom-boom* of the reggae music from the dance-floor as it reverberated downstairs in the cavernous main *sala* of the dance club. '*Hot-hot-hot . . . it's hot-hot-hot.*'

That was Kroon's favorite song. Buster Poindexter was

so '*jai yen*' cool, yet so '*bplack jai*' hot at the same time
. . . You never knew what was going to happen when the
dance-crowd began to snake-dance into a frenzy. Guys and
girls, girl-guys and guy-girls, hopping three steps up, two
steps back in rhythm, holding on to the gyrating hips ahead
of them in the line. Like one long prolonged orgasm . . .

Kroon snapped his compact shut. He could see the
Chaweng Stadium from his window. The fight-crowd was
already gathered outside the doors waiting to be let in. He
ran his hands through his platinum-blond hair that hung
down to his shoulders tonight, and squeezed his breasts
into shape.

'Hot-hot-hot . . . *feeling hot-hot-hot* . . .' The internal
lyrics flowed through his heart.

Do the snake, baby. Do the snake, Kroon thought to
himself as he walked over the couch where the two boys
were now resting. They fondled each other idly as they
watched their boss approach them. 'What! You're tired
already?' Kroon scolded them saucily. 'You need a
vacation? Get back to work!' He hiked up his skirt. He was
so hard. The two boys didn't waste any time.

Two mouths on him. Two more mouths to feed . . .
Kroon swooned in ecstasy for a moment, his eyes closed.
Then he slapped their faces away.

'That's enough for now, you're ruining my make-up.'
Kroon had painted his dick red tonight. That was his
favorite color. Red as blood, red as the *chi* that was
flowing from Butterfly these days now that they had put
him on an intravenous regimen of nectar from the wild red
hibiscus blossoms they fed him.

They were holding Butterfly in one of the sheds behind
the Chaweng Stadium, ready for delivery to Khun Wing Fat
after the fight. Production was up. Kroon was very pleased
at how things had turned out.

He lowered his skirt and blew the boys a deep-throat kiss
with his tongue wagging at them.

'Don't go anywhere. I'll see you after the fight is over.'

•
Stone Age Steak

A canvas curtain separated the two halves of the corral where the fight was to take place at 8:30 p.m. this Saturday night in the Chaweng Stadium. White Saga, the killer kick-boxer, and Stone Age Steak, the killer *kerbau* water buffalo, would be facing each other for the first time in Thai kick-boxing history.

The indoor stadium was packed to overflowing with a crowd of two thousand drunken and jeering spectators. Bookies were everywhere, pacing the floors, taking bets on the spot and shouting into their cell-phones. Drink vendors prowled the aisles selling ice-cold Singha beers, colas, and bottles of Samui mineral water.

Bottles of caramel-colored Mekong whiskey and Sangthip cane liquor were selling briskly at the concession stands along with cuttlefish jerky, crispy-fried crickets, and peanuts.

Thais and *farangs* alike were crowded together in the bleacher seats high up in the stadium, while down below in the more expensive front-row sections the high-rollers hooted and whistled. They were mostly all men. This was a true *mai bin rai kas* sport.

Women and children got into the fight at half-price. This was one of Kroon's eccentric Buddhist merit-making gestures. The *mai bin rai kas* present consisted mainly of wide-eyed young European *farangs* in skimpy halter-tops and tanned thigh-revealing shorts, and toothless Thai crones in black cotton pajamas.

The old crones jabbered lewdly to each other about the size of the water buffalo's equipment as they rolled cheroots of *chaiyo* 'victory' leaf tobacco from giant tubes of paper. The *farang* women clutched their Thai or foreign boyfriends' hands and took swigs from their bottles of beer.

There was a nervous buzz in the air of excitement,

anxiety – so much money was exchanging hands – and of fear. Fighting *kerbau* were known to bolt suddenly in the middle of a bout, even as their horns were locked, and to stampede through the crowd.

It was not unheard of for a few unlucky spectators to get crushed or maimed during a match. Chaweng's only ambulance was parked in front of the stadium with its red lights flashing in readiness. The paramedics sat on the stretcher in the back of the ambulance playing cards and smoking.

Young children, some as young as four or five, were restricted to the scaffolding that had been specially erected for them at the side of the stadium. They clung like monkeys to the bamboo frames, swinging their legs as they hung from the rungs of the makeshift jungle gym.

The suffocating heat of so many bodies pressed together cast off such intense waves of energy that the cheap plaster walls appeared to be sweating tears mixed with soot.

A nervous roar erupted throughout the stadium as the crowd spotted Stone Age Steak, the champion *kerbau*. He was being led in a solemn procession by his Thai handler and four burly assistants. They had appeared from a side-door of the hall.

The massive black *kerbau* lumbered along grudgingly towards the ring, halting and snorting as his handler yanked at the leather cord that was attached to a brass ring in his flared-out nostrils.

Every few steps or so it seemed, Stone Age Steak would stop in his tracks and thrust his curved horns at any spectator foolish enough to reach out and touch his rippling black hide to ensure good fortune for their bets.

Two of the handler's assistants now lifted the long bamboo poles at the entrance to the corral to let Stone Age Steak into the ring. The intelligent black eyes of the *kerbau* radiated nervous fury as his Thai handler led him to his designated corner of the dirt-packed ring.

With a deft slipknot, the handler now secured the *kerbau*'s tether to an iron stake that had been hammered into the ground on his side of the canvas curtain.

The handler, a middle-aged Thai dressed in a white shirt with rolled-up sleeves, black pants, and a heavy gold Rolex-Seiko watch on his wrist, brought out a vial from his pocket. He splashed some magic spirits over the *kerbau*'s red-and-gold ribboned long horns and whispered secret incantations into the bull's twitching ear.

Flies buzzed the *kerbau*'s muscled hump as Stone Age Steak whipped his tail at them and gouged his hooves into the ground. He knew what awaited him on the other side of the billowing canvas.

The crowd roared as Stone Age Steak suddenly lunged at one of the handler's assistants who had gotten too close with his whisk broom and dust-pan as he went about his task of sweeping the *kerbau*'s king-sized buffalo patties off the floor.

The young Thai, who was wearing a torn t-shirt that read 'Santa's Sleigh,' jumped away just in time, leaving one of his rubber *zori* sandals behind him in the muck. The crowd laughed and applauded. It was all part of the evening's entertainment.

The Thai fight-announcer launched into a series of announcements over the public address system, working the crowd up into a frenzy.

'That's Stone Age Steak! Stone Age Steak! White Saga, the demon kick-boxer, will be on his way to the ring any moment now, ladies and gentlemen! White Saga will confront Stone Age Steak in a fight to remember! Place your bets now before it's too late!'

Kroon, the Boss Bitch of the Rasta Palace, made his swanky appearance surrounded by his bodyguards, waving and blowing kisses at the crowd. He settled into his own private box-seat in front of the ring with a young Swedish *farang* boy-toy. Kroon ran his hand through the boy's curly brown hair and laughed, showing off his own set of perfectly white teeth.

Inside one of the dilapidated sheds outside the stadium that served as his dressing-room, White Saga sat on a stool and stared at the cracked mirror that hung from a nail on the wall. A bare light-bulb dangled from an electrical cord in the ceiling.

Tham, his personal attendant, was rapping on the door. 'Five minutes left before the fight,' Tham called out. 'Can I get you anything?'

White Saga grimaced at his reflection and bared his teeth. Pressing his ear to the door, Tham heard the devil-freak pound his hairy chest with a vicious tattoo of drum-beats.

Tham stepped away from the doorway, shivering as he hurriedly left to inform the manager that the monster was almost ready.

White Saga grinned as he heard the footsteps recede. Then he stood up and studied his reflection again. A mask of sorrow lay under his grotesque white pancake make-up. Nearly all of Tommy Kok Lau's humanoid expressions had fallen apart by the time he had crossed into Thailand from the Malay border-town of Padang Besar. Only the sorrow was left. And that was his best-kept secret.

Tommy had hitched a ride up north with a Thai trucker who was half-drunk, and half-cranked up on 'Dr Cap' *shabu*. A lonely bastard who wore his heart on a sleeve during the entire trip. He had kept pining about the daughter he had sold to some brothel in Bangkok, about the wife who had abandoned him, and about his elderly parents in a village somewhere who had cursed him with their gratitude.

With the last of his human *karma* slipping away from him, Tommy had snuffed the truck-driver. It was his first kill. The taste of first blood was like *tantra* in his heart.

Tommy could still remember the eyes of the man and the death-rattle in his throat as he squeezed and squeezed 'till there was no breath left to squeeze any more. 'Thank you for the ride, sir,' he had addressed his victim. 'You are better off dead. Believe me, I am doing you a great service. Your world will no longer torment you. You are now safe. You are free.'

Ugly, you are so ugly that you have become beautiful. White Saga regarded his image with a critical eye.

He had a woven head-band tied around his skull with its coarse black hair, a bulging forehead, deepest brown eyes without mercy, a square chin, sloped hairy shoulders over a heavy torso built like a battering-ram, a pair of long hairy black arms (an arm-band on his left arm, part of his kick-boxer's get-up, like his head-band), no gloves (he was fighting a *kerbau*, it was explained to him), powerfully muscled short hairy legs that stood out in dark contrast against the red satin of his boxing-trunks, and his feet – his feet! His deadliest weapons: hammer-heeled feet, taped around the soles, with toes that could grip and choke and gouge.

Tommy closed his eyes and gripped the edge of the dressing-table, moaning softly with his cheek against the mirror.

Pinang was far behind him now. That life and all it represented, Ma, Pa, all his friends. How had he come to this pass? And where was he going now?

He knew but didn't know. He didn't know but he knew. *Nita!* Tommy's teeth chattered against the glass.

Your voice is silent. You have stopped calling me. And you no longer hear me. Not any more. What have they done to have silenced you? All that loves can no longer love. Only this hatred remains – that is my love letter to you . . . This is the vengeance of the shattered heart.

Tham was about to knock on White Saga's door again for the final call when he heard the sound of breaking glass. *What was the monster doing now?* He trembled. Suddenly the door swung open and White Saga stood there in the doorway like a vision unhinged from some Thai hell.

'I . . . I was just about to . . . to remind you . . .' the trembling Thai blurted out. 'That . . . that it's . . . time.'

'I know,' White Saga replied in a gruff rasping voice. 'I could smell you coming.'

● ● ● ● ● ● ● ● ● ● ● ● ● ● ● ● ● ● ●
Kerbau Karma

The crowd in the stadium went wild when White Saga walked in on all fours. He scurried down the aisle followed by a small retinue of handlers.

'*Sa-ga! Sa-ga! Sa-ga!*' the crowd began to chant in unison as they clapped to the rhythm of his name. '*Sa-ga! Sa-ga! Sa-ga!*' That was followed by a resounding '*BOOO!!*' when he pulled off his red silk fighter's robe, trampled it on the ground, and showed them his hairy behind. The crowd booed even more furiously when he did the next unexpected and most unpardonable thing. White Saga tore off the tri-colored Royal Thai flag that draped on the side of the ring and began to piss on it.

You could hear the sound of his pissing all the way from the upper-galleries. There was stunned silence in the vast hall.

Sitting in his box-seat, Kroon couldn't believe his eyes. He gripped the hand of his *farang* boy-toy and gaped at the fighter. For the first time in his life, he felt the rigid certainty of his own fear. It was visceral, on a gut-level. Here was something more evil and more dangerous than any of his own dirty tricks, power plays, and intimidation. White Saga was much more sophisticated in his display of natural vulgarity.

The crowd came to its senses as soon as White Saga concluded this uninhibited demonstration of his disdain. They began to throw things at him, bananas, bottles, cans, balled-up programs, anything they could get their hands on. White Saga raised his hands like a victor. He had gotten them into the state that he wanted. Wild.

Stone Age Steak, on his side of the curtained corral, stiffened as a tremor ran down his front legs. He now could smell the adversary. The *kerbau*'s eyes showed confusion. There was no other scent of *kerbau* in the air. The beast snorted. *This fight of no fights . . .* His nostrils flared around the ring in his nose. *What was he going up against . . . ?*

Water dripped down Stone Age Steak's flanks as his handler hosed him down. *Any minute now.* The *kerbau* smelled the strangeness of his rival more than he did the frenzy of his adrenalinized system. The water buffalo was kicking his hind-legs frantically now, pulling at his tethered nose-ring despite the echoing sensation of pain.

His Thai handler aimed the hose at Stone Age Steak again to cool off the beast's angst. '*Jai yen, jai yen,*' he kept repeating over and over to his prized champion buffalo. 'Cool heart, cool heart . . .'

'*I can't believe he just did that!*' Paul Sykes exclaimed as he gripped Trevor Gobi's arm excitedly.

'Hey, watch what you're doing!' Trevor recoiled. Trevor had some kind of a digi-cam out and was taping a Kirlian Beta version of the event. The digi-cam was practically the only thing Trevor had stowed in his backpack except for a few clothes. Sykes never realized that his new friend was such a film buff. Such an indie.

'Sorry,' Sykes apologized. 'Hope I didn't ruin your shot.'

'Not to worry,' Trevor replied as he resumed the filming. 'It's all part of the story.'

Paul Sykes and Trevor Gobi had arrived on the island of Kho Samui on the afternoon of the previous day. Their VIP bus had transferred on to the car-ferry from Surathani and they had steamed into the port at Nathon. A heavy marsh-like smell hung in the air from the receding tide on the adjoining stretch of beach beside the ferry-pier. Stalagtite-shaped dark clouds hung from a blue, blue sky above. 'It's almost the brainy season,' Trevor had joked. 'You never know when it's going to pour. I get some of my best ideas this time of year.'

Trevor knew his way around. He'd been on Samui a couple of times before, he told Sykes. They'd hopped aboard an open-air *songthaew* taxi-mini-bus and headed straight to Bhoput, a small village on the eastern side of the island. There they booked two rabbit-hutch-sized bungalows on stilts at Boon's for 50 *baht* a day. That was two dollars a night. And all the banana pancakes you could eat across the road at Boon's café.

Palm trees ringed a village path that meandered along a beautiful beach where topless French *farangs* tanned themselves while the local dogs went fishing in the surf up to their necks. The canines were hoping to snag a few fish free from the fishing-nets that were slung into the water from pastel-colored Thai fishing boats anchored off-shore. There was one enterprising dog – Sykes had never seen this happen before – that boogied its butt on to a surf-board and dog-paddled out a short distance with his muzzle in the water.

It was paradise, all right, and Paul Sykes was looking forward to the upcoming Full Moon party on Kho Phangan island, and maybe snagging one of those *farang* chicks, until Trevor spotted a flyer pinned to the bark of a palm tree.

It was one of Kroon's flyers announcing the fight between the White Saga and Stone Age Steak.

Suddenly, Trevor's face had assumed an intense and serious expression. 'This we gotta see,' he told Sykes.

'What? A kick-boxing fight between a man and a water buffalo?' Sykes retorted. He was surprised to witness such prurient interest from Trevor Gobi, son of the black interactive sun. 'It sounds gross to me.' Still, Sykes felt compelled to scrutinize the photograph of White Saga on the poster.

Where had he seen that same expression before? Not this expression of anger and contempt that radiated from the fighter's eyes, but something that lay on a deeper level than that. Something primeval and fatalistic. Something that had once seen the true face of love. It bewildered Sykes. How could someone so fierce be so gentle at the same time? Something stirred deep within him, and Sykes felt a heavy sadness in his heart. He blinked. *I know you.*

'Suit yourself,' Trevor snapped at Sykes. 'But I'm going.' Paul stared at Trevor for a moment. This guy was something else. He was ticking, too. Just like White Saga. Just like Sykes was ticking somewhere inside himself, even though he didn't want to admit it. He wanted to see the fight, too. And he knew whom he was rooting for. For both of them – for both the fighting water buffalo *and* the haunted kick-boxer. Because they were up against a world that demanded to see damnation before final victory.

'Okay, okay, if you think there's something meaningful there, let's go, by all means,' Sykes pretended to concede. 'I need to stretch my legs out from that cramped bungalow anyway.'

But secretly, he knew that the fight was some kind of a *rendezvous* between love and the hatred of love. The *yin* and the *yang* of the damned and the saved. And the real referee was the black interactive sun.

Trevor Gobi laid his Kirlian digi-cam down for a moment as White Saga leaped over the bars of the corral, and hurried towards his corner on all fours.

Trevor's face was flushed with excitement. 'Sorry I was so abrupt with you, Paul. I wanted to catch the aura around his eyes. It tells a whole story.'

'You're an odd bird, Gobi.' Sykes shook his head wonderingly. Then his own gaze returned to the figure of White Saga. The fighter was being rubbed down by his handler as he sat on a stool staring impassively at the canvas curtain that separated him from Stone Age Steak.

There was definitely something familiar about that weird-looking man-ape with the white facial make-up.

'Hey, what are *you* doing now!' Sykes turned to Trevor Gobi who was filming the expression on *his* face.

Trevor laughed. 'Like I said, Paul. You're part of the story, too.'

'You're crazy.'

'That makes two of us, Paul. You see something, don't you? Hey, I'll give you a tip if you want—'

'What is it?' Sykes joked. 'Invest in banana pancakes?'

'No, Paul. It's this.' Trevor smiled. 'Use the black sun. Go ahead, and tune in. You'll see the real show that way. But I think you already know that.'

Up in the far reaches of the bleacher seats, high above the stadium floor, Tara O'Shaughnessy Evans-Wentz Gobi turned to her husband. 'Frank, this is just dreadful.'

'I know,' Frank Gobi replied. 'But what can we do? We're not going to stay and watch the whole thing, honey. Soon as the musicians start jazzing up and the hokey-pokey starts, we'll slip out. This is perfect for us. They're all into this bullshit. They won't be paying attention to anything except this fight. Too many big bucks are riding on it.'

'I hope so,' Tara said. There were signs of obvious distress on her face.

Frank Gobi squeezed her hand. 'They're holding the poor bastard inside one of those sheds behind the stadium. That's where the Butterfly is now, baby. They've moved him from another bungalow earlier this evening. That means they're probably going to move him again, probably after the fight. So we'll do what we've planned. I'll leave through one of the side-doors and check it out. If I can, I'll spring him. They won't be expecting anyone. They'll be so preoccupied with this crap. Meanwhile, you get the

Jeep ready and be waiting at the rear of the stadium. Okay?'

'You'll be careful, won't you, Frank?' Tara gave him a worried look. Ever since they'd hang-glided down from Wing Fat's dirigible whorehouse that hooked for tricks high above the streets of Bangkok, Frank had been on some kind of a *chi* rush. They had landed in the courtyard of the Wat Arun, the Temple of Dawn, and had scared a couple of Thai monks half to death. Tara made Frank fork up some *baht* to pay for some new robes. The monks had ripped theirs as they tripped down the stairs of the *wat*.

His attitude reminded Tara of the day when Frank had finally made up his mind and gone into Satori City after it had crashed. There was no stopping him then. There was no stopping him now. He was one of the most ferocious peace-loving men she had ever known. Especially when it came to standing up to the voodoo of injustice. He was a real tiger, which was his animal sign according to the Chinese zodiac. But she loved him and she had all the faith in the world in him.

'Of course, I'll be careful,' Frank promised her. 'You remember how to work that stick-shift, right?'

'Yes, Frank, I do—hey, *Frank!*' Tara suddenly exclaimed as she leaned sharply forward on the hard wooden bench. 'Look! *Do you see what I see* down there in the stadium!?'

Frank Gobi snapped his head around to look in the direction that she was pointing. 'Where, Tara?'

Tara rubbed her eyes. 'No, it can't be. I must be imagining things.'

'Honey, what is it?'

'Over there, Frank! It's him!' Tara pointed again at the floor of the stadium. 'Eight rows down from the main pillar, about the middle of the row, in that group of *farangs* . . . that blond guy.'

'I wish we had brought the binoculars.' Gobi shook his head. 'Who is it?'

Tara bit her lip. 'I really can't be certain. But I think it's Jordan, Frank. Our dear friend who split from Xiang Gang so abruptly. Terry Jordan.'

Terry Jordan was in the black sun now. These people all around him had such paltry auras. Too much pig-fat and Mekong whiskey. Lard in their souls. He was much more impressed by the kick-boxer, White Saga.

Not bad, Jordan thought to himself. *All that self-torture is draining out of him slowly. He's coming to his center now. He's going to jack in to the big picture, and when he does, the real fight will start . . .*

Then Terry Jordan thought about Butterfly. He now addressed him. *Butterfly, I know you're watching this, too. You're going to be in the ring with the rest of us. But we're going to remove that big pin they've stuck in your heart. Do you hear me, Butterfly?*

Contact. Butterfly heard him. Jordan felt the rustle of his wings. The chrysalis was on the move again.

Hang in there, good buddy. Pretty butterfly.

Contact again. Number two, this time.

Terry Jordan let this one tickle the back of his neck. The black sun opened its shutter-window wider. *Not Butterfly. Someone else.*

Terry Jordan slowly turned around to identify the fresh contact. It was coming from somewhere in that crowd that was still tossing down rubbish and shouting abuse from the upper gallery.

Then he smiled and waved.

'Frank, look!' Tara exclaimed. 'He's waving. He knows we're here!'

'Why not?' Frank Gobi replied. 'Don't you think he's been expecting us?'

'You ever fought a *kerbau* before?' the Thai handler asked White Saga as he iced the kick-boxer's taped fists. White Saga was sitting on a stool in his corner watching the canvas curtain flutter in the rush of hot air that was fueled by two thousand breathing *hantus*.

Ghost people. They just didn't know it. Maybe they would never know it.

White Saga spit out his mouth-guard and replied, 'You ever fuck the Buddha?'

The Thai handler, a thin, wiry bantam-weight ex-kick-boxer, with a broken nose and a blue Khmer tattoo that ran riot down his forearms, shrank back in horror. 'What's the matter with you! Don't talk like that! You're profaning the Lord Sakyamuni!'

'You do that every second your heart beats,' smirked the White Saga good-naturedly as he rose slowly from the stool.

Kroon gave the signal to the fight promoter who gave the signal to one of the men in the ring who pulled a string that was attached to the curtain that separated Stone Age Steak from White Saga.

The curtain dropped to the ground and was quickly yanked away off to the side. Stone Age Steak's manager whispered a final incantation into the ear of the *kerbau*, as he undid the slipknot that tethered the beast's nose-ring to the stake in the ground.

Then he abruptly kicked the stake away and ran for safety on the outside of the bamboo corral. The musicians seated at ring-side began to furiously strike their percussion instruments and pipe their *pii* oboes in a manic approximation of snake-charming music.

The fight had begun.

Phase 4
························
Butterfly

The Kiss *Mudra*

Frank Gobi hesitated. He felt torn between his impulse to rescue Butterfly and his desire to confront Terry Jordan while he still had the chance.

Tara sensed his frustration. 'Just go, Frank,' she told him. 'What you're doing is so much more important. I'll try and keep an eye on Jordan as long as I can.'

Gobi nodded stoically. 'I think you're right. We'll catch up with him later. It's a small enough island. See you soon, baby,' he said as he kissed her cheek. 'You be careful, too, okay?'

He rose to leave. There was a long row of screaming fans he had to squeeze past in order to reach the stairs that led to the rear stairway of the stadium.

'Honey?' Tara called out to him.

Gobi paused to look at her. Tara blew him a kiss with her hand. He felt the energy transmitted directly into his heart center like a butterfly alighting on a fragrant flower. It was a kiss *mudra*.

He blew one back to her and disappeared into the roar of the crowd.

White Saga approached Stone Age Steak with all the respect and concentration that the animal deserved.

Once the *kerbau* had been set free from the oval prison of his nose-ring, Stone Age Steak had chosen to exercise his freedom by running around the corral in frenzied circles. Now he stopped dead-center in the middle of the ring. His glaring black eyes began to input the creature in the red trunks that was slowly but surely making its way towards him.

Stone Age Steak snorted and mashed his hooves into the dirt. He was breathing heavily now, buffalo hyper-ventilating. When the dizzy feeling of freedom settled, he would charge the intruder. His twitching ears already sensed the jetstream of death that raced around the inside of the corral like an invisible tornado.

Now the *kerbau* began to back his 600-pounds of buffalo rage into a slow reverse, as he built himself up to the moment when he would let it all loose.

Stone Age Steak pulled his weight into his shoulders and charged. But White Saga did not budge. He did not make a move. He simply stood there and opened his arms wide to receive the *kerbau* in the complete fullness of his acephalous embrace.

Nita! Tommy sent a silent scream up to the heavens, beyond the rafters of the stadium. *Beautiful Nita, beautiful dead Nita, here I am coming to life in your world! It's me, Nita, I'm falling . . .*

Two thousand screaming spectators became one silent caterpillar crawling on a green leaf. The leaf quivered, and the branch that the leaf grew from vibrated under the caterpillar's incoming caboose.

'My God!' thought Tara. *He's committing suicide.* She recognized all the colors of acedia that raced above White Saga's head like splashes of an inhuman sunset. *Acedia, that hatred for all life that leads a person to suicide. There is never any feeling of loss because there is nothing left to lose. It is so final. So endlessly final . . .*

Tara let her tears flow. *How cruel it is, how cruel it is, how cruel it is . . .*

Stone Age Steak came to a puzzled stop. There was no reflection of aggression in the mirror of the water buffalo's mind. It saw green bamboo shoots, felt a gentle wind, smelled a female *kerbau* and was confused by all the she-buffalo's feelings of longing that were radiating towards him.

Tommy!

White Saga opened his eyes abruptly, shaken out of his death-welcoming trance.

He had heard her voice again!

Tommy! I love you! I will always love you, my love . . . I will always love you . . .

Stunned, Tommy looked around for Nita. Instead, he saw Stone Age Steak, the killer *kerbau*, lower his head as he began to lick the salt off Tommy's hands.

Terry Jordan stood up in the audience and began to applaud. That was the only sound in the otherwise hushed stadium. Kroon, in his front box-seat, managed to tear his eyes away from the disaster of his demon kick-boxer making lovey-dovey *ram muay* with what should have been the most vicious fighting *kerbau* in Chaweng.

'Who is that idiot?' he demanded. Krik, his bodyguard, recognized the *farang* instantly. He understood the dimensions of such reckless self-exposure because he sensed the invisible ring of protection around it. 'It's that *farang*, Boss.'

'*Which* fucking *farang*?' Kroon lashed out at Krik in a spitting fit.

Krik felt the slap land hard across his face and saw the movement repeated across a vast distance as if it were a shooting star instead of a slap.

'The same one who touched the *katoey*, who made Butterfly a Butterfly Queen . . . It's Dr *Chi*, Boss,' he explained as he felt the hot sting on his cheek.

'Well, *go* and *get* him, you idiot! *NOW!!!*' Kroon ordered.

'Boss, look!' Krik was pointing at the ring. White Saga had mounted Stone Age Steak and they were both riding out of the ring, crashing through the bamboo barrier.

'*What the fuck is going on here!* Kill that bastard Saga! And kill that fucking *kerbau*!' Kroon was temporarily deranged. He had shrewdly bet two small fortunes on the bout – one on White Saga, and one on Stone Age Steak. Now he had lost both bets, the match being officially declared a draw.

'Right away, Boss—' Krik ran off at a trot, waving at the rest of Kroon's goons to join him in the pursuit of the escaping kick-boxer and the fleeing *kerbau*.

'*Wait a minute!*' Kroon called out to his foot-soldier.

'Get *him* first, you idiot! Get that *farang*! Get Dr *Chi*!'

But Kroon's voice was drowned in the general uproar that flooded the stadium.

Tara was desperately trying to keep her eyes on Terry Jordan, but that was proving to be impossible. Two thousand irate fight-fans were tearing up the stadium, throwing chairs, beer bottles, getting into fist-fights, as the ring-side musicians kept on playing their madcap snake-charming music. They were on to their second rendition of the 'King Cobra Suite' now.

The scene was one of complete and utter pandemonium with a capital P. Not even her caterpillar rain-dance experience in Xiang Gang had prepared Tara for this terrifying fireworks display of total chaos.

She had lost sight of Terry Jordan, and was now concerned about Frank. *What was Frank doing?* Tara was supposed to *rendezvous* with him behind the stadium in the Jeep, and *he* was supposed to be there with Butterfly, and they would fly away together . . . But there wasn't time. There couldn't have been time.

Where was *Frank?*

She hurried outside to look for him. It was chaos outside the fight-stadium as well. It was hot-hot-hot.

Ziggy Stardust's

The full moon above Bhoput unwound its sarong of clouds. It was now floating naked above them in the crystal fruit-bowl of the clear star-lit sky. Frank and Tara had been watching the electric light-show at the beach before returning to their bungalow.

They had watched the soft pulses of light zig-zag above

the moonlit waters of the Gulf of Thailand. The throaty grumble of thunder echoed in the distance from the scattered palm-and-coconut archipelago of the Anthong Marine National Park.

The scattered shore-lights of Samui's closest neighboring island, Kho Phangan, offered a more accessible counterpoint to the orgone blossoms that burst so radiantly in the velvet aquamarine sky.

Frank and Tara were sitting on a rattan settee on the veranda of their bungalow at Ziggy Stardust's. They heard the lowing sounds of a *kerbau* in the thicket of a grove nearby, followed by the smoldering croaks of an army of amorous toads.

Tall palm trees hid the moon from their view, but the mood was still peaceful, still beautiful. Down the road from them, at 'Rasta Baby's,' they could hear the rhythmically throbbing reggae beat of steel-drums. It was a Rasta Baby night.

The sweet smell of flowers from Ziggy's tropical garden made Tara feel as if she was in the intensive care unit of an aromatherapy institute. She felt mildly intoxicated, mildly crazy, and very much in love with Frank Gobi. 'Oh, Frank!' she exclaimed. 'If we weren't already married, I think I'd propose to you.'

'Wouldn't that be rushing things just a little?' Frank asked with a tender smile as he kissed his wife's full lips.

'What a night . . .' Tara marveled as she scratched at the hair on his chest with her fingernails.

'Yes, what a night,' Gobi agreed. He was naked except for his bikini briefs which Tara had purchased for him as a souvenir aboard Wing Fat's dirigible Patpong whorehouse. Tara was wearing an extra-large-size 'Rasta Palace' t-shirt with Bob Marley's face printed on it, and with nothing underneath.

She gave Frank a playful nibble on his ear as she sprawled out across his lap. 'Listen to you, Mr Understatement! I thought I'd *never* find you in all that madness. I couldn't even find the Jeep! They'd overturned it and rolled it over into the lagoon!'

'Never underestimate a crowd of disappointed fight-fans.'

'You can say that again! Tell me again what happened—' Tara asked as she sat up on the settee. She pulled Bob Marley's face down over her knees and clasped her arms around them.

'Well—' Frank repeated the story that he had already told her. 'I heard all the commotion coming from the stadium. By this time, of course, I had already slipped out the side-door. Thank God, it wasn't a Fire Exit. They keep *those* locked at all times, as you know. Anyway, I had no trouble at all getting to that row of huts or shacks or sheds or whatever you call them. The guard wasn't anywhere in sight. I guess he was watching "The Fight" from some convenient vantage point, who knows?'

'I was really worried about you.'

'And I was really worried about you, too, honey,' Frank said as he kissed Tara again. 'I checked the huts out one at a time. I even poked my head into White Saga's locker-room. Jeez Mite! What a haunted feeling. Who would have imagined . . . ?'

'Go on—'

'I came to this weird room. It was full of medical equipment. An operating table. And bunches and bunches of flowers. Red blooms, all of them. Wild hibiscus, I think. And I found this poor frail, delicate creature. It was the Queen Rim in person. I had the strangest sensation, almost like a flashback, when I saw him. Or *her*. Or *it*. He/she/it's a *katoey*. A Thai transsexual.' Frank paused. 'Or a polymorphous-something. I didn't get the feeling he was attached to any of the dominant sexual persuasions. He was almost beyond it, really. He had this almost translucent skin and he had a tube inserted into his abdomen, into his *hara*. His reservoir of *chi*. Where they've been harvesting him.'

'Those blood-sucking SOBs,' Tara said darkly. '*Then*

what happened?' she asked as her eyes brightened up.

'Okay, I was standing there looking at him, just wondering what I was going to do, how I was going to disconnect him – I didn't know where to begin.'

'Uh-huh.'

'Then he opened his eyes and looked at me and then he spoke to me.'

Tara shook her head and rubbed her neck. 'What did he say?'

But Frank said, 'Turn around, honey, I'll give you an Ancient Gobi massage.' He began to knead Tara's neck and shoulders with his strong hands.

'Oooh, that feels s-o-o-o good,' Tara murmured. 'Don't stop.'

'What I'm doing or what I was telling you?'

'Both.'

'Right.' He continued to massage her neck. 'Butterfly asked me the strangest question. He opened his eyes wide and asked, "*On what do you feed and where do you come from, dear butterfly?*"'

'He thought *you* were the Butterfly? He thought *you* were *him*?'

Gobi chuckled. 'My first impression was this poor guy's so disoriented. Come on, let's get him out of here. But he *meant* it. He really thought I *was* a butterfly . . . I must have looked like one to him.'

'Hmm,' Tara mused as she gave Frank one of her intuitive looks, one that processed the answer to her question before she even asked it.

'Either that, Frank, or else . . . you *are* a butterfly on some level that you're not even aware of.'

'Sort of like the Zen finger pointing at the moon, right? Is it really the finger or the moon? Or the dream of that ancient Chinese poet who dreamed he was a butterfly, then woke up, and discovered he was a butterfly dreaming that he was human.'

'Yes.'

'That's something to think about, I suppose. But just when I was about to help Butterfly sit up, the mustard hit the fan. There was another huge ruckus – and there *he* was. Sitting astride that water buffalo as if he was just taking a little ride, picking flowers on a Sunday outing. White Saga riding on Stone Age Steak. That just about shocked me out of my Tevas. And they were in second gear.'

'I can imagine,' Tara sighed. 'The monkey-knight on shining water buffalo.'

'Anyway, I took one look at White Saga and White Saga took one look at me. Then he jumped off the *kerbau*, scooped up our precious little Butterfly in his arms and rode away again. Just like that!'

'Just like that?'

Frank Gobi snapped his fingers. 'Just like that! Needless to say, I didn't hang around. There was a bunch of goons chasing them with baseball bats and shotguns . . . They looked quite pissed-off. I watched White Saga ride across the lagoon on that long wooden bridge that leads from the Rasta Palace to Chaweng town.'

Tara shook her head again and laughed. 'They didn't get very far, did they? The goons, I mean?'

'No,' Frank Gobi agreed. 'You know how much those water buffalos *weigh*? Tons probably. And that bridge was put together with planks and termites, you know. It was creaky and wobbly to begin with. Then when Kroon's bunch went after White Saga and Stone Age Steak and Butterfly on their motorcycles, the inevitable happened. That entire bridge collapsed, it fell completely apart, and they all went into the drink!'

Tara let out another laugh, then sighed. 'I'm sorry that I lost sight of Terry Jordan. He just vanished with some other *farang* who was with him. Another "child of *Chi*," I suppose.'

'No, don't be sorry, honey.' Frank put his arm around Tara and hugged her. 'I have an idea about that. I think I know where to find him. I'm beginning to get some ideas about our Terry Jordan.'

Frank looked out across the garden and sat in silence for a moment. Tara touched his cheek. 'What is it, Frank? What's the matter?'

'It's difficult to put into words. Have you ever heard of the interactive black sun, Tara? It's sort of a mental triggering device. A mythical Shambhala technology, but in the here-and-now. It's *chi*-software. The "children of *Chi*" are supposed to use it to get from here to there.'

'From here to where, Frank?' Tara asked.

'Remember Satori City, Tara? When I went in . . . ? When I was looking for Trevor in that crashed-out wreck of Virtuopolis?'

Tara nodded.

'Those lost kids . . . in Gametime. *That's* how they moved from one sector to another. They clicked on the "black sun." It's sort of a cheat-sheet escape-mechanism. The key was buried in the program. But you had to know how to use it. The kids were always one step ahead of the collapsing structure of Satori City. I used to wonder how they did it.' Frank took a deep breath. 'Almost like White Saga, Butterfly, and Stone Age Steak being one step ahead of disaster on that bridge which collapsed tonight . . .'

'What are you getting at, Frank?' Tara's tone had changed. She was sensing all kinds of shapes in the night now. *What were they? Spirits, or travelers of some sort?* All she knew, all that she *felt*, was that they had been traveling along this axis for a long time. They weren't Thai, they weren't even aboriginal. They were the *Now* beings . . .

'The black sun *does* work in this dimension, too, Tara,' Frank said to her quietly. 'Not just in Omnispace. And it's a lot bigger than just a little black dot, a secret escape-hatch icon that you click on if you've mastered the higher levels of some kids' game.'

'But where are they *going*, Frank?' It was funny how

Tara zeroed in on the essence of things before they had even assumed a shape.

'It's a beautiful full moon tonight, Tara,' Frank said to her as he held her closely. 'Do you hear that sound?'

She cupped his hand against her breast and listened together with him. 'That sounds like motorboats. Engines.'

Frank Gobi nodded. 'That's right. Motorboats. Speedboats. There's a Full Moon rite happening tonight at Kho Phangan. Those speedboats are ferrying all these backpackers across the straits. Did you notice how many young people there were in Bhoput tonight? Thais, *farangs*, everyone, including those *others* whom we can sense but can't see— They've been gathering at the ferry pier waiting to cross over.'

Tara got off the settee and stood facing Frank. He noticed that she had goosebumps on her arms even though it was a languorously warm tropical evening. 'It won't take me but a sec to get ready, Frank. Let's get going. I think you're right. I think we'll find him there.'

He didn't reply for a moment. Then he glanced at her and asked, 'Who do you think we'll find there, Tara?' He was just touching bases with her.

With both hands on her hips, and with a determined note in her voice, Tara answered, 'You know *who*, Frank . . . I think it's time we had a talk with him. He's really taken it too far.'

'I should have done that a long time ago,' Frank said, feeling a sudden weariness about all the mistakes he'd made in his life. 'How was I supposed to know?'

'You're a good man, Frank,' Tara said. 'And he's a good boy. A good young man, I should say. There's *got* to be some reason. An explanation. Maybe even an apology due.'

'I agree, honey,' Frank said as he rose to his feet and held Tara close in his arms again. 'But I think I probably owe him one, too. I just saw him as being someone different, that's all. I went into Satori City and came out.

In a sense, he never did. He's got an inner life on some plane I know practically nothing about.'

'It's not your fault, Frank,' Tara said gently.

'I know. But I feel almost as if I'm related to an earthquake and the needle on the seismograph is beginning to melt.'

. . . .

The Kinnari

'**W**ell, Mir, it looks like he's not coming after all,' Deedee Delorean reckoned as she set her glass of 'Big Buddha Ice Tea' down on the table. It tasted a little bit like the American 'Long Island' version, but with a dash of Sangthip cane-liquor instead of bourbon. 'Wing Fat's full of shit. And don't tell me he's not. He's ever so subtle, but he's still full of it,' she insisted.

Deedee and Mirabelle Myers, her VP of product development at *Chi* Memory Systems, were sitting at a table on the terrace of the Verandah Bar in the main *sala* of Le Royal Meridien Baan Taling Ngam. They had booked a villa at this luxury resort that sat high on a bluff overlooking the Gulf of Thailand on the south-west corner of Kho Samui Island.

Their Thai-style villa was a teakwood duplex filled with rare antiques and all the comforts of palace-life including super-fuzzy logic geckos that kept an eye on things for the guests from the walls. The lizards were fluent in Thai Omnispace, room-service, were expert travel-guides, and were licensed real-estate brokers linked to a vast network of intelligent geckos all over the Southeast Rim.

Deedee and Mir had waited paitently for Wing Fat to deliver his demo to them at the villa. 'He's the ultimate *chi*-projector,' Wing Fat had assured them. 'Just hook him up to an IV and download into any bio-Cray. You'll never run out of material. His name is Butterfly, and he's more beautiful than Grace Kelly. I'll bring him over this evening to demonstrate the latest in *chi* mediatainment.'

Wing Fat was supposed to catch a flight from Bangkok to Kho Samui that afternoon. It was only a 70-minute flight from the Thai capital, but Wing Fat never showed up.

Exasperated, yet ravenous, Deedee ordered one of the Royal Meridien's golf-carts to pick them up at their villa and bring them down the hill to the main *sala*. They had dinner at the Lom Talay, an open-air Thai restaurant that overlooked the hotel's cliffside pool and palm-thatched floating bar.

They had enjoyed a delicious dinner of fresh sea bass and lobster prepared in the Thai style with a dessert of banana fritters flambéd with Armagnac and mango ice-cream. But their mood remained edgy and restless.

The blazing scorpion tail of sun had long since dropped its stinger somewhere beyond the horizon, and a purple roll of silk had dropped out of the heavens to envelop the three mysterious islands that lay a few miles off-shore. The full moon was hidden behind a frond of clouds, a glowing coconut ready to drop at the slightest gust of wind.

A fleet of Thai fishing-boats was trawling the black waters, shining their spotlights into the surf as they dragged their driftnets through the brackets of night.

'What is that thing?' Deedee asked as she pointed at a large bronze sculpture that stood in a corner of the high-ceilinged *sala* of the Royal Meridien. It looked like a half-woman on top and a half-bird on the bottom. She had large pointed breasts and her head was crowned with a layered diadem. Her tiny waist disappeared into a carved maze of wings, tail feathers and birdlike feet.

'*It's a "Kinnari*,"' answered a chirping voice from Mir's handbag.

'Good grief,' Mir exclaimed as she opened her bag to take a look inside. 'It's one of the geckos from the room! It must have crawled into my bag when I wasn't looking,' she said as she shook her head in disbelief.

'A "*Kinnari*" *is a mythical Thai creature, half-bird, half-woman, related to . . .*' the pale-skinned gecko began to explain.

'That's enough! I've had it!' Deedee scowled as she grabbed the tiny gecko in her hand. She raised her arm and was about to toss the damned thing over the precipice when it chirped out another message. '*Urgent communication from Mr Wing Fat.*'

Deedee froze her pitching arm and studied the wriggling gecko whose eyes were anxiously blinking a red diode light.

'What did you just say?' Deedee asked as a frown creased her brow.

'*Urgent communication from Mr Wing Fat. Urgent communication from Mr Wing Fat. Urgent communication from . . .*'

'Don't hold it so tight, Deedee,' Mir advised her. 'They've got very delicate operating systems.'

Deedee set the gecko down on the table. 'Go ahead, I'm listening.'

'Mr Wing Fat regrets that he is unable to meet with you personally this evening. He has urgent business in Singapore to take care of. He suggests you meet with Mr Min, his trusted associate, instead. A speedboat has been reserved for you at the Royal Meridien Baan Taling Ngam boat-pier on the beach in front of the hotel. Please be ready to depart in fifteen minutes.'

'I don't believe this!' Deedee looked up at Mir. She grabbed at the gecko again and squeezed its body harder this time. 'You better talk! Where exactly are we supposed to be going on this fun boat-ride? What's this all about?'

The gecko remained silent as Deedee shook it in her hand. 'What's the matter with this goddamned thing?' She cursed loudly as she held the gecko up to her ear hoping to catch a final word.

'I think it's dead, Deedee,' Mir declared with a thoughtful

expression on her face. 'Maybe the battery needs to be recharged.'

'Damn!' Deedee cursed again. She waved her hand at a guest relations officer who was walking towards their table. The pretty Thai girl wore a traditional sarong and had an orchid pinned to her long beautiful black hair.

She stepped up to their table and bowed. 'May I be of assistance, Madame?'

'I certainly hope so,' Deedee replied as she thrust the gecko into the startled woman's face. 'What's the matter with this thing? The power just went out, right in the middle of an important message. Can't you do anything about it? Maybe you can retrieve the message on your central system? Or else trace the call?'

'Let me see it please,' the young Thai woman said with a studious air. She examined the gecko carefully, then handed it back with an apologetic smile. 'I am sorry, Madame, but this is not one of ours.'

'What!' Deedee gave her an astonished look.

'This gecko does not belong to our hotel. Our geckos have little purple spots on their bellies. This one has green spots.'

As Deedee and Mir stared at her in surprise, the guest relations officer made another startling announcement: 'The speedboat you have ordered is ready to depart at your convenience. The cart is ready to shuttle you to the Baan Taling Ngam pier.'

'Where is the speedboat supposed to be taking us?' Deedee's eyes narrowed.

The Thai woman paused before replying politely. *Farangs* were always such unpredictable creatures. 'Why, Madame, just as you have ordered, it will transport you to Hat Rin Beach on the island of Kho Phangan for the Full Moon party. Will there be anything else?'

Deedee shook her head as she gave Mir a curious glance. 'No. No, thank you. That will be all. It will just take us a minute to get ourselves ready. Thank you very much again.'

The Thai guest relations officer gave them a bow, turned, and left their table. Deedee and Mir watched as she walked past the large sculpture of the Kinnari in the main *sala*. Then they noticed that she had discreetly tucked the non-resident gecko underneath a napkin on their table.

'Let's give the poor thing a decent burial at sea, shall we?' Deedee said as she dropped the inert lizard into a dish of curry.

....
'Long Neck'

'**A**ll right, Long Neck,' Wing Fat admonished his customized Otis elevator. 'What's this all about? This isn't about another raise, is it? Your information, lately, has not been that reliable, you know. Granted, you spotted Gobi and his wife on that elevator aboard the Patpong air-ship. But I'm still holding you personally responsible for letting them get away.'

'Long Neck' was not only one of Wing Fat's most valued informants, linked to the entire network of Otis lifts in Asia, but for some time now the 650-pound Chinese had been carrying on a secret love affair with his private elevator as well.

Wing Fat's servant Little Min had turned a blind eye as usual, but what was the point in worrying his master about the perils of sexual contact with an elevator that had a shaft 30-stories deep?

Besides, the Mountain's massive girth had outgrown the dainty machinations of his stable of petite concubines. And Little Min had become weary of his role as middle-man making sure that the master's minuscule *yang* jade-stalk connected with every visiting Peony's *yin* jade-gate. The last three girls had been crushed under his weight, and it was, quite frankly, a mess to clean up afterwards.

Anyway, what was the harm of a little flirtation between man and machine? Little Min had witnessed the master swoon with his member caught between Long Neck's rubber-flanged doors as they automatically opened and closed until the final culmination of his ecstasy. It was not a pretty sight, Little Min had to admit.

But then, as Little Min well knew, decadence is not limited to the basement level of man's desires any more than propriety belongs to the roof-top. In the final analysis, all that mattered was 'The Well.' As the Last True Empress, Her Imperial Majesty the *I Ching*, had truly declared: '*The town may be changed, but the well cannot be changed. It neither decreases nor increases. They come and go and draw from it.*'

If you lowered the bucket into muddy water, or if the rope did not go down all the way, or if the jug broke, well, that was another matter . . .

'So why are you refusing to move? Why are we stuck here between the twenty-eighth and twenty-ninth floors?' Wing Fat demanded. 'Say something, you sniveling umbilical moron!'

Little Min had rolled Wing Fat from his apartment into the Long Neck elevator. After navigating his master's collapsible Ming dynasty wheel-chair palanquin into the lift, Min had set off on the staff elevator to await Wing Fat on the ground floor of the highrise luxury condo building.

'Long Neck, I'm warning you,' Wing Fat used his most threatening voice. 'If you don't move your ass right away, you're fired.'

Long Neck remained mute. Wing Fat now began to sweat. The air-conditioning in this metal-box was not working. 'Long Neck,' the Chinese giant now pleaded. 'I have a plane to catch. I need to get to the airport. Come on, hurry up!' He punched the buttons on the control panel. 'Get going!'

Silence.

Wing Fat reached out his hand to lift the emergency phone. There was obviously some malfunction in the system. He'd have to get Little Min to summon the maintenance crew and somehow get him out of here. But there was no tone. The phone was dead. *Something was seriously wrong here.*

Wing Fat was beginning to sweat profusely now. He felt the heat radiating from both sides of the elevator. He touched one of the panels with his hand. *It was blistering hot!*

'Curse you and your elevator ancestors!' Wing Fat swore suddenly, feeling the knot of fear growing in the sand-bag of his gut. He pressed the Emergency Alarm button. No ringing sound. Meanwhile, he was beginning to really cook in here.

'Long Neck!' Wing Fat suddenly had glistening tears in his eyes. 'Do something! I'm broiling alive! You're turning into a hot-plate on me! *Please!* Twenty-five thousand more shares in Otis Manila, how's that? Do we have a deal? Get me down!'

No response.

Something clicked in Wing Fat's head. A trace of his old shrewdness reasserted itself in the *wok* of his brain. 'Listen – you're not . . . you're not getting *jealous* on me, are you? If it's that elevator in the Krung Spratly building – *pshosh!* She doesn't mean anything to me! It was just a casual fling, that's all! I never went all the way with her, the way that I do with you! Long Neck . . . Long Neck . . . please!'

Wing Fat tore at his diaphanous black silk robe in desperation. He was running out of air.

'Have it your way,' he said with finality. 'Twenty-five thousand shares of Otis Manila, thirty thousand shares of Otis Indonesia, ten thousand more shares of Otis Brunei, and I'm not budging another inch.'

Long Neck lurched suddenly and dropped down two floors in a freefall. Wing Fat screamed as he held a hand against the wall to steady himself. The third-degree burn on his palm did not register as pain as much as the sound of the whirring overhead captivated his attention.

Wing Fat stared at the air-conditioning grille in the ceiling of the elevator. There was a hissing sound coming from the grille, almost like the sound of thousands of tiny flapping wings. The hissing rose to a crescendo as Wing Fat screamed again. He covered his eyes, and flailed. 'Get them off me!' But it was too late—

When Long Neck's doors finally opened down below on the ground floor, Little Min did not recognize his master. He was covered from head to toe with thousands of ravenous yellow caterpillars that were in the process of consuming both flesh and silk as if they hadn't eaten a single mulberry leaf in a thousand years.

Little Min stepped back to analyze the situation. This was no time to equivocate. He sniffed the slime in the air. *Ku* caterpillars. Someone had put a Chinese black-magic hit on Wing Fat. No question about it.

Little Min did some quick calculations. *Each silkworm needed to consume at least ten thousand times its bodyweight each day to survive.* (Being Chinese, Little Min knew his silk-bearing *Bombyx Mori* caterpillars.) *His master weighed, let's see . . . At that rate, it would take these infernal silkworms – what? a hundred years? – to turn Wing Fat into something approximating the size of a petticoat. But then again, the silk of Wing Fat's soul was hardly what you would call gossamer . . .*

You couldn't weave a purse from a sow's ear.

Little Min made up his mind as neatly as he made his master's bed each afternoon when the Mountain awoke. He reached into the elevator and pressed the > < button, then quickly hit the auto-pilot control.

Apart from Wing Fat, only Little Min knew the code to operate Wing Fat's private elevator. His master would be riding this elevator for a very long time. In his mind, Little Min was already making the necessary arrangements for the memorial service. By his reckoning, it would have to be conducted on every floor in the building as the hydraulic coffin made its vertical pass-by.

Therefore, 30 Chinese funerals would suffice to send off Wing Fat into the next world . . .

Up and down, Little Min reflected. It was all the same destination in the final end.

Then a sudden realization hit the faithful servant. It was his final act of subservience to the bloated creature whom he had served since the Mountain's childhood.

Little Min didn't take the other elevator. No sense in pushing his own luck. He ran up the entire flight of 30 stories, 'till he reached his master's palatial apartment on the top level.

Little Min unlocked the front door, walked briskly through the lavishly decorated living room, stepped past his master's beloved Ming dynasty rosewood opium couch – what memories he had of preparing the pipes! – then through the sliding doors that led to the balcony overlooking the flowing brown muscles of the Chao Phraya River.

He approached the traditional Thai spirit-house that stood high on its crimson pillar. Once again, apart from Wing Fat, only Little Min knew the secret combination that would open the door to the disguised Toshiba Cray bio-supercomputer. This was Wing Fat's satellite link-up to his worldwide network of *chi* brokers. Little Min paused to '*wai*' the spirit-house with his hands folded as a sign of sincere reverence.

When Little Min opened the red door to the spirit-house, he gasped then ran to the balcony where he threw up the contents of his stomach.

Steady yourself, Little Min thought as he heard the little barking sound echo from the interior of the spirit-house. *More ku black magic, that's all . . . Perhaps it was a final practical joke of his late master?*

Little Min now felt the tug of little teeth at the cuffs of

his cotton Chinese trousers. He looked down at his feet. *Put on a happy face, that's all you can do.*

The servant squatted down and patted the silky grey fur of the panting, growling Pekingese dog. *It was Xiaoling.* Not that long ago, one night when the Bangkok rain had come down in blinding sheets, Little Min had stood here on this very balcony, and at his master's command he had dropped the dog thirty stories into the flowing river below.

'There's good dog, Xiaoling,' Little Min said as he continued to caress the animal's fur-matted head. The dog yapped and ran in circles around him. *The ghosts are coming home where their bones are buried,* Little Min thought to himself.

The tide of the chi *must be turning.*

'You must be hungry. Why don't I go and fix you your supper then?' Little Min asked in a soft voice. 'A little hundred-year-old carp steak prepared just the way you like it? With some sweet and sour sauce? What do you think about that? Come on—'

Xiaoling wagged her tail and barked again. She followed Little Min inside the apartment.

Epilogue
• • • • • • • • • • • •

The Children of *Chi*

Kho Phangan

The speedboats were coming from all directions –
from Kho Tao, from Kho Samui, and from the
Thai mainland. Brightly lit ferries leaving from the pier
at Big Buddha Beach on Samui were packed with
revelers, young *farangs* and Thais, all bound for the Full
Moon celebration at Hatrin on Kho Phangan island.

Paul Sykes and Trevor Gobi were sitting on the top deck
of a Big Buddha ferry, getting into the party spirit. The Big
Buddha himself, a 40-foot kitschy gilt statue of Maitreya,
the Buddha of the Future, sat on his knoll at the Wat Phra
Yai temple-complex on Koh Fan, observing the comings
and goings of the crowd with a tolerant smile.

Trevor had his Kirlian digi-cam out and was recording
the scene. He laid his camera down and grinned at Sykes.
'They say there are lots of beautiful temples in Samui but
not very many monks. I don't think that's quite accurate.
Just take a look around. We're all pilgrims, bro.'

'Doing our full moon meditation, I quite see your point,'
Sykes replied. 'Pass that joint, if you don't mind – thanks.'
Trevor reached over and handed Sykes a lit Rizla that a
smiling blond Swedish chick held out to them.

She blew out a lungful of *ganja* smoke and addressed
Trevor. 'Hi there, haven't we met before? You look
familiar. Goa? Katmandu? South Carolina?'

Trevor shook his head shyly. 'Haven't been to any of
those places.'

'Wait a minute,' the Swedish chick said as she scratched
the tattoo on her left breast. She was wearing a gauzy see-
through Nepalese blouse and a Spanish gypsy skirt with bare
feet showing, a gold ring on her right toe. 'Jah, I got it!
Phnom Penh, right? You've been to Angkor, haven't you?'

Trevor smiled shyly again. 'It's possible.'

'I never forget a face,' she said as she relapsed into a happy stupor. 'Wow! Look at all the phosphorescence in the waves, that's cool!'

'I must be really stoned,' Sykes said to Trevor. 'Those two old guys over there. That chap in the Hawaiian print shirt. I swear, he looks like Yeats, y'know. He's a spitting image of William Butler Yeats. The English poet. "*Slouches towards Bethlehem . . .*" That lot. This stuff is potent, man! And that guy he's with, he must be German or Swiss. Shit!' Sykes laughed. 'He looks like Carl Jung, if I didn't know better. Or else it's his great-great-grand-twin-brother. This must be the Love Boat of the Collective Unconscious, man! Ha! Ha! Ha!'

Trevor laughed softly and resumed filming, focusing his camera on the two older European *farangs* who were engaged in a quiet conversation with each other. ' "*Where love rules, there is no will to power*," ' Trevor quoted a bit of Jung as he filmed the old *farangs*. ' "*And where power predominates, there love is lacking. The one is the shadow of the other*." '

'You're blowing my mind, man,' Sykes said as he pulled up his legs to allow a heavy-set Thai deck-hand to squeeze past him on his way to the wheelhouse. The Thai was wearing a ragged t-shirt that had Day-glo letters on it announcing: '*Hat Rin Full Moon Party, 2038.*'

There were various commemorative graffiti on the t-shirt, scribbled by the *farang* passengers. The graffiti radiated from the Day-glo central image of the full moon. Sykes noticed that one of them read: '*Have a top day,*' while another graffiti pointedly declared: '*Fuck off, fatty.*'

Sykes himself was wearing a t-shirt he had bought at a stand at Big Buddha Beach. It had cost him one hundred of the king's *baht*, or $4. He had decided to splurge because it seemed like a real collector's item.

Sykes' own t-shirt read: '*Happy End of the World.*'

It was a five-minute walk from the Kho Phangan pier to the Hat Rin beach where the Full Moon rave was in full swing. The path led Frank and Tara Gobi through a village that resembled a sprawling flea-market with cafés, European bakeries, falafel stands, and retro-psychedelic tekno-bars.

The place was swarming with young *farangs* with long hair, body-piercings, and tattoos. They wore all kinds of jewelry, some of which caught Tara's eye.

'Look, Frank.' She nudged him. 'Some of those pieces look like direct knock-offs of Salvador Dali's costume jewelry. Check out that one over there.' She pointed at a dark-skinned Thai girl who had the look of an angel that had just climbed off a Harley.

Frank glanced at the girl who was dressed in a leather bodice which was revealingly laced open at her breasts. She wore a kinetic amethyst sculpture that resembled a praying-mantis from Atlantis.

'Animal and insect motifs seem to be "in" this season,' he observed.

'You know what Dali said, don't you?' Tara mused. 'He was very anthropomorphic in his jewelry designs. He said he saw the human form in trees, leaves, and animals; and the animal and the vegetable form in the human.'

'He'd be right at home here then,' Frank replied. 'This place is crawling with them. Anthropomorphism for the masses. Animal, vegetable, mineral, what have I left out? They're all here for the party.'

They followed in the direction of the steel-drums. The rhythmic beat led them straight through the village until they arrived at a long curved white sand beach that was framed between two craggy bluffs on either end.

Bonfires blazed up and down the length of the shore. Palm trees decorated with fairy-tale strings of lights swayed in the breeze, their fronds rustling as the choreographed fire-flies flitted on their strings.

The music hit them right away, a mesmerizing tekno-reggae beat that riffed their bodies like lyrical fingers massaging each of their nerve-endings at 135-beats per second.

'Wow! It's Disco Shambhala!' Tara exclaimed as she slipped off her sandals and wriggled her toes in the sand. 'I feel like I'm eighteen again, Frank! How about you!'

'Uh, better make that twenty-five.'

'Come on, it looks like the real party's down that way!' Tara said as she grabbed Frank's hand and dragged him towards Dance Central at the far end of the beach.

There were fish-nets hanging above the dance-floor on the sand. The nets were decorated with empty water-bottles and starfish that had been painted with Day-glo spirals. Five hundred or more bodies – some of them naked and painted with Day-glo colors, others more modestly clad in tribal garb from all over the globe – shimmied and trance-boogied on the sand.

A procession of *katoey* shamanesses was moving slowly on stilts around a fire.

Someone standing next to Frank and Tara laughed, 'That's Mama Choosri and her Dancing Falafels! Wait 'till they set off their fireworks! Those stilts are loaded with Catherine-wheels and *chi* fire-crackers!'

Frank Gobi turned his attention away from the dancing for a moment. Then he turned back with a start and blinked – Tara was dancing with an Orang-utan! *No, it couldn't be.* The fellow was just hairy and wearing some sort of black furry Spandex outfit. *Funny, how the optics can play tricks in the tropics . . .*

It was a magical scene, all right. The full moon hung above the sea like a mother-of-pearl deejay with a pink boa of clouds slung from around its neck.

Longboats were still arriving from the other side of the island, from remote corners like Bottle Beach and Mae Hat and Cholok Lam. The new arrivals were letting themselves down from the bobbing boats into the surf and wading ashore to join the party.

Gobi blinked again. There was a lone water buffalo standing in the sea up to his rump, with a little boy pouring buckets of water over him and scrubbing down his sleek black hulk. *Looks like that fighting* kerbau, Gobi thought to himself. *Stone Age Steak. But then they all look alike . . .*

Further down the beach, there was a little intimate nightclub scene happening. Partyers sat on mats around little low tables lit with little Thai kerosene lamps. They were talking quietly amongst themselves, laughing as they took swigs from bottles of Singha beer or sipped fruit smoothies from coconut shells.

At one table, Frank Gobi saw two young foreigners sitting together. One had a digi-cam in his hand and was filming the passers-by. Then the camera turned in his direction. Gobi could feel the Kirlian close-up recording his chakric reflexes, as he recognized the young man behind the camera.

'*Tara!*' Frank called out to his wife who was doing a whirling-dervish minuet with the Orang-utan in the Spandex. She didn't hear him. She was caught up in the feverish monkey dance.

'I'll be right back, honey,' he muttered to himself as he began to walk towards the young man who was sitting on the sand still filming him.

He'd have it out with Terry Jordan. *This was really* his *party, wasn't it?*

Paul Sykes glanced up at the towering *farang* who was wearing a white t-shirt and a pair of blue Thai fisherman's trousers tied at the ankles.

'Hey, he's dressed just like you!' Sykes turned to Trevor. 'Who is this dude?'

Trevor still had his eye through the view-finder. As he put the Kirlian digi-cam down, he grinned and said, 'Hi, Dad. I'd like you to meet Paul Sykes, a friend of mine. Paul, this is my father.'

'Hello there, Paul,' Frank Gobi greeted the young man as he lowered himself onto the mat. He sat cross-legged on the sand, and stared at his son from across the table.

'You're *Trevor's* Dad? Dr Frank Gobi? *The* Frank Gobi?' Sykes appeared flustered. 'What an honor it is to meet you, sir!' Sykes turned to Trevor. 'You didn't tell me your father was going to be here!'

'He wouldn't have missed this for the world,' Trevor replied with a grin. 'Would you have, Dad? It's *your* party, too. You realize that, don't you?'

Frank Gobi shook his head in wonder. '*Trevor*. Or should I call you "Terry" now? Terry Jordan's your *nom de plumeria*, isn't it? You've turned into a homeochromatic mime. You blend right into the jungle landscape like a strangling fig.' He paused. 'Or are you still going by "Kundalini Kid"? That was your handle when you went on-line into Satori City wasn't it? Or was it the "Kundalini Kameleon"? I forget.'

'It does seem appropriate somehow,' Trevor conceded. 'I'm glad you and Tara could make it.' He glanced at his watch. 'The show is just about to start.'

'More Chinese *ku* magic, Trevor?' Frank Gobi demanded. 'What is it going to be this time? Last time it rained golden caterpillars. Before that, it was the Queen Rim butterfly fluttering across the mindscape of Xiang Gang. What's next on the entertainment channel? Acrobatic snails?'

'You'll see, Dad,' Trevor laughed. 'I was just following in your invisible footsteps. But leaving my own mark.'

'So *that's* what this is all about,' Frank Gobi said.

Tara appeared behind Frank and laid a hand on his shoulder. 'What was it you once told me about Trevor, Frank? It was one of his favorite expressions when he was a child . . . You thought it was cute at the time.'

Frank sighed and repeated, ' "*Like father like son, only son is more devious.*" He used to say that a lot.'

'That's right.' Tara sat down beside Frank on the mat and eyed Trevor. 'So, maestro, *Mr Jordan*. I had a feeling you were involved in this. But I didn't want to worry your Dad.' She squeezed Frank's hand.

Trevor gave Tara an apologetic look. 'I'm sorry I put you guys through the head-trip. But I knew I could rely on you. You were very, very good, Tara,' he said to her. 'I had to borrow your *shakti*. There was no other way. Mr Chin agreed that you were a natural *tao nai nai*. Born to the *ku*, as they say.'

Trevor turned to his father. 'Dad, did you know that you're married to a powerful sorceress? I'll bet you didn't.'

'Says my son, the sorcerer,' Frank Gobi retorted.

'The sorcerer's *apprentice*, Dad,' Trevor corrected his father. 'The sorcerer's *apprentice* . . . That's part of the equation which you can't overlook. I guess you weren't prepared for all the consequences.'

'Tell me, Trevor . . .' Frank Gobi raised an eyebrow. 'Exactly *what* consequences are we talking about here? I raised you to be a practicing devil-worshipper? Is that it?'

'Worship the devil and you're really worshipping God, Dad. It's like the elections back home. When you vote a Democrat for president, you're really electing a Republican. You know how it works.'

'Bullshit.'

'Where's your sense of humor, Dad? I was just making a little joke. You know as well I do that duality is simply the glue that keeps the One from falling apart. You taught me that when I was nine years old.'

'I did?'

'That and a whole lot more.'

'That's a scary thought,' Frank Gobi said pensively.

'Uh.' Paul Sykes shifted uncomfortably on his cushion. 'If I'm interrupting a private family discussion, then maybe I ought to—'

'*Paulie!*' a familiar voice called out to him. 'Is that *you*, Paulie?'

'*Blimey!*' Paul Sykes spilled his drink as he shrank into the sand. '*Mum*, what are *you* doing here!'

'Charlie brought me, he's around here somewhere with his boyfriend,' replied Sykes' mum, an old raver with a musical-chime for a nose-ring and a daub of psychedelic blush on her face.

The painted spirals on her cheeks made her look younger

than her age, which was mid-sixtyish, give or take a few tabs of E.

'Hadley's a good egg, son. He's here looking for a storyline for his next production, "*Hailey's Kismet*," I think it's called. We flew in from Bali. But we had to leave your Dad in Singapore. He's having trouble adjusting to the Orient. He keeps insisting that Joseph Conrad is a fraud. I told him, "Bill, at least try and make an effort. Why can't you admit this is a wee bit more exotic than Lancashire? This is Lord Jim country." "Don't bloody *Lord Jim* me," snaps your father . . .

'Oh, excuse me,' Mrs Sykes paused, bringing her hennaed hand to her mouth.

'I *do* go on and on.' She looked around. 'It's such a lovely party, isn't it? I hear they're expecting UFOs. I *do* hope that's not the case. You've seen one, you've seen them all, that's what I say. Back in '28, when we were camping near Stonehenge . . . *No*, what we need is something truly original. Something that's definitely *authentic*. Hadley's counting on it. So is Charlie. And so am I.'

'Then I'm sure you won't be disappointed, Mrs Sykes.' Trevor gave her an encouraging smile.

Paul Sykes jumped to his feet and took his mum by her arm. 'Come on, Mumsy. I hear they're serving psilocybin shakes at the "Shroom Shack" just down the beach. See you all later then.' He nodded at the Gobi family.

'Cheers,' Mrs Sykes said as she waved goodbye to them. 'Lead the way, Paulie, dear.'

'I hope she doesn't get stoned and decide to go swimming,' Trevor remarked after they had left. 'Last time that happened at Hat Rin, this German guy got eaten by a shark, and the shark had a bad trip.'

Tara and Frank exchanged glances. This was far more serious than they had ever imagined.

'Oh, shit!' Paul Sykes blurted out on their way to the 'Shroom Shack.'

'What is it, Paulie? Did you forget something? That was such a nice young man. You have the coolest friends. You and Charlie both do. Hadley's been ever so decent to the family – why, I think it's probably because he doesn't have one of his own! He and Charlie are thinking of adopting, don't you know? They've been having serious discussions about it. They want to adopt a Thai *katoey*. Do you know what that is, dear? The poor child – he's an orphan – is only 27 years old. That means that Butterfly, that's his name – isn't that quaint? – would be older than Charlie . . .' Mrs Sykes giggled.

'Older than his own adopted father, imagine that!' she laughed. 'To think that in my own lifetime, I've seen the basic family unit go from nuclear to fractal, well, the mind just boggles, Paulie dear . . .'

'That's enough, Mum,' Paul replied darkly as he felt a shiver run through him. There was a scene happening at this beachside bar they were passing. The Café Hiatus, it was called. Sykes' black sun was spinning like a roulette wheel, and its little ball was tumbling around and around as it skittered into its fated slot.

There. Sykes blinked. He saw three Butohs standing at the bar. They were Japanese. They were naked except for their loincloths, their bodies powdered white as usual. Practically invisible. They were having a drink. Watching a Japanese Butoh dancer knock down a Jack Daniels on the rocks is a protracted affair, under any circumstances. The fingers tighten ever so slowly around the glass, the glass breathes, the fingers relax, the fingers tighten, the elbow begins its slow angular ascent . . . Of course, by the time the glass has reached a quarter of its way to the Butoh's lips, the ice has totally melted.

'*Mizuwari*,' *the drink is called*, Sykes' black sun database interpreted for him. So it *was* a calculated drink order, after all. Japanese planning! What they really wanted was a plain whiskey-water, those Butoh boozers.

But no. That wasn't the issue. At the end of the bar,

watching the Butohs, and siphoning their Butoh energy through a *chi* straw, was that *creature* again. That half-woman, half-bird. The one Sykes had seen on Khao San Road in Bangkok with the brilliant plumage on her head, and with the two Amazon parrots grafted to each shoulder.

She was wearing a naval blue jacket with brass buttons and cuttle-bones attached in the place of epaulets. These epaulets, when the Amazons were not otherwise occupied with preening themselves, the parrots would sharpen their beaks upon. Those sleeves would need cleaning, Sykes observed. Parrot droppings are a gnarly business.

The parrot-woman was smiling at him again. She had turned her gaze on Sykes, and her twin parrots were suddenly on the alert, ruffling their feathers and bobbing their little heads with their beaks open like can-openers at the ready.

Sykes recalled Trevor's warning at Peachy's guest-house. There was a serial eye-ball gouger on the loose, preying upon travelers who had the 'green eye.' The green *chi* eye that signaled the high *chi* content of a 'child of *Chi*.'

Who was she supplying with those purloined eye-balls? There was some nefarious black market for green *chi* eyes, no doubt, Sykes concluded.

For a moment, Paul Sykes panicked, vowing that in future he would never travel without wearing a pair of colored contact-lenses. Preferably ones with a dark tint . . .

'Wait here just a second, Mum,' Sykes told his mother, his courage returning to him. He'd have to do his duty, warn those Butohs off, and confront this demon bird-person face to face. He would tell her that he was on to her dirty tricks.

'I don't think she's your type, Paulie,' his mum called out to him as she watched her son walk up to the bar.

'You,' Sykes addressed the bird-woman. The woman looked at him with an amused smile.

'Yes?' Her voice was soft, almost musical. Her eyes had a mesmerizing quality to them.

Sykes had to shake this feeling off. *Damn, she was beginning to look rather attractive to him!* Something about her, something in her genes perhaps, exuded a natural sex appeal. Almost as if she was a sexy movie-star on a set. And *he* was the set . . .

'You have such beautiful green eyes,' she said to him. 'I'm attracted to men with green eyes.' She gently laid a hand on his.

'Er.' Sykes struggled to retain his composure. This was more than he had expected. She was already drawing him in.

'Would you care to have a drink with me?' she asked coyly. 'My name is Kinnari. But you can call me Kimberly. And you are?'

'*British*,' Paul Sykes declared, suddenly asserting himself.

'I just *love* British men,' Kinnari said as she moved in even closer. Sykes felt the soft warmth of her breasts against his arm, and he began to melt. *So beautiful*, he thought to himself dreamily. *This can't be happening. I've finally met the woman of my dreams. So what if she's got two birds growing out of her shoulders? We can all get along together, can't we? We'll have parakeets.*

'You find me attractive? Pleasing to you?' Kinnari breathed into Sykes' ear as she slipped her thigh between his legs. He was sitting on a bar-stool feeling quite saturated, full of something – *indefinable*.

Sykes drew his arm around her waist and pulled her close. 'Umm, yes I do find you indeed *very* attractive,' he murmured.

'A Piña Colada,' she said. 'That's what I'm having. Would you like one?' He nodded dumbly. 'Bartender!' she snapped her fingers at the bar-man. Her parrots squawked, bobbing their heads. 'One more of the same.'

'So tell me,' Kinnari asked him. 'How's your eye-sight? Is it twenty-twenty?' She ribbed him gently. 'I'm just kidding. I've just met you and I'm already worrying that you'll find some other woman more appealing. I wouldn't want to lose you, you see. There are so many beautiful women here tonight. I know men. They like to stray.'

'Not me,' Paul Sykes declared his innocence. 'I'm at home with your body.' He blushed. 'What I mean to say,' he became flustered, 'is that I'm really a *home-body*. I mean, I'm no gigolo.'

'And I'm no gigolette,' Kinnari cooed at him. 'I stand by *my* man.'

The bartender brought them two Piña Coladas. Kinnari gave Sykes another seductive smile and leaned over to kiss him with her parted lips. Sykes could sense the kiss coming. The bliss of it. 'That's enough out of you, you hippy harlot!' a sharp voice cut through his reverie.

Paul Sykes opened his eyes to find his mum standing at the bar beside him. 'Is that you, Mum?' he asked dazed.

'Who *is* this bitch?' Kinnari spun around to face the unwelcome intruder.

The spell broken, Paul Sykes said meekly, 'It's my mother. Mum, what's going on? What are you doing here?'

'I saw her slip the mickey into your drink, son. You can't be too careful with strange women. They'll soon have their way with you. What's that you just poured into my son's drink, miss? LSD? Let me see that. I'd like to try some myself, just to be sure—'

'You're out of control!' Kinnari swore at Mrs Sykes. 'This is your *mother*?' She turned to Paul Sykes. 'That is the dumbest thing I've ever heard of! Bringing your mother to a rave! What are you, some kind of an infantile *creep*?'

'That's no way to talk about my boy!' Mrs Sykes said defensively. 'I'd like to see *your* mother, what with those feathered lamp-shades growing out of your neck!'

The pair of Amazons screeched and hissed. Paul Sykes shook his head clear of the first *chakra* sexual cobwebs enmeshing him. *Jeezus, he had come* that *close to disaster!*

'Thanks, Mum,' he whispered gratefully to his mother. The Japanese Butohs at the end of the bar were watching them with curiosity.

Sykes shocked them by addressing them directly. 'I don't know what the Japanese word for it is, but watch out for *her*.' He yanked his thumb in the direction of Kinnari. 'She's bad news. She's been sucking the *chi* out of your *hara*, you guys. And you didn't even notice. You've been too preoccupied with performing the *kata* for drinking your *mizuwaris*.'

One of the Butohs blanched. 'You can *see* us? Actually *see* us?'

'Well, what do you think?' Paul Sykes replied. 'Of course, I can see you. Why are you guys trying to pass yourselves off as being invisible anyway? What's the point?'

The other Japanese Butoh explained with a chagrined expression, 'Otherwise, they charge us Japanese rates. They think we are very, very rich in Japan.'

'Well, just be careful you don't get your *chi* ripped off trying to save a few *yen*.'

'*Domo arigato*, thank you very much for the warning.' The Butoh bowed.

'She also goes for eye-balls, too,' Sykes said as the Butohs began to disconnect themselves from the bar. It was going to take them a while to leave. He may as well chat with them for a bit.

'I do *not*! Why are you spreading such deliberate lies about me!' Kinnari swore at Sykes. 'Lies! All lies!'

'Oh, yeah? Lies, are they? I've been warned about you. You're the eye-ball gouger. Admit it!'

Kinnari drew herself up defiantly. 'The person who made those allegations against me is not *luk phu chai*, a gentleman,' she protested. 'He can choose for himself whether he is a *luk phee*, a ghost's son, or a *luk maa*, a dog's son . . .'

'Easy for you to say.' Mrs Sykes glared at her. 'What is *your* genealogy, if I may be so bold as to ask? There's something about your looks . . . You look vaguely familiar. I can't quite place it. You'd be quite attractive, in fact, if you weren't covered in so much bird-shit.'

Kinnari fluffed up the bird feathers on her head with her hand, and replied haughtily before she stalked away, 'My DNA, Madame, is certainly superior to yours. I'll have you know that I come from an impeccable line of beauty products and celebrity genes carefully handed down through the ages.'

'So you were hatched from Mary Poppins? Is that safe to assume?' Mrs Sykes sneered.

'No, Madame,' Kinnari replied disdainfully as she turned up her nose. 'In point of fact, if you *really* want to know, *my father is James Dean and my mother is Elvis.*'

Then she walked away.

'That explains everything,' Mrs Sykes said. 'Now, where's that "Shroom Shack," Paulie? I believe we were headed there before we were so rudely side-tracked.'

'I think we need to have a little talk, Trevor,' Frank Gobi said to his son as he glanced at Tara. She nodded in agreement.

'I know your intentions are good. But you're behaving like, what's the word I'm looking for?' Frank turned to Tara. This was more difficult than he thought. He felt suddenly tongue-tied.

'An Omniopath,' Tara interjected.

'That's right. You can't go around restructuring reality as if it were some sort of a Gametime bleed-through from Omnispace. I know you want to change the world. It *does* need changing. I'm not saying it doesn't. But there are certain limits that you can't – that you *don't* – cross.'

'That sounds hypocritical coming from you, Dad,' Trevor replied as he fingered his digi-cam. A little picture sprang to life on the viewing-screen that was mounted on the side of the camera.

'I mean, you've been searching for the Holy Grail of Omnispace for how long now?' Trevor turned his green eyes at his father. 'You know the entire system is corrupt and in danger of collapsing. Both on the outside *and* on the inside. Omnispace is just the mirror. A living mirror, yes, but a mirror nonetheless. There *is* an opening – and you've managed to come pretty damn close to it. But you never went through all the way. How come?'

'What's *that* supposed to mean?' Frank Gobi demanded, his face flushing. 'You know I've been working all my life to improve the channels between the – between the *dimensions*. Between Omnispace and Real-Time. Between this world and everything that exists beyond it.'

'That's just the point, Dad. For you, the unknown's just another *channel*. For human consumption. We're turning into a race of cosmic consumers now. Everything is fodder for recycling into human consciousness. But there's so much more – so much more . . .'

Trevor fiddled with the digi-cam. 'You'll see soon enough.'

'Frank,' Tara said nervously. 'That's some kind of a *ku*-projector he's got there.' She turned to Trevor. 'Is this the Big One, Trevor? Before you slam shut the clap-board and yell, "*Cut!*"? What are you planning to do? Do you think you're Alfred Hitchcock or something? You'd better think carefully before you go through with it, whatever it is. There may be no turning back.'

'I *have* thought about it carefully, Tara,' Trevor replied as he shrugged his shoulders. 'Dad, do you remember that hypothetical algorithm you were playing around with? To jack into Greentime? Into Gaiaspace? It really *does* work. With a few modifications, of course. I just want you to know that.'

Frank Gobi stared at his son. 'You lifted it, didn't you? I tried to access it from the datafiles of the *Interspecies Insider*. That was my only copy, Trevor. I wanted to check it out one more time, but it was gone. Erased from memory.'

'I was covering for you, Dad,' Trevor said. 'You'd forgotten all about it. But there were others who wanted it. Wanted it badly enough that they were ready to kill for it.'

'What are you saying?'

'Your old buddy Mort Wisenik. Remember him? The ex-con golemtologist? He got through all right, Dad. Into Greentime. So did Paul Sykes. But Wisenik gave a taste of it to some very bad people. Some really terrible people, Dad. And they killed him for it.'

'Wisenik's dead?' Frank Gobi felt a brick going through the glass of his heart. He remembered the look of sadness in Terry Jordan's eye – when Trevor was miming Jordan – in the lobby of the Mandarin Hotel in Xiang Gang. When he and Tara had walked in on him. He had felt as if they had been interrupting some sort of a wake Trevor was having with Old Ming, that potted palm in the lobby.

'That's right, he's dead, Dad. He paid the price.'

'Who's got it now? That algorithm for the chlorophyll search-engine?' Frank Gobi asked anxiously.

'No one, Dad,' Trevor answered with the same depth of sadness in his young face. 'I beat them to it. Don't worry, they haven't gotten their hands on it. It's in a safe place.'

'Where is it?' Tara interjected. 'I mean, where is it *right now*?'

'It's all loaded and ready to go.' Trevor looked at her in the eye as he patted the digi-cam. 'They had their own plans for it. Stupid plans. Stupid men. Stupid women. Stupid. Stupid.'

'What did they want to do with it, Trevor?' Tara asked him gently. 'Maybe we can make sure that it never happens. You don't always need to go all the way. There are safe-guards, controls.'

'To make sure that no one ever presses the button that nukes our souls? No, I don't think so.' Trevor shook his head. '*Homo sapiens* think too highly of their human pedigrees. It's a basic flaw in their programming.'

'In *their* programming? Wait a minute, you're not including yourself in this group?'

'Look, Tara, see that speedboat over there with the two *gringas* from Silly Putty Valley?' Trevor pointed at the shore where a motorboat was unloading two women passengers. They were struggling to balance themselves in the surge of the waves that crashed onto the beach.

'They think they've come here to make a deal. But they're a little too late for that. Excuse me a moment.'

Trevor got up and began to walk towards the speedboat.

'What the fuck is this, Mirabelle?' Deedee Delorean swore as she felt the salt water seep up into her pantyhose and soak her crotch. 'Is this some kind of a Woodstock for cannibals or what?'

'I'm not sure, Deedee,' Mir replied as she grabbed Deedee's arm to steady her. 'It's a Full Moon rave, that's what the skipper told us. It's a monthly thing. Moon trippers, that's what they are. Harmless pagans.'

'They'd better be,' Deedee swore again. 'So where's Min? He's supposed to meet us here, isn't he?'

Shit. Deedee tripped and sat down hard on the beach. She rose awkwardly and brushed the sand off her rear end.

'There he is,' Mir said. 'He's heading down our way now.'

'Great, the son-of-a-bitch better have a good explanation for all this.'

'Welcome to Kho Phangan,' the Chinese said to them. 'I'm sorry that my master Mr Wing Fat was unable to meet you in person. He had another pressing engagement.'

'I heard all about that,' Deedee scoffed. 'So what's it to be?' She glanced at the digi-cam that the Chinese was holding in his hand. 'Is that it? You've got it with you? The works?'

'The works, Ms Delorean.' The Chinese bowed.

'Why did we have to come all the way out here?' Deedee asked, suddenly suspicious. 'Why couldn't you have shown it to us in our hotel?'

'This is a better venue. It is a full moon, you see.'

'Full moon, full shmoon. This had better not be a joke. I'm getting tired of all the run-around. I want the real thing.'

'No run-around, Ms Deelorean.'

'What the fuck!' Deedee turned to Mirabelle Myers. 'We've got company. Is this your idea of a private negotiation, Mr Min? You invited some of your friends to bid against us?'

Frank and Tara Gobi were walking hand in hand towards the three figures on the beach. The tekno-reggae beat was working itself up to a climax in the dance-pit under the glowing fish-nets. The procession of shamaness *katoeys* on stilts was shooting off a series of colorful fireworks from under their asbestos party-dresses.

A shimmering mandala of a Catherine wheel spun into the sky, whizzed, and exploded into a thousand radiant *yin* and *yang* symbols.

'You have to trust him, Frank. After all, he's your son,' Tara said to Frank.

'Do I have any choice?'

'Well, you could disown him. But somehow I don't think you would want to do that.'

'Nah,' Frank Gobi said. 'Too much paperwork.'

'I thought you liked paperwork.'

'I like *paper*, Tara, not paperwork. We'll just have to see what happens.'

'Mr and Mrs Gobi, what a pleasure it is to see you here.' Deedee Deelorean beamed at them with sarcasm. 'Are you buying or selling?'

'Buying or selling *what* exactly?' Frank asked puzzled.

Deedee turned to the Chinese. 'I don't get it. Are they in the picture or not?'

'In a manner of speaking. But not entirely.' Min bowed his head apologetically.

'Well, I guess you'll get to see it with the rest of us peons.' Deedee winked at Frank and Tara. 'Then we can all judge the quality of the material and negotiate the distribution rights. But I'm warning you right now, if it's the real thing you can't afford it. Not a chance in hell.'

'What is she talking about, Trevor?' Frank Gobi asked his son.

'Trevor?' Deedee scoffed at Frank Gobi. 'So you and Min are on a firstname basis already. Isn't that charming? What do you think about that, Mir?'

Mir was looking up at the full moon, shielding her eyes against the glare of brilliant moonlight that was beginning to assume various animated shapes. 'Look, Deedee – the moon!'

The Hat Rin beach became an outdoor theater. Several thousand Full Moon partyers took a break from their dancing and festivities to sit on the sand and watch the movie that was beginning to roll its giant credits across the craters on the silver screen.

'I have to apologize,' Trevor said to his guests. 'It's still in its black-and-white stages, and it's *not* a talkie. Not yet. It's a silent film. There's room for improvement, I guess.'

'There always is, son,' Frank Gobi said as he put one arm around Trevor's shoulders and his other arm around Tara. 'There always is. But this – this is beautiful! Really beautiful. Congratulations.'

'Thanks, Dad,' Trevor said. 'I really appreciate that, coming from you. From one director to another.'

'You're giving it all away free!' Deedee shrieked. 'I had the syndication rights pre-sold to the Spratly Studios! You idiot! Just the foreign rights *alone* are worth a fortune! Think of all the animal and mineral life on the planet. And the commercial spin-offs! Under-shell deodorant for snails, giant posturepedic mattresses for whales, dental floss for monkeys, language cassettes for mynah birds . . . We'll use the barter system at first, of course, then work our way up from there. Give them a line of credit. What *are* you *doing*? Stop! I can't stand this! I'm going to go out of my mind!'

'Shush, let's just watch this—' Mir said as she pulled Deedee down to the sand. 'Ooh, they look so gorgeous, maybe we can sign them!'

It was the first interspecies tear-jerker ever produced. The entire living, breathing, organic and inorganic audience on the planet was tuned in to the premiere of *Chi*, a Gaia-Gobi Films co-production. It was the story of Tommy and Nita and how they were reunited at the very end on the dark side of the moon.